KU-319-212

A LAETITIA RODD MYSTERY

The Mystery of the Sorrowful Maiden

KATE SAUNDERS

BLOOMSBURY PUBLISHING

LONDON · OXFORD · NEW YORK · NEW DELHI · SYDNEY

BLOOMSBURY PUBLISHING
Bloomsbury Publishing Plc
50 Bedford Square, London, WC1B 3DP, UK
29 Earlsfort Terrace, Dublin 2, Ireland

BLOOMSBURY, BLOOMSBURY PUBLISHING and the Diana logo are
trademarks of Bloomsbury Publishing Plc

First published in Great Britain 2021
This edition published 2022

A catalogue record for this book is available from the British Library

Library of Congress Cataloguing-in-Publication data has been applied for

ISBN: HB: 978-1-4088-6692-4; PB: 978-1-4088-6693-1;
eBook: 978-1-4088-6694-8; ePDF: 978-1-5266-4521-0

2 4 6 8 10 9 7 5 3 1

Typeset by Integra Software Services Pvt. Ltd.
Printed and bound in Great Britain by CPI Group (UK) Ltd, Croydon CR0 4YY

To find out more about our authors and books visit www.bloomsbury.com
and sign up for our newsletters

For my fellow 'Angels', Jo, Shelley, Carol,
Shirley and Claire

One

1853

SPRING WAS A LONG time coming that year. Though the winter had not been especially cold, it had been so damp that everything I touched seemed to be speckled with black mould, and Mrs Bentley had suffered a bad attack of pleurisy. By the time she was well enough to come downstairs and sit beside the kitchen fire, it was the week after Easter, and a few timid rays of sunshine had finally pierced the general gloom.

After I had settled Mrs B in the Windsor chair, wrapped in a heap of shawls and blankets, I found a letter, hand-delivered, on the doormat.

Dear Mrs Rodd

I understand that you have a reputation as a private investigator, specializing in matters requiring discretion. If convenient to you, I shall call this afternoon at three o'clock, to discuss the possibility of a professional engagement.

Yours respectfully
Benjamin Tully

Mr Tully, a retired actor, was one of our neighbours in Well Walk. We exchanged bows and smiles when we met in the street, but he was far better acquainted with Mrs Bentley, and so I gave the letter to her. 'Do you happen to know what he wants, Mary?'

It was exactly the tonic my dear landlady needed; I rejoiced to see the 'snap' returning to her pale blue eyes as she pored over the single sheet of paper.

'No, ma'am; your guess is as good as mine. But Mr Tully's a nice sort of fellow, and a good neighbour too. He keeps those cats, for one thing, and this terrace hasn't seen a mouse for years.'

'Should I receive him in the drawing room, or will he be more comfortable down here? Dear me, I don't know what to do with an actor!'

In those days, theatrical people were still regarded as a race apart, both morally and socially. Though certain actors were starting to be considered as serious artists, it would not be appropriate for them to be received as equals by someone like me – the widow of an archdeacon and the very epitome of respectability.

'I'd say down here, ma'am,' said Mrs Bentley decidedly. 'If you sit in the drawing room, it'll mean another fire, which we can't afford – because that coal merchant you like so much is an out-and-out robber.'

I laughed at this, for it made me so happy that she was well again, and up to criticizing. She had nearly died, and I would have been grievously lonely without Mary Bentley; our friendship amounted to so much more than the usual bond between a landlady and her lodger. When we first met, five years before the time of which I am writing, I had just lost my beloved husband and was almost penniless.

Everyone had expected me to move into my brother's house in Highgate. Fred's wife had assumed that I would then teach her swarms of children for nothing out of 'gratitude' and she could dismiss the governess. Much as I loved those children, however, I was having none of it; independence was everything to me, and so I set about looking for lodgings.

And a dismal experience I found it; I will spare the reader a complete account of the mean and shabby little rooms, the slatternly landladies and the shocking prices. Mrs Bentley's narrow house in Hampstead did not appear especially promising at first glance, but it suited me, and so did she; I was pleased to learn that many years before, when her five red-headed sons were small, she had let lodgings to John Keats and his two brothers (how they all fitted in is still a mystery to me), and I had taken this as a hopeful omen.

Mr Tully had been living in Well Walk, four doors down from us, for ten years. He was an odd-looking little man, small and slight of build, with a silken floss of grey hair and bright blue eyes in an innocent, ageless face. His movements were quick and graceful, though he was lame in one leg and walked with the aid of a cane. He knocked briskly on the door at precisely three o'clock, carrying a seed cake on a plate, which he presented to me with a bow.

'I made it this morning, Mrs Rodd; I know Mrs Bentley's fond of my seed cake.'

He did not mind in the least that I led him downstairs to the kitchen, but bowed to Mrs B with a courtly flourish, and settled easily beside the fire. His cake was excellent; soft and sweet and moist, with just the right quantity of caraway to give it a delicate flavour. I was very pleased that Mrs B accepted a slice, for her lack of appetite was a constant worry to me.

'I hope you can forgive my approaching you directly,' said Mr Tully. 'I'm doing it on behalf of a very old friend, who knows your reputation for discretion.' He raised his eyebrows in a meaningful way. 'She – this old friend – is acquainted with a family by the name of Heaton.'

Mrs Bentley and I exchanged sharp glances; the Heaton case had been my first great success as a private investigator, and it was still (as Mrs B liked to say) bringing in customers.

'Not that my friend's situation is in any way similar,' Mr Tully said quickly. 'There are no dead bodies – no actual crimes at all, in fact. It's simply a … a *situation* that requires very careful handling.'

'Of course I understand, Mr Tully,' I hastened to assure him. 'I do not sit in judgement, and it's next to impossible to shock me. How may I help you?'

'This friend of mine,' he said, 'is very well known in theatrical circles; her name is Transome.'

'As in Thomas Transome?' I knew very little about the theatre, but even I had heard something of this celebrated actor-manager.

'Yes, ma'am.' His eyes had a gleam of pride. 'Thomas Transome and his family hold the lease of the Duke of Cumberland's Theatre in the Haymarket. Before my retirement from the stage, I spent some very happy years with his company.'

'Tell her about the fire,' said Mrs Bentley.

'Dear me, yes,' said Mr Tully. 'Ten years ago, when we were still at the King's Theatre in Drury Lane, there was a terrible fire – the cause of my retirement.' He placed a hand upon his lame leg. 'I was badly injured; my memory of that night is imperfect, but Tom Transome always said I saved his life. Whether I did or not, he staged a grand benefit performance and gave me the proceeds so that I could live out my days in comfort. He is capable of great generosity.'

'Indeed.'

'But I won't talk about the theatre; Mrs Bentley thinks theatres are sinful places. And I'm not calling on Tom's behalf. My friend is his wife, Mrs Sarah Transome.'

'You must forgive my ignorance,' I said. 'Do I take it that she acts too?'

'She does, ma'am – in her day, she was a great actress – one of the very best. And her three daughters are also on the stage.'

'Why does she need my services, Mr Tully?'

He was sorrowful now. 'To put it plainly, because Tom Transome has fallen in love.'

'I beg your pardon?' I had not expected this, and had no idea how to respond.

'He has fallen head-over-ears in love with a girl by the name of Constance Noonan, who is currently playing Juliet to his Romeo. She is eighteen years old. Tom has had what you might call "intrigues" with certain actresses in the past – but he always kept them out of the way of his wife. This is different. He has quite lost his mind, and is talking about setting up home with this girl.'

'Disgraceful!' said Mrs Bentley.

'I'm inclined to agree,' I put in, not wanting to discourage Mr Tully when he was just getting up steam, 'but we ought to suspend any judgement until we have heard the facts – why does Mrs Transome need my assistance?'

'She needs someone to speak up for her interests.' His pale face reddened a little. 'Her husband wants to turn her out of the house.'

Mrs B's lips formed the word 'disgraceful'.

'Has he cited any reason for turning her out, apart from his own infidelity?' I asked.

'He has accused Mrs Sarah of being a neglectful mother to her girls when they were small children,' said Mr Tully. 'Which is arrant nonsense, and simply his latest attempt to do her out of what is rightfully hers. She needs to consult a lady like yourself, with whom she can be absolutely candid.'

'Oh, you can't shock her!' said Mrs B, nodding at me.

'She's very troubled, Mrs Rodd! It makes my heart ache sometimes, to see her so anxious and unhappy. Tom is angling for a legal separation, on terms that are frankly stingy; I don't know what's got into him! And she doesn't know who she can trust.'

'What about the daughters; don't they live with her?'

'Only the youngest, Cordelia, aged nineteen and Tom's pride and joy; she's not speaking to her father, and that has only made the situation worse. The middle sister, Olivia, at the tender age of twenty-four, has taken Tom's side and left her mother's house. And the oldest, Maria – now Mrs Maria Betterton – is away in America, on tour with her husband. She is twenty-seven. She sent her father a letter that made him furious, to the point of smashing things. The name "Betterton", of course, only added insult to injury!'

He nodded at us knowingly, saw our blank faces and went on, 'There is a famous feud between the Transome and Betterton families, strikingly similar to the state of affairs between the Montagues and the Capulets.'

'Let us return to the requirements of Mrs Sarah Transome.' I sensed this was a tale that could fly off in a hundred directions, and it was important to keep things as simple as possible. 'I would be very happy to meet her, and to speak on her behalf in the matter of making a settlement – if I can be of real help.'

'Thank you!' cried Mr Tully, radiant with relief. 'You will find her at home in Pericles Cottage, Ham Common, on any day convenient to you.'

My conscience troubled me that evening. I was the widow of an archdeacon, and dignitaries of the Church did not frequent places of public entertainment. My beloved Matt could never conquer a sneaking fondness for such places, and had occasionally 'treated' our nephews to a pantomime, but this did not mean he approved of the theatrical world. I could not help knowing he would not have approved of my involvement with the Transomes.

On the other hand, Mrs B's illness had been costly (I had not told her the half of it), and I needed the money – yes, the argument that so often trumps all the others. This was my excuse for taking on one of the saddest cases I have ever encountered, though it was not sad to begin with.

In true theatrical style, the programme commenced with a farce and ended with a tragedy.

Two

TWO DAYS LATER, DIRECTLY after breakfast, a most extraordinary carriage arrived in Well Walk to take Mr Tully and myself from Hampstead to Ham Common; a four-wheeler of a rather bright shade of blue, drawn by two horses and with a coat of arms upon the door.

'It's not a genuine coat of arms,' Mr Tully said happily. 'Tom designed it himself and got the scene-painter from the theatre to execute it; he enjoys cutting a dash.'

A small crowd of local children gathered to admire the carriage. I had installed twelve-year-old Hannah Bentley, one of Mrs B's army of red-headed grandchildren, to sit with her while I was out, and she waved us off from the drawing-room window as if we were royalty.

Upon closer examination, the paintwork and fittings of the showy equipage turned out to be rather faded and frayed.

'Tom left this at Ham for Mrs Sarah,' said Mr Tully. 'He lives in Herne Hill at present and prefers to drive himself to and from the theatre in his cabriolet. And there's talk that he's buying a brougham for the girl – though it may be just talk.'

'He must be very wealthy,' I suggested.

'Indeed he is, Mrs Rodd. The Duke's has proved to be an absolute goldmine. The fire at his last theatre nearly ruined him, but he confounded the naysayers with one triumph after another.' Mr Tully had brought a covered basket, which he opened to show a pewter flask and a number of little bundles wrapped in whitey-brown paper. 'I have some ham sandwiches, some slices of pound cake and a flask of sherry, if you would care for refreshment.'

'Not at the moment, thank you.'

'You're quite right, it's too early. Perhaps later.'

'I'm impressed by your handiness in the kitchen, Mr Tully.'

'Cookery is a favourite pastime of mine, especially since my retirement.'

I could not help looking at his injured leg, which was thinner than the other and slightly twisted. 'If you don't mind my asking, what was the cause of that fire?'

'A broken footlight,' said Mr Tully. 'The whole place went up like a tinderbox. Very fortunately the theatre was closed at the time, or hundreds might have perished.'

'You said that Mr Transome was inside the building; where were his wife and daughters?'

'The girls were safe at home. Mrs Sarah was in her carriage, halfway back to Ham Common, when the fire broke out. The play that night was *Romeo and Juliet*; she was playing Juliet to her husband's Romeo.' He was smiling, yet I caught a flash of calculation on his guileless face. 'The fire was the cause of their first great falling-out – you may as well know it before you meet her. Tom went into a ridiculous amount of debt to fund the move to the new theatre.'

'Was there no insurance?'

'Yes, but not sufficient to pay for everything. Tom knew he could not survive unless he opened the Duke of Cumberland's with a sensation, and he made a very bold move – he decided to revive his production of *As You Like It*, but with his oldest daughter as his leading lady, instead of his wife. He said she was too old.'

'Poor Mrs Transome!'

Mr Tully sighed. 'It was harsh of him – but life is harsh, and Tom was proved right in the end. Maria's performance as Rosalind, opposite her father's Orlando, was a stunning success.'

'Correct me if I'm wrong, for I'm anxious to get the details right,' I said. 'Maria is the daughter who became Mrs Betterton – in defiance of the animosity between the two families?'

'Yes, and the betrayal cut Tom to the heart.'

'Do you know what is behind their rivalry?'

'Not precisely – but those Bettertons are slippery customers, ma'am. They claim to be related to the actor Betterton who was so famous during the Restoration, but I've never believed a word of it. James Betterton hauled himself out of an Irish bog, and plenty of folks will tell you that in those days his name was Jimmy McGinty.'

'Mrs Betterton must be a spirited young woman,' I said, trying to arrange the pieces of the Transome family in my mind, 'to defy her father so openly.'

'Well, she's the image of him, that's the trouble.' A glint of mischief sparked in his eyes. 'They're both very stubborn, and very fond of their own way. Between ourselves, Maria never paid much attention to her mother, and after she took her place as Tom's leading lady, she seemed to despise her. Tom and his daughter adored each other and were the toast of the town – until Maria happened to meet young Betterton. He's the second of the sons—'

'Mr Tully,' I interrupted, 'you must spare me another family tree when I'm still getting to grips with all these Transomes! What of the one who followed her father?'

'Olivia.'

'Thank you: Olivia. I assume she is another actress. Did she take her sister's place at Mr Transome's side after Maria married?'

'Oh, dear me, no! And thereby hangs another tale, ma'am. Poor Olivia isn't a patch on either of her sisters. She's perfectly good in her way, but Maria and Cordelia inherited the lion's share of Tom's genius and put her thoroughly in the shade. She knows it and is jealous of them. That's why she took Tom's side.'

'Is the bond between them especially close?'

'Well – she all but worships her father, Mrs Rodd, and of course he's extremely fond of her, but anyone can see that he favours the others. He was inconsolable when Maria eloped; you could hear his sobbing all over the theatre.'

'When was this, exactly?'

'Three years ago,' said Mr Tully. 'The family were still together in those days. Olivia begged Tom to let her take over Maria's roles, but he turned her down and gave them to little Cordelia, who had just turned sixteen.'

'Olivia must have been angry,' I said.

'That's putting it mildly, ma'am. She was beside herself.'

'Yet she forgave her father, to the point of leaving her mother's house!'

'She'd forgive that old rascal anything, if you ask me.'

'Wasn't Cordelia rather too young to make such a grand debut?'

'In most cases you'd be right, but Cordelia had been training since she could walk; her first appearance was as a fairy in the *Dream* when she was six. Her debut at the Duke's was an absolute triumph.'

We were driving south and after passing many gleaming new streets and squares, and seemingly endless plots of new houses in various stages of completion, the roads became leafy and surrounding us were fields and gardens. It was pleasant to see the clusters of daffodils and primroses, which had not yet appeared in any great numbers upon Hampstead Heath.

'Before I meet Mrs Transome,' I said, 'I would like to know when her husband met Miss Noonan.'

'Everything was going so well for him,' said Mr Tully, rolling his eyes. 'Isn't it always the way? It was a year ago, Mrs Rodd. Tom saw her at the Theatre Royal in Wakefield. She was playing the lead in a dreadful verse drama called *Boadicea*, specially written for her by the local Chatterton – every provincial town has its dreadful poet. And Tom was enslaved at once, though only in a professional sense at first. He could not rest until he had brought Miss Noonan down to London, to play Juliet opposite his Romeo.'

'I would have thought him rather too old for the role.'

'His appearance onstage is very youthful. When he plays the ardent young lover opposite Miss Noonan, you'd swear he was no more than a boy. It was a vast success and, before long, he had lost his heart. He had said he would never play Romeo again after Maria ran off; not even with Cordelia. The Noonan girl changed his mind.'

'I see,' I said. 'That must have angered his family.'

'As I have said, ma'am, it tore the family asunder.'

The fitful sun broke through the clouds just at the moment the carriage turned into Ham Common, drenching the broad expanse of green in sharp spring sunlight. I was struck by the beauty of the woods and grassland so close to the city, and the glimpses of fine houses I caught through the new leaves. Mr Tully drew my attention to the lodge at the gate of the magnificent Ham House, ancestral seat of the Earls of Dysart, exclaiming how lovely it was to be out in the 'countryside'. I grew up in the countryside and knew that this suburban idyll was nothing like it, being far too clean and tidy.

Pericles Cottage, half-hidden behind a red-brick wall, was a long, low-built house of white stucco, surrounded by smooth lawns. Mr Tully and I were admitted by a stout middle-aged Irishwoman with grey hair neatly pinned beneath a cap of black silk. She asked us to wait for a few moments, and Mr Tully whispered to me that she had once been Mrs Transome's 'dresser' in the theatre. 'The two of them go back a long way, ma'am, to the days before she met Tom.'

The hall was bright and spacious, with black-and-white tiles on the floor and walls crowded with paintings that I would have liked to look at more closely – all of actors and actresses in wondrous costumes and dramatic poses. There were some portraits of women, strikingly handsome; the lion's share, however, were of men: in fact, of the same man – Thomas Transome, attired in togas and breast-plates, tights and medieval jerkins, and always wonderfully good-looking.

The housekeeper returned to show us into a sunny sitting room, rather sparsely furnished, with great windows that overlooked a garden gay with crocuses and daffodils.

'Mrs Rodd, I am very glad to see you.'

Now I had eyes for nothing save Sarah Transome. All these years later, I still struggle to describe her; she was neither young nor pretty, yet there was something vivid, something arresting about her that gave an impression of beauty. Her eyes and hair were of a soft dark brown. She wore no cap, and no 'cage' or crinoline beneath her black velvet skirts, and her slender figure moved with a kind of sinuous freedom. She must have been well into her forties but something in her air was indefinably girlish – particularly when Mr Tully bent to kiss her hand and she smiled.

13

'My dear Ben, what a courtier you are! Please sit down beside the fire, Mrs Rodd, and Murphy will bring us something refreshing. You are most kind to visit me, when you must be well aware that this is a house of shame.'

'That's a bit strong, my darling!' Mr Tully gently protested (I was not yet accustomed to the familiarity with which theatricals addressed one another, and made an effort not to raise my eyebrows). 'Nobody thinks it's your fault.'

'I know of no shame attached to you, or to your daughters,' I hastened to assure her. 'You cannot be blamed for the behaviour of your husband.'

'You are very kind,' said Mrs Transome.

I sat down in an armchair that was covered with rather musty-smelling red plush.

Mr Tully went to look out of one of the long windows. 'There's Cordelia! She can entertain me while you are speaking with Mrs Rodd.'

Out in the garden, a beautiful young woman in a loose-fitting green robe, her dark hair unbound and streaming down her back, drifted slowly across the lawn.

'My daughter,' said Mrs Transome, with a sigh of exasperation. 'I suppose I should be thankful that she's getting some fresh air; she spends most of her time in the boudoir upstairs, sprawled across the daybed.'

'Has she been unwell?' I asked.

'Oh, there's nothing the matter with her, except that she has barely spoken a word since she left her father's theatre. Ben, my dear, do try to cheer her up before she sulks us all to death!'

He bowed to us both and left the room. Mrs Transome took the chair on the other side of the fireplace. Gazing down at us from above the mantelpiece was a painting of Thomas Transome as Julius Caesar, with a laurel wreath upon his brow and a storm raging behind him.

'Yes, that's dear old Tom.' Mrs Transome smiled to see how my eyes were drawn to him. 'It was done shortly before Cordelia was born. He named her Cordelia because she was his third daughter, and he wanted to do *King Lear* when they were all grown up.'

'I'm sure,' I said, 'that you are thankful to have her at your side now.'

'I suppose so,' said Mrs Transome. 'Frankly, I was a little surprised; she loved being her father's leading lady. And he didn't start making a fool of himself with the Noonan girl until after Cordelia left him. That is to say, he was already up to his eyes in the infatuation and the whole theatre was gossiping about it – but he didn't actually lose his head until the falling-out with Cordelia.'

'Do you know what passed between them?'

Her face turned sour. 'She was getting jealous of Noonan, that's the bottom of it. The last straw was when she heard that Tom had cast the girl as Juliet; only then did she remember her duty to her poor deserted mother. Out she flounced – and she has been moping and weeping here ever since.'

The conversation was making me uncomfortable. There was a hardness to the way this woman spoke of her own child, and a kind of careless flippancy in her attitude that grated on me. And yet I had no doubt that Sarah Transome had been grievously wounded; the hard shell could not conceal her pain.

'Mrs Transome,' I said, 'Mr Tully has told me a little about what you require of me, but I would like to hear it from you.'

'That won't take long. Tom and I have come to the end, and a final settlement must be made between us. He wants me to live as cheaply and obscurely as possible. I think he wishes I would simply disappear.'

15

Murphy, the dresser-turned-housekeeper, burst into the room without knocking, bearing a tray with a bottle, a plate of fancy cakes and two mismatched glasses.

'The butcher's at the back door again, Mrs Sarah; he won't go away till he gets something on account.'

Mrs Transome, not the least put out, sighed irritably. 'Tiresome man! Let him have five shillings, but only if he carries on bringing us meat. You see the position I'm in, Mrs Rodd; until my husband grants me an income, I am quite helpless!'

Despite her avowed penury, the entertainment was generous to the point of extravagance. Once Murphy had departed to placate the butcher, Mrs Transome offered me a cake that was evidently purchased from some West End patisserie and a glass of excellent Madeira.

'Have you sought legal advice?'

'Only in an informal sense,' said Mrs Transome, 'sufficient to convince me that the law is not on my side. I am a chattel; my husband can dispose of me like a set of spoons if he sees fit. I shall only need a lawyer when we reach a proper agreement. Before that, I need an advocate to assert my moral rights as Tom's wife and the mother of his children. He wants me out of this house so that he can sell it. I have warned him that I refuse to be budged unless he gives me enough money and somewhere decent to live.'

'That is perfectly reasonable,' I said carefully. In truth, I did not care for an assignment that would help Thomas Transome to commit adultery – but if the mischief was already done, his wife certainly stood in need of someone to defend her interests. 'Has your husband appointed his own advocate?'

'Yes,' snapped Mrs Transome. 'One of his cronies from the Garrick Club; a very well-known barrister by the name of Frederick Tyson. Perhaps you have heard of him?'

I had indeed heard of him and, though my heart sank, I had to make an effort not to laugh.

Three

'M Y OWN SISTER — this is the best joke I've heard in years!'

'Fred, do be serious! I tried to tell her we couldn't possibly work on opposing sides, but she refused to listen to me.'

My brother, Frederick Tyson, was the most celebrated criminal barrister in London, famed for his flamboyant performances in court. We were sitting in his study, at the front of his large red-brick house in Highgate, where the walls were decorated with examples of the cartoons and sketches of him that constantly appeared in the popular press. As a little boy he looked like a plump cherub, and led his 'sensible' older sister into all kinds of mischief. At the age of fifty-two, he was stout, with a mass of grey curls, and as fond of mischief as ever.

'Nonsense, my dear! The more I think of it, the better I like the idea. The Transomes will never settle properly if their advocates are at odds. And on my side, it is only an informal thing — a favour to a friend. So I have Punch and you have Judy, and between us we can stop them killing each other.'

It was early evening and above us we could hear the distant thumps and shrieks that meant the smallest of his eleven children were being put to bed. Beneath us were the muted sounds of dinner being prepared in the basement kitchen. Fred's wife was also upstairs, dressing for a dinner party to which I had been (grudgingly) invited at the last minute.

Fred stopped laughing and refilled our wine glasses. His study was large and wondrously comfortable, lined with legal tomes and questionable French novels, and the extravagant fire was hot enough to make my eyes water.

'Do you know Thomas Transome well?' I asked.

'He's an acquaintance of mine at the Garrick, and I've seen him perform many times.'

'Do you like him?'

Fred grinned at me. 'I can see that you don't like him in the least.'

'I think his behaviour is abominable – shameful!'

'Yes, I suppose so.'

'Suppose? My dear Fred, he has deserted his wife and family! He consorts openly with his mistress! Why do his audiences put up with him?'

'Because he is a genius.'

'That is beside the point.'

'Take a word of advice,' said Fred. 'Actors are commonly treated as outsiders, which means they are able to behave as outsiders – living in their own little world, with its own laws and customs. You must accept this, or you'll get no sense from any of them. Consider yourself a traveller in a strange country and suspend your disapproval.'

I could see the sense in this, but still did not like it. 'I don't approve of double standards, and I'm very reluctant to make allowances for anyone – genius or not.'

'I'll take you to see him in action, and then you'll understand the particular spell he casts over his audiences.'

'Have you seen his wife onstage?'

'Of course – and all three of his daughters. Sarah was a charming little thing when she was young. What did you think of her?'

'I'm not certain,' I said. 'I didn't quite like her manner, though she was perfectly friendly and courteous.'

'She's very angry.' My brother drained his glass of claret and poured himself another. 'You should make allowance for that. You are only concerned with making the poor woman a fair settlement; I warned Transome that I would not support any attempt to cheat her of her moral rights, and got his assurance that he wished to treat her fairly. He's really not a bad fellow.'

'Hmm.'

'Look how decent he was to that little neighbour of yours.'

'Mr Tully saved his life when the last theatre burned down.'

'Ah, the fire – a dreadful business!' said Fred. 'Fanny and I were there just the night before; it was a mercy the place was empty.'

I had been thinking a great deal about the famous fire. 'I was told the cause was simply a broken footlight.'

'That was the coroner's conclusion – though naturally there was a babble of gossip about arson.'

'Surely not!'

'I'd say of course not, but actors love to spice up a dull story. The rumour was that it was the work of Transome's great rival, James Betterton. He had apparently placed a "spy" in Transome's company, who ran off somewhere before any charges could be made.'

'Was there any truth in it?'

Fred gave one of his rich, rumbling, vinous laughs. 'Not a scrap! My personal opinion is that Transome and Betterton keep up the rivalry because it's good for business – though he was certainly furiously angry when Maria went over to the other side and eloped with his rival's son.'

'Has he forgiven her yet?'

'They staged an official reconciliation, and then Maria and her husband conveniently went off to America. We'll have to see what the weather's like when she returns. She's no lover of Miss Constance Noonan, that I do know.'

'You've seen the Noonan girl at work, I'm sure,' I said. 'She must be very beautiful.'

'She is a divinity,' said Fred. 'Her hair is spun gold, her eyes are sapphires, and she has the voice of an angel.'

'I presume she is already living with Mr Transome.'

'You presume wrong. The young lady is still officially living with her mother in Pentonville. The word is that she's holding out for a "settlement" of her own.'

'Indeed!'

'Now, Letty, don't purse up your mouth like that! I shall escort you to the theatre tomorrow night, and you'll see the leading players for yourself.'

The Duke of Cumberland's Theatre was a magnificent edifice of white stone, with a great pillared portico before it, and powerful flares of gaslight burning on either side of the entrance. The Haymarket was crammed with people; my brother's carriage inched along in a line of other carriages, some of which were very grand, with genuine coats of arms painted on the doors. The crowd that surged around them was a noisy, jostling, mostly good-natured mixture of all kinds and classes – gentlemen in silk hats, beggars, loafers and thieves.

Fred laughed at my dazzlement. 'When was the last time you went to the theatre?'

'Matt and I saw Macready as King Lear; it was a private performance for the Archbishop of Canterbury.' I stopped gaping out of the window. 'I'm not accustomed to such crowds of people.'

'Well, this is *Romeo and Juliet*, played by Transome and Noonan, and the sensation of the hour,' said Fred happily, brushing crumbs of pastry from his capacious white waistcoat. 'Fanny and I have seen it, judges and bishops have seen it, and even the clerks from my chambers; the man must be raking in a fortune. And how splendidly apt that we should first see our star-cross'd lovers masquerading as star-cross'd lovers!'

'I'm not sure that I care much for *Romeo and Juliet*,' I said. 'The tragedy is so dreadful and the lovers are both so silly!'

'I'm sure you would've settled the silly pair in a moment – and the whole of Verona, while you were at it,' said Fred. 'Try to get into the spirit of the thing. By the end of the evening, your hard heart will be in absolute shreds. Poor Fanny's eyes were swollen for two days!'

'I'm not hard-hearted,' I returned. 'Only sensible.'

'I bet you half a crown you'll shed copious tears.'

'Nonsense! I don't waste my tears upon made-up stories.'

'You won't be able to resist! I warn you now – I shall be weeping like a watercart.'

We had arrived at the great portico; my brother helped me from the carriage and led me through the crush at the entrance to the theatre. Through a forest of heads, I caught a glimpse of two large portraits on the wall – a slender, dark-haired young man and a beautiful girl with a luxuriant heap of golden hair.

An elderly maid in a cap and apron showed us into our box on the Grand Tier and took charge of my black cloak and bonnet and my brother's silk hat. Fred told her to bring us a bottle of sherry and tipped her a shilling.

'So much!' I could not help protesting.

'It's not extravagance,' said Fred. 'That old woman used to be an actress, and the tips she gets for serving the boxes probably make up most of her income.'

'Really? Poor thing, what a precarious way to make a living.' I settled myself in one of the spindly gilt chairs and stared about me at the wall of faces in the packed theatre (I had noted every door we passed in case there was a fire). I was dazed by the roar of conversation, the glare of gas-light, the musicians tuning their instruments in the pit. Most of the noise came from the gallery at the very top of the auditorium; Fred called it 'the gods', though the people were decidedly ungodlike in their behaviour: when the blue velvet curtains parted, they broke out in whooping and stamping that drowned out the orchestra.

I do not know enough about the theatre to describe this production of Shakespeare's tragedy in detail; my brother was soon sobbing into his sherry, but my main interest was in the players rather than the play.

Mr Transome's first entrance was greeted by the gallery with a mighty roar and a thunderous outbreak of stamping that made the whole building tremble. He acknowledged the audience with one brief nod, then waited patiently for the noise to die down. Fred had described him as 'youth-ful' and I admit that I was startled by his boyish appearance; there really is no other word to describe him. Transome's figure, so gaily got up in red tights and a velvet jerkin, was slender and elegant. He moved with an effortless grace; his head was beautifully shaped and his voice was as naturally lovely as birdsong. Though he did not reduce me to tears, I found myself believing this man was an ardent boy.

And whatever opinion I had formed of Constance Noonan, my first sight of her took my breath away. For once Fred had not been exaggerating. Her hair was of the purest gold, her eyes as blue as periwinkles, her soft and plaintive voice brought out the sweetness of the poetry. And love shone out of her; she blazed with love, filling the entire theatre with it, until even my sensible eyes were moist.

'Now you see it,' Fred said at the end of the performance, blowing his nose vigorously. 'I don't blame Transome for falling in love with her; I'm half in love with her myself!'

The maid returned, to conduct us past the row of boxes to a baize-covered door in the wall at the end of the passage. Through this door we entered another world, the hidden world behind the stage that sent my head into a spin. Fred was very much at home here; he led me up a dank stone staircase crowded with insolent, semi-clad people who conversed in shouts and took absolutely no notice of us; I did my best to look unconcerned, but the bare arms and bosoms made my face hot with embarrassment.

The door of Thomas Transome's dressing room was opened by a neat, cheery man of around my own age, with grey hair trimmed very short around a bald pate. He wore a coarse apron with the bib stuck full of needles and pins.

'Mr Tyson! Good evening, sir.' He gave me a friendly, slightly-too-familiar bow. 'Ma'am.'

'Good evening, Cooper; is Himself presentable?'

'Yes, sir; he's expecting you.' Cooper ushered us inside and called out, 'They're here, dear! And one's a lady – a real one – so let's all mind our language.'

The dressing room was a good-sized chamber with a small fireplace, flowered wallpaper, a daybed covered with chintz, three soft armchairs and a large dressing table in a glare of gaslight; I was most interested to see sticks of coloured greasepaint laid out in tidy rows upon a towel.

Mr Transome himself erupted out of an inner door. 'You are Mrs Rodd; Ben Tully told me we'd managed to engage both Tyson and his sister, and I think it's a most excellent wheeze, besides which I've heard Johnny Heaton singing your praises any number of times.'

I was startled by this sudden rush of intimacy when we had just met, and could only mumble 'How do you do?' (Despite my confusion, I made a mental note of the fact that Mr Tully was still in touch with Transome; the loyalties of these people seemed flexible, to say the least.)

'And Tyson – how are you, my boy? Mrs Rodd, please forgive my *déshabillé* and take the armchair nearest to the fire; Coopsy, give her the footstool.'

He was wrapped in a sumptuous dressing gown of dark red velvet. He had scrubbed the paint from his clean-shaven face and removed the romantic wig he wore for Romeo to reveal his own smooth black hair. This was not the ardent youth I had just seen onstage; there were streaks of grey at his temples and a very faint crazing of wrinkles around his fine dark eyes. And yet in his brisk energy and the almost overwhelming charm of his manner, there was still something youthful about Thomas Transome.

While Fred and I reclined in our chairs, Mr Transome roved about the room, looking at things without seeing them, and pouring forth a cataract of friendliness. 'By the by, Tyson, before you congratulate me for my performance – as I'm sure you will – I must congratulate you for yours! The word at the club is that you *floored* the jury yesterday, and cheated the hangman once again; when I finally murder someone, I hope you'll defend me.'

'Thank you,' Fred said, smiling. 'It was one of my better shows.'

'And so you were in tonight? How did you find it?'

'Magnificent,' said Fred. 'Even better than last time. Your death nearly broke my heart.'

'You're very kind; I felt it went rather well, but Cooper says I was "off" in the first swordfight.'

'That you were, sir,' said Cooper. 'You fluffed the footwork something shocking, dear.'

'You see, Mrs Rodd? No actor is a hero to his dresser!'

'I was most impressed by your performance, Mr Transome,' I said. 'If there was anything wrong with it, I didn't notice.'

'Thank you!' Mr Transome gave me a graceful bow. 'Do you hear that, Coopsy? Stop picking holes in your betters and go and fetch my dinner!' He added to me, 'You must forgive my bad manners, ma'am; Cooper gets my dinner from the tavern after every performance; it is the only proper meal I have upon a working day, and I must eat it or perish.'

'What – you fast before a performance?' Fred cried out, laughing. 'I could never do that in court; I can only deliver on a full stomach.'

'My dear Tyson, there is no comparison! Nobody cares how fat you are because nobody expects you to impersonate Romeo. I have to mind every morsel or I'll burst out of my costumes.'

His manner was so droll that I found myself chuckling before I knew what I was doing, and Fred roared with laughter, patting his great stomach complacently, not the least offended.

'I find it a lot harder to maintain my figure nowadays.' Mr Transome examined his lissom reflection in one of the several mirrors. 'When I was a boy, I could eat anything with impunity. It's only quite recently that I've had to take care – not having any ambition to play Falstaff just yet.'

Cooper pulled on a blue coat, without removing his apron. 'Will it be the usual, Mr Tom?'

'Yes, don't forget the mustard pot this time.'

'Right you are, sir.' Before he left the room, Cooper paused to scoop up a little heap of coins from a large heap of silver and copper, carelessly scattered on a shelf.

'I'm forced to deal in ready money,' said Mr Transome. 'None of the local taverns will give credit to theatricals. I daresay this is born of bitter experience on their part and I can't say I blame them for it; actors have been dodging their bar bills since the days of Roscius in ancient Rome.' He sat down on the daybed, not exactly theatrically, but with a natural flourish. 'Now, as to why you are here – well, you've met my wife, Mrs Rodd, and she has doubtless told you of my many acts of wickedness.'

'She is mostly anxious about money.' I was determined to be practical, without appearing to approve of his careless, cynical manner. 'And she refuses to leave the house at Ham Common until she is found a suitable house of her own. That is surely reasonable.'

Mr Transome let out a sigh of exasperation. 'It would be reasonable, if the woman didn't have such grand ideas! I'll admit that my initial offer, the small house in Edmonton, was on the niggardly side – but she has no need for a large establishment like Pericles Cottage. Two of our girls have flown the nest, and I'm prepared to bet that Cordelia will see sense eventually and come back to me.'

He stopped, gave me a shrewd glance and adjusted his expression to one of sober penitence; this was a man well able to assess his audience and to fine-tune his performance accordingly, and he saw through my attempts to hide my disapproval.

'I beg your pardon,' he said quietly. 'My feelings are running off in all directions; the tearing apart of my family is my fault, and that only increases the general misery.'

'It is a shame,' I said, 'that your daughters have taken opposing sides. Before any kind of agreement is drawn up, you and your wife ought to decide where they are to live.'

He was a little taken aback. 'Yes, of course; Maria is married and settled with an establishment of her own, and there's plenty of room for the others in the new house at Herne Hill.'

'Mr Transome!' It was all I could do not to snap at him. 'You must be aware that they cannot possibly live with you!'

'Why not? It's a delightful little place.'

'Because they would be ruined, Mr Transome! You cannot expect them to live under the same roof as your mistress!'

I had put it as plainly as possible, amazed that he appeared not to understand me, and he simply shrugged his shoulders. 'That sort of thing doesn't really matter in the theatre.'

'Doesn't matter!'

Fred shot me a warning glance, and I forced myself to calm down.

'According to Mr Tully,' I went on, 'there are reports that you have accused your wife of being an unfit mother.'

'Oh, you may ignore that,' said Mr Transome breezily. 'Certain things were said in the heat of the moment. I'm afraid I was still angry with Sarah because she helped Maria with the elopement business.' His face lit up with a dazzling smile. 'My dear Mrs Rodd, if you raise your eyebrows any higher, you'll never get them down again!'

'I beg your pardon,' I said faintly (doing my best not to look at Fred, who was obviously enjoying my discomfiture). 'Mrs Transome told me nothing of this; there was no hint that she actually assisted the young couple.'

'She did it to get back at me, and she has always been under Maria's thumb.'

'I understood that you and Mrs Betterton had kissed and made up,' said Fred. 'Don't tell me that touching scene was a sham!'

I thought this impertinent; Mr Transome merely laughed.

'I wasn't about to give those Bettertons a chance to cast me in the role of Heavy Father – but one benefit perform-ance doth not the reconciliation make!'

My brother was mightily amused, and this encouraged Mr Transome to launch into an imitation of Maria's hus-band playing Laertes in breeches that were too tight. He was so dreadfully funny that I could not help laughing, and Fred nearly laughed himself into a seizure.

Cooper came back halfway through this impromptu performance, carrying a stack of covered dishes and with a knife and fork sticking out of his top pocket; he chuckled while he laid out Transome's supper on a folding card table, and muttered, 'He'll be the death of me one of these days!'

Mr Transome sat down to a homely meal of roast beef, potatoes and gravy (good tavern fare, straight from the kitchen fire; the man was not dainty in his habits). He ate quickly and neatly, not in the least self-conscious about being watched, and keeping up a cheery conversation with Fred.

At the cheese stage he produced a decanter and showed us how he 'gargled' with a mouthful of brandy to relax his throat. 'You should try it in court, Tyson, next time you have a long summing-up!'

While the two men laughed and drank brandy, they forgot about me. I was free to observe Thomas Transome at close quarters and could quite understand why Fred liked him. I had never before encountered a person so shamelessly disgraceful, and yet so difficult to resist.

Four

B
Y THE TIME FRED and I left the theatre, we had managed to sketch out the bare bones of an agreement between husband and wife. Mr Transome, though bored by the facts and figures, was neither vindictive nor ungenerous. I even thought the business might be settled quickly. As far as I was concerned, I could not wash my hands of the theatre and its myrmidons quickly enough. I am always careful not to sit in judgement but I worried that I could not touch pitch without being defiled. I sat over the empty grate in my little drawing room until far into the night.

Above the fireplace I had installed my dearest possession, the portrait of my beloved husband by Edwin Landseer. It was what is called a 'speaking likeness', which caught exactly Matt's warm, quizzical expression; oh, how I wished I could really speak to him now. He was the kindest of men, but I had an uneasy feeling he would not have approved of this latest case.

Over the next fortnight, a number of letters passed between my brother and myself and the warring couple. Punch had reached the point of allowing Judy a small carriage; Judy had reached the point of considering a modest yet pretty house in Maida Hill near Paddington.

The next development in the case happened when I was not thinking about actors, but about the noisome slums in the area known as Seven Dials, situated near to the top of St Martin's Lane. I was the Honourable Secretary of a committee for the building of almshouses for the people who lived there (oh, what a long process this turned into; it took several years to find a suitable piece of land and several more to raise the funds for its purchase, and there were times when I longed to bang together the heads of certain ladies). Our meeting that morning had been at a house in the Strand, in the shadow of St Martin-in-the-Fields and Nelson's Column.

The day was beautiful and I could not resist strolling around those bustling streets when the meeting was over; I have always loved the way that a really fine spring day makes everything – and everybody – look cheerful. I went to the market at Covent Garden, revelling in the dirt and debris, the rumble of cartwheels upon cobblestones and the cries of the costers and their donkeys. It was the start of May and the first strawberries were in; the sweet scent of the scarlet fruit took me back to my dear mother's strawberry bed at home (she had a net to keep off the birds, but no net could save the berries from my greedy brother).

I walked along Drury Lane in the direction of the turnpike at St Giles, intending to take the omnibus to Camden Town. The area of Covent Garden, then as now, was a lively mixture of quality and cabbage-leaves, and I avoided the smaller streets and alleyways that ran off the principal thoroughfares.

One section of the street was covered with scaffolding and shrouded in tarpaulins. In those days new buildings were springing up like mushrooms; I slowed to a dawdle, enjoying the sunshine as I watched the labourers at work with their pulleys and barrows. There was a stationer's shop opposite with a window that displayed portraits of leading actors, and I frittered away yet more time gazing at these.

Thomas Transome was here, alongside a large picture of a noble-looking man with fair hair – his rival, James Betterton. In the centre of the window was an elaborate, rather garish hand-coloured print of a youthful king and queen, both richly attired and impossibly handsome; I was most interested to discover that they were Mr and Mrs Edgar Betterton, otherwise known as Maria Transome and the man with whom she had eloped.

I was startled out of my reverie by a dry voice at my elbow.

'Well, I never, it's Mrs Rodd! You do have a way of turning up, ma'am.'

'Inspector Blackbeard! What has brought you here?'

I was sincerely glad to see him, though our friendship had not always been harmonious. In his younger days (about which I knew next to nothing), Thomas Blackbeard had been a sergeant in the army. He was now an inspector in the Metropolitan Police, in which capacity his mania for doing everything 'by the book' had caused me great annoyance during certain of my investigations.

'Just the usual, Mrs Rodd; a nice corpse.' He was dry and buttoned up, spare and inexpressive, with the rigid stance of a soldier and the obstinacy of a granite boulder. His clothes were drab, his hair was shaved down to stubble, his mouth was a slit of disapproval. I knew him well enough by now to see the glint of humour in his eyes. 'Do I dare to hope, ma'am, that you haven't come sniffing round with a view to interfering?'

'You may rest easy, Mr Blackbeard; my business today has nothing to do with your corpse.'

'I'm glad to hear it; I'd like to get this one dealt with quickly.'

'Are you able to tell me anything?' I could not help being curious; my dear mother used to say curiosity was my besetting sin, and I dearly loved to hear of an interesting corpse.

'Hmm,' said Blackbeard (that 'hmm' was a stock response of his, and in the past it had irritated me to the point of madness). 'I might've known you'd start your questions! The street's blocked at this end; please allow me to escort you back to Long Acre.' He touched his hat and began to walk off without waiting for my reply.

I had to break into a half-trot to keep up with him. 'Where is the body now – and when was it discovered?'

'The men working at the theatre found it early this morning,' said Blackbeard.

'Which theatre?'

'That one.' He nodded at the site covered with tarpaulin. 'The King's.'

'The King's!' I was very curious now. 'That's the one that burned down ten years ago when Thomas Transome held the lease.'

'So it did!' He gave me a sharp sideways glance. 'The place was boarded up for years – theatre people being superstitious about such things. Whoever took up the lease after the fire, they never did anything about it and let the place lie empty, but now it has been taken by one Edgar Betterton.'

'Indeed? I thought he was in America.'

'I must say, ma'am,' said Blackbeard, slowing his brisk pace, 'I'd never have guessed you were fond of the theatre.'

'That is putting it a little strongly,' I said. 'At present I am working amongst actors, and though it's a private matter, I'll tell you all about it – if you'll tell me about the corpse.'

He halted and turned to face me. 'You've made one of your connections.'

'Only because all theatricals seem to be connected in some way, and it happens that Betterton is the son-in-law of my client.'

'Hmm,' said Blackbeard. 'Let's have it, then.'

As briefly as possible, I outlined my business with the Transomes. 'Now you will understand why I'm interested. Quite apart from the matter of the corpse, Mr Transome will be most annoyed that his daughter and her husband are setting up as rivals. And since he was the last person to perform at the King's, you will presumably want to speak to him.'

Blackbeard stared at me in flinty silence for a few moments, then said, 'I'll give you what I've got, and if you don't mind risking your fine clothes, you can come and see the corpse for yourself, exactly as he was found.'

'Thank you, Inspector.' Though ladies were not supposed to take an interest in corpses, he knew me well enough to know that I would jump at the invitation. 'Do you know how long it has lain there? Could it be one of the builders, or perhaps a vagrant sheltering in the ruins?'

There was no hurrying Blackbeard; he ignored my questions and wound back to the beginning. 'At around seven this morning, two of the labourers fell through some rotten timbers into a cellar directly underneath the remains of the stage, thus dislodging a corpse in an advanced state of decomposition.'

'Is it possible to say how long it has been there?'

'I'm waiting for the surgeon's opinion about that,' said Blackbeard. 'Seeing as the place has lain waste since the fire, it's tempting to say ten years, but it might be more. The clothes are quite well preserved; he died in some sort of fancy coat and tights.'

'So he was evidently an actor,' I said. 'Has he been identified?'

'Not as yet, ma'am, but actors are easy to track down. I'm hopeful that your Mr Transome keeps good records.'

One of the labourers held aside the sheet of canvas so that we could enter the theatre. There is something very forlorn about the ruins of a place of entertainment, haunted by ghosts of pleasures past. The interior of the King's was halfway between a builder's yard and a charred suburb of the underworld. Through a spider's web of scaffolding, we saw the remains of the auditorium and heard vigorous hammering; the men had resumed their work in the principal part of the theatre.

'Watch yourself, Mrs Rodd!' Blackbeard guided me down a long (and alarmingly decrepit) staircase, where unexpected patches of daylight yawned out of large holes in the wall. 'Grab a hold of my arm, ma'am.'

We ducked under the half-burnt remnants of the stage and were plunged into a dusky glow of lamplight. Two policemen stood on guard here, and it was now possible to see where the timbers above us had broken, and where those unfortunate labourers had found the corpse.

The police surgeon, a rosy-faced young Scot, had just finished his examination and was rolling down the sleeves of his shirt. 'I've got as far as I can here; you may take him away now.'

'This is Mrs Rodd,' said Blackbeard. 'I brought her down because she's fond of dead bodies. Mrs Rodd, this is Dr Reid.'

Dr Reid did not appear to think this strange and acknowledged me with a friendly nod.

I am not afraid of the dead; as the wife of a country vicar I had many times helped to lay out corpses, often pitifully disfigured by illness. In my current incarnation as a private investigator, I had several times examined the remains of people who had been murdered. I said a private prayer for the soul of this poor creature, and then bent over to get a proper look.

It was a skeleton, still with a shock of dust-coloured hair and the last vestiges of a face. The clothes were better preserved than the flesh; this man had died in a coat of antique cut and a pair of tights, now faded to tatters of indeterminate duns and greys.

'Is it possible to ascertain how long he has lain here?' I asked.

'Difficult to be exact, ma'am,' said Dr Reid. 'I'll know more when I have more light to see him by. He's in pretty good condition due to the lack of air in his tomb; the foreman here says he was shut away in a kind of cistern under the floor. The trapdoor that was above him is burnt on one side, which suggests he was placed there before the fire.'

'A long time before?'

'I'd say not,' said Dr Reid, 'or there'd be less of him left.'

'He didn't get down here by accident, I'll bet,' said Mr Blackbeard. 'What's the cause of death?'

'You know I'm usually too canny to give an opinion right off,' said the doctor. 'In this case, however, the cause of death is only too obvious. There's a hole in the back of his skull.'

'A hole?'

'I found a bullet.' The doctor held out a small piece of lead. 'I think it's safe to say that someone shot him.'

'So it's murder,' said Blackbeard, with a certain grim relish. 'I had a feeling.'

'And there's a name stitched into the jacket,' said Dr Reid. 'Tybalt.'

'Tybalt!' I exclaimed. 'He was in *Romeo and Juliet* – and that was the play on the night of the fire!'

'Well now,' said Blackbeard. 'You've saved me some trouble, ma'am; all I have to do is hunt through a pile of old playbills.'

'You may not need to hunt very far, Inspector,' I said. 'Thomas Transome was playing Romeo in this theatre, with his wife as Juliet, and plenty of people will be able to name the other members of the cast.'

My head whirled as the connections slotted together. It was possible that this man (for the moment unknown) had been killed on the same night that Mr Transome had nearly died. In which case, the rumours of arson might not be as far-fetched as they seemed.

The two policemen came forward to wrap the body and place it upon a stretcher, and Blackbeard escorted me back to the blessed sunshine of the street.

'I believe I must thank you, Mrs Rodd,' he said. 'You've saved me quite a bit of work.'

'Inspector, may I beg a favour?'

'The police don't do favours, ma'am.'

'I would like to be present when you speak to Transome.'

'I daresay you would!'

'It's not merely curiosity on my part.' (I was intensely curious, but strove to hide it.) 'It might be nothing more than a tragic coincidence, not remotely connected to my client. But you don't believe in coincidences – and nor do I.'

Five

O N THE DAY FOLLOWING, when the clocks had just pealed noon, I found Blackbeard waiting on the steps of the Duke of Cumberland's Theatre.

'I hope I'm not late, Inspector.'

'Not at all, Mrs Rodd; you're always bang on time.'

It was strange to see the theatre foyer in daylight, empty but for two old women who were busily sweeping the litter of tickets and playbills from the carpet. This, according to the timetable of the theatrical world, was early in the morning, before the working day began in the evening. Mr Transome's dresser hovered beside the door to the stalls.

'Good afternoon, Mr Cooper,' I said. 'This is Inspector Blackbeard, from Scotland Yard, come to speak to Mr Transome.'

'Oh, dear, dear!' sighed Cooper. 'That dead body on top of everything else! He's expecting you, Mr Blackbeard, but you won't get much change out of him – he's in a shocking temper today.'

'I'm sorry to hear it,' I said. 'Has something happened?'

'He's just heard about his daughter and her husband setting up at the King's.'

'I didn't imagine he'd be pleased by that.'

'Oh, dear, dear – he flew off the handle, Mrs Rodd, and started smashing things right and left. I saved the stuff he usually smashes but I was too late for the mirrors; Lord knows how many years' bad luck we'll have now!'

'So he's given to outbursts of violence,' said Mr Blackbeard.

'He never hurts anybody,' Cooper assured us. 'And in the normal way of things, he's gentle as a lamb!'

He pushed open the heavy mahogany door to the stalls, and we immediately heard the famous Transome voice shouting angrily – and using such dreadful language that barely a sentence is fit to print here. The gist of it was the wicked 'ingratitude' of his daughter and her 'idiotic' husband. He was stamping around on the bare, drab stage in a kind of demented dance, watched by a dozen of his fellow-actors. They were silent, unrecognizable in their everyday clothes, and they looked resigned, as if they had seen it all before.

A string of particularly disgraceful epithets made Cooper wince.

'Mrs Rodd don't care about bad language,' said Blackbeard. 'But us policemen are ever so delicate and easily shocked. You'd better tell him to shut up.' This was his idea of a joke, but delivered in such a way that Cooper turned pale and scuttled through the rows of empty plush seats to the stage.

He tugged at Transome's coat and murmured urgently in his ear. Mr Transome stopped shouting and stamping, took a few deep breaths and said in a more temperate tone of voice, 'Take an hour, boys and girls.'

With many inquisitive glances at Blackbeard, the actors hurried off into the wings – all but one young woman in a modish blue silk bonnet, who ran to Transome's side and took hold of his arm.

'Tom, who are these people?' Her voice was soft, but carried over the footlights. 'Why do they want you? Is it your wife again?'

I saw the blue eyes and golden hair under the brim of the bonnet and recognized Miss Noonan.

Mr Transome whispered in her ear and kissed her little gloved hand, and she ran off after the other actors. He then called out, 'My dear Mrs Rodd, please accept my humblest apologies! I had no idea anyone was listening,' and hurried down the temporary wooden steps on one side of the orchestra pit.

'Your actors were listening,' I could not help saying. 'And several of them are young women.'

'They're used to him,' said Cooper.

'We're rehearsing our new comedy – *The Country Girl* in a splendid new version by George Lewes – and you caught me just as I heard something that upset me most grievously,' said Mr Transome. 'Something that cut me to the heart.'

'About your daughter and her husband, and the new theatre,' I suggested.

'Yes! The sheer insolence makes my blood boil. But you don't want to hear about that.' He sat down upon one of the plush-covered benches in the 'pit' at the very front of the auditorium. 'You've come about the dead body at my daughter's lovely new theatre; the whole of London is tattling about it.'

'I understand you were the last person to perform at the King's, sir, before it was burned down,' said Mr Blackbeard.

'Yes,' said Mr Transome. 'What a night that was, though I don't remember much about it.'

'The play was *Romeo and Juliet*,' I put in. 'And the dead body was found still in his costume – at any rate, in someone's costume – for the role of Tybalt.'

'Maybe you can tell us the name of the actor who was doing him,' said Mr Blackbeard. 'That would be a start.'

'Reynolds,' said Cooper promptly. 'Davey Reynolds.'

'So it was,' said Mr Transome. 'And he wasn't at all bad – tall, dark-haired fellow, very handy with a sword – but I could swear he escaped the fire. And I could also swear that I saw him afterwards, alive and well and doing small parts with the Kemble company.'

'When would that have been, sir?'

'Now you're asking! Cooper, do you remember? It was the year we went to Derby for the races.'

''Forty-seven,' said Cooper.

'That was four years after the fire,' I said. 'And this man would hardly have gone to a ruined theatre in full stage costume.'

'We're assuming he was murdered before the fire,' said Blackbeard. 'How long before I couldn't say. It would help to know how long you'd been doing that play.'

'That's easy,' said Transome. 'We'd only been open for a matter of five weeks, we were a huge success – it was heartbreaking! At first I was inclined to blame Jim Betterton, who certainly did nicely out of my misfortune. But even he wouldn't go to such lengths to get rid of me. I think I must take the blame myself, for not maintaining those wretched footlights properly.'

'We are no closer to naming our corpse,' I said. 'And I do wonder why he was not discovered at the time; did no one miss him? Was there no roll call taken after the fire?'

'The place was empty, apart from myself and this unfortunate corpse,' said Mr Transome. 'And the chaos was simply dreadful; by the time I had recovered my wits, my actors had scattered far and wide.'

'Our corpse got hidden away,' said Blackbeard, watching Transome intently. 'We found him in a sealed space under the stage.'

'That sounds like the remains of the old cistern,' said Mr Transome. 'It was once lined to hold water, and there was some pipe arrangement that supposedly flooded the stage. I never made use of it.'

'Thank you, sir; that's very helpful.'

'I'm sure I hope so. Cooper will provide you with a complete list of everyone in my company at the time.' Transome leapt to his feet in one easy, quicksilver movement. He shook hands with Blackbeard and bowed to me. 'I'm anxious to help in any way – and, Mrs Rodd, I'm sure we'll meet soon about the other matter.'

Blackbeard and I took our leave.

'Not much to go on,' said Blackbeard, once we were back on the grand stone steps. 'I'll find this Reynolds, just to rule him out.'

'Inspector—' Cooper came bursting through the door of the theatre. 'I'm glad I caught you! I suddenly remembered something about the night of the fire, and Mr Tom said I must tell you at once.'

'Were you in the theatre at the time?' asked Blackbeard.

'Not when the fire broke out, but I was there during the performance. Mr Tom don't recall it, but I do; Reynolds didn't turn up and I had to put him down for a fine of five shillings. His understudy went on in his place and I stitched the boy into his costume. His name was Francis Fitzwarren.'

'Well now, I'm grateful to you, Mr Cooper,' said Blackbeard. 'And I'd be more so if you can tell me anything else about this man. How old was he? Who were his friends?

Did he have enemies? Are we certain he hasn't been seen since?'

Cooper was shaking his head. 'He was young, sir; that's all I can give you.'

I was not sure I believed him – up to this point, his memory had been excellent – but Blackbeard appeared to be satisfied, and said, 'Thank you, sir.'

A neat, shiny closed carriage drew up at the foot of the theatre steps.

'That's all we need!' exclaimed Cooper, rolling his eyes. 'The entrance of the Queen of Sheba!'

'Who is it?' I asked.

'It's Miss Olivia; you'll have to excuse me.' He bustled down the steps to hand her out of the carriage.

I was most interested to see the young woman who had taken her father's side in the family war. Olivia Transome was slender and sinuous of build, like Mrs Sarah, with handsome dark eyes in a sallow face and a sour twist to her mouth. She wore a fine dress of lilac silk and a grey silk bonnet, and she looked at Blackbeard and myself as if we were less than the dust beneath her little buttoned boots.

'I suppose you will want to talk to her,' I suggested, once the door had closed behind this vision. 'Though she was a mere child at the time of the fire.'

'She can wait,' said Blackbeard. 'I need to account for the people who were in that theatre on the night it burned down – it's quite a crowd. I think you said, Mrs Rodd, that you are acquainted with another member of that company?'

'Yes, my neighbour, Mr Tully.'

'Perhaps you can have a word with him, ma'am, and save me a journey; you have such a nice soft manner, and I haven't much patience with actors and their flimflam.'

Six

THE NEXT MORNING, WHILE I was in the act of writing a note to Mr Tully, I saw the man himself through my drawing-room window – flurried, hatless and hopping down the street on his lame leg like a bird.

I beckoned him to my front door, so that Mrs Bentley would not be agitated by his knock and try to hurry up the kitchen stairs (she was not nearly as well yet as she made out; we argued at least ten times a day over my attempts to save her strength).

'Mrs Rodd, forgive this intrusion, ma'am—'

'Good heavens, Mr Tully, what is the matter?'

'Mrs Sarah sent me round a letter by special messenger, in the middle of last night when I was in my bed. It's Cordelia.'

'Is she ill?'

'She's left her mother, ma'am. Oh, such an upset!'

Once I had established that nobody was dead, I made Mr Tully sit in the easiest chair, and would not let him tell his story until I had given him a glass of the good port wine that I kept for visitors.

'May I see the letter, Mr Tully?'

He took the sheet of paper from his breast pocket and handed it to me; it was only a few scrawled lines.

Pericles Cottage
Weds. night

My dear Ben

Something dreadful has happened and I am at my wits' end. Maria has returned from America and she came here tonight without a word of warning. She refused to speak to me but went straight upstairs to Cordelia, and a short time later the two of them departed in her carriage.

My youngest child has left me and I am utterly alone! I swear before Heaven that I do not know why my daughters are so angry with me. What have I ever done to them? And what shall I do? Tom will not give me sixpence now. Come to comfort me, my dear, and please tell Mrs Rodd,

Sarah Transome

'I shall go to her this very morning,' said Mr Tully, his voice shaking with emotion. 'Poor darling!'

'This is a strange turn of events,' I said (privately wondering if the drama contained a modicum of 'flimflam'). 'Do you think Miss Cordelia planned to run away with her sister?'

'No, I do not; I didn't even know she was on speaking terms with Maria.'

Everything I heard about the determined Mrs Betterton made me more curious to meet her. 'It's very singular; first she falls out with her father, and then she treats her mother in this heartless manner! Do you have any idea what has set her against both her parents?'

'She has joined the other side,' said Mr Tully, 'and turned herself into a Betterton.'

'But what is the point, if nobody knows what started the rivalry between the two families in the first place?'

'Whatever started it don't matter now, ma'am. It's my belief that Cordelia will join Edgar Betterton's new company at the King's. Tom won't like it one bit. He thought that if Cordelia left her mother, she would come back to him. This will be a savage blow to his pride.'

'I visited the King's Theatre yesterday, Mr Tully,' I said, seeing an opportunity to ask a few questions on behalf of Blackbeard. 'It is in the process of being rebuilt, and the workmen made a most tragic discovery.' Briefly, and with the least possible flimflam, I told him about the dead Tybalt, finishing with the name Francis Fitzwarren.

The effect upon Mr Tully was striking (I took care to hide the intensity of my interest in his reaction). He was shocked, he was confused; he hugged himself with his arms and was haggard with fear, which he tried to conceal.

'I'm very sorry,' I said gently. 'It must be painful for you to think of that terrible night, but I thought you might find it easier to talk to me and not a policeman.'

'Why would the police want to talk to me?' squeaked Mr Tully.

'They will need to talk to everybody who was there.'

'But I don't know anything!'

'Let me give you a cup of tea.' I hurried from the room and called down the kitchen stairs; not to Mrs B who was strictly forbidden to hoist kettles or carry trays, but to granddaughter Hannah, who was in attendance again. She had just that moment made a fresh pot, and brought two cups up to the drawing room.

The tea revived Mr Tully and made him more cautious. 'It's not the memories of the night that hurt, it's the lack of them. They come at me in fragments, and none of them make any sense.'

'Does the name Francis Fitzwarren mean anything to you?'

'He was covering Tybalt on account of what's-his-name being drunk again,' said Mr Tully. 'I always assumed that he escaped the fire.'

'Do you know his age?'

'Twenty-three, twenty-four … tall, fair boy – handsome too.'

'Did he have any enemies in the company?'

'None that I ever heard of.'

He was hiding something; I changed direction as if I had not noticed. 'What was your role in the play, Mr Tully?'

'Mercutio. Tom always said I was the best he'd ever seen. That entire production was a triumph – the end of my career, but also the crown of it. Like all truly great actors, Tom sheds his light over everyone else on the stage. And it was the last time Sarah played Juliet.' He had dropped his caginess now, and was confiding once more. 'She was a lovely Juliet, so graceful and sweet, and I'll never forget what a beautiful pair they made onstage.'

'And it closed after only five weeks,' I said. 'Such a pity! Were you present when the fire broke out?'

'No – it happened several hours after the curtain came down. I was in a nearby tavern, the Fox and Grapes, along with some other members of the cast, when the cry went up that the King's was in flames. I knew that Tom was still inside and ran in myself, with the intention of saving him.'

'How splendid of you,' I said. 'You were very brave.'

'It was reckless rather than brave – to this day I don't know what got into me. I have one distinct memory of finding Tom on the stage, unconscious from the smoke. I managed to drag him to the street but was quickly overcome myself. I don't remember anything else, and can only tell you what they told me later. The fire took hold up in the flies – that is, the space above the stage, from which they raise and lower the backdrops and certain pieces of scenery. It is filled with ropes and paint, and is one of the places most susceptible to catching fire. A beam fell across my leg and I was discovered lying across Tom's body to shield him. If I had not pulled him most of the way out, neither of us would have survived.'

'Do you remember your last sighting of Francis Fitzwarren?'

'The curtain call,' said Mr Tully, after a hair's-breadth pause. 'And immediately after, when all the men in the company carried him to his dressing room – it was a custom we had for understudies. Nothing after that.'

'I see.' It was strange and sad that this young man could apparently disappear, and not be missed by someone. 'You've been most helpful, Mr Tully; it looks as if you have confirmed the identity of that unfortunate corpse.'

In the afternoon I sat down in my drawing room to write an account of the meeting for Inspector Blackbeard. I had barely begun when I was interrupted by thunderous knocking at my front door. It was an expensive special messenger, with a letter for me.

20 Vale Crescent
Holloway
Thursday

Dear Mrs Rodd

You are working on behalf of my mother, Sarah Transome, in the ghastly dispute between my parents, and you will have heard by now that I have taken my youngest sister into my home. I would be most grateful if you could call on me tomorrow morning at the above address.

Yours etc.
Maria Betterton

I sent the messenger away with a brief note of acceptance, most intrigued to be summoned by the oldest of the three Transome daughters, and avid to know what she wished to tell me.

In those days before the arrival of the railway, the district of Holloway in north London was quieter and more genteel than it is now. Vale Crescent was a row of white-painted villas, close to Seven Sisters Road and the area now known as the Nag's Head.

The door was opened by a respectable-looking maidservant, who showed me into a pleasant back parlour, where a young woman, dressed in a plain gown of dark blue silk, stood before the fireplace.

'Mrs Rodd – how do you do. I am Maria Betterton.'

'Mrs Betterton.'

We exchanged stiff bows, and I sat down in one of the chintz-covered chairs. I noted the slightly haphazard arrangement of the furniture; the chairs were new, and stood about awkwardly, like people who have only just been introduced, and several pictures were stacked against the wall, waiting to be hung.

Maria Betterton was a beauty; a feminine version of her father, with masses of dark hair bundled carelessly into a net, and wondrous black eyes (and she was a great deal handsomer, I could not help thinking, than her sister Olivia).

'You find us at sixes and sevens, Mrs Rodd,' she said. 'We have only lately taken possession of this house.'

'I know you have been in America,' I said. 'Your father tells me you were a great success there.'

'Ha, that must've killed him,' said Mrs Betterton. 'He wanted us to fail.'

'Surely not!' I protested.

'You've heard all about his ridiculous feud with my husband's family.'

'Well – yes.'

'It's all moonshine, Mrs Rodd; a distraction from the real feud between my father and myself. He thinks I have betrayed him.'

'You took your sister Cordelia away from your mother's house.'

'Yes – and I'd do it again.'

'I beg your pardon, but I'm not sure I understand why you are at odds with your mother; I know she is greatly distressed at being left alone.'

'I daresay,' said Mrs Betterton. 'I acted as I did because my sister needed my protection. You won't meet her today, I'm afraid; she is unwell.'

'I'm sorry to hear it.'

'Our mother is not fit to take proper care of Cordelia, and she can't possibly go back to my father's theatre. When she is recovered, she will join my husband's new company at the King's.'

I had a strong sense that she was sizing me up, trying to decide how much to tell me; I kept quiet to encourage her.

'You are assisting with the arrangements for my parents' separation,' she said.

'Yes … '

'That's moonshine too.'

'I beg your pardon?'

'There's no money,' said Mrs Betterton shortly. 'My father's box office takes in plenty of cash, but he's up to his ears in debt.'

'That is certainly not the impression he gave me,' I said. 'He has purchased a fine new house in Herne Hill.'

'Purchased? Nothing of the kind! He has put down a sum of money for the first few months' rent, and that is all the landlord will ever see.'

If this was true, it would make nonsense of any 'settlement' between the Transomes, and I was alarmed. It was possible, however, that Maria Betterton's anger exaggerated the facts; her beautiful face was hot with spite.

'What about the house at Ham Common?' I asked.

'Pericles Cottage belongs to him. He wants to sell the place because Noonan refused to live in any house that had been lived in by his lawful wife.'

'Mrs Betterton, you haven't told me why you wanted to see me.'

For a moment there was an expression of pain on her face and I saw how unhappy she was underneath her anger. She sank into a chair, avoiding my eye, and we were silent for a spell.

And then she looked up and said, 'My husband doesn't know you are here and I'd rather he didn't find out.'

'Can you not confide in him?'

'I'll tell him eventually, when the time is right. Papa calls him an "imbecile", which is a beastly lie, but I'll admit my dear Edgar is not the sharpest of men.' Her lovely face lost every vestige of spite as she spoke of her husband, and she smiled. 'I protect him from vexation wherever I can. He's at the theatre this morning, consulting the architect and the builder about when we can open.'

'I was there a few days ago,' I said, 'and it didn't look anywhere near ready.'

'You saw the body.'

'I did.'

'That is the reason I wanted to see you,' said Mrs Betterton. 'Nobody will tell me anything.'

'At present, there is not much to tell.'

'Has the body been named?'

'Not definitely … '

'Please – I beg you!' Mrs Betterton cried out. 'Was it Francis Fitzwarren?'

'Yes.' I did not have the heart to deny it. 'He was wearing the costume for Tybalt, and your father's dresser remembered that the understudy went on in place of—'

'Oh, dear God!' Her eyes filled and her face crumpled. 'I should have known it!' She covered her face with her hands; it was a stagey gesture, yet there was no suggestion that she was acting. She let out a single sob, then proudly removed her hands. 'I have been most cruelly deceived!'

'What do you mean?'

'All these years, I have believed that Frank Fitzwarren ran off after the fire. He sent me a letter, saying he had left my father's company and would not be returning.'

'When did you receive this letter, Mrs Betterton?'

'A week or so afterwards, with no clue as to where he had gone. But he couldn't have written it, could he? Oh, how I have wronged him!'

'Did you know Mr Fitzwarren well?'

'We were engaged to be married.'

'Indeed?' This was most unexpected. 'Your father did not mention—'

'No, he wouldn't,' said Mrs Betterton furiously. 'When I told him we were in love, he flew into one of his rages and said I was too young to know anything about it. I had to beg him – literally on my knees! – not to throw Frank out of the company, which would have ruined him when he was just beginning his career.'

'Did you break off your engagement?'

'That's what everyone believed; we concealed our true feelings, and took care never to be seen together. But we still loved each other, and the letter – the letter that I

51

thought was from Frank – shocked and hurt me very much.'

'You thought he had abandoned you,' I softly suggested.

She nodded. 'I was only seventeen, and I allowed myself to be persuaded. Papa was kind to me, seeing that my heart was broken. He said the experience would help my acting.'

'And what of your mother?'

'She took his side,' Mrs Betterton said icily. 'As she always did in those days – before he decided she was too old to play Rosalind at the new theatre.'

Silence fell between us, and I allowed it to stretch into minutes while I watched her.

Eventually, she looked at me directly, and said, 'You'll inform the police of this, I'm sure.'

'I think I must.'

'Tell them there was only one person who would want Frank out of the way,' said Mrs Betterton. 'Tell them my father is a murderer.'

Seven

I HAD AN APPOINTMENT THAT afternoon at my brother's chambers in Furnival's Inn, and I hastened there
(via an omnibus from the Nag's Head) directly after
taking leave of Mrs Betterton. I had made an effort not to
react when she brought out the word 'murderer', though I
was certainly startled, and wondered very much what
Blackbeard would make of it.

For the moment, however, my main concern was Mr
Transome's financial situation. I arrived a little early and
took the opportunity to speak to Fred in private.

'We have assumed he can afford to keep all his great
promises, without really looking into the matter.'

'So we have,' said Fred. 'And I must admit that it never
occurred to me to question him; he is so confoundedly
plausible! I saw the crowds at the theatre and took the
money for granted.'

'His daughter claims that he has enormous debts but
I'm not certain how much she is to be believed.'

'We had better get to the bottom of it, or you and I are
wasting our valuable time.'

Mr Transome had agreed to meet us in the chaos of
Fred's private office, where every surface was heaped with
papers and covered with dust. Mr Beamish, my brother's
confidential clerk, was making a last-minute attempt to

tidy the place by wiping the dust off two chairs, and setting Fred's white wig neatly upon its wooden stand.

The sounds of scuffling and whispering in the outer office heralded Mr Transome's arrival.

'They all want a look at him,' said Beamish. 'It's not every day we get a visit from a famous actor.' He left the room to rescue Mr Transome from the intense curiosity of the younger clerks.

Not the least put out, Mr Transome breezed into Fred's office a few minutes later, looking most elegant in white trousers and a blue coat.

'Good afternoon, Mrs Rodd! Well, Tyson – how fascinating to see you in your private lair. I'm really most grateful. Do I take it that we're close to a final settlement?'

'Sit down and have a glass of my better sherry,' said Fred. 'My sister had an interesting encounter this morning, which has thrown up a couple of questions.'

I told him I had met his oldest daughter, and repeated her claim about the money.

His brow darkened ominously. 'You don't want to take her word for it, Mrs Rodd. My daughter and her wretched husband only wish to blacken my name.'

'Naturally, I'm aware that Mrs Betterton is not without prejudice,' I said. 'But we need to know if there is any truth in what she says about your debts.'

Mr Transome sighed. 'Well, of course I have certain debts; good God, what actor-manager does not? A theatre is a monster that eats money. I had to borrow thousands when I took on the Duke of Cumberland's. I throw bits of cash at the debt collectors from time to time, to keep them satisfied.'

'Can you put a figure to it?' asked Fred.

'No – it's all such a tremendous bore! If I had to fret over figures, I'd never do anything.'

'What reserves of cash do you have?'

'I couldn't say exactly.' Mr Transome shrugged irritably. 'You had better ask my banker.'

I said, 'Your daughter is a little sceptical about your new house at Herne Hill, and suggests that you have not actually purchased the freehold.'

'For your information – and hers – I bought a lease of five years.'

'You see the difficulty, I'm sure,' said Fred. 'If you undertake to settle an income upon your wife, you'll need to produce a lot of hard cash in a hurry.'

'I can always raise money when I need it,' said Mr Transome, as if a little irked by our line of questioning. 'You saw how much I'm taking in at the box office. People love to lend me money, because they know I'm such a good bet. If I happen to fall a little short, I simply do a few more performances.' His fine dark eyes – so like his daughter's – watched me narrowly. 'Pay no attention to Maria and her accusations.'

'As I have said, I make allowance for her personal feelings.'

'How is she looking?'

'Very well, as far as I could see.'

'I'm sure I'm glad to hear it,' said Mr Transome. 'As long as she's not in the family way.'

'I beg your pardon?'

'I can't afford to be a grandfather, can I? Not while I'm playing Romeo.'

This piece of selfishness shocked me to my marrow. I looked helplessly at my brother, who was trying not to laugh.

Mr Transome noticed nothing and airily refilled his glass. 'And did you happen to meet her great troll of a husband?'

'I did not,' I said. 'He was out at the new theatre.'

'You've heard, I'm sure, about the two of them kidnapping Cordelia; did you see her?' His attitude was still easy and casual, yet I had a sense that he was on his guard.

'Mrs Betterton said she was unwell.'

'Unwell?' He could not hide his alarm. 'Is it serious?'

'I don't think so—'

'No, no, of course not, or she would have made sure I knew about it. She's quite capable of using her own sister as a stick to beat me with.'

I had intended to keep the rest of my meeting with Maria Betterton to myself until I had spoken to Blackbeard, but could not now resist seeing how Mr Transome reacted.

'Mrs Betterton claims that she and Francis Fitzwarren were engaged to be married.'

'Stuff and nonsense!' said Mr Transome. 'Good God, is she still harping on about that? There was some sort of youthful infatuation on Maria's part, and I put a stop to it – as any father would. The man was simply using her to get on in the company.'

'Are you sure about that?' Fred was all eyes and ears now.

'She thinks you murdered him,' I said.

'Oh, I daresay,' said Mr Transome airily, not the least put out by this terrible accusation. 'The poor girl refused to accept the truth, but every young and ambitious actor knows the value of making love to the manager's daughter.' A smile flashed across his face. 'I did it myself; Sarah's father was manager of a theatre in Manchester when I met her and, though I loved her with all my heart, the advantages of the match did not escape me.'

'I believe you, my boy,' said Fred. 'But you ought to take this more seriously, you know.' Though my brother's manner

56

was as light as ever, there was a sharper edge to his attention now. 'A man was unlawfully killed and you have presented me with the most beautiful motive for killing him.'

'Me? That's absurd!' Finally, Mr Transome was rattled. 'You know me – do you really believe I'm capable of killing anyone?'

'Personally, no,' said Fred. 'But my personal belief is neither here nor there. Take a piece of free advice and stop talking about it – unless you want your next public appearance to be at the Old Bailey.'

Inspector Blackbeard reacted to Mrs Betterton's accusation with all the vivacity of a gatepost.

'Gammon and spinach, ma'am!'

'You don't think it worth looking into?'

'I didn't say that, but where is the evidence? I've spent the past few days working through a long list of names, trying to track them all down – some to theatres out of town, a few to the graveyard – and nobody's given me a scrap of anything solid. I don't mind telling you, Mrs Rodd, that I've never had such a sense of people hiding things.'

The two of us were in a plain black police carriage, struggling through the snarl of morning traffic at the end of Upper Street in Islington. In those days, this long thoroughfare was dangerous, noisy and crime-ridden, and filled with some highly questionable places of entertainment; local people called it the 'Devil's Mile'. In the light of day, it was merely very dirty indeed, and choked with carts and carriages headed for the City Road.

At the Angel Inn, we took the turning into Pentonville, with its trim, quiet streets of flat-fronted houses that were then falling out of fashion and into a state of slightly forlorn respectability. Miss Constance Noonan and her mother lived in a dull little square set around a dusty garden. This was where Blackbeard had arranged to meet Mr Transome two days before, as far as possible from the rampant flimflam of the theatre.

'I had a fine murder here, back in 'forty-five,' said Mr Blackbeard nostalgically, tugging at the bell of the Noonans' house. 'A publican's wife did away with her husband, and had the manners to do it in front of some excellent witnesses. I had her strung up in a matter of weeks, ma'am – neat as you like.'

'I'm afraid this murder is bound to be rather untidy,' I said. 'It happened years ago, the witnesses have scattered and all the traces were destroyed in the fire. Of one thing, however, I am certain; actors have memories like elephants, and one of them will remember something significant.'

I was a little uneasy about the propriety of meeting Mr Transome in the house of his mistress, but told myself that I knew nothing concrete against Miss Noonan. If she was to be believed, she had not yet taken the ultimate step to her disgrace.

The door was opened by a woman I took to be the parlourmaid, until she introduced herself as Margaret Noonan. She was very thin, with a pronounced stoop, a frizz of faded red hair and a sullen look to her face; I afterwards learnt that she only looked like that to hide the fact that several of her teeth were missing, and was in fact rather gentle and shy.

'Mrs Rodd, Inspector!' Mr Transome burst out into the hall to shake our hands. 'It's awfully decent of you to come here; the truth is that I'm dodging my daughter Olivia. Do please come into the parlour.'

'Why are you "dodging" your only remaining daughter, Mr Transome?' I asked.

'Oh, it's merely a professional disagreement, but she's behaving like a harridan; I couldn't face her last night, so I slept at the theatre.'

He ushered us into a small, square front parlour, which was clean though shabby and very plainly furnished. Miss Constance Noonan stood before the fire like a great bird of paradise, with her vivid red-gold hair loose and lying against the rich colours of her paisley shawl. By daylight and at close quarters she was every bit as splendid as she had been onstage.

There was a tea-table, strewn with crumpled napkins and the remains of a lavish breakfast; I saw coffee, cream, muffins, strawberry jam and bacon.

'Today is one of my eating days,' Mr Transome told us airily. 'Maggie, bring us a fresh pot of coffee, there's a dear.'

This was no request, but the kind of order one would give to a servant; I was evidently not the only person to mistake Mrs Noonan for the parlourmaid. She acknowledged him with a nod that was nearly a curtsey, took the coffee pot and left the room.

Mr Transome set chairs for us, and Blackbeard and I sat down.

'Connie, my darling,' said Mr Transome, 'you needn't stay; they want to know about the night of the fire, and you were still in pinafores then.'

'Oh, that everlasting fire!' sighed Miss Noonan. 'It's such a bore; another obstacle put in our way!'

'I know – the very stars in their courses, and all that – but one must oblige the police.'

'Very well.' She left with a shake of her great mane of hair, and shut the door behind her rather pettishly.

Mr Transome picked up his half-drunk cup of coffee. 'Miss Noonan is a little put out this morning, due to a

59

private disagreement – the same disagreement that led to my spending an uncomfortable night on the couch in my dressing room.'

'You didn't stay here, then,' said Blackbeard (this was uncomfortably blunt, but echoed my own thinking exactly).

'I did not,' said Mr Transome. 'Connie's awfully strict about that sort of thing. How may I assist you, Inspector?'

'We're assuming, for the moment,' said Blackbeard, 'that the night of the fire and the night of Fitzwarren's murder were one and the same. Upon that understanding, sir, I'd like to go over the details with you again.'

'If you wish, though as you know, I don't recall very much. I was unconscious for two days, until I woke up in my bed at home.'

'Any little thing might be significant, sir. We're trying to establish the victim's movements.'

'No great mystery there,' said Mr Transome. 'He went on in the role of Tybalt, observed by hundreds of people.'

'You claimed not to remember the young man,' I reminded him.

'I didn't at first – the business of opening the new theatre drove everything else from my mind – but dear old Cooper has been jogging my memory, and one or two things have come back to me. For instance, that I was annoyed because Reynolds didn't show up; I don't generally like playing with an understudy at short notice. Sarah kept whispering at me not to frighten the boy; when it came to the point, he was actually very good.' He caught my eye and added, 'I didn't like him any better for his "romance" with my daughter; that is beside the point. In the theatre the performance is all that matters.'

'What was your last sight of Fitzwarren?' Blackbeard asked.

'Well, there was the curtain call, after which we carried him back to the green room on our shoulders, according to custom.'

'And then what?'

'I spoke to my wife and saw her into the carriage.'

'Why didn't you go home with her?'

'I had some business to attend to.'

'What sort of business would that be, sir?'

'It's … delicate,' said Mr Transome, looking steadily at me. 'You won't like this, ma'am.'

'Nothing you say can shock me, Mr Transome,' I told him (not entirely truthfully, but I was determined not to allow my deep disapproval of his immorality to stand in the way of solving a murder).

'If you insist, I'll let you have it, and then you will understand why I kept it out of the original enquiry. I had arranged a private meeting in my dressing room with a young member of my company.'

'Female?' asked Blackbeard.

'Yes.' Mr Transome's manner was jaunty, yet he had the grace to look a little uncomfortable. 'You will doubtless want a name: Miss Arabella Fenton. She came to me after the performance and took her leave at around one in the morning.'

'Did you escort her as far as the street?'

'No,' said Mr Transome. 'She poured a half-pint of iced champagne over my head and escorted herself.'

'So you were in your dressing room when the fire started?'

'Yes – and that's the point at which my memory shuts down. I think I must've smelled the fire and tried to escape, since poor old Ben found me up on the stage.'

I was convinced he recalled more than he was letting on. Before I could ask him anything else, however, there was a violent banging on the front door and a female voice cried out, 'Papa – let me in! I know I've caught you and I'm not going away! I'll stand here until I knock the house down!'

'Oh, God, God, God!' Mr Transome let out a soft moan. 'Olivia!'

There were footsteps in the hall.

'Go away!' shouted the voice of Miss Noonan. 'You have no business here!'

'I demand to see my father, you scheming little witch. I know what you're up to!'

'He don't want to see you!'

'Open this door!'

(I have omitted the coarsest part of this fishwifely exchange, which makes it appear to be briefer than it was; the two were, as Mrs Bentley would say, going at it hammer and tongs.)

Blackbeard looked at Mr Transome, until that gentleman rose from his chair and went out into the hall to admit his shrieking daughter.

Miss Noonan tried to block his way. 'You're always on her side – you don't care how she treats me!'

'I can hardly leave her on the doorstep!'

A moment later the two young women burst into the parlour, in a great flurry of skirts. Neither took the slightest notice of me or Mr Blackbeard.

'Is it true, Papa?' Miss Olivia clutched her father's arm. 'Tell me it's not true! This creature says I can't live with you at Herne Hill!'

'I'm not going if she's there!' cried Miss Noonan. 'Tell her, Tom – you said it was to be my house!'

'Girls, please!' said Mr Transome.

'How can it be my house when she's there giving me orders?'

'Papa, I'm your daughter! Does that count for nothing? Will you let this creature turn me out into the street?'

'Livvy, my dear, nobody's being turned out—'

'Where am I supposed to go?' Miss Olivia's pale face was pinched with fury. 'I took your side – is this all the thanks I get?'

'You can always go back to your mother,' said Miss Noonan. 'Tom, you promised it would be just us two, our own little refuge from the world!'

'I can see this is a private matter,' said Mr Blackbeard. 'We'll leave you to it.'

I was only too glad to leave these people and their squalid argument, which flared up again the moment we were out of the room.

Mrs Noonan was waiting beside the front door, and she put a diffident hand upon my arm.

'I don't know how to stop them,' she said softly. 'But I wish I could save her!'

Eight

BLACKBEARD WAS QUIET AND thoughtful while we drove back to Hampstead, and I could not guess how the cogs of his brain were turning. To my slight surprise, he insisted on coming into the house to pay his respects to Mrs Bentley, who was very pleased to see him. She sent little Hannah out to the nearby tavern for a jug of ale, and Blackbeard sat with us beside the kitchen fire.

'This is very domestic and pleasant, ma'am,' he said. 'It reminds me of my wife.' He had lost his wife at around the same time I had lost my beloved husband, and I knew that when he spoke of her, his guard was down. 'We spent many a happy hour talking about murder, and she was a good deal sharper than some of my superiors.'

'Do you know what Mrs Blackbeard would have made of this murder?'

'She wouldn't have cared for some of the morals,' said Blackbeard. 'But she wouldn't have let the moral side of things get in the way.'

'I know what I think,' declared Mrs Bentley. 'I reckon it was Transome.'

'But we have no hard facts,' I said. 'Merely unfounded accusations from his enemies.'

'Who else had a reason to want the man dead?'

'We may very well find someone else, and Mr Blackbeard is only interested in facts.'

'You've kept very quiet about your instincts, Mrs Rodd!' said Blackbeard. 'And it's not like you at all.'

'I'll admit that it's not,' I said. 'In this case, however, I am confused. Do you have any instincts of your own?'

'I prefer to call it a "smell", ma'am,' said Blackbeard. 'And something about Transome don't smell right. I'm working along the lines that he's guilty, until I find proof that he ain't. What about you?'

'Well … ' I was hesitant. 'He is our strongest suspect at the moment, but I simply cannot imagine him shooting anyone.'

'Somebody killed Fitzwarren, ma'am. And so far, all roads seem to lead but one way.'

Mr Transome had given us another name – that of Miss Arabella Fenton.

'She weren't too hard to track down,' said Blackbeard. 'She's left off being an actress and nowadays she's Mrs Dupont, married to a wine merchant. I asked you to join me because I have some ticklish questions for her, and she's more likely to be forthcoming with a lady present.'

'I'm very glad to help,' I said. 'But I'm afraid all we'll get is more about Mr Transome's immorality, and nothing about the murder.'

Nearly a week had passed since the scene we had witnessed in Pentonville, and the police carriage was taking us into the heart of the city. I am always rather excited by the energy and bustle in this part of London; the pavements solid with men in a hurry, the continual grind of traffic and the clamour of bells from the many old churches.

Mrs Dupont lived in the ancient street of Bucklersbury, close to Leadenhall Market. The ground floor of the house was given over to the offices of Dupont and Villard, Wholesale Wine Importers. Blackbeard knocked at the door, and we were admitted by an ink-stained young clerk who showed us to the family's private quarters on the floors above.

The drawing room on the first floor was large and expensively appointed, and would have been perfectly bright if the two long windows had not been choked with several layers of lace. The furniture was all of dark wood, elaborately carved, and slightly too large for the setting. A very old lady, her face wrinkled and brown like a withered apple, sat beside a solid red blaze of a fire.

'This is my husband's mother,' the younger Mrs Dupont said. 'You needn't mind her; she's deaf, and not all there.' This sounded a little unfeeling, but I noted the tender expression on her face as she tucked a rug over the old lady's knees.

She was a handsome woman of around thirty years old, in a black dress of the utmost plainness; I saw not a hint of her theatrical past in either her looks or her manner.

'I'm glad to assist the police, sir,' she told Mr Blackbeard. 'As I said in my letter. That unfortunate part of my history is long past, however, and I don't like to return to it.'

'The inspector is always very discreet,' I hastened to assure her. 'He simply wishes to know everything you remember about the night of the fire.'

'Everything?'

'We heard about the business in Transome's dressing room, ma'am,' said Blackbeard.

'Oh.' Mrs Dupont was startled, and shot an alarmed glance at her mother-in-law.

'You must not be afraid of us,' I said. 'Mr Blackbeard is not interested in old scandals; he is simply trying to build a picture of Francis Fitzwarren on what we assume was the day of his death.'

'Well … ' She was quiet for a moment, sizing us up. 'Naturally I remember him; we were in the same company.' She gestured to us to sit down, as far as possible from the old lady. 'I did small parts for Mr Transome, but I was mainly employed as a dancer; we performed a ballet between the acts.'

'Did Fitzwarren have any enemies, ma'am?' asked Blackbeard.

'Not in the company,' said Mrs Dupont. 'Frank was a thorough gentleman, and very well liked.'

'We've spoken to Mrs Maria Betterton, ma'am.'

'You know about that business?' She sighed, as if relieved. 'Yes, Maria was head-over-heels in love with Frank, and her father was very much against it. Do you think he did the murder, then?'

'He's the only person with anything like a motive,' said Blackbeard. 'Can you tell us when you last saw Mr Fitzwarren?'

'I can't be certain.'

'He was still inside the theatre when you left, ma'am.'

'Oh – was he?'

'It stands to reason,' said Blackbeard, 'seeing as he was in his costume. He'd hardly go out into Drury Lane in that get-up.'

'I'm afraid I don't remember.' Mrs Dupont's defences were thoroughly up now; she was every inch the prosperous City lady, no trace of the ballet-girl she had once been.

'Do you remember what time it was when you left Mr Transome's dressing room?' I asked.

'You said he told you about the dressing room.' She glanced again at her mother-in-law and lowered her voice. 'He summoned me, and I'm sure you can guess what he was after; all us girls knew what it meant to get one of his invitations. You couldn't turn him down or you'd lose your job. I chose to fight him off.'

'And he dismissed you for it?' I was dismayed; it was very difficult to imagine the charming Transome behaving so abominably.

'I saved him the trouble,' said Mrs Dupont. 'I told him I was leaving – and I left.'

'Were there any signs of the fire when you left the building?'

'No, and I would've noticed; theatre folk live in terror of fires.'

'It was late and the streets were dangerous,' I said. 'Where did you go?'

'I had a room nearby, in Monmouth Street. And a few days after, I went to the Bettertons' theatre and James Betterton gave me a job there.' The ghost of a smile softened her stiff, wary face. 'He doesn't indulge in that sort of thing himself; he pays less than Transome, but he's a decent man, and he treats his actors like ladies and gentlemen.'

'How refreshing,' I said, 'to hear something nice about Mr Betterton, for a change!' (Blackbeard was getting impatient and trying to catch my eye; I ignored him because I was encouraging Mrs Dupont to speak freely: it was my turn not to be hurried.) 'Now, let us go back to Mr Transome's dressing room. At what time did you leave it?'

'I can't say exactly; some time after one o'clock.'

'Did you see Fitzwarren on your way out?'

'I don't recall if I saw anyone, the state I was in.'

'Did Mr Transome run after you?'

'No,' said Mrs Dupont. 'He called me a few names, that's all.'

'Thank you, ma'am,' said Blackbeard. 'Is there anything else you can tell us about the murder?'

'One thing,' said Mrs Dupont. 'I read in the paper that Frank was shot; I saw Mr Transome's pistol.'

'Did you, now?' Blackbeard almost smiled. 'Are you sure it was a real pistol, ma'am, and not one of them pop-guns he uses in plays?'

'No, it was real, all right; he kept it for when he drove home alone, in case of robbers. And I saw it on his dressing table.'

'Splendid, ma'am!' declared Blackbeard. 'We're building up a nice case against him – provided you're willing to speak out in court.'

'In court?' Mrs Dupont jumped to her feet. 'I can't do that – my husband is the best of men, but none of the people in his circle know of my past – his pride won't stand for it!'

'Some people would reckon it's no more than your duty,' said Blackbeard.

'I can see that this is hard for you,' I said, sincerely sorry for her dismay. 'Unfortunately, you are the only person we have found who can tell us about that particular night.'

'The only person? Ha! Why haven't you asked Cooper, or Transome's wife?'

'We've spoken to Cooper,' said Blackbeard. 'And Mrs Transome left before the fire started.'

'Well, you'd better speak to them again,' said Mrs Dupont. 'They know a lot more than I do. Ask Mrs Sarah what *she* thought about Maria's fiancé.' She bowed to us. 'Good morning.'

The interview was over. Refusing to throw us another word, Mrs Dupont rang for the clerk and he escorted the two of us back into the street.

'I'm certain she knows more than she's telling,' I said. 'Like practically everyone we speak to.'

'But we're getting warmer, ma'am,' said Blackbeard, with a faint yet unmistakable gleam of satisfaction in his eye. 'It's all pointing in the same direction – and we've nearly got him. Would you oblige me by taking another little trip?'

Nine

O UR 'TRIP' WAS TO Ham Common, the next day. Blackbeard said very little during the journey, yet I knew him well enough to detect a certain jauntiness in his manner.

'We're closing in, Mrs Rodd!'

'I can see that your mind is made up, Mr Blackbeard; you have decided Transome is guilty, and now you are only waiting for an excuse to arrest him.'

'Oh, here we go!' said Blackbeard. 'I've been wondering when you'd start.'

'I beg your pardon?'

'You're going to bring in your feelings, ma'am. You're going to tell me you have one of your "instincts" that the old tomcat is innocent.'

'I wouldn't go so far,' I said, smiling. 'It's simply that I find it hard to believe the "old tomcat" is capable of any action as serious as murder.'

'Hmm,' said Blackbeard. 'He's bamboozled you, that's the trouble – this is a man who makes his living bamboozling folks.'

'I don't care for his shameless immorality, but you can't arrest him for it.' I had spent a sleepless night fretting over the flimsiness of the case against Mr Transome. 'I'm afraid that if we look too hard for evidence against him, we might miss something that points to the real culprit.'

'I'm as open-minded as anyone, ma'am,' said Black-beard. 'Let's see what his wife makes of it all.'

'Very well.' Experience had taught me that it was quite useless to argue with him, or I would have pointed out that his mind was not in the least 'open', but closed as tight as an oyster-shell.

Pericles Cottage was showing signs of neglect since my last visit. In the garden the lawn needed cutting and trimming and the borders were full of weeds. The house was emptier; the pretty piano in the drawing room had gone, along with at least half a dozen of the paintings, including the portrait of Mr Transome as Julius Caesar. Murphy, the dresser, appeared to be the only remaining servant.

Mrs Transome herself was looking somewhat frayed about the edges, yet she held herself as proudly as a queen. 'I know Ben has told you about Cordelia, Mrs Rodd, and how she let Maria take her away from me.'

'Yes,' I said. 'I called on Mrs Betterton.'

'Did you see Cordelia?' She spoke as if she did not care, yet could not hide her anxiety; once again, I sensed a deep, fierce pain in her, and wanted to be comforting.

'I did not see her,' I said. 'Her sister said she was unwell, but I gathered it was nothing serious.'

'I'm glad to hear it,' said Mrs Transome. 'You haven't come here to talk about my daughters, of course; this is more ancient history. Ben told me the police were speaking to everyone who was present on the night of the fire. I left directly after the performance, and saw no signs of it; that is all I can tell you.'

'Never mind the fire, ma'am.' Blackbeard would not sit down, but stood at attention beside the empty (and unswept) fireplace. 'This is a murder enquiry now. I'd be much obliged if you could tell me about Francis Fitzwarren, and the last time you saw him alive.'

'Poor man!' Her cool, collected manner did not waver, yet I felt her guard going up. 'I saw him at the curtain call. And then, about ten days later, we assumed that he had survived the fire because my daughter Maria had a letter from him.'

'It can't have been from him, seeing as he was lying dead under the stage at the time,' said Blackbeard shortly. 'Can you think of anyone else who might have wrote that letter, Mrs Transome?'

'No,' said Mrs Transome. 'It was obviously the work of the murderer, to make everyone think Fitzwarren was still alive. Who have you spoken to?'

'We met Miss Arabella Fenton,' I said, 'who is now Mrs Dupont. You may not remember her; she was one of the dancers.'

'I remember her perfectly.' Mrs Transome gave us a wintry half-smile. 'She married a rich old Frenchman.'

'And she claims she had an assignation with your husband that night,' I said, 'in his dressing room.'

Mrs Transome showed no surprise, but only sighed rather impatiently. 'I daresay she did; Tom never could leave off interfering with the ballet-girls.'

'Weren't you angry, ma'am?' asked Blackbeard.

'I was the first time it happened, but constant dripping will wear away a stone.'

'Mrs Dupont said to ask Mrs Sarah what she thought of Maria's fiancé,' said Blackbeard.

'Ah,' said Mrs Transome, 'I wondered if Maria would tell you about her so-called engagement.'

'Your husband freely admits he was against the match,' I said. 'I take it you were of the same opinion?'

'Maria was seventeen years old, Mrs Rodd; barely out of the nursery. Fitzwarren was a very well-favoured young man, and it was my belief at the time that she nagged him into proposing to her. She was a termagant from the day she was born.'

Once again, I was disturbed by the harshness of her tone when she spoke of her own child.

'Mr Transome was more inclined to blame Fitzwarren,' I said, 'for taking advantage of Maria because she was the manager's daughter.'

For a moment, her face wore an expression of intense caution and calculation. My instinct was that the woman was trying to work out what to say next. There was a spell of silence, and then she spoke. 'Tom was jealous; Frank was handsome and gentlemanly, and half the girls in the theatre were in love with him. More than that, Frank was young, and my husband has a horror of getting older; in fact, a horror of old age in general. The first thing he noticed when he woke up after the fire was that I looked too old to play Rosalind.'

'That must have been very painful for you,' I suggested.

'It was bound to happen sooner or later,' said Mrs Transome. 'At the time I blamed Maria for pestering him. I had to admit, however, that her performance was quite remarkable.'

'It's Mrs Betterton's opinion,' said Blackbeard, 'that her father murdered Francis Fitzwarren. What do you say to that, ma'am?'

'I had no idea she would go that far,' said Mrs Transome, not the least shaken. 'My husband has many faults, Inspector, but I will swear in any court you like that he could not possibly commit a murder – the very idea is ridiculous. His character simply isn't deep enough.'

'Very well, let's say it wasn't him,' said Blackbeard. 'Who else might have done it?'

'I really don't know; as I told you, and as my husband told you, I left the theatre long before any fires or murders.'

'Did you go straight home?' I asked.

'I did,' said Mrs Transome.

'Perhaps someone in your household can recall the time of your arrival here?'

'I no longer have a household; the servants we kept then are long gone.'

'What about Murphy?'

'In those days she was still my dresser at the theatre, and did not live with us.'

'We'll have a word with her anyway,' said Blackbeard, 'while we're in the neighbourhood.'

'Yes, of course.' Mrs Transome rose from her chair and rang the bell, with the queenly grace of a tragic heroine on the stage.

Murphy knocked on the door in a matter of seconds, very much as if she had been listening outside it, and came briskly into the room.

'This is Inspector Blackbeard,' said Mrs Transome. 'And you know Mrs Rodd. They want to ask you about the night of the fire.'

'You haven't told them, have you?' Murphy folded her arms defiantly. 'The fire was years ago – this is far more important. Mrs Rodd, you ought to know that Mr Transome's left us without a penny piece. He promised to send us some money weeks ago! She's written to him three times and got no answer – we've taken to pawning the furniture and the house is as empty as a drum!'

'I will speak to Mr Transome,' I said. 'Perhaps there has been a mistake.'

'Look at her! She hasn't a ring or a necklace left to her name! If this carries on, I shall march right down to his theatre and take the money off him myself!' Murphy's indignation made her Irish brogue more pronounced. 'Isn't it bad enough that he's shamed her with his wickedness and taken away her children?'

'Never mind about all that now, my dear,' said Mrs Transome, smiling at her with real affection. 'Mr Blackbeard only wishes to ask you a couple of questions.'

'He can ask all he likes!' snapped Murphy. 'I have nothing to hide.'

'I'll leave you to it,' said Mrs Transome, 'so the inspector will know for sure that you're speaking freely.'

'I always speak freely,' said Murphy, glowering at Blackbeard.

Once Mrs Transome had left the room, Murphy stood proudly (and somewhat defensively, I thought) in the middle of the hearthrug.

'Please sit down,' I said, as cordially as possible. 'The inspector will only ask you the same questions he has asked of everyone who was present.'

Murphy sat down on the sofa, holding herself stiffly and watching Blackbeard with intense suspicion.

'This is good of you, Mrs Murphy,' said Blackbeard. 'I'd like to know when was the last time you saw Francis Fitzwarren, if you please.'

'I couldn't tell you what time it was by the clock, but it was after the curtain came down. There was a lot of larking about in the green room, as you'll often find when the understudy goes on. Mr Frank was cock of the walk amongst the actors and Mrs Sarah twitted him for still being in his costume, not to mention as drunk as a lord. And then she went off in the carriage and I set her dressing room to rights.' She pursed her lips defiantly, as if daring us to challenge her. 'And then I went home.'

'Mrs Transome told us you did not live with the family in those days,' I said, knowing full well that she was prevaricating, but pretending not to see it.

'I had a lodging in Adelphi Street,' said Murphy, 'close to the river. It wasn't much, but most of my time was spent at the theatre, and it was mighty handy for Drury Lane.'

'You were Mrs Transome's dresser for many years; when did you meet her?'

'The best part of thirty years ago, in Manchester. I was born in County Kildare and crossed the Irish Sea in search of work. Mrs Sarah's father, Mr Clifton – may God rest his soul, for a kinder gentleman never lived – hired me as a cleaner and laundress, and then Mrs Sarah made me her personal dresser. This was just before Mr Transome came on the scene.'

'You've known the man for a long time, ma'am,' said Blackbeard.

'Yes, indeed,' said Murphy. 'And he wasn't a great man in those days – far from it! But he was a handsome creature and Mrs Sarah fell head-over-ears in love with him. That is why Mr Clifton gave him his chance.'

'And he has been successful ever since,' I said. 'Mr Clifton must have been delighted.'

'I wouldn't go so far, ma'am,' said Murphy. 'Oh, he was happy to have the money the two of them were bringing in but he didn't like the match, and he didn't quite trust Mr Tom. Thankfully, the poor man died before he had to see what his daughter's husband got up to with ballet-girls and suchlike.'

'I can see that you don't like it either,' said Mr Blackbeard. 'But that's not our concern. I need to know what you saw on that particular night.'

'I did not see any sign of the fire before I went home,' said Murphy. 'I knew nothing about it till the next morning.'

'That must have been a great shock to you,' I said. 'Are you quite certain that Mrs Sarah came directly back to this house?'

'Of course she did!' snapped Murphy. 'Where else would she be going, at that time of night? I've told you everything, and now you must get some money out of Mr Tom – ready money – before we run out of credit entirely.'

'I shall certainly look into the matter,' I said. 'I cannot imagine Mr Transome withholding money intentionally.'

'There's a lot you can't imagine about him,' said Murphy. 'I saw nothing that night, and have nothing I can pin on him, but it wouldn't surprise me if he shot that poor young fellow. He has no conscience, particularly when it comes to his daughters; he's the one who set them against their poor mother – oh, she won't say it herself, but it made me sick sometimes, the way he treated those girls – as if they were nothing more than his playthings.'

She stopped herself, and looked at us as if she had been about to tell us something, but had abruptly changed her mind.

'How do you mean?' I asked, taken aback by her sudden lash of anger. 'I understood that Mr Transome has always been a most devoted father.'

'Devoted, you call it?' Murphy pursed up her lips and her face reddened. 'Tom Transome is only devoted to one person – and that is himself!'

She would say no more, but looked at me in a meaningful way, as if willing me to understand something that could not be uttered.

Ten

THE BUSINESS OF THE money had to be addressed as quickly as possible, and so I fired off a note to my brother (delivered by the little boy next door at the cost of one penny) as soon as I came home. The following morning, Fred and his carriage swept into Well Walk to carry us to the Haymarket.

'It never rains but it pours,' he said jauntily. 'I was beginning to think that the next time I saw Transome would be in a cell on a murder charge! I certainly did not expect to be shaking him down for money at this stage of the game. When's Blackbeard planning to arrest him?'

'When he has sufficient evidence.'

'Good old Blackbeard – never makes a move until it's all watertight!'

'You believe Mr Transome is guilty of murder?'

'Oh, my dear, of course he's guilty!'

'I thought you liked him.'

'He's enormously likeable, as murderers can be sometimes – I've defended many a good sort with a rotten conscience. And I hope with all my heart that he remembers his promise to engage me for his trial. This will be the sort of case to make a man's fortune and it couldn't have come at a better time; Fanny is still determined to have her new carriage.'

'You shouldn't count your chickens before they are hatched.' (In my opinion, the new carriage was a ridiculous extravagance, but now was not the time to bring this up.) 'No one has been arrested yet.'

'It won't be long.' Fred finished the slice of game pie he was guzzling and flicked away the crumbs with his handkerchief. 'I must say, I'm surprised that he's already trying to dodge his obligations to his wife, after all our toing and froing.'

There was to be more 'toing and froing', for we arrived at Mr Transome's theatre only to find that he was absent.

'There's been an upset, Mrs Rodd.' Cooper bustled down the steps to speak to us through the carriage window. 'Olivia and Miss Noonan had another bust-up, and Olivia's left her father's house.'

'Oh, dear,' I said. 'Has she returned to her mother?'

'She's gone into lodgings with one of the young ladies in the cast,' said Cooper, 'a Miss LaFaye. And ten to one that's where you'll find Mr Tom now – over in Golden Square, trying with all his might to smooth her down.' He lowered his voice dramatically. 'She sent him a letter this morning that turned him as pale as a ghost! He's lost without her, that's the trouble.'

'I understood that Miss Olivia did not play important roles.'

'She took over managing his money, and his correspondence and suchlike,' said Cooper. 'And now she has him on a string.'

'Perhaps we should leave this for another day,' I suggested to Fred. 'Since it's a private family matter.'

'My dear Letty, we're already up to our ears in the private business of this family and you said yourself that Mrs Sarah's situation must be addressed at once.'

'Yes, but—'

'Besides, my blood is up now.' Fred shouted instructions to his coachman on the box, and the carriage began to move away through the maelstrom of traffic.

Golden Square, in Soho, had been rather a grand address when it was built in the last century. It had fallen into decline since then, and was now a place of shabby boarding-houses, much favoured by the foreign musicians who flocked around the opera houses. Three of these men stood on the pavement outside Miss LaFaye's house, talking loudly in Italian, while someone played a violin behind an open window. Mr Transome's carriage, incongruously clean, waited at the kerb.

We heard raised voices as soon as we were on the door-step, and my brother had to pull the bell several times before anyone thought of letting us in.

Eventually, the door was opened by a flurried young woman who was evidently not a servant; she wore a gown of bright flowered stuff, modishly cut with an enormous skirt, and her light-brown hair bristled with curl-papers.

'I suppose you can come in,' she said, with a doubtful glance upstairs. She led us into a bare and somewhat dirty hall and cried out, 'Livvy – visitors! Shall I bring them up, or what?'

Silence fell, and then a disembodied voice called, 'Let them come up!'

'Won't you come up, please?' She giggled a little at the absurdity of the exchange. 'We'd better pretend we didn't hear anything, but they've been at each other's throats since Mr Tom got here.'

'You are Miss LaFaye, I believe,' I said, as Fred and I followed this gaudy little figure up the stairs.

'Yes, I'm Paulina LaFaye; that's my stage name, anyway.' Miss LaFaye threw us a friendly smile over her shoulder. 'My real name's Polly Higgins.'

'A rose by any other name would smell as sweet,' said my brother gallantly.

'Oh, go on!' Miss LaFaye showed the dimples in her pretty pink cheeks (I was a little confused by my readiness to like this flaunting, ribboned creature; her speech was pert and her manners lamentable, yet she had a droll charm to her that was difficult to resist).

The room upstairs was in great disorder, with an open trunk spewing out a jumble of dresses and the fireplace littered with pieces of broken china. Mr Transome stood beside one of the long windows, his face buried in the velvet curtain. Miss Olivia clutched the mantelpiece with her back towards us.

'Miss Olivia.' I had a shocking moment of wanting to laugh at the sorrowful tableau. 'Mr Transome.'

The tragedians uncovered their faces; both were breathless and in tears.

'You have a talent for finding me at my worst,' said Mr Transome.

'It's a private matter,' said Miss Olivia. 'Polly – fetch us some tea.'

'Indeed I will not!' said Miss LaFaye. 'I'm not a servant, I won't be ordered about in my own lodgings. And don't expect me to pay for all the china you smashed!' She left the room with a great tossing of her curl-papers.

'I'm afraid we have chosen an awkward time to call,' said my brother. 'But it's a matter of some urgency, concerning your wife.'

'Please sit down.' Mr Transome was recovering himself with violent face-mopping and nose-blowing. 'You caught us in the midst of a professional dispute, for which I offer you the most abject apologies.'

'I wouldn't call it "professional",' rejoined Miss Olivia. 'I have been forced out of my father's house, Mrs Rodd, by a wicked and designing person who has set him against his own flesh and blood.'

'My dear girl, if you will only listen to me!' sighed Mr Transome. 'What can I do? She has me over a barrel! But let's leave it alone for the moment; Mrs Rodd and Mr Tyson are here for quite another purpose.'

We sat down, and I gabbled out my account of Mrs Sarah's poverty as fast as possible, while I had his attention.

'There must be some mistake,' said Mr Transome. 'You know the terms we agreed; my wife was to receive a certain amount to tide her over, while we were still thrashing out the final settlement. If she has been forced to pawn the furniture, as you say, she should have told me of it sooner!'

'She claims to have written to you three times,' I said.

'Three? I haven't received one letter from her, let alone three!' He looked blank for a moment, and then the storm clouds gathered on his brow and he glared at Miss Olivia. 'This is your doing!'

'I don't know what you're talking about,' said Miss Olivia coldly.

'I gave you the money and you swore you'd send it to her!'

'You gave me a long list of bills to pay – and a sum of money that wasn't enough to pay them all. Most of it went on the actors' wages; my priority had to be keeping the theatre running. My mother was at the back of the queue.'

'She wrote me three letters; what did you do with them?'

'They're in my writing case,' said Miss Olivia. 'You may see them if you wish.'

'Why didn't you give them to me when they arrived?' Mr Transome cried out, in an anguish of fury and remorse. 'Why did you keep them from me?'

'There wasn't any point in your seeing them.' In stark contrast to her agitated father, Miss Olivia was now entirely calm and matter-of-fact. 'They were all the same – begging for money. I ignored them because we didn't have any to spare.'

'How could you be so heartless?' Mr Transome stared at his daughter as if seeing her for the first time. 'Your own mother!'

'Much you care about her!'

'I care a great deal; we're separated but I'm not an absolute brute!' He remembered us and made a visible effort to wrestle down his anger. 'Mrs Rodd, I'm grateful to you for bringing this to my notice, and I'll send poor Sarah all the cash I can scrape together in a hurry; she may have it this very day, if you come to the theatre this evening.'

'Thank you, Mr Transome.' It would have been useful to ask him the questions that had arisen from my encounter with Mrs Dupont, but I did not like to do so in front of Miss Olivia and decided to wait until I saw him at the theatre.

Our mission being accomplished, Fred and I took our leave.

Miss LaFaye scampered into the hall to intercept us; she had taken out the curl-papers and her head was now a profusion of bouncing ringlets. 'It's gone awfully quiet up there. I hope you haven't killed them!'

'I was tempted to,' said Fred, chuckling. 'What turbulent company for you, my dear!'

'I didn't invite her to move in here,' said Miss LaFaye. 'Princess Olivia invited herself because Noonan chucked her out of the fancy new house at Herne Hill – and Noonan ain't even living there herself yet!'

'It is a pity,' I said, 'that Miss Olivia did not feel she could take refuge with her mother, or her older sister – as Miss Cordelia has now done.'

'Cordelia had her own reason for running home to Mother.' The little creature dimpled at my brother and shook her curls at him. 'And it was nothing to do with Noonan.'

'Oh?'

'I heard quite another story – which was that she fell out with Papa on account of a certain young man.'

'Are you able to give me his name?'

'No – and even if I could, it'd be more than my job's worth. Good morning!'

The door shut smartly in our faces.

'She's an engaging little morsel,' said Fred. 'And I'll say one thing for Transome – he might be a danger to other people's daughters, but he's pretty fierce when it comes to guarding his own! I wouldn't care to be the chap who meddled with Miss Cordelia.'

My brother was unable to accompany me to the Haymarket that evening, due to a dinner party that Fanny would not allow him to miss. He sent me his carriage, however, to spare me fatigue in crossing London again, and I was quite happy to go to the Duke of Cumberland's Theatre on my own. I was determined to get my hands on some cash to help Mrs Sarah, and I was still hoping for a chance to speak privately to Mr Transome.

I arrived an hour before the curtain was due to go up, and found the street already crowded with onlookers, and hawkers of everything from hot pies to ballad-sheets. The front entrance being closed, I went to the stage door, which was in a narrow alley at one side of the building. Mr Cooper was waiting for me.

'Good evening, Mrs Rodd; he's expecting you, and I'm to take you to his dressing room.'

The area behind the scenes was calmer than I had last seen it; though still noisy and chaotic, there was an air of purpose and industry. I caught a glimpse of the stage, dressed for the opening scene of *Romeo and Juliet*, where a line of dancers, including a very scantily clad Miss LaFaye, practised their steps.

Cooper rapped on the door of Transome's dressing room and led me inside without waiting for an answer.

'Ah, Mrs Rodd; I knew you would be punctual to the very second!' He was in his red velvet gown at the table, busily covering his face with thick flesh-coloured paint. There was a woman with him, stooped and black-clad and evidently not one of what his wife termed his 'ballet-girls'. She gave me a timid greeting and I recognized her; it was Margaret Noonan, mother of Constance.

'All right, Maggie,' said Mr Transome. 'We'll finish this later.'

She nodded obediently and hurried from the room, closing the door behind her.

'More money, Mrs Rodd!' said Mr Transome, now painting a youthful blush upon his cheeks. 'I'm beset on all sides by demands for money; that establishment in Pentonville is another expense. All Connie's doing, of course; she won't come to me at Herne Hill until all her conditions have been met – well, you heard Olivia this morning.'

'Did you find something for your wife, Mr Transome?'

'Indeed I did! Cooper spent untold hours this afternoon going through all my pockets and so forth, and found nearly twenty pounds in ready cash; will that do?'

'Yes, Mr Transome; it will be a great help to her, until the final agreement is made.'

'I'm afraid I can't hand it over to you as I intended, for Murphy has been hanging about here all day, like some dreadful Irish bird of ill omen. I had to give it to her before I had time to put you off, and I can only apologize to you for your wasted journey.'

'Please don't mention it – I am grateful to be spared another journey to Ham Common.'

'Cooper, my dear, kindly give Mrs Rodd a glass of sherry – the good sherry, not the one that strips varnish. No, ma'am, I insist; it's the very least I can do.'

Although I had not intended to linger, I found myself back in the chintz-covered easy chair with a glass of excellent sherry. It was fascinating to observe the great actor as he applied his paint with a sure, swift hand, transforming himself into the character of Romeo.

'It's just as well we got the money out of the building before Miss Olivia got wind of it,' said Cooper. 'She had no idea there was such a nice sum right under her nose!'

Both men chuckled merrily at this.

'Too late!' said Mr Transome. 'Mrs Rodd, is the redoubtable Blackbeard any closer to finding his murderer?'

I could not reply, for at that moment he astonished me by jumping from his chair to strip off his dressing gown, revealing himself in a decidedly scanty attire of tights and shirtsleeves. I nearly choked on my sherry, but Mr Transome did not appear to notice my embarrassment, and pulled on his velvet jacket as if quite used to removing his clothes before ladies he barely knew.

'If he wants to arrest me, I wish he'd hurry up! I object to being hanged, but a brush with the law might be rather good for my box office.' He studied his reflection in the long glass. 'I'm most awfully sorry about the scene you saw this morning.'

'It is quite forgotten, I assure you,' I said.

'Do you have any searching questions?'

'Perhaps now is not the time.' I did not have his full attention and I was reluctant to question him in front of Cooper. 'You are about to begin your performance.'

'Well, you know where to find me.' With a friendly and disarming smile, he buckled on his stage sword, and stuck a long dagger into his belt. He then sat down again, for Cooper to put on his wig. 'It's all quite ridiculous, of course; Blackbeard must know by now that I couldn't murder a fly!'

The door was rudely wrenched open and Miss Olivia stormed into the room.

'Papa—'

'For God's sake, child! Am I to have no peace?'

'You are here again,' said Miss Olivia, glaring at me. 'Why are you here?'

'Livvy!' Mr Transome was pained. 'Mrs Rodd is here because I invited her!'

'Very well – but I am not to blame if she don't like what she hears – that girl has moved herself into my dressing room here, and says you gave her permission to do it!'

'Yes, I did – she is my leading actress and must have her own room.'

'You had no right!' snapped Miss Olivia. 'That room is mine!'

'I never said it was yours.'

'I am your own flesh and blood, and you gave it freely enough to Cordelia!'

'I gave it to Cordelia as my principal actress. It had nothing to do with blood.' Mr Transome paused to paint a line of white under his eyes. 'She is my Juliet and you are merely her understudy.'

'You promised me a principal role,' said Miss Olivia, now pale and still with anger. 'You refuse to see that

Noonan is making a fool of you! She's not in love with you, Papa – the whole theatre knows it!'

'My dear girl, this is nonsense.'

'Oh, is it? You think that when you've done everything she wants, she will give herself to you and live with you as your wife, but she has no intention of doing any such thing! She's carrying on with someone else right under your nose!'

'These are the forgeries of jealousy,' said Mr Transome. 'I refuse to listen to your gossip-mongering; you are very well aware of how matters stand between Constance and myself. She has sacrificed a great deal for my sake – it's disgraceful of you to suggest there is anyone else.'

'She never made a sacrifice in her life!'

'This is not an attractive side of your character, miss.' Mr Transome kept his tone even, yet his black eyes flashed pure fury. 'First you sniped at Maria and then at Cordelia, and this is simply more of the same.'

'But it's not fair!' Miss Olivia cried out passionately. 'What must I do to prove to you that I'm as good as Noonan? I ought to kill her this minute – then you'd be forced to give me my chance!'

She left the room, violently slamming the door.

Eleven

THE DAY AFTER THIS encounter, I saw a far better example of a father and daughter. It was the seventeenth birthday of my oldest niece, dearest Tishy (short for Laetitia; I am her godmother), and her mother being ill with a cold, it fell to me to accompany her and her father to the theatre.

'This should be quite a contrast to our last outing,' Fred assured me. 'One of my grateful customers presented me with a very decent box at the Princess Theatre, which is run by none other than James Betterton. He's opening a new production of his famous *Hamlet* – with every single impropriety cut out, so that it's entirely suitable for maidens of seventeen and quite a bit shorter. Betterton sets great store by his reputation for respectability.'

I knew that I could trust my brother not to expose his treasured child to anything in the least questionable, and gave myself up to the enjoyment of the occasion. All these years later, I can see Tishy as she was that night, shy and graceful as a fawn, and so pretty in her new gown of rose-pink silk; she wore a nosegay of rosebuds in her bosom, and the little string of pearls that I had given her around her slender neck; it was pleasant to see the loving expression in my brother's eyes when they rested upon her.

Naturally, I was most interested to see Mr Transome's greatest rival in action. The first difference between the two actors was evident before we entered the theatre; here were the same numbers of people I had seen outside the Duke of Cumberland's, yet this crowd was quieter and better behaved, and we were able to reach our box without too much pushing and shoving. Even the people in the 'gods' were more subdued, and greeted Mr Betterton's first entrance with a short burst of clapping instead of a prolonged riot of shouts and stamping.

James Betterton was tall and rather heavily built, with a handsome face and thick fair hair that appeared to be his own. His Prince of Denmark was serious and intelligent, and he commanded the stage with real authority. Most interesting of all, the role of Ophelia was played by his daughter-in-law, Maria, while her husband, Edgar, played Laertes.

The stage lights made Maria look very young, very beautiful and (somewhat disturbingly, under the circumstances) very like her father. Also like her father, she was a performer of natural brilliance. Maria's husband, as even I could tell, did not have the same magnetism. He spoke well, however, and was strikingly good-looking – like a fairer, more graceful version of his father.

At the curtain call, James Betterton made a short speech about how proud he was of the young couple's success in America, and urged the audience to wish them well in their new theatre.

Fred and I exchanged smiles at Tishy's face, radiant and transfixed.

'Well, my dear?' Fred asked. 'What did you think?'

'Oh, it was wonderful!' sighed Tishy. 'I didn't want it to end – but it was so dreadfully sad! Did you like it, Aunty?'

'Very much,' I said, sincerely. 'I thought I was familiar with the play, because I'd seen it once at a creaky old theatre in the country; Betterton has shown me something

91

else entirely, and he makes the words sound so magnificent that they're still marching about inside my head!'

'I have fond memories of that creaky old theatre,' said Fred, smiling at Tishy. 'The *Hamlet* we saw there was played by a shocking old mountebank with a red nose, who kept dropping the skull. Betterton is the new type of actor – an educated gentleman, like Macready or Kemble.'

There was a knock at the door of our box; it was a little, wrinkled, spry old man with white hair.

'Beg pardon, sir, but are you Mr Tyson?'

'I am,' said Fred.

'Mr Betterton spotted you during the curtain calls, sir, and begs the favour of a word.'

'What – now?'

'If you'd be so kind, sir.'

'Are you acquainted with Betterton?' I asked, surprised.

'We have met a couple of times at the Garrick,' said Fred. 'That's all; I'm impressed that he remembers me.'

'Tishy and I can wait in the carriage while you speak to him.'

'Beg pardon, ma'am,' said the old man. 'If you are Mr Tyson's sister, he'd also like a word with you, and I'm to escort you to his dressing room.'

'That is quite out of the question,' I said at once. 'Please explain to Mr Betterton that we're with my brother's daughter, and cannot possibly—'

'Oh, I don't see why not,' said my brother.

'Fred – are you out of your mind?' I gasped, recalling what I had witnessed behind the scenes when we visited Mr Transome.

'Keep your hair on; I wouldn't allow my Tishy anywhere near Transome's gaff, but Betterton is a famous Bible-basher, clean as a whistle and moral enough even for you.' Fred gave me the wicked grin he had used to wear me down since the day he was born. 'And aren't you dying to know what he wants?'

'Well—' Of course I was curious, and Tishy's awestruck face persuaded me to ignore the 'Bible-basher'. 'If you really believe it will do no harm ... '

I was still uneasy, but found that I had already lost the argument. Fred took a firm hold of Tishy's hand and we followed the old man to the baize-covered 'pass' door that led to the backstage area.

I saw the difference to Transome's theatre as soon as we entered. There was no clamour of insolent shouting, no rude shoving of strangers, no flaunting of bare flesh. The staircase and passages were busy with actors, but here they were decently covered, they spoke quietly and stood aside politely to let us pass.

Mr Betterton received us in his private dressing room, which was considerably less luxurious than Transome's; the furniture was plain, the walls were unpapered, and there was a tea urn in place of the bottles and decanters.

The man himself – fully dressed in a dark coat and stiff collar – bowed to us, and solemnly thanked us for answering his summons. It was strange to see the Prince of Denmark transformed into an ordinary gentleman, with a gentleman's manners and deportment. His treatment of Tishy won me over immediately; he bowed to her as if she had been a queen, accepted her stammering compliments with a smile of real kindness and wished her many happy returns when Fred told him it was her birthday.

'I didn't know you had done me the honour of bringing your daughter, Tyson; I envy you, for my late wife and I were only blessed with our four sons.'

'Mr Edgar Betterton was a fine Laertes,' I said.

'Thank you, ma'am; he's a good lad, and fully aware that his wife acts him off the stage.' He was about to say something else, but glanced at Tishy and set about pouring tea.

'They will be opening their new theatre soon,' I said. 'Do you know when it will be ready?'

'Edgar says next month; I think it will be longer. The building is in a very bad condition.'

He handed us tea, in fine bone-china cups. Fred took his without enthusiasm.

'I have heard a great deal lately about the animosity between your family and Transome's,' I said, 'and I'm very curious to know how it began.'

Mr Betterton sighed and looked pained. 'That is an old story, Mrs Rodd. I can only assure you that there is no animosity on my side.'

Once again he seemed to be about to say something more, but glanced at my innocent niece and stopped himself.

'Let's hear what you want with us.' Fred was starting to be impatient. 'Is it connected to Transome?'

Mr Betterton set down his cup and saucer, deeply serious. 'I believe it might be. As I'm sure you know, the world of the theatre is very small; everyone knows everyone's business, and there has been a great deal of talk about the police enquiry into the fire and the murder. I remember that night, and I think I might have some useful information, which you must feel free to pass on to the police. First of all, I was acquainted with poor Fitzwarren.'

This was unexpected and Fred's interest sharpened. 'I wouldn't have thought he was your sort of thespian – when did you last see him?'

'We met on the morning of the fire, in this very theatre. Our business was professional, but he had a connection to my family.'

'The police will be happy to hear it,' I said. 'They haven't been able to find any of his relations.'

'We were not related by blood,' said Mr Betterton. 'He was a cousin of my late wife, and I took an interest in him for her sake. On the morning of the fire, I offered Fitzwarren a position in my company – which he accepted.'

'Well, well!' said Fred. 'Did Transome know?'

'I believe not. Fitzwarren appealed to me because he had got himself into a difficult set of circumstances.'

'Oh, yes – he was secretly engaged to Miss Maria.'

'Indeed,' said Betterton. 'And there was something else, which I won't go into now.' (Another glance at Tishy.) 'I tried to warn him against it.'

'I know that several of Transome's actors came to your company after the fire,' I said. 'Weren't you surprised, Mr Betterton, when Fitzwarren simply disappeared?'

'I'm sorry to say that I was annoyed, ma'am; I thought he had run away from his obligations. Naturally I now regret that I did not look into it further. And there was something else, but I'll write it down.'

Mr Betterton found a scrap of paper and a pencil, rapidly scrawled a few lines and folded it several times, before he presented it to Fred.

Fred did not open it until we had taken our leave and were driving home. 'Oho!' he said, laughing. 'This certainly isn't something he could say in front of my daughter!'

He pushed the paper into my hand, and I read it by the light of the carriage lamp.

F was embroiled in a love affair with Mrs Sarah T. On the night of the fire, I saw Mrs T in Manchester Square.

Twelve

I FIRED OFF A LETTER to Blackbeard first thing the next morning (after a restless night of mulling over the new information and wondering if *anyone* had been telling the truth). My brother kindly stopped at Well Walk on his way to the City to pick up the letter, which he promised to deliver to Scotland Yard without delay.

'The inspector must know of this as soon as possible.' I was in the street and addressing Fred through the open window of his carriage. 'He often talks of "motive and means", and Mrs Transome has both – her motive was love, and she had the means to do it because she was not in Ham Common.'

'Steady on,' said Fred. 'Her love affair gives Transome another good reason to murder Fitzwarren. My money's still on him. Where do you go next?'

'Not very far; I shall be speaking to Mr Tully.'

I was now certain that my neighbour had not told me anything near as much as he knew, and knocked at his door as soon as Fred's carriage had departed.

'Mrs Rodd!' He was surprised to see me so early, I thought, and was also rather uneasy.

He looked more uneasy when I told him I had met James Betterton, but ushered me into his little drawing room with his accustomed politeness.

The room was spotlessly clean and perfectly neat, though he kept no servant. There were a couple of nondescript pictures on the walls, a framed playbill or two, a shelf of books and furniture that was shabby yet well maintained. His three fat ginger cats sat in a row upon the brocade sofa, and stared at me with scornful indifference until Mr Tully shooed them away so that I could sit down.

As concisely as possible, I described my encounter with Betterton and showed him the pencilled note.

'Oh – I see. Yes, of course.' He looked stricken and confused. 'But I wouldn't set much store by anything he says.'

'Come now, Mr Tully!' I was rather touched by his loyalty and wanted to be kind, but I was taking no more flimflam. 'I know that Mrs Transome is a friend of yours, and I'm sure you have the best reasons for trying to protect her reputation. It is too late now, however, and you cannot help her unless you tell the truth.'

'I was afraid of this!' He shook his head mournfully. 'I knew she would be misunderstood!'

'Was she in love with Francis Fitzwarren?'

'Yes, she loved him – but that sort of thing is more common – more easily accepted – in the world of the theatre.'

'Mr Betterton claims to have seen her in Manchester Square, when she told the police she was miles away at Ham Common.'

'He could have been mistaken.'

'Mr Tully, I beg you!'

'Oh, very well.' He let out a long sigh. 'Fitzwarren lived in Camden Town, but Sarah kept rooms in Manchester Square so that they could meet in private.'

'Wasn't that very expensive?'

'There was plenty of ready money around in those days, and the Transomes' credit was still good,' said Mr Tully.

'She only had to put down a couple of pounds on account for the rooms, and that's where she went on the night of the fire.'

'Did her dresser know of this?'

'I assume so.'

'Did her husband know?'

'He was aware of the affair,' said Mr Tully. 'I couldn't say if he knew they were meeting on that particular night.'

'And what of Maria?'

'Maria knew nothing – I'm certain of that.' His tone was firm now. 'She was little more than a child. Sarah moved heaven and earth to keep her in the dark.'

'Let us be clear, Mr Tully; do you mean that Mrs Transome was involved with this man at the same time as he was wooing her daughter?'

'Yes.'

'I see.' Try as I might, I could not keep my horror out of my voice; I had not dreamt that she was capable of such flagrant immorality.

'It looks very bad, I know,' said Mr Tully. 'The fact is that the Transomes had not lived as husband and wife for many years. Rightly or wrongly, they both considered themselves at liberty to … to fall in love with other people.'

'The police are only concerned with their movements on the night of the murder. When Mrs Sarah discovered that Fitzwarren was not at Manchester Square, did she return to the theatre?'

'I don't know – I didn't see her – as I told you, I was in the Fox and Grapes, and only went back into the theatre when it was burning.'

I was silent for a spell, while the three cats stretched and yawned on the faded hearthrug, and Mr Tully rearranged his version of events.

'If you or anyone else saw Mrs Sarah returning to Drury Lane on that night, she will be suspected of murder.'

'No!'

'Do you consider her to be capable of killing someone?'

'No, Mrs Rodd – upon my life I swear that she could not!' His unearthly blue eyes were bright in a face that was deathly pale. 'I will admit that I held back one or two things from you, but now you may have it all; she was involved with Frank for a good two years before the fire. He came along at a sad time in her life. Tom was philandering, of course, and she was accustomed to that. But now Tom turned cold on her; he ignored her, and had eyes and ears only for Maria.'

'Surely Sarah could not object to that,' I said. 'There are too many fathers who take no notice at all of their daughters.'

'He didn't pay his girls a great deal of attention when they were very small,' said Mr Tully. 'That changed round about when Maria turned fifteen. She had grown up into a beauty, but that wasn't all; she took to spouting Shakespeare around the house, until Tom couldn't help being struck by her talent – positively bludgeoned by it, you could say. This was when he began to train her seriously, and not merely from fatherly pride. He was looking to the future. Maria was a new lease of life for the company; the possibilities were endless.'

'Why did he wait until after the fire to launch her?'

'Rosalind was her official debut, Mrs Rodd, but Tom started her off in smaller roles at least a year before the fire.'

'So there was a time when father and daughter were in perfect accord,' I said.

'Not exactly perfect, for they were constantly falling out and shouting at each other. Poor Sarah didn't get much of a look-in. Nobody was surprised that she took up with young Fitzwarren. It was an open secret in the company.'

'In which case, why didn't Maria know it?'

'You've seen how it works,' said Mr Tully. 'There's a kind of code in these matters. Nobody spoke of it in front of Maria; she was the manager's daughter and people were afraid for their jobs.'

'But did no one say anything when she became engaged to Fitzwarren?'

'As I said, ma'am, they were afraid. Nobody wanted to be the bringer of bad news.'

'Did Mrs Sarah know about it?'

'She did,' said Mr Tully. 'I know she did, because we discussed the matter. I don't think, however, that she believed the engagement to be genuine.'

I felt a stirring of sympathy for Maria; she had been only seventeen years old, the same age as my beloved Tishy, and she had lost her heart to a man who was 'carrying-on' (as Mrs Bentley liked to put it) with her own mother.

'You and Mrs Sarah are great friends,' I said. 'Do you know where she went after Manchester Square?'

'I assumed she went straight home to Ham Common,' said Mr Tully. 'I did not see her anywhere near the theatre, nor did anyone else. That is all I can tell you. She loved Fitzwarren very deeply – her heart was quite broken when his letter came, and she thought he had run off after the fire.'

'Did you happen to see a dancer, Miss Arabella Fenton?'

'Who? Oh, wait a minute, she's the girl that married the rich old foreigner.'

'She claims she had an assignation with Mr Transome, in his dressing room.'

'I didn't know about that, and I didn't see her,' said Mr Tully. 'But I wouldn't be surprised; Tom has a well-known fondness for dancers.'

'Did Mrs Transome know anything about this particular assignation?'

'Probably – I don't know – she might've done.' His voice was more forceful now. 'It wouldn't have given her any reason to kill Fitzwarren. She loved him. Why would she kill the man she loved?'

'You speak as if people never did such a thing,' I said. 'I find that surprising in someone who has worked in the theatre, Mr Tully; you must have noticed how often it happens in plays, and for once art is only imitating life. Love and hate are but two sides of the same coin.'

Thirteen

'Very nice work, mrs Rodd; very nice indeed. But you've upset the apple cart, as you always seem to do.'

'How do you mean, Inspector?' I was a little disappointed by his calm reaction to my great revelation.

'I was all set to arrest Transome,' said Blackbeard. 'Now I have to start again with a new suspect. I'll admit to you that before you came up with all this, I wasn't looking at that wife of his.'

'Neither was I; she is evidently an accomplished liar, or at the very least, an expert at withholding information.'

'Hmm,' said Blackbeard. 'So now I'm to arrest her instead? I'm not ready to let her husband off the hook just yet, ma'am.'

He had sent the police carriage for me that same morning, and we were muttering in a dark corridor of the magistrate's court in Bow Street, on the edge of Covent Garden Market.

He opened a heavy door and ushered me into a large panelled room, furnished with a long mahogany table and a dozen ponderous chairs. Upon one of these sat Mr Transome, incongruously bright and elegant in his blue coat and gaily patterned silk waistcoat.

'Mrs Rodd, Inspector!' He leapt to his feet when we entered. 'It is, of course, an enormous pleasure to assist the police once again, but your summons caught me in the middle of a rehearsal for my new piece, and if you are not going to lock me up, I wish you would allow me to get back to it.'

'Believe me, sir,' said Blackbeard, 'I'd be happy to lock you up, only I ain't got enough on you to do it today.'

This made Mr Transome laugh, wiping years from his face. The three of us sat down around the table, and he said, 'Let's have it, then!'

With admirable brevity, Blackbeard told him of our meeting with Mrs Dupont, and the new evidence given by James Betterton and Mr Tully. I watched his reaction narrowly; his manner was suitably serious now, yet his expression gave nothing away. His lustrous dark eyes moved from Blackbeard to me; he allowed the silence to stretch when the inspector finished.

And then his only comment was, 'So you've heard at last; I knew it was only a matter of time.'

'I suppose you know, sir,' said Blackbeard, 'that withholding evidence is a crime?'

'Now, wait a moment – I was trying to protect my wife! Is that a crime?'

'Yes, sir, if she murdered her lover.'

'This is precisely why I said nothing – because I knew you would condemn her for the mere fact that she was involved with Fitzwarren, without seeing that she couldn't possibly have killed him.'

'How can you be sure of that, sir?' asked Blackbeard. 'Is it because you did the killing yourself?'

'No!'

'You said you saw her off in her carriage; were you aware that she was going to see Fitzwarren in Manchester Square?'

'Well, of course I was aware of the possibility; they often met after a performance. It was a marriage in all but name.'

'Mr Transome,' I said, wincing at his careless disrespect for the institution of holy matrimony, but pushing it aside (I was getting used to swallowing my disapproval), 'when your wife did not find Fitzwarren as she expected, did she return to the theatre?'

'I didn't see her there; as the charming Mrs Dupont doubtless told you, I had other matters on my mind.'

'According to James Betterton,' I said, 'he met Fitzwarren on the day of his death and offered him employment.'

'Did he, indeed?' Anger flared in Mr Transome's face; he was all attention now. 'I suppose I shouldn't be surprised – that dull old prig has always loved getting at me! And now he has Maria to egg him on!' He leapt from his chair and began to pace around the room. 'She has set her heart on seeing me hanged – her own father! And I taught her everything she knows, which is more than any Betterton will ever know! I poured my whole soul into that girl, and she repaid me by shackling herself to another yellow-haired imbecile. Edgar is simply another Fitzwarren – she's never forgiven me for that – I beg your pardon for flying off the handle, Mrs Rodd – but how in heaven's name could I permit my daughter to marry a man who was entangled with her mother?'

He flung himself back into his chair and slumped into silence (I have done my best to convey the disjointed, galvanic nature of his outburst) which lasted for a few minutes. The inspector, also silent, briefly looked at me and raised his eyebrows; I knew of old that this meant he wished me to take over the interrogation.

'Are you absolutely certain,' I asked gently, 'that your daughter did not know about the entanglement? I find it difficult to believe such a thing, yet Mr Tully implied that it was common knowledge.'

'Some things are known about but never spoken about,' said Mr Transome. 'I did not like my daughter to get too confidential with the other actors in the company, and they all knew it. Maria was kept apart from the others – though it didn't stop her losing her head over Fitzwarren.'

'Mrs Betterton claims that she only pretended to break off their engagement; were you aware of that?'

'No, I was not.'

'Was your wife aware of it?'

'You'll have to ask her, but I would say she was not – or why would the boy go begging James Betterton for sanctuary? How do you know he wasn't working with Betterton all along? It wouldn't surprise me if he set the fire on Betterton's orders!'

'I have heard that there were such rumours at the time,' I said. 'Having met the man, however, I don't think it likely.'

'What is it that you fellows are supposed to ask? *Cui bono?* – who benefits? Well, let me tell you, there was only one person who benefited from the fire, and that person was James Betterton! He poached my best actors with remarkable speed, for all the world as if he'd been prepared!'

'That is a serious accusation, Mr Transome,' I said. 'Do you have any evidence?'

'No, but I haven't gone looking for it. That's your job, Inspector.'

'I don't tell you how to do your work, sir,' said Blackbeard. 'So kindly don't go telling me how to do mine. The coroner found no evidence of arson; I shall go along with that until somebody tells me different. I'm only interested in one corpse with a bullet hole in his head, and you had a gun. Mrs Dupont saw it.'

'Lots of people saw it.' Mr Transome was calm, eyeing us both keenly. 'As I explained at the time, it was one of a pair of pistols I purchased, to defend myself on the roads. There had been a spate of robberies.'

'Was it on your person, sir, at the time of the fire?'

'No, I'd given up carrying it by then. I only fired the thing once, at a plaster cherub on the front of the dress circle. And I missed.'

'I'll set my men a-searching for it in the ruins,' said Blackbeard. 'And I'm sure they'll find it, sir – so long as someone didn't take it away with them.'

'I certainly didn't,' said Mr Transome.

'You say the gun was one of a pair; do you know what happened to the other one?'

'The other one? There's a good question!' He was interested now. 'Good Lord, I haven't thought about it for years. I'm pretty sure I gave it to my wife, though she didn't like it – she said she was more frightened of the pistol than she was of any highway robbers, and begged me to take it out of the house. I can't remember whether or not I did.' He stood up again. 'And now, if you have everything you want from me, I need to get back to my rehearsal.'

'Not everything, sir; not by a long chalk,' said Blackbeard drily. 'But we're finished for the moment.'

'You will soon see that I am innocent, Mr Blackbeard.' Mr Transome picked up his hat and gloves. 'I have great faith in British justice, even when it doesn't seem to have any faith in me!'

The gaiety of his manner drew a reluctant and rusty smile from Blackbeard. 'Wish you good day, sir.'

'Mrs Rodd, it's pouring with rain and I have my carriage – please allow me the pleasure of conveying you home. No, no, I will hear no protests!'

The rain was terrible that day, and had already taken its toll upon my bonnet, shoes and best umbrella. I accepted his offer most gratefully. The two of us dashed across the muddy pavement (I resigned myself to spending yet another evening cleaning the hem of my second-best black silk gown) into the same smart and commodious carriage that I had seen outside the theatre.

The interior was lined with soft dark red plush and wonderfully comfortable, with the windows tightly sealed against the weather and the racket of the street.

'This is most kind of you, Mr Transome.'

'Not at all, Mrs Rodd.' He was sat facing me, his back to the driver, those great black eyes of his fixed upon me (I had a sudden, disconcerting moment of thinking how my dearest husband would have laughed, to see his spotlessly respectable wife shut up in a carriage with a famous actor and notorious libertine). 'You are very brave, when for all you know I'm a murderer.'

'You may very well be,' I returned, 'but I'll risk it to escape this horrid weather.'

Though he smiled at this, his gaze was unusually thoughtful and penetrating. 'Even if I wished to murder you, I'd hardly do it in the middle of the Strand.'

'I should hope not!'

'That Blackbeard fellow is an interesting study for an actor. I've never seen a face that gives so little away. You know him of old, of course; is he always like this?'

'Yes, Mr Transome. I believe he's proud of his inscrutability.'

'As far as I can guess, he thinks I killed Fitzwarren. I can feel him circling above me, like a bird of prey preparing to swoop. When he summoned me this morning, I was half-expecting him to arrest me.'

'Mr Blackbeard never swoops until he is absolutely certain.'

'And what about you, ma'am? What is your opinion in the matter?'

'My personal opinion is neither here nor there.'

'You are quite right; we should not be having such a conversation. We had better talk about something else.'

'Very well.' I was happy to change the subject. 'How is Miss Olivia?'

He let out a sigh that was half a comical groan. 'She's back in my house at Herne Hill, if you can credit such a turn of events. She and Miss Noonan have made some sort of truce, though Lord knows how long it will last. By the by, my wife sent me a note to say that she had received the money I sent her.'

'I'm glad to hear it.'

'I'm still furious with Olivia. Between ourselves, I wish someone would marry that girl. In my lowest moments, I find myself wishing she had eloped with Betterton, and not Maria. I would've endured it so much better!' Mr Transome scrutinized me for a moment, and then observed, 'But I have shocked you again.'

'I simply do not understand how you can speak of your own child in such an unfeeling way.' (I was assailed by a memory of Fred as a cherub of four years old, cheerfully admitting to our dear father that he had stolen a pie and wasn't sorry; Transome had the same air of sublime insouciance.) 'Miss Olivia was the only one of your daughters to stand by you.'

'Oh, to be sure,' said Mr Transome airily. 'And naturally I was grateful to her – but she really isn't much use to me in the theatre. While her acting is perfectly good for farces and pantomimes, she doesn't have the voice or the bearing for the great roles – unlike her sisters. As a father I love them all equally. As the manager of a theatre, I must think of my takings at the box office, and Olivia simply doesn't pull them in like the others. I've told her so to her face and she refuses to hear it. She loves to spend my money but there won't be any more money unless she stops plaguing poor Constance, and I wish she'd see it! Now that Maria and Cordelia have forsaken me, where else will I find a leading lady?'

'Is that why you said Miss Noonan had you "over a barrel"?'

'Oh – you heard that?' Mr Transome was, fleetingly, annoyed. 'I may as well tell you, since you know so much about my affairs, that Constance threatened to take her talents off to another company.'

'Which company?'

'She did not mention any names, but the hint was enough. She can go anywhere she likes, now that I have made her famous.'

'But – I understood that she had promised to live with you as your wife!'

I blurted this out without thinking, and Transome's sad smile sweetened. 'You know, Mrs Rodd, you sometimes remind me powerfully of my sister Eliza, who brought me up after our mother died; any shreds of decency in my character are entirely due to her.'

'You are fond of making yourself out to be wicked and devoid of conscience,' I said. 'But I think you have more decency than you will own.'

'That is because you are kind, Mrs Rodd; in fact, I am a complete scoundrel of the deepest dye.'

'Is this a confession, Mr Transome?'

'No – I am not a total fool. I am nevertheless a thoroughly wicked man.'

'What have you done?'

'Nothing, as far as the law of the land is concerned. The law of Heaven is another matter.' He was still smiling at me, yet the smile had an inward quality, as if he had a private joke. 'Perhaps, if you haven't anything better to do, you might pray for me.'

We had arrived at the Haymarket and the carriage stopped outside Mr Transome's theatre. He leapt out with his accustomed grace, touched his hat to me and was gone.

Fourteen

THE NEXT ACT OF the tragedy unfolded upon the following day, which began with a disagreement between myself and Mrs Bentley. The innocent cause of our argument was her granddaughter, dear little Hannah. Mrs B's health was greatly improved, but it was plain to me that she was not yet well enough to take up all her old work, and I had made the bold suggestion that we should keep the child as a permanent member of our household.

'I know she is only twelve years old,' I said. 'But she has been a blessing to us, and I would see to it that she goes to the parish school to finish her education. As you told me yourself, her parents are poor and hard put to feed and clothe all their children. Hannah is a clever girl, sensible and handy beyond her years, and when she is older I can help her to an excellent place in a good family – as I have already done for several of her cousins.'

'But I'm as fit as a fiddle, ma'am, and I've done my own work in my own house all my life! If I have help, the next thing will be everyone expecting me to give up and sit quiet in the chimney-corner!'

'My dear Mary, nobody expects any such thing, and you are simply being stubborn. You must admit that Hannah has already benefited from living with us; she was a skinny little scrap when she first came, and look how she has grown!'

'It's another expense, ma'am, when we have to look out for every penny.'

'My brother has received a very nice sum for the Transome business, which will allow us a few small comforts.' (I had been surprised when Fred handed me the little sheaf of grubby banknotes; having heard about Mr Transome's improvidence, I had begun to wonder if I would ever get paid at all.)

'We'll run through that soon enough.'

'The Lord will provide.' (I do not say such things lightly.) 'Hannah may well be a part of His plan for us; knowing she is here with you greatly improves my peace of mind when I am away.'

'You worry too much about nothing. Still … ' Mrs B was yielding. 'She's a good girl, and it would be a help to her poor mother, I'll give you that.'

'She would have her own little room and plenty of good food. And think how quickly she learns everything you teach her; before long, she will be ready for a fine situation in one of the best families.' (I cannot resist adding that this last promise was one I did not honour, for Hannah was destined to become such a vital and beloved part of our household that I could never bear to let her go, and she stayed at Well Walk until she got married.)

Sensing that I had won this dispute, I did not press my point any further and turned my mind to the business of the day. Maria Betterton had sent me a brief letter, in which she hinted that she had something more to tell about the murder, and so off I went to Holloway.

I arrived at Vale Crescent in the early afternoon and immediately saw that something was amiss. There was a carriage waiting outside the house and upheaval within it; the maid who admitted me into the hall was agitated in her manner, and still clutching an armful of what appeared to be bed-linen. I noticed a pervasive smell of illness, that smell of bodily waste and decay that is so well known to anyone who has watched in a sickroom.

'It's Miss Cordelia, ma'am – she's been took bad and the doctor is up with her now.'

'I'm sorry to hear it,' I said. 'Please tell Mrs Betterton that I will call again another day.'

'Mrs Rodd?' A man emerged into the hall from the back parlour. 'My wife wishes to see you, if you will be so kind.'

I knew him, for I had seen him playing Laertes to his father's Hamlet. 'Mr Betterton, I don't like to intrude—'

'You will not be intruding, ma'am.' Seen at close quarters, Maria's handsome husband looked a little older than he had done on the stage, and more manly. 'You have caught us in the middle of – well, I'll leave it to my wife to tell you.'

He showed me into the room in which I had interviewed Maria Betterton. She was there, and so, to my surprise, was Mrs Sarah. Both mother and daughter were tearful, and I had the impression that they had only just stopped weeping.

'Maria sent for me this morning,' said Mrs Sarah. 'My youngest child is gravely ill, Mrs Rodd. When I got here, I was afraid I had come only to say goodbye to her!'

'She took poison,' said Maria, in a shaking voice. 'The servant found her lying on the floor, as cold as death, amidst signs that she had suffered terrible sickness and terrible sorrow.'

'But – how dreadful!' I was profoundly shocked, and could not help asking, 'Did she mean to do away with herself?'

'No!' said Mrs Sarah sharply.

'Yes – of course she did!' Maria cried out passionately. 'I told you, Mamma – it's far too late to think of covering it up. Cordelia took poison because she wanted to kill herself, and now this whole family will be mired in shame and scandal!'

'Do you know why she would do such a thing?' I asked, as gently as possible.

'Cordelia has been very unhappy ever since we brought her here,' said Mr Edgar, with an anxious, sideways look at his wife. 'I have barely seen her; she has hidden herself away in her room; she has spent night after night weeping as if her heart had broken.'

'Just as she did when she was at Ham,' said Mrs Sarah. 'I knew she hated to leave her father's company; I thought it was him she was pining after, and her fine life as a leading actress – may Heaven forgive me! But you should not have told her that he was a murderer.'

'I might have known you'd try to blame me!' snapped Maria. 'I told her nothing of the kind, but I am more certain with every passing day that he killed Frank Fitzwarren!'

Mrs Sarah flinched at the sound of his name, and shot me a fearful look that convinced me she had said nothing to her daughter of her own love affair.

'My dear,' said Mr Betterton softly, placing a tentative hand upon Maria's arm. 'Now is not the time for this.'

There was a loud rap at the door, and a man entered; a brisk and sharp-eyed man in his middle years, with a neat head of grey hair; he wore a dark frock-coat and carried a large black valise, of the kind commonly used by doctors. His expression was stern.

'Mr Betterton.' He addressed himself to the man in the room and took no notice of the rest of us. 'I'm able to tell you that the young lady is out of danger.'

'Thank God!' gasped Mrs Sarah.

'She is very weak; I left your girl to watch beside her, and I suggest that you engage a professional nurse. The young lady did not intend to harm herself; she took a dose of pennyroyal, and her reason for doing so was only too plain. She has lost the child she was carrying.'

Maria let out a hoarse cry, and slid to the floor in a dead faint.

In my time, I have watched beside many a sickbed; this is my excuse for taking charge after the doctor had departed. The small house was in a decidedly unhealthy state of upheaval. Maria and her mother wept, Mr Betterton fussed ineffectually, and the poor invalid had been left at the mercy of a frightened servant-girl who had no idea what to do.

I sent her out to fetch a nurse whom I had briefly employed to help me care for Mrs B; a very capable and clean young woman named Mrs Plant, who lived conveniently close by in Barnsbury.

With the assistance of the other servant, I pulled the bed away from the wall to allow the air to circulate freely around the sick girl. I opened the window and swept the grate so that the coals did not smoke. I set a pan of beef broth to simmer upon the kitchen range (I commandeered the fresh meat intended for that night's dinner; too many people make their broth with nothing more than a few leftover bones, but this is not sufficiently nutritious for an invalid). I demanded fresh linen, fresh water, towels and good soap. My dear husband would have called me a 'whirlwind'; order was imposed in a remarkably short time.

While we awaited the nurse, Mrs Sarah and I sat beside the bed.

Mrs Sarah had recovered her composure. She held her daughter's hand, gazing at her with the brooding look of all-consuming love that you see on the face of a mother with a sick child. There was a strength to her that I had not seen before, but she had lost her youthful air. She was lined and careworn, and I had never liked her so well.

'Do you know when I may give her something to eat, Mrs Rodd?'

'I would try a few spoonfuls of beef tea when she wakes and, if she says she is hungry, a soft-boiled egg. If she is thirsty, you may give her weak tea with boiled milk, or water that has been boiled and left to cool. But the nurse will advise you better than I can.'

'My poor little girl – what a burden she has carried!'

Miss Cordelia, the daughter I had not met and only glimpsed through a window, was very like her eldest sister: a dark-haired beauty with a face of carved ivory. She lay very still, yet her breathing was easy. The doctor had told us of a great loss of blood. She had sinned – first by being with child, and then by swallowing oil of pennyroyal to correct the situation – but I could not bear to condemn her for it. The sadness in her young face cut me to the heart and made me remember the limitless compassion of our Saviour.

Mrs Sarah murmured, 'I wish I had known – if only she had told me! But she wore loose clothes that revealed nothing, and kept herself apart from me. And I thought she was angry about leaving the theatre! What a fool I have been!'

'Were there really no signs?' I asked softly.

'Perhaps, but I was too blind – too absorbed in my own silly affairs – to see them.'

'Do you know the name of the man?'

She shook her head. 'I know nothing of her life before she suddenly came home to me.'

'Do you think your husband might know?'

'Possibly; he will have heard all the gossip in the company.'

'Forgive me, but should he be sent for?'

'My husband should be told, but I will take care of it – my God, this will break his heart! Cordelia is his darling, his pride and joy. Now at least he will understand why she left him.'

'Mrs Transome,' I could not pass up this golden opportunity to question her about the murder, 'Mr Blackbeard wishes to speak with you again. There is some new evidence.'

'Oh?' She could not take her hungry gaze from the face of her child.

'You were not entirely candid about Francis Fitzwarren.'

She glanced at me sharply. 'What have you heard?'

I told her of my encounters with James Betterton and Mr Tully. Her face twitched as if I had touched a nerve, but she listened quietly and was quiet for a long stretch when I had finished.

And then she said, 'I loved him, you know; the appearance is shameful, but my love for him was not.'

'That is not my concern; the police only wish to know your movements on the night of the fire.'

'James Betterton is one of those fearsome types who never tells lies, and if he says he saw me in Manchester Square, it must be true.'

'Your husband says he saw you into your carriage, after the play.'

'Yes, that's true,' said Mrs Sarah. 'But unlike Betterton, my husband loves lies and is very good at lying. I wouldn't believe everything he says.'

(We were conversing in whispers barely louder than breath, across the still figure of a young girl who had nearly

117

died; I think it was this that shamed Mrs Sarah into being serious.)

'You may tell Mr Blackbeard that I went to Manchester Square that night. I did not see Betterton but he evidently saw me; I believe his father lived there at the time. I waited for Frank until gone two o'clock. I now know that I ought to have been anxious about him; I was only annoyed. I woke my coachman and went home to Ham Common.'

'At what time did you hear of the fire?'

'Five o'clock in the morning, when they brought home my husband. Cooper told me everything.'

'Cooper claims not to have been in the theatre.'

'The dear old thing loves my scapegrace of a husband so devotedly that he is happy to lie for him. Though I left the theatre directly after the play, I am sure Cooper stayed a little longer than he claims. In the usual manner of things, Tom would not send him away until he wanted to be alone with his ballet-girl.'

'Mrs Transome, please forgive me – but was Maria really unaware that you loved Fitzwarren?'

'I believe so.'

I found this very hard to believe, and resolved to talk again to Maria when the present crisis had simmered down. In the meantime, I did not like to leave the house until I was certain that Miss Cordelia would have the care she needed, and waited there until the arrival of Mrs Plant. I instructed her myself, saw her safely installed at the bedside and only then went downstairs to find the rest of the family.

Mr Betterton met me at the foot of the stairs. 'How is she?'

'I think she is a lot better,' I said, as cheerfully as possible. 'She is young, and will quickly recover her strength. The nurse knows what to do. How is Mrs Betterton?'

'I've never seen her so upset.' He was pale with anxiety. 'She wouldn't stop crying until I gave her a few drops of laudanum, and now she is sleeping. Did I do the right thing?'

'I would say so, though you shouldn't give her any more.' I was rather touched by his faith in me. 'She has had a bad shock, and sleep is the best medicine for her.'

'She's so fond of Cordelia, you see – her baby sister, and all that. I suppose you'll go now.'

'I'm leaving her in very good hands, Mr Betterton.'

'It's most awfully decent of you – that is, you have been so kind – I don't know what we would have done—'

'Please don't mention it; I'm afraid I was officious and I apologize for firing out orders at you, but I could hardly stand by and do nothing.'

'I wish I could send you home in our two-wheeler,' said Mr Betterton. 'Unfortunately, it has gone off to Ham, to fetch Murphy.'

'Now I am completely easy about leaving you all, for she strikes me as a woman of great good sense.'

'If you will wait a little longer, I can dash out and fetch a cab.'

Night had fallen; I was aware, all at once, of how many hours I had been in the house (my disagreement with Mrs Bentley now seemed like another lifetime), and longed to escape into the cool, sharp evening air.

'Please don't trouble yourself; the rain has stopped and I will easily catch the last omnibus.'

'I can't allow that,' said Mr Betterton more decisively. 'Tell you what – let me walk with you to the Nag's Head, and then I'll gladly stand you a cab home. It's the least I can do.'

'Well … ' I saw that he was longing to leave this house as I was, and it occurred to me that it might be interesting

119

to talk to him. 'Thank you, Mr Betterton; you are most kind.'

The gaslighting was intermittent in those days and I had to hold my escort's arm. In the shadows, however, distracted by looking out for puddles and potholes, the young man was more confiding.

'I'm not much good in an emergency, Mrs Rodd. I tend to lose my head. My father says I gibber like a monkey. He is trying to cure my chronic stage-fright.'

'I have had the pleasure of meeting your father.'

'Oh, yes; Maria told me you were in for the first night.'

'It was splendid,' I said. 'How does the work go with your new theatre?'

'Slowly – and expensively! My wife is full of plans for the plays we will put on, and I can only see our money disappearing. Left to myself, I'd sooner keep it and carry on working for my father. My wife is more ambitious, however.'

'That is a good thing, surely?'

'Oh, yes; it's just that I sometimes feel as if I'm tied to the tail of a rocket.' He smiled as he said this, and I could see how proud he was of Maria. 'She hates being idle and having nothing to do in the evenings. That is the reason she was so eager to appear with my father's company.'

'She was a marvellous Ophelia, I thought.'

'I quite agree, but she has commissioned a new version of *Phèdre*, by what's-his-name—'

'Racine?'

'That's the fellow! And now she can think of nothing else.'

'Mr Betterton, your wife had something to tell me; do you know what it was?'

'I'm afraid – that is, she must have told me – it all got blown away because of poor Cordelia.'

'Never mind,' I said reassuringly. 'I daresay it will keep.'

'It was something to do with a disagreement she had with her father on the day of the fire – but the two of them were always falling out, you know.'

We had come to the main road now, which was busy with carts and carriages, and illuminated by occasional flares of gaslight outside the larger shops. Mr Betterton helped me into the most respectable-looking cab at the stand and gave some money to the driver (a nice amount, judging by the driver's grin, and his sudden attack of courtesy).

Mr Betterton paused before shutting the door. 'Thank you, Mrs Rodd – you know – for taking charge when we were all at sixes and sevens.'

'I was happy to be of use,' I said. 'And now you can go back to being the head of your own household.'

'I'm not the head of the household!'

'Oh?'

'That's my wife – she always knows what's what.' By the light of the cab's lamp, I saw that he was smiling, yet not joking. 'Good evening, ma'am.'

I was very tired when I got home to Hampstead. I had no idea of the time, but it was late; Mrs B had sent Hannah to bed, and she ordered me to sit down while she prepared me a nice little supper of toasted cheese.

Afterwards, drinking our favourite brandy-and-water over the kitchen fire, I told her of this latest crisis in the Transome family.

'Dear, dear!' She shook her head solemnly. 'I can't help pitying that poor girl, ma'am! I had a friend who did just the same, and died of it. Do they know the name of the man?'

'No – Miss Cordelia has said nothing yet. Her mother says it must be one of the actors in her father's company.'

'Maybe he's married,' said Mrs Bentley. 'The scoundrel who led my friend into disgrace was married. What'll you tell Mr Blackbeard?'

'I really don't think this has anything to do with the murder, but you know I never hide anything from Blackbeard if I can help it, and I shall write him an account tomorrow.'

The reader will be familiar with the old saying, 'Man proposes, God disposes.'

I wrote my letter to Blackbeard first thing next morning (I sent it by the penny post, since I did not consider Miss Cordelia's situation to be a part of his investigation; in the days before the telegram was in general use, the sending of messages was very expensive).

The day after this, when the church clock had just struck eleven and I was busy at my desk writing letters and paying bills, a policeman came to my door, bearing a laconic note from Inspector Blackbeard.

Dear Mrs Rodd

Thomas Transome is dead. Please come to the Duke of Cumberland's Theatre.

Yr servant
T. Blackbeard

Fifteen

HE WAS IN HIS dressing room, lying upon the chintz-covered daybed, as if he had fallen on to it backwards. His hands were bloody, as if in his final moments, he had tried to pull out the dagger that was embedded in his chest. The blood had welled up around the handle of the dagger, leaving a great black stain upon his striped waistcoat. One thick stream of blood had wound its way down to the floor and congealed in a pool upon the flowered carpet. His handsome face was frozen into an expression of startled anguish, which was very distressing to see.

I remembered the last time I had seen him; he had asked me to pray for him.

I said a private prayer for him now.

Dr Reid, the young police surgeon I had met in the ruins of the King's Theatre, pulled out the dagger (the sound of it scraping against the dead man's ribs was hideous) and presented it to Blackbeard. 'If you've seen enough, Inspector, I'll take him away for a closer look – but I don't think there's much of a mystery about the cause of death.'

'You'd better cover him up and carry him out the back way,' said Blackbeard. 'We don't want an audience. The newspaper fellows are already hanging round outside, and

I can't say I'm surprised, ma'am, for this murder's a big 'un.'

His manner was rough, yet I was glad to observe that he removed his hat respectfully while Mr Transome was covered with a sheet, and borne out of his dressing room for the last time.

'It's a sad business,' said Dr Reid. 'I saw him as Romeo, not two months ago; he looks older than he did on the stage.'

Once he and the body had departed, Blackbeard and I were left alone, in this room that was filled with reminders of the dead man – his face paint, his bottles and glasses, his dressing gown of red velvet.

'You're shocked, Mrs Rodd; do you need to sit down?'

'No, thank you; as you know, I am not the sort to faint or go into hysterics.'

'Well, that's a mercy,' said Blackbeard, ramming his battered, shapeless hat back on his head. 'Everyone else in this place is weeping and wailing, until I'm at my wits' end!'

'At what time was he discovered?'

'He was found shortly before nine o'clock this morning by Mr Cooper,' said Blackbeard. 'The place was empty, saving the night watchman, who ran outside to fetch a policeman. This policeman sent for me, and had the sense not to touch anything in here. And that's when I sent for you, Mrs Rodd.'

'I'm very glad you did.'

'You can talk to these theatre-folk without losing your patience.'

'Do you have any idea of who did this?'

'Not as yet, ma'am. Transome wasn't short of enemies.' Blackbeard still held the bloody dagger, which he now wrapped up in his threadbare handkerchief. 'This looks like one of his stage properties, what with the fancy carved handle and all. You might ask Mr Cooper, when the man has stopped crying and started to talk sense, if he recognizes it.'

'Poor Cooper, this must be terrible for him,' I said. 'He was devoted to Mr Transome.'

'Hmm,' said Blackbeard. 'Every single one of them claims they was devoted to him.'

'Mr Transome always maintained that he did not kill Fitzwarren; I suppose this proves his innocence.'

'It don't prove nothing, ma'am,' said Blackbeard shortly. 'If he killed Fitzwarren, as I'm still inclined to believe he did, this could've been his wife looking for vengeance.'

'Of course you must look into all possibilities,' I said. 'I have come to know Mrs Transome better, however, and think it highly unlikely. Has anyone informed the family?'

'I sent a man to the house at Ham Common, and Miss Olivia is waiting upstairs. The actors all turned up at ten for their rehearsal, and you never saw such a commotion.'

He took me up to the grand foyer of the theatre, where I saw the commotion for myself.

Cooper sobbed loudly upon a gilt chair. An old woman (the same woman I had seen serving the boxes, when I had visited with Fred) sat beside him upon another gilt chair. A large group of actors, many of them in tears and all talking at once, crowded around Miss Constance Noonan at the foot of the staircase. A much smaller group stood around Miss Olivia, including Miss LaFaye, who had an arm about her and clutched a bottle of smelling-salts.

Miss Olivia's face was swollen by a storm of weeping. She had lost the father she adored, and she sobbed into her friend's shoulder with absolute abandon.

'There, there, Livvy!' murmured Miss LaFaye. 'Don't take on so, my love!'

'I should have known when he didn't come back last night,' gasped Miss Olivia, between sobs. 'I thought he was with her!'

The inspector fastened his chilly gaze upon the young policeman who stood guard at the door. 'Purvis, get everyone's names and addresses.'

'Yes, sir.'

'Ladies and gentlemen.' He did not raise his voice, yet it cut across the babble, 'Give your names to the constable and tell him where you live, and then you'll be spoke to in due course!' He added, 'And nobody talk to the papers!'

Miss Noonan had been sitting upon the stairs. She stood up proudly, her lovely face distorted with tears; unlike Miss Olivia, she was perfectly self-possessed. 'He was not with me, Mr Blackbeard. I must be very clear about this. I went directly home to Pentonville after the performance. You may ask my mother.'

'Thank you, ma'am,' said Blackbeard.

'I suppose the rehearsal's off,' piped up Miss LaFaye. 'I'd like to know what happens to us, now that Mr Transome's gone. Well, I only asked!'

The crowd outside the theatre had swollen, and none of the actors appeared to have taken the slightest notice of Blackbeard's order not to talk to the press, for they all began talking the moment they left the building, to anyone who would listen.

'Good luck to 'em,' said Blackbeard drily. 'They'll hear sixty different stories, and not one word of sense. Now, Mr Cooper—'

Cooper had managed to calm himself a little. The old woman brought him a glass of spirits and he gulped it like a draught of medicine.

I pitied him from my heart, for he was wild-eyed with grief. 'Perhaps we should leave this until—'

'No, no!' He interrupted me eagerly. 'I want to talk, Mrs Rodd – I want to tell every single detail, while it's fresh in my mind. My own life ended when I found him!'

'Mr Blackbeard tells me you found him at nine o'clock.'

'It was a few minutes before nine; I heard the hour striking. I'm always in at that time, especially lately, when he's slept at the theatre overnight. I had his clean shirt, and I was all set to shave him before I fetched his breakfast.'

'Was he planning to stay last night?'

'Not that I knew – he didn't always know himself.'

'What was the last time you saw Mr Transome alive, sir?' Blackbeard asked.

'He dismissed me shortly after midnight.' Cooper blew his nose loudly. 'He said, "Off you go, Coopsy." Those were his last words to me – spoken so kindly! And so I left him.'

'This dagger, sir – do you know it?' Blackbeard quickly showed him the horrid thing.

Cooper nodded. 'It's part of his costume for Romeo.'

'I thought stage-weapons were meant to be harmless,' said Blackbeard. 'Which this one ain't.'

'It's not a stage-weapon. It's a real one – an antiquity, and it cost a fortune. Mr Tom loved the look of it, that's all. He never used it for fights.'

Blackbeard again wrapped the dagger in his handkerchief and put it back into his pocket. 'Where did you go after you left him?'

'I went to the tavern across the road, and stayed there until about one o'clock. And then I walked home to my lodgings at Stables Court, off the Strand.'

'How did he seem that evening?' I asked. 'Was he troubled, or anxious?'

'Not a bit of it!' said Cooper. 'He was quiet and thoughtful but in good spirits. I would've noticed otherwise; after all these years I could read him like a book. And the performance – his last performance! – was perfect.'

'Were you aware of any arguments he might have had yesterday?'

'Only the usual, with Miss Olivia. She was on at him for a bigger part in the new piece. Mr Tom was short with her; she woke him up when he was having his rest in the afternoon.'

'Did he have any visitors?'

'His wife called, maybe two hours before the curtain went up.'

'His wife?' This surprised me. 'I understood they were not on speaking terms!'

'Not officially – but all those years together can't be undone in a moment. Mrs Sarah said she'd come to thank him for the money he sent her, and she wanted to talk to him about the girls. I don't know what about, exactly; Mr Tom sent me out for a bottle of gin and a couple of lemons. By the time I came back – not more than half an hour later – Mrs Sarah was taking her leave. I thought Mr Tom looked a bit shaken; the truth is that he was always rather shaken up after they'd met. It's my opinion that he loved her more than he let on.'

'Did Mrs Sarah go home to Ham, or to her daughter's house in Holloway?' I asked.

'I don't know,' said Cooper. 'She didn't say – but it can't have … she would never hurt a hair of his head! I've known the two of them since before they were married.' His eyes brimmed again. 'They were deep in love, and a love like that don't just crumble away into nothing.'

'He was well known for his skylarking with ballet-girls and suchlike,' said Blackbeard. 'Which gives his wife a fine motive for stabbing him. But she left this theatre too early to put herself in the picture – unless she came back later. Did she, Mr Cooper?'

'Not as far as I know. When I left Mr Tom, and oh, how I wish to God I had not, there was only Potter, the night watchman, left in the building. And I doubt he saw anything; he's drunk most of the time. I had a terrible job waking him up this morning.'

'Thank you, sir,' said Blackbeard. 'That's all for the moment.'

'May I go back to his dressing room now?'

'Hmm. I don't see why not.'

'I must set it all to rights, you see, just as he liked it.'

Mopping his face forlornly, Cooper hurried away to carry out his duties for the last time.

Blackbeard's gaze travelled around the theatre foyer, now empty of actors, and he fell into one of his silences. I knew him well enough to know that he was thinking deeply, and allowed the silence to stretch into minutes.

'Well, Mrs Rodd,' he said eventually, 'here's a nice mess. I'll admit to you that I'm nonplussed.'

'I am nonplussed too, Inspector.'

'If we're going along with what Cooper says, our corpse was alone in this theatre from just after midnight, with only a drunken night watchman for company. Any number of people might have come and gone during that time.'

'Did you read the letter I sent to you, concerning Miss Cordelia?' I asked.

'I did, ma'am, though I haven't got around to working out where it fits in.'

'I think Cordelia must have been the reason for Mrs Sarah's visit yesterday; she said she was going to tell him, and it would explain why Mr Transome was "shaken" afterwards.'

'Hmm,' said Blackbeard. 'The trouble is, Mrs Rodd, it don't explain anything else. It just makes the whole thing more of a puzzle. There I was, looking for any good reason to arrest Transome for murdering Fitzwarren, and now he's gone and spoiled it by getting murdered himself!'

'Yes, but it is still possible that Mr Transome committed the first murder.' I had never seen Blackbeard so downcast, and found that I had an absurd wish to cheer him up. 'It is far too soon to rule anything out.'

He fell into another silence, and then said, 'You know how I like to work, ma'am. There are only three reasons why folks go murdering other folks—'

'Love, money or the fear of discovery,' I finished for him, having heard him say it many times.

'I've been assuming this case is all about love, and there's just too much of it.'

'I beg your pardon, Inspector?'

'I'm tired of hearing about who loved who, that's what. Too many motives, ma'am!' His stony grey eyes fastened upon me narrowly. 'What do you think, then?'

He did not often ask for my opinion so directly and I did my best to be truthful. 'We have two murders, ten years apart, but I am inclined to think there is only one murderer.'

Sixteen

READERS OF MY YEARS are likely to remember the sensation caused by the death of Thomas Transome. The lower sort of newspapers and ballad-sheets carried lurid and most unlikely pictures of villains brandishing daggers. The outside of the Duke of Cumberland's Theatre was festooned with black crêpe, and the stationer's windows were filled with soulful portraits of the dead man. Mr James Betterton closed his own theatre for a night, as a mark of respect. On the following night, he made a solemn curtain speech – widely reported – that contained the phrases 'goodnight, sweet prince' and 'we shall not look upon his like again'.

The inquest, which I did not attend, was held in the upstairs room of the tavern across the way, and the verdict – murder, by person or persons unknown – surprised no one.

He was laid to rest in the cemetery at Kensal Green, attended by a huge crowd of inconsolable mourners and a long line of empty carriages blazoned with aristocratic coats of arms. It was not the custom in those days for ladies to attend public burials; I read the service to myself at home and prayed for the dead man's soul.

The area of Brixton, on the south side of the river, was still a quiet district at that time, with market gardens and strawberry fields instead of the endless brick terraces that sprang up a few years later. Blackbeard and I drove through it the next morning, on our way to the neighbouring suburb of Herne Hill, where Thomas Transome had intended to set up home with Miss Noonan.

The wide road was lined with large and showy villas that sat in enormous gardens, like country estates in miniature. Mr Transome's house was only too easy to find; a crowd of several dozen tradesmen waited outside the gates, and they set up an angry clamour when the police carriage halted.

'The butcher, the baker and the candlestick-maker,' said Blackbeard. 'They're always the first to come out after a death.'

'I was afraid of this,' I said. 'Maria Betterton told me of her father's improvidence with money, and Mr Transome himself told me of his debts.'

The gates were opened by a grey-headed man in a shabby livery, who was sullenly impervious to the shouts of the creditors. The house itself was on the small side compared with its neighbours, yet very pretty to look at; newly built of grey brick, with large windows, and surrounded by wide expanses of lawn. I saw signs of neglect that had begun long before Mr Transome's death – the grass was too long and the gravel drive studded with weeds.

Blackbeard tugged at the bell and, a few minutes later, Miss Olivia herself opened the door. She was very pale, dressed all in black and merely shrugged to hear why we had come.

'I suppose I should be grateful that you're not after money.'

Her trunk – the same that I had seen at Golden Square – stood in the middle of the wide marble floor, alongside a plush-covered sofa with its gilt feet wrapped in brown paper.

'That's brand new,' said Miss Olivia, following my gaze. 'And now it's going back to Gillow's – without ever being sat upon, let alone paid for. I did my best to manage his money. I couldn't stop him spending it on all sorts of silly things. As you see, this house has never been properly lived in.'

'Are you alone here?' I asked.

'Quite alone, apart from the man you saw outside, who was our old coachman.' Her voice shook and she held her head up proudly. 'My father hadn't got around to engaging a proper staff. *She* was going to do that.' The word was uttered with bitter emphasis. 'This is all because of her.'

'I take it you're talking about Miss Noonan,' said Blackbeard. 'Are you saying she done the murder?'

'No – but she might as well have done it. I blame her for the ruination of my family. Nothing went wrong until she came.'

Her sour black eyes flashed a challenge at me, which I ignored; it seemed to me that all sorts of things had gone wrong well before the advent of Miss Noonan, but I did not have the heart to argue when Miss Olivia was clearly half-mad with sorrow.

She led us past rooms that were empty, or furnished only with wooden crates and wisps of straw, into a small sitting room at the back of the house. Here we found a collection of mismatched chairs, and not much else.

'This house was meant to belong to me as much as her,' said Miss Olivia. 'It was my father's house and I had a perfect right to live here with him – but she wouldn't come until she had bullied him into throwing me out on the streets.'

'You had another set-to with your father on the day he died,' said Mr Blackbeard. 'I'd like to know what it was about, if you please.'

'I don't remember,' she said impatiently.

'You were very fond of him,' I put in, hoping to smooth her down. 'This is very hard for you, I know. Did you expect your father to return here after that last performance?'

'Yes,' said Miss Olivia. 'But I can't say I was surprised when he didn't. Papa never really lived here; he meant it for his lovers' bower with that creature.'

'At my last meeting with him, he claimed that you and Miss Noonan had reached a truce.'

Her thin mouth twitched irritably. 'I allowed him to persuade me, mainly because I couldn't bear those horrid lodgings. There was no truce on her side, I assure you.'

'Let us go back to your disagreement; Cooper claims it was over your father's reluctance to give you more prominence in his company.'

'You put it very sweetly, Mrs Rodd. In the world of the theatre, there is no division between the professional and the personal. Papa was considering *Hamlet* – in direct opposition to James Betterton – and his flat refusal to give me Ophelia cut me to the quick. He let my sisters play any roles they wanted.'

'Maybe he didn't think you were up to it,' suggested Blackbeard.

'I'm every bit as good as they are!' snapped Miss Olivia.

(I recalled Mr Transome's dismissive remarks about her acting ability, and found that I pitied her too much to pursue this when she was already broken-hearted.) 'I understand that your mother came to the theatre before the performance; did you happen to see her?'

'I did, and our encounter was perfectly cordial; my mother and I are not enemies.'

134

'And yet – forgive me – you left her, you risked your reputation, to take your father's side when they parted.'

'I am an actress,' said Miss Olivia. 'More than that, I am a Transome. My place was at his side – until Noonan made such a fool of him. I'd be his leading lady now, if not for her.'

'And yet when your sister Maria eloped,' I said, 'he overlooked you, and favoured Miss Cordelia, and that was long before Miss Noonan's arrival.'

'Cordelia was the family baby, and Papa's little pet.' Her lips quivered and she shot me a look of pure fury. 'When she ran off back to Mamma, I naturally assumed that my father would turn to me. Instead of which, he let that woman take my place. I freely admit that I was angry with him; I daresay the whole theatre heard us arguing, and I daresay you think I murdered him because of it. But of course I did nothing of the kind. I loved my father with all my heart.' Her red-rimmed eyes filled with tears. 'If I'd been in the mood to kill anybody, it wouldn't have been him.'

'Who was it, then?' asked Blackbeard bluntly. 'Do you have an opinion, miss?'

'I do not.'

'What was your last sight of Mr Transome?'

'We did not part in anger – we never did, for our arguments died down as quickly as they blew up. He and I had a dance together during the ball scene and he squeezed my hand in the special way he had and smiled at me. And after the curtain, he gave me a quick kiss outside the green room and whispered, "Don't be cross, my pet!" Those were his last words to me.' She let the tears spill down her cheeks. 'I'm glad to think of it now.'

'It must be a comfort to you,' I agreed and found myself wondering if she had ever known what it meant to fall in love; had she kept all the passion in her nature for her father? 'Where will you go, once you have left this house?'

'Home – to my mother. We need each other, and I cannot possibly go back to those lodgings.'

I suppressed the unkind thought that Miss LaFaye would be relieved to hear this. 'Did your mother tell you about Cordelia's illness?'

'Yes, she told me everything,' said Miss Olivia.

'Pardon me, miss,' said Blackbeard, 'do you know the name of the man who got your sister into trouble?'

'She is still too unwell to speak. There was a little gossip, a few months ago, that she was fond of some fiddle-player or other – Joseph Barber. I haven't seen him for ages, however, and don't think it likely.'

'What was your father's opinion of him?'

She shrugged listlessly. 'I doubt he knew the man well enough to form an opinion. The musicians are hired on a daily basis, by whoever is conducting, and they come and go. What does it matter now?'

'Is Miss Cordelia still at Mrs Betterton's house?' I asked.

'For the moment,' said Miss Olivia. 'She will go home with our mother when she is well enough.'

I wondered if Maria had promised Olivia a place in her new company, but it had no bearing on the murder, and I decided I had asked her enough for the time being.

Blackbeard and I took our leave and drove away through the crowd of shouting creditors.

'She didn't do it,' said Blackbeard.

'I'm inclined to agree with you, Inspector – she loved her father too much to hurt him. I suppose it might be interesting to find this musician, if only to rule him out. Where do you go next?'

'Not to any place you can follow me, ma'am. That part of London is swarming with thieves and streetwalkers and suchlike. And though they don't make respectable witnesses, they've got perfectly good eyes and ears. You mark my words, Mrs Rodd; someone saw our murderer in the right place at the right time, and that's all I need.'

Seventeen

THE WEATHER WAS WET next day, and I was thankful not to be going out again, for the journey to Herne Hill had tired me more than I liked to admit. In the afternoon I sat in the kitchen with Mrs B and Hannah, and the three of us worked quietly upon two new gowns for Hannah (one of printed cotton-calico and one of more formal black) to replace the much-mended and outgrown garments the child had brought with her to Well Walk. Mrs B's hands were swollen with rheumatism, yet she could still sew a straight seam and cut out the pieces with wonderful accuracy, and Hannah and I meekly followed her directions.

It was pleasant to see Hannah's happy face; according to her grandmother, she had never had a new dress in all her life, and she handled the workaday material as if it had been the finest silk.

Shortly after four o'clock there came a soft knock at the front door. Hannah eagerly jumped up to answer it and came back to tell me I had a visitor.

'It's a lady who says she wants a word with you, ma'am; her name's Mrs Noonan and I've put her to wait in the drawing room.'

'Who?' Mrs Bentley looked up from her work. 'Not that young actress!'

'Her mother,' I said. 'How very interesting!'

'What's she doing here, then? Were you expecting her?'

'No, this is most unexpected.' I quickly set aside my sewing and brushed the bits of lint and thread from my dress. 'Hannah, you may bring us some tea – served in the willow-pattern set.'

'Yes'm.'

'I'd like to hear what she wants,' said Mrs B. 'If I wasn't so stiff, I'd stop outside the door to have a listen.'

'Never mind, I'll give you a full report later.'

I hastened up the stairs and found Margaret Noonan standing awkwardly before the empty fireplace in the drawing room. She wore the same black dress that I had seen at the house in Pentonville, and a black straw bonnet – all perfectly neat and respectable, yet I was struck once again by the contrast between her thin, stooped figure and that of the magnificent Constance.

'Please sit down, Mrs Noonan,' I said. 'How may I help you?'

She did not sit down until I did, and then perched diffidently on the very edge of the easy chair. 'My daughter doesn't know I'm here, and she won't like it when she finds out. It's just that I'm not quite comfortable about what she told that policeman.'

'Indeed?'

'She says she came straight back home on the night of the murder. And she didn't. She went off somewhere – I don't know where – and didn't come back until daybreak.'

She stopped abruptly and put a hand to her mouth, watching me all the while with the utmost wariness.

I waited for her to speak again, and then softly asked, 'Do you know where she went?'

'She wouldn't tell me.' Mrs Noonan's hands were in her lap now, but twitched as if ready to fly to her mouth again. 'She said it didn't concern me. She went off in a cab

139

directly after the performance, and it wasn't the first time, either.'

'Did Mr Transome know of this?'

'No!' She uttered this with a shudder. 'I mentioned it just the once, and she turned on me in a fury, and said I was not to say a word to Mr Tom.'

I was not forming the highest opinion of Miss Constance. 'Do you suppose she has been meeting another man behind his back?'

'That was my suspicion.'

'Did you ask her about it?'

'No.' Mrs Noonan gave another shudder and hugged her elbows. 'I didn't want her to fly at me. I don't know the half of what she's up to.'

'Forgive me, Mrs Noonan – the last time we met, I was a little shocked by the way your daughter spoke to you.' Seeing her blank face, I added more forcefully, 'Her tone was disrespectful to the point of rudeness. Has she no idea of what is due to you as her mother?'

'Constance is my sole support, Mrs Rodd. I have depended on her since she was a child – since the first moment she put her foot upon the stage. Some folks say that I pushed her, that I used her, but the truth is that I couldn't stop her.'

'Were you on the stage yourself?'

'Yes – and so was her father. He died when Constance was a baby and I got by doing small parts, and little bits of mending and laundry and suchlike. It was very hard for a few years.'

'I can imagine.'

'I tried with all my might to keep her out of trouble. But then Mr Tom saw her, and fell in love with her. And that was the last time she ever took heed of me.'

There was a knock at the door and Hannah came in with the tea tray; I broke off my questioning to take the heavy tray from her and make the tea. Once we were alone again, I thought Mrs Noonan seemed a little easier.

'Last time we met,' I said, 'you whispered to me that you wished you could save her. I took it that you did not approve of the agreement she made with Mr Transome.'

'What mother could approve of such a thing? She was all set to live with him as his wife! They hadn't reached that point yet; Constance made all sorts of demands before she would give herself to him, and he was still jumping through hoops when he died.'

'I'm sure you were as shocked and grieved by his death as anyone,' I said. 'Were you also rather relieved?'

'I didn't want him dead – I certainly didn't murder him, if that's what you're suggesting. But it's an ill wind, as they say, and I did think it a blessing for Constance.' Mrs Noonan's voice was firmer now. 'I had a wedding ring upon my finger when she was born and I wanted her to have the same. All she thinks about is the theatre, and the great roles she means to play. She doesn't see why the outside world matters.'

'Did you like Mr Transome?'

Her eyes widened with surprise. 'Oh, yes; I couldn't help being fond of him. I knew him years ago, round about when his youngest daughter was born.'

'Oh?'

'He engaged me to play small parts in his company. You wouldn't credit it now, but I was a pretty girl in those days; Mr Tom said he liked my red hair because it lit up so nicely on the stage. He was always kind to me.'

'Do you have any idea who killed him?' I asked.

'No – that is—' Mrs Noonan stopped and her sallow cheeks reddened. 'I didn't tell Mr Blackbeard, you see. I

141

told him I was at home in Pentonville that night and it wasn't true. I had been suspicious of my daughter's behaviour – coming back at all hours – and though Constance ordered me to stay at home, I went to the theatre. My intention was to spy on her after the performance and find out what she was up to. I knew she and Tom were quarrelling because I heard them at it, every time he visited. I took his side because I couldn't endure for her to fall any further! Do you see?'

'She placed herself under his protection,' I said. 'If she had left him, it would have looked very bad.'

'Yes – she simply does not understand the world, and how cruel it can be.'

'Her success came too early,' I suggested, 'and her head was turned.'

'She's a good girl underneath.'

'I'm sure she is. At what time did you reach the theatre?'

'Just gone eleven o'clock,' said Mrs Noonan. 'I made sure to be good and early. I waited outside, pretending to watch the street-tumblers, and out she came, all wrapped in an old grey cloak so that I nearly missed her – she's always had a talent for disappearing when it suits her. There was a cab waiting; I heard her tell the driver something about "Brompton". That was all I needed to confront her and so I jumped out and cried, "Where do you think you're off to?" Well, she was beside herself. I accused her of sneaking off every night behind Mr Tom's back. She said, "Oh, now you're his advocate, are you?" She told me to mind my own business and off she went.' She eyed me warily. 'Will you tell the police?'

'You know that I must, Mrs Noonan; I'll do my best to see that you don't suffer by speaking the truth.'

'Thank you, ma'am.'

'After your daughter had driven off, did you go straight home?'

'Yes. I walked all the way, and then I sat up and waited for her.'

'And did you question her again when she came home?'

'I wanted to,' said Mrs Noonan. 'I asked her where she'd been – but she just laughed at me, and told me to make her a cup of coffee. She said, "Oh, Mother, Mother, isn't love a wonderful thing?" And then she wanted me to heat up some water so she could bathe, and she was singing to herself. I thought she must have somehow made things up with Mr Tom.'

'Is this what you came to tell me, Mrs Noonan?'

'I saw Tom's wife.' She forced this out, and once more her hand flew to her mouth.

'I beg your pardon?' I was confused. 'You saw Sarah Transome – when, exactly?'

'She was in the crowd outside the theatre, a few feet away from me.'

'And this was after eleven o'clock?'

'Yes, it was just after Constance had gone. I don't think she saw me.'

Though I kept my composure, my heart leapt; I had assumed that Mrs Sarah left the theatre several hours before this. Here was someone with a motive and someone else who had seen her near the scene of the murder. 'Are you certain it was Mrs Transome?'

'Oh, yes.'

'Would you be prepared to swear to it in court?'

The word 'court' made her flinch. 'If I have to.'

'Thank you, Mrs Noonan,' I said. 'I shall tell Mr Black-beard.'

'I – I don't want any trouble.'

'Telling the truth should not lead anyone into trouble. He will only be grateful to you for coming forward.' I said this with as much confidence as I could muster, though my mind was turning somersaults. 'Are you still at the house in Pentonville? That is, I know Mr Transome's financial circumstances—'

'Tom only paid the rent for the first month.' Mrs Noonan cut me short, with a wry half-smile. 'After that, my daughter paid it. She has a hard head for money. You needn't worry that we're about to be thrown out.'

'I'm glad to hear it,' I said. 'Mr Transome lived as a wealthy man, but it was based on nothing more than his own imagination – he was simply playing the role.' This was a man, I remembered, who had designed his own coat of arms, and had the nonsensical thing painted on to the door of his carriage. 'His death has exposed his amazing improvidence.'

'It was all a game to him, you see,' she said sadly. 'Love as well as money. When he wasn't onstage, he wasn't properly alive.'

Eighteen

MRS NOONAN'S SINGLE SIGHTING of Sarah Transome 'in the right place at the right time' was enough to set the wheels of the juggernaut in motion. I wrote a message to Inspector Blackbeard that very afternoon, and considered it sufficiently important to deliver in person.

I had met Mrs Sarah, I had even liked her. The fact remained, however, that she was now the person most likely to have killed her husband, and I was fully prepared to hear that she had been arrested.

News travelled more slowly in those days than it does now, and it was two days later that I received a most extraordinary letter. It was written in a distinctive, untidy hand, with no address and no date, and it was from Sarah Transome.

Dear Mrs Rodd

I write this to you, partly because you already know so much about my affairs, but also because I think you have a kind and compassionate nature. Now that I am face to face with eternity, I have discovered that I am not after all a godless woman and the prospect of heavenly judgement makes me very frightened. All I can do now is confess my sins and hope for mercy.

I killed my husband and ten years ago I killed Francis Fitzwarren. I loved them both with all my heart but there is evidently something very wrong about my manner of loving. I have a jealous nature; if I feel that I have been slighted or betrayed, a dreadful fury takes hold of me that is beyond all reason, all control.

For ten years I have worn my remorse for Frank like a cloak of lead, but it is amazing what a person can get used to, and I had learnt to push it to the back of my mind. I persuaded myself that his body was safely concealed and would never be discovered, even when Maria and her husband took over the theatre.

On the night of the fire, I went to the rooms I kept in Manchester Square, fully expecting to meet Frank. My husband knew of our love and turned a blind eye — he could hardly have done anything else, for his own behaviour at the time was utterly shameless.

I was burning with anger, having just found out that Frank was still carrying on his intrigue with my daughter, though both had sworn it was over. I had a pistol, given to me by my husband. It is strange now to remember the intensity of my feelings that night. I don't think I set out to kill him, but will admit that I wanted him to suffer as I was suffering.

Frank was not at Manchester Square. I did not wait for him until two o'clock as I think I told the police. I went back to the theatre. I don't know what time it was. The stage was dark and the place more or less deserted. I found Frank in the wings, still in his costume and very drunk. The men of the company had 'treated' the understudy until he could barely stand up. Angry words were exchanged between us. He turned away from me and I shot him in the back of the head.

My husband heard the shot and it was my husband who helped me to hide the body inside the old cistern under the stage. He urged me to go home, saying he would cover our tracks. He then set fire to the theatre but miscalculated and would have died himself, if Ben Tully had not risked his own life to save him.

When Tom recovered from his injuries, matters between us were very different. He said he could not 'play the lover' with me any longer, that my crime rose up between us whenever he looked at me.

146

This was his principal reason for pushing me aside in favour of Maria.

All in all, though he kept my secret, Tom's silence came at a high price. He treated me with contempt and encouraged our daughters to do the same, until I was less than nobody in my own house. His behaviour became more and more profligate; his extravagance became more extreme.

The last straw was my discovery that he had lied to me regarding Pericles Cottage. I understood that he owned the place absolutely and then I learnt that he had sold it behind my back. I saw then that any 'settlement' we had reached was as utterly worthless as every other promise he ever made to me. I was to be nothing and nobody and to live nowhere.

On the night of my husband's death, I waited until the theatre was empty and then I cornered him in his dressing room and stabbed him with his antique dagger that he wore to play Romeo.

The remorse will torture me for the remainder of my life. I cannot endure it, and my life will soon be ended – one way or another. My sins are so great that one more won't make much difference. As the saying goes, I might as well be hanged for a sheep as for a lamb; though the truth is that I do not wish to be hanged at all, and have therefore decided to take full responsibility for my own death. I am writing this in a certain inn, on a certain road out of town. Please tell Mr Blackbeard not to waste his time searching for me. He will not find me.

I was not a good mother to my three girls. I always loved them and my last thoughts and prayers will be for them. I know that I do not deserve their forgiveness.

Sarah Transome

I read it twice, and said a private prayer for Mrs Sarah in the solemn knowledge that she might be dead. And then I covered my head with a shawl and hurried down the street to knock at the door of Mr Tully.

He was at home, and he did not try to hide the tears that streamed down his face.

'I know why you're here, Mrs Rodd – but I didn't help her – I wish I had!' He was clutching a single sheet of paper, which he offered to me.

My dearest Ben

I have confessed to everything and now I am going away. I beg you not to follow me, or try to find me. You have been a most beloved friend. God bless you.

Sarah

'I can't say I'm not surprised,' said Mr Blackbeard, 'but that's neither here nor there. I can't allow it to stand in my way. My job is to deliver the woman to justice.'

'You may be too late,' I said. 'She clearly states her intention to kill herself.'

'Alive or dead, ma'am; it makes no odds to me. I can't tie it all up until I find either Mrs Transome or her corpse.' Blackbeard had appeared on my doorstep after the dinner hour, and was crouched beside the kitchen fire.

'Do you believe her confession?'

'It looks all right to me.' I had given him permission to light his pipe (I abhor the habit of smoking, but knew that it helped him to think; in fact, I found his rough tobacco far less offensive than my brother's cigars). 'She had the motive and the means, Mrs Rodd, and she wrote it all down as neat as anything. My superiors are very happy about it.'

'I'm not sure that I believe she committed both murders,' I said. 'I'm not entirely convinced that she murdered anyone. I have the same sense that I've had throughout this case – that the wool is being pulled over my eyes, and I am missing some vital thing.'

'She might be covering up for someone,' said Mrs Bentley. 'One murder's enough to hang her, so she threw in another one because it made no difference.'

'Sarah claims she has bouts of uncontrollable rage; I don't believe a word of it. A woman who is capable of killing two men would show some signs of violence in her everyday behaviour; she would not be able to help herself. And Mrs Sarah is one of the most self-controlled people I have ever met. I simply cannot imagine her shooting or stabbing anyone!'

'Whether you can imagine it or not, ma'am,' said Blackbeard, 'it's pretty clear that she's guilty and I expect to have her arrested by tomorrow morning.'

'Has anyone seen her?'

'Not as yet; I've got my men watching all the big roads and railways, and suchlike.'

'Mr Tully was adamant that he had no idea where she had gone, and I'm sure he's telling the truth. Have you spoken to Murphy?'

'Hmm,' grunted Blackbeard. 'Murphy was drugged.'

'Drugged?'

He pulled the pipe from his mouth. 'My officers went to Ham Common to bring in Mrs Transome for questioning. The bird had flown by that time. They searched the house and found Mrs Murphy upstairs in her bed, sleeping like the dead. Mrs T knocked her out to make certain the woman wouldn't follow her. The local doctor brought her round somewhat, though she was too fuddled to tell us anything useful.'

'Oh, dear,' I said. 'This is the strongest indication I have seen that Mrs Sarah intended to take her own life, and there are so many questions—'

'I might've known!' said Blackbeard, making the grating sound that was his version of a chuckle. 'Just when I've got my murderer, you're going to tell me she's innocent!'

'No – it is simply that I am not satisfied. The solution is too neat, there are too many threads left hanging. The fire, for instance. Do we really believe Transome burned down his own theatre? If the poor woman has killed herself, the whole case will be put away and forgotten, and we will never know the truth.'

'We'll catch her alive, ma'am, and leave it to a jury to decide the ins and outs.'

'I pray that you are right, Inspector.'

'Hmm.' He squinted at me thoughtfully through a veil of smoke. 'If it weren't Mrs Transome, who was it? I had the tomcat husband in my sights until he was murdered himself. She wouldn't protect the man when he's already dead, would she?'

Blackbeard's mind was made up; I knew he would not listen to anything he termed 'fanciful' and so I kept my arguments to myself.

Older readers will remember the drama of the police search for Sarah Transome. There were numerous false sightings of her, in all kinds of strange places, but the weeks passed, the months passed, and not a trace of her was found.

Life goes on and new sensations sweep away the old.

In November of that year, Maria Betterton and her husband reopened the King's Theatre with a vastly successful production of *Macbeth*. I did not see it (I have always considered it a violent tragedy with no hint of redemption), but my brother did, and assured me that it was 'superb'.

'Edgar Betterton is a passable Scottish warlord and not much more,' he told me. 'That doesn't matter; I had eyes and ears only for Maria. Oh, how I'd love to defend her Lady Macbeth! What jury on earth could resist such an out-and-out stunner? "Had he not resembled my father as he slept, I could have done it" – good God, the power of the woman!'

'It is a macabre choice of play,' I said, 'considering what happened to her real father.'

'My dear Letty, that only adds salt to the story – and gold to the box office!'

The next theatrical sensation was even greater. Mr James Betterton opened a new production of *Much Ado About Nothing*, in which he played Benedick opposite a Beatrice who quickly had the whole town at her feet. It was none other than Constance Noonan. To everyone's astonishment, Betterton had married her.

It was now only too clear what the young lady had been up to in the last weeks of Thomas Transome's life. I did not know whether to condemn her hard-headedness or praise her good sense. She had cast off the scandal of her intrigue with Transome so completely that she was invited to do a special performance at Buckingham Palace for the Queen and the Prince Consort. I was glad for Mrs Noonan's sake, and curious to know what Maria thought of the whole business; did she enjoy the fact that her greatest professional rival was now her mother-in-law?

I got my chance to find out a few weeks before the end of that year. It was a mild, dry, bright morning in early December and I was out on Hampstead Heath, where

quite a few people were taking advantage of the unsea-
sonal weather. I stood aside to make way for an invalid
carriage, like a large wicker chair on wheels, and was startled to be greeted by the woman who was pushing it.

'Mrs Rodd!'

I knew her as soon as I looked at her properly. 'Mrs
Murphy!'

The invalid reclining inside the carriage was Miss Cordelia Transome. She was very thin and her naturally pale
skin seemed almost transparent. Though apparently wide
awake, she did not look at me, but kept her listless gaze
upon the nearby pond.

'Good morning, Miss Cordelia,' I said.

Those beautiful, sad, dark eyes turned to me then, yet
she did not speak; I might have been a shadow.

'We like to give her an airing when we can,' said Murphy.
'It does her the power of good. Please don't expect her to
talk, ma'am; she can say little bits of things now and again,
but that's all. She can see and hear and move, though she
is so wasted away, but she spends her days in a little world
of her own.'

'I am sorry she has been ill for such a long time; I was
sure she would be recovered by now.' I fell into step beside
Murphy (and behind the invalid, so that I could not see
her face). 'What do the doctors say?'

'Doctors! We've had dozens of them trooping through
the house, and each man says something different. The
poor dear has been dunked in cold water and dosed with
goodness knows what, but nothing helps; I've told Miss
Maria to her face that she's wasting her money. It's lucky
there's plenty coming in from the new play.'

'I am old-fashioned, Mrs Murphy, and in my opinion a
little country air would be better for this poor young lady

than a hundred doctors. Can they not send her away to some quiet place where she can recover in peace?'

'Mr Edgar wanted to send her to his aunt in the countryside, but Miss Maria didn't like to think of her sister being so far off. She's been as jumpy as a cat ever since her mother left us.'

I had wanted to raise the subject of Mrs Sarah. 'I have not been keeping up with events as I should – has there been any news at all?'

'No.' She was aware that I was watching her for any sign that she knew more than she was letting on. 'She's dead; may God rest her soul.'

'Do you really think she is dead?'

'You know how she left me,' said Murphy, her voice thickening with emotion. 'She slipped me a sleeping-draught to stop me running after her, for she knew I'd follow her to the ends of the earth.'

'Do you believe she committed those murders?'

'I don't know – and I don't care! Tom Transome only got what was coming to him.'

'That is harsh, Mrs Murphy.'

'It's no more than the truth. I saw how he treated those girls he said he loved so much. Mrs Sarah didn't know the half of it.'

'What do you mean?'

'I mean—' Murphy flushed angrily and pursed her lips, as if she had regretted the words as soon as they were uttered. 'I saw how he set them against each other.'

I was not satisfied, but changed my direction. 'How is Miss Olivia, now that both her parents are gone?'

'Oh, deary me!' sighed Murphy. 'She made it up with her mother before they parted, and I'm thankful; she was the one that Mrs Sarah worried over most.' For one fraction of a second, there was calculation in the glance she flicked at me. 'Maria offered to take her into the house in Holloway, but she chose to go her own way and she's in lodgings with a friend.'

'Was there a disagreement?'

'Well … ' Murphy considered for a moment, and then decided to tell me. 'The trouble is that Miss Olivia had got too accustomed to being important in her father's company. She couldn't endure doing only small parts in Mr Edgar's new set-up, which is all she was offered.'

'That is a shame,' I said. 'It must be doubly hard for her, in the shadow of Maria's success.'

'Indeed it is, ma'am – and you may add to that the success of the other Mrs Betterton, as used to be Miss Constance Noonan. All of a sudden the Bettertons are everywhere, and the Transomes nowhere. While Miss Cordelia is ill, Miss Olivia is the last of them, and there was a flare-up due to her turning down Mr Edgar's offer. She took herself off to a low sort of establishment in Charing Cross.'

'The theatre seems to me to be a cruel business, Mrs Murphy.'

'I agree with you there, ma'am.'

We had reached the end of Millfield Lane, where a large and gleaming carriage waited at the junction with West Hill. A young man, with his hat pulled down low over his face, paced to and fro beside the two fine horses, puffing at a cigar. He crushed out the cigar, and when he removed his hat, I recognized him.

'Good morning, Mr Betterton.'

Edgar Betterton shook my hand, with a charming smile. 'Mrs Rodd, how nice to see you.'

'I ran into Mrs Murphy quite by chance, and she has kindly given me all the latest news of your family. Please give my regards to your wife.'

'Thank you, I shall.'

'I am sorry to see Miss Cordelia in such a sad way.'

'We hoped she'd be better by now; Maria worries about her dreadfully.'

I watched as he gently lifted the fragile girl in his arms, like a broken lily, and placed her inside the carriage; though my opinion of actors as a class was not high, I was impressed by Mr Edgar's kindness to his sister-in-law. He and the coachman hoisted the wheeled chair on to a kind of bracket attached to the back of the carriage.

'That was my invention,' he said cheerfully. 'See how well it fits?'

'It is very clever, for now you can take her anywhere.'

'Precisely! Even my father was impressed.'

'I believe I must send your father my congratulations, Mr Betterton; I hope he and his wife will be very happy.'

'Thank you, ma'am; Maria cut up a bit at first, you know, but I'm coming round to my new stepmother. She's really not a bad sort.'

We wished each other the compliments of the season, and I watched as the carriage drove away. As far as I was concerned, the whole grievous case was wrapped up and finished.

Nineteen

YOU MAY CALL IT a coincidence; I prefer to see it as the workings of Divine Providence.

A chance remark, at a chance meeting, set me off in a new – and most unexpected – direction.

It was March, very nearly a year since my first encounter with the Transomes. A fresh case (of which I may write at a later date, if spared) had come and gone, pushing that unfortunate family to the back of my mind, when I happened to attend a charitable tea party given by the Bishop of London.

My beloved husband would have described it as a 'scrum' – a great gathering of ladies and clergymen, all milling about in a vast hall somewhere in the City. I wore my newest black silk gown and bonnet; I listened to several dull speeches; I purchased a hideous painted vase from one of the stalls set around the walls. The room was hot, the tea was cold, and the noise prodigious. After a couple of hours, my feet were aching furiously, and I found a chair in a remote corner.

And it was here that I was hailed by an old friend. 'Mrs Rodd, I hoped I'd run into you!'

I was very glad to see Mr Roland Pugh, who had been one of our curates during our time in Herefordshire. He was an easy-going man in the middle thirties; Matt called him 'Esau' because he was 'a hairy man'; tufts sprouted in his ears and on the backs of his fingers, and the light-brown thicket on his head defied all attempts to make it look tidy. He was no intellectual, but he had been much liked in the parish, and (as most of our curates did) he had married a local girl.

'My dear Roly, you are a sight for sore eyes – and sore feet, come to that. Do sit down and give me all the news. How is Dinah? How are the children?'

'All blooming, Mrs Rodd, thank Heaven.'

'Is it four now, or five? I beg your pardon for being so dreadfully out of touch.'

'It's five,' said Mr Pugh, smiling. 'Don't worry, I lose count myself sometimes. May I bring you some tea and cake?'

'Tea would be welcome – I don't care how cold it is – I wish I knew why this sort of occasion makes one so fatigued!'

Mr Pugh dived into the crowd around one of the refreshment tables, and returned with a good cup of hot tea. He then sat down beside me and kindly allowed me to interrogate him about the latest happenings in Herefordshire.

'Now, this will interest you, Mrs Rodd; of course you remember Titus Mallard?'

'Yes – poor man.'

'Believe it or not, he has married again.'

'No!'

'I knew you'd be surprised. It's the talk of every tea-table for miles around.'

Mr Mallard, the vicar of Newley Castle near Ross-on-Wye, had lost his first wife and infant daughter some twenty years ago, during an outbreak of typhoid fever. The tragedy shattered him; though punctilious in carrying out his duties as a clergyman, grief had gripped and paralysed his life like a hard frost. As time passed, many people wished him to marry again, but he would never look beyond that little white stone in his churchyard. I had settled him in my mind as an eternal widower.

'Who is the lady? Have you met her? Where did she – oh, dear, I'm bombarding you with questions, but my curiosity knows no bounds!'

'Nobody knows her,' said Mr Pugh, smiling. 'She came out of nowhere, and Mallard fell in love with her when he saved her life; you will have to ask Dinah for the fine details, but it was a splendid piece of knight-errantry. I didn't think that dry old biscuit had it in him!'

'I am happy for him; I often used to think he cried out for a woman in his life. If you happen to run into him, Roly dear, please pass on my good wishes.'

Mr Pugh and I parted cordially and I forgot about Mr Mallard until he was pushed back to the forefront of my mind by another 'coincidence'.

Mr Tully asked Hannah to feed his three cats for the next fortnight, while he went away on a visit.

'He treats them like princes,' Hannah told us, giggling. 'They eat better than we do! Mr Tully made me come into the house, so he could show me where they like to sleep, and their special little china bowls and such. I wanted to laugh, but I didn't, for he's such a kind gentleman and he gave me half a crown!'

'I dunno,' said Mrs B, shaking her head at the extravagance. 'Half a crown, and you could buy all three of them cats for sixpence!'

'Mr Tully has not stirred from his home for months,' I said (the day was chilly and the three of us were in a confidential huddle around the kitchen fire). 'Did he say where he was going?'

'I saw it written on his baggage,' said Hannah promptly (she had inherited her grandmother's powers of observation). '"Tully, The Red Lion, Newley Castle".'

'Newley Castle?' The name leapt out at me. 'Are you sure?'

'Yes, ma'am.'

It might have been nothing more than an odd coincidence, but as I have said before, I do not believe in coincidences. That evening I wrote a letter to Mr Pugh, and a few days later I got my reply; not from him, but from his wife.

> *The Rectory*
> *Holyard*
> *Herefordshire*
> *14th March 1854*

Dear Mrs Rodd

My dear Roly told me he had met you in London, where you spoke of Mr Titus Mallard. He was trying to write to you with the full story but kept asking me questions and getting things wrong until I decided to do it myself. Though my writing is not as elegant as Roly's, I know far more about what he calls 'gossip', which I prefer to call 'news'.

Mr Mallard met his new wife towards the end of last year and as you may imagine the marriage caused a great sensation. I did not believe it until we saw him in October, and the change in him was quite remarkable, for he looked so young and brisk. I don't know if you ever visited him at Newley but oh, what a gloomy place – miles from anywhere and hidden behind black trees.

He was out walking one day beside the river and his dog started to worry at something in the reeds. It was the body of a woman and at first he thought she was dead, until he dragged her on to the bank and saw some signs of life, whereupon he carried her back to his house and called the doctor. For several days this poor woman hovered between life and death and Mr Mallard nursed her most devotedly. Naturally there was talk about how she got into the river – was it an accident or had she tried to take her own life? And the next thing we knew he had married her.

I have never seen Mrs Mallard. She goes to church but otherwise keeps to herself. My sister Catherine who married John Wickes of Knots Farm caught a glimpse of her at Christmas and told me she was rather old and thin and striking-looking rather than handsome. The rumour is that she was a widow and in poor circumstances. That is all I can tell you which is precious little. I do not even know the lady's Christian name.

We are all very well here and often think of you. How fast time passes! The baby is walking now and I am to be confined again in September.

Yours affectionately
Dinah Pugh

———

'It might be something, Mrs Rodd,' said Blackbeard. 'On the other hand, it might be nothing. The lady might be anyone, and your neighbour might have any number of reasons for visiting that particular place.'

'Mr Tully never goes anywhere, Inspector. That is what makes me suspicious. I have kept an eye on him over the past few months, and this is the first time he has left Hampstead since Mrs Transome vanished.'

The day was windless and overcast, and we were walking near the ponds on the Highgate side of the Heath. Mr Blackbeard's shabby, mud-coloured coat was only just on the right side of respectability, and yet there was something soldierly in his ramrod bearing that gave him an air of authority. He had answered my summons, he had read Dinah's letter, and now the wheels of his mind were turning.

'I agree that it looks odd, ma'am, but I don't see how I can base any new investigation on something you heard at a bishop's tea party.' He counted the points on his fingers. 'Some vicar you know gets married, Mr Tully goes on a visit to the same part of the country, and that's enough to convince you that this vicar's wife is a famous actress who's wanted for murder.'

'Oh, dear, it does sound far-fetched when you strip it down to the essentials!' I chose my words carefully, for I sensed beneath his scepticism a glimmer of interest. 'This is not merely my "instinct", however; Mr Tully was absolutely devoted to Sarah Transome and she trusted him to the utmost. If she is alive, he is the one person she would wish to contact.'

'Hmm,' said Blackbeard. 'Not her daughters?'

'I am sure she wants to see them, but she dares not risk "blowing her cover", as my nephews would say.' I was gaining in confidence now. 'I think Mr Tully may be her one remaining link with her old life. It would make perfect sense; I have never been quite satisfied that she died. No body was ever found. Mrs Transome was an actress, well able to disguise herself.'

'Well now, Mrs Rodd,' said Blackbeard. 'I can't go arresting some vicar's wife for murder – not without proper identification. My superiors have put the Transome case on the shelf, so to speak, and they won't be inclined to listen to a lot of stuff about disguises. On the other hand, I think you've got something.'

'Thank you, Inspector!' This was all I had wanted from him. 'Now, may I suggest how we should proceed?'

'Let's have it, then.'

'If I am right and this lady is Mrs Transome, the smallest hint that her cover has been blown will be enough to scare her off. Nobody, however, will take much notice if I visit that part of the country on my own account, and I have the advantage of knowing the lady, so it will be a simple matter of identification and I can contact you at once.'

'On that understanding, ma'am,' said Blackbeard, 'I shall be ready and waiting.'

Twenty

S OME OF THE HAPPIEST years of my life were spent in Herefordshire. My husband's parish was situated in one of the delightful villages that nestle in the folds of the rolling green hills between Hereford and Ledbury. In those halcyon days before the railway, the countryside was wilder than it is now, and its settlements more remote; a heavy fall of snow could cut us off for weeks at a time.

I had not been back for years and was fully prepared to find the same dismaying changes that had come to so many other places in the name of 'progress'. Once I had left the railway behind, however, it was both pleasurable and painful to see that this beautiful region had scarcely changed at all. I made the rest of the long journey in a succession of old-fashioned coaches and carts, and distracted myself from the rattling of my bones by gazing out at the steep hillsides dotted with sheep, the rushing streams and the black-and-white houses that were older than the Book of Common Prayer.

I knew that discretion was essential, and for that reason I had told no one of my visit. Fortunately, the small market town of Newley Castle was many miles from the countryside around my old parish, and there was little danger that I would be recognized by one of my former neighbours – besides which, as I have often observed, nobody takes any notice of a lone, middle-aged female, and my plain black dress and bonnet were as good as a cloak of invisibility.

The only person I needed to avoid was Mr Tully, in case he warned Mrs Mallard before I made my 'swoop'. He was staying at the Red Lion, a crooked, half-timbered inn that overlooked the market square. I stayed at the Coplestone Arms, on the opposite side of the square. I arrived there in darkness, without any kind of fuss or fanfare. The Coplestone Arms was a little more genteel than the Red Lion; a long, flat-fronted red-brick built in the previous century, with a busy stableyard and panelled walls blackened with smoke. My room was shabby but comfortable; the pattern on the faded chintz curtains gave me a pang of nostalgia for the old chintzes in my dear mother's parlour.

Mr Mallard's parish was not in Newley Castle itself, but in a village named Newley Bridge, some four or five miles outside the town, depending upon which road you took. The morning after my arrival was fine and cool, and it was market day, which suited my purpose very well; the square was noisy and bustling, and all the roads into town were busy with horses and carts.

I left the Coplestone Arms as early as possible, threaded my way through the crowds that milled around the stalls and struck out on the road to Newley Bridge, constantly looking about for Mr Tully. I did not see him. After a mile or so the road was clear (and mercifully dry), and I began to fret over the task I had set myself. If I had indeed found Sarah, how much did her husband know about her past? I liked and respected Titus Mallard, and here I was, preparing to destroy his new-found happiness.

My road passed between high hedgerows, which opened to reveal the bridge that had given the village its name; a broad and sturdy old stone bridge over the rushing waters of the Severn. The square tower of Mr Mallard's church,

St Michael and All Angels, was visible behind a thick grove of evergreens. The rectory beside it was a large white house surrounded by lawns and shrubberies; as Mrs Pugh had said, it was a 'gloomy' situation: whenever a cloud blew across the sun, the shadows seemed to rise up around it.

The maid who opened the door to me was in her morning gown, and plainly startled to see such an early caller.

'I would like to see Mr and Mrs Mallard,' I told her. 'On a matter of urgency.'

'Who shall I say, ma'am?'

'Mrs Rodd.' My heart was thudding uncomfortably now. I waited while the maid went into a room leading off the hall, and thought what an unlikely setting this was for Sarah Transome – this dark, dull house in the middle of nowhere.

The silence that followed the mention of my name told me, beyond all doubt, that I had come to the right place. The maid returned to show me into a dining room, where I found Mrs Sarah and Mr Tully sitting at breakfast – never will I forget the expressions on their faces.

Mr Tully looked anguished and wrung his napkin in his hands.

Mrs Sarah stood up proudly, her gaze locked into mine. She told the maid to bring a fresh pot of tea and another cup, and her gaze did not waver once the three of us were alone.

'I think you are my nemesis, Mrs Rodd. I should have known you would hunt me down. I won't ask how you found me.'

'It was my fault,' Mr Tully said wretchedly. 'It must've been, and I thought I had taken such care!'

'You mustn't blame yourself, my dear,' said Mrs Sarah. 'I am sure you have heard of my marriage, Mrs Rodd. My husband is from home at present.'

'I am acquainted with Mr Mallard,' I said. 'How much does he know about your history?'

'Nothing! The poor man has no idea that his wife is a murderer, and you must see to it that he is not punished for helping me.'

She had lost none of her poise, nor her air of youthfulness; now that she had got over the initial shock of seeing me, she was even able to give me a wintry smile.

'I am almost relieved that it is all over; you need not fear that I will run away again.'

'I trust you,' I said. 'And there would not be much point in your running away now.'

'How did you find us?' Mr Tully burst out. 'You must've been spying on me!'

'I know Mr Mallard, and was very much struck by the news of his sudden marriage. I made the connection when Hannah Bentley told me the address on your baggage.'

'I told you, my dear,' said Mrs Sarah tenderly, 'you are not to blame yourself. This was pure chance.'

'But if only I hadn't—' Mr Tully stopped himself as the maid returned, bearing a fresh pot of tea and a willow-pattern cup and saucer.

Mrs Sarah made me a cup of tea and asked Mr Tully to leave us alone.

I had got over the first drama of discovery by now, and no longer felt as if I were sitting at the table with a ghost. She leant back in her chair and waited, with the utmost composure, for me to say something.

'You haven't asked about your daughters,' I said. 'I take it Mr Tully has been keeping you informed.'

'Yes, he fires off regular bulletins and I am thoroughly up to date,' said Mrs Sarah. 'He knows how anxious I am about Cordelia. I can't tell you how many times I was tempted to give myself up for one more sight of her!'

'Do they really think you are dead?'

'Why not? You did.'

'You have not communicated with them?'

'No, I have not,' Mrs Sarah said. 'The risk of exposure was too great and I didn't want to be hanged. Besides which I had my new life to think about.'

'Your new husband,' I said. 'Please tell me honestly, how much does he know about your past?'

'I thought you knew him,' said Mrs Sarah. 'Titus is the most truthful being on earth, and the most unbending moralist. Never mind the murders – he has no idea that I am a mother, since my body is not the type to show any signs of childbirth that he would recognize, and he knows nothing about my liaison with Frank. I told him I was the widow of a naval officer and that I had appeared on the stage in my youth. I gave my name as Sarah Clifton, which was my father's name.'

'He is in for a considerable shock.'

She sighed. 'Poor man, I wish I could spare him. I am shocked now, to think of the lies I told him but it didn't feel like lying at the time. I felt that I had been reborn and given the chance of a new life. Please, Mrs Rodd, as a great favour, let me be the one to tell him the truth.'

'Yes, of course, if I can.'

'It's a relief, in a way, like a burden being lifted. The happier I was with him, the more I lived in terror of discovery. Now I hate myself for breaking his heart – and do you know, Mrs Rodd, I wasn't in love with him when I married him? I was only thinking of myself and my own safety. I fell in love with him before I knew I was doing it.'

'The story is that he saved your life,' I said.

'I tried to drown myself and very nearly succeeded. I came to this part of the country quite by chance, because it is so far from everything I know. I remember standing for a long time on the riverbank, where the water was deep, and saying farewell to the world. I remember the moment I flung myself into the water's embrace. And then, out of the darkness, I awoke in this house. That was the moment I ought to have given myself up to the police. I had tried to escape being hanged, but God was having none of it.'

In the hall, we heard the front door opening and the sound of footsteps.

'That's Titus,' Mrs Sarah said softly.

Mr Mallard came into the dining room. I had not seen him for many years, and was disconcerted by the change in him. He was a thin man of about fifty, with meagre lips, a balding head and a face heavily lined with sorrow and self-denial – no one's idea of Sir Galahad – but now the lines had been erased by the love that shone out of him when he looked at his wife.

'My dear,' said Mrs Sarah, 'I believe you know Mrs Rodd.'

'Why – yes—' In his last moments of happiness, he looked at me and recognized me. 'Mrs Rodd – a friend from the old days! This is a pleasant surprise—'

The words died on his lips as he saw our faces; there was a short spell of silence.

Mrs Sarah (wonderfully calm and collected) touched my arm. 'You know what I have to do; it won't take long. I will take it as a great kindness if you leave us alone until I'm done. You need not worry that I'll jump out of the window.'

'Sarah?'

I could not endure to look at Mr Mallard's face and quickly left the room.

There was a drawing room across the hall, in which I found Mr Tully weeping silently beside the empty fire-place. I pitied him, and hoped he would not get into trouble for helping his old friend.

'It's all over,' he said.

'Yes,' I said. 'All over.'

'What will happen to her now?'

'She is in my custody, until I'm able to hand her over to the police. After that she will probably be taken to London to stand trial.'

'And then they'll hang her.'

'I'm very sorry, Mr Tully.'

He wiped his streaming eyes with his handkerchief. 'I thought she had died, like everyone else; I was so happy when I got her letter and learnt that she was alive. She trusted me to keep her secret.'

'You are a faithful friend and I know you acted from the best of motives. But the law applies to her as it applies to everyone, and she has confessed to killing two men.'

'I don't believe it – I have never believed it! I have known Sarah, and shared the secrets of her inmost heart, since she fell in love with poor Tom. She adored that man, Mrs Rodd, and forgave him – time after time – for his dalliances with other women. She knew his nature, and often told me that she didn't care what he got up to, because she knew he would always come back to her. She did not allow herself to get involved with other men until poor Tom went cold on her.'

'Other men – where there more besides Fitzwarren?'

'I meant Fitzwarren, of course.' Mr Tully was confused for a moment, and went on too quickly, 'There was a long estrangement after Maria was born, but then they went off to America together, where they were a great success, and Olivia was born shortly after they came home. He called her Olivia because she was their olive branch, and Cordelia arrived a couple of years later – oh, they were riding high in those days! And when I think of everything Sarah had to put up with – her patience, her forbearance – I simply cannot imagine her hurting anyone, let alone killing them!'

'I agree that it seems unlikely,' I said. 'I have observed, however, that people can turn violent after years of apparent forbearance. She says she is guilty; perhaps we should take her at her word.'

'It's too hard,' said Mr Tully.

He fell to weeping again, and mopping his eyes, and we were both quiet until Mr Mallard came into the room. I had been expecting him to revert to his old, wrecked self, yet though his face was filled with pain, there was still that new light in his eyes.

'I have ordered my carriage, Mrs Rodd; my wife and I will accompany you wherever you must take her.'

Twenty-one

MRS SARAH WAS BROUGHT to London and locked up in the recently opened Holloway Prison. Mr Mallard followed her, and his demeanour during those awful days impressed me very much. He was splendidly strong and calm and his devotion to his wife never wavered. He braved the crowds of reporters outside the prison to visit her as often as possible, and yet he did not question the truth of Sarah's confession.

'She has repented and I have forgiven her,' he told me proudly. 'It is no more than my duty as a Christian. If I love my wife without reserve, I must forgive her in the same whole-hearted manner – for any wrong that she has done to me, I mean, since it is not my place to forgive the wrongs she has done to others. Only God can do that.'

We were standing, at the time, in a whitewashed prison corridor, and I could not resist asking, 'Do you truly believe that she is guilty?'

'I must believe my wife, Mrs Rodd – or how can I help her? God brought us together for a purpose, to save her immortal soul.'

I could not argue with such iron certainty; his faith was the only thing keeping the poor man alive. I visited Mrs Sarah myself, as often as I was permitted, and found something awful in her resignation. She waited in the shadow of the gallows with an extraordinary coolness – 'like she was a-waiting for the omnibus!' as Blackbeard put it. When I visited, she received me with an offhand cordiality, and with occasional flashes of humour that confused me greatly.

'You should have a glass of port or perhaps gin, Mrs Rodd,' she told me on one occasion. 'No, you should have several glasses. It would do you a power of good to get thoroughly tipsy, and I am positively drowning in strong drink! Every actor in the world who didn't like my husband has sent me a bottle of something, as a thank you.'

I nearly laughed aloud, though it would have been most inappropriate in these surroundings. 'Thank you, but I don't care to get tipsy.'

I had come to like Mrs Sarah, and I think she liked talking to me, yet there was always a distance between us; a sense of something being held back. None of her daughters had come to see her, though Maria's house was practically on the doorstep, and I knew this made her sad, though she spoke of them lovingly and never reproached them for it. Cordelia was too ill to be moved, and it was doubtful that she would have known her mother. Maria and her husband had closed their theatre and were doing their best to shun the public gaze.

Miss Olivia, however, seemed to yearn for the public gaze. She denounced her mother in the papers, and generally made such a noise that she was given larger roles at the questionable theatre in Charing Cross. She was busy raising money to build a vast tombstone for her father. I thought her quite shameless, yet Mrs Sarah refused to utter a word of criticism, and never showed a single sign of the ungovernable passion that had driven her to commit murder. I began to worry, in my lowest moments, that there had been a most dreadful mistake.

'It might be nothing, Mrs Rodd,' said Mr Blackbeard. 'I rather hope it is nothing; I don't want to go upsetting any more apple carts at this stage. My superiors won't like it one bit. But it must be looked into, and I'd like to hear your opinion.'

He had sent the police carriage for me early that morning (as usual without a word of explanation), and he was waiting for me in Golden Square, outside the lodgings of Miss Paulina LaFaye.

'I understood that Miss LaFaye had given a statement to the police,' I said. 'Do I take it that she has changed her mind?'

'She reckons she knows something significant,' said Blackbeard. 'She sent me round a letter last night.'

'It must be something to help Mrs Sarah – she would hardly take the trouble to provide more evidence against her.'

'Hmm,' said Blackbeard. 'That's what I thought, ma'am, but let's not run ahead of ourselves.'

'No, of course not.' Though I strove to hide my excitement, my mind was racing.

Blackbeard tugged at the bell; we stood there for several minutes, listening to sounds of a piano nearby, and a woman singing scales in a piercing soprano.

The door was eventually opened by a grubby little servant-girl, and we found Miss LaFaye in the upstairs drawing room, attired in a frilled and beribboned morning gown and with her ringlets freshly combed out.

'Well now,' said Blackbeard, standing at attention before the (unswept) fireplace. 'What have you got for us?'

'I hope it's not going to get me into trouble,' said Miss LaFaye. 'That's why I didn't say anything before.'

'Are you alone here, Miss LaFaye?' I asked.

She caught my meaning at once. 'You needn't worry about Olivia Transome, she don't live here these days. We had a difference of opinion.'

I sat down upon the sofa beside her. 'Do you have new evidence about the murder?'

'I read Mrs Sarah's confession.' (Her letter to me had been released by the police, and printed in the newspapers.) 'I knew I had to say something, because she wasn't anywhere near the theatre on the night Mr Tom was killed – I know because I saw her somewhere else.'

My heart leapt at this, for if Mrs Sarah could be placed elsewhere on that night, it cast a deep shadow of doubt across the entire case. 'Are you certain it was Mrs Sarah you saw?'

'Yes, it was her all right,' said Miss LaFaye.

'Did she see you?'

'I doubt it,' said Miss LaFaye. 'She was too busy.'

'When you gave your account to the police,' said Blackbeard sternly, 'you said you went straight home after the play.'

'Oh, I know that's what I said. Only it wasn't exactly true.'

'Lying to the police is a serious matter, miss.'

'Yes, but I had to lie, because everybody was listening and I didn't want them to know. After the play, I attended a private party in Cremorne Gardens.'

This was a so-called 'pleasure garden' beside the river in Chelsea, a place of music, dancing and low morals; I was not surprised that Miss LaFaye had not liked to tell anyone she was there.

'Was it a large party, Miss LaFaye?' I asked.

'No.' She reddened, and held her head up with a hint of defiance. 'There were only two of us – me and a certain gentleman I know – all quite innocent, I assure you.'

'I'll need his name,' said Blackbeard.

'What for? He didn't see anything!' She was alarmed now. 'And if you ask him about me, he'll deny he ever met me, not that we were doing anything wrong.'

'I'm sure you were not,' I hastened to say, afraid that Blackbeard would scare her away before she had told us anything useful. 'Where did you see Mrs Sarah, exactly?'

Miss LaFaye's gaze shuttled between Blackbeard's face and mine for a few minutes, and then she gave a little shrug of resignation. 'They have these private booths, you see – like rooms in a house – the walls are made of trellis and covered with flowers, to stop people from looking inside – and the waiter don't come unless you ring the bell. My friend and I wanted to have a quiet conversation, which is why we had our dinner in one of the booths.'

'How did you see Mrs Transome, then?' asked Blackbeard.

'Through the leaves,' said Miss LaFaye. 'There's ever so many gaps. She came into the booth next door and sat down at the table.'

'Was she alone?' I asked.

'She came in alone and waited for a good half-hour. And then a man came in and sat down with her, and they talked for a long time.'

I asked, 'Did you know him?'

'No,' said Miss LaFaye. 'I'd never seen him. He was tall, with black hair and whiskers, and got up like a gentleman. Mrs Sarah gave him a little parcel of something and he put it in his coat pocket. And then they had some supper, and she was still there when my friend and I left.'

Blackbeard and I exchanged glances now, and though his face was as expressionless as ever, I knew him well enough to know that he shared my excitement.

'Look here,' said Miss LaFaye, 'I know I should've told you before now, and I'm sorry for it. But I can't have any trouble.'

'It was good of you to come forward,' I assured her. 'I'm sure Mr Blackbeard will do everything possible to spare you.'

'I hope it'll help; I don't want Mrs Sarah to be hanged.'

'Depends when you left the gardens, miss,' said Blackbeard. 'What time was that?'

'Oh, dear – you will think I'm so bad! I'm afraid it was dreadfully late.'

'Miss LaFaye,' I said, 'we are not in the business of judging your character. You may be able to save a woman's life.'

'Very well, but please don't go spreading it about, or I'll lose what's left of my reputation. My friend and I happened to … to fall asleep after we'd had our supper.' She turned as red as a turkey cock. 'When we woke up it was daylight, and they were still talking in the booth next door. And I can tell you exactly what time it was. My friend looked at his watch and said, "Oh b— oh botheration – why did you let me fall asleep? *It's half past six!*"'

I was excited; surely this was enough to cast doubt on Mrs Sarah's guilt?

'Thank you, miss,' said Blackbeard. 'That's very interesting, and I'm greatly obliged.'

'You can see why I didn't want to tell,' said Miss LaFaye. 'I was afraid people would get the wrong idea, and it was only a little bit of supper with a friend.'

'I quite understand, Miss LaFaye,' I said, 'and I'm sure the inspector will be as discreet as possible.'

We took our leave and I followed Mr Blackbeard back to the street, extremely curious to know what he was thinking. Instead of climbing into the waiting carriage, he stood stock-still in the middle of the pavement, his stony face unreadable. I knew that these were the outward signs of inner turmoil in the Blackbeard brain, and simply waited.

Eventually, he said, 'Mrs Sarah could easily have slipped off and done the murder while them two were sleeping. But the fact remains that she was not where we thought she was – if LaFaye is to be believed.'

'I believe her; the poor thing was blushing up to her eyes.'

'Hmm,' said Blackbeard. 'I'll bet that don't happen often.'

'You must see that her evidence changes everything – for instance, Mrs Noonan cannot have seen Mrs Sarah at the theatre that night. And if Mrs Sarah lied about her visit to the Cremorne Gardens, it makes nonsense of her entire confession!'

'But why would the woman confess to a murder she didn't do?'

'I can't imagine – but surely that is beside the point. In my opinion, Mrs Sarah is innocent, and it is our duty to prevent an innocent woman from being hanged.'

'Hmm.' He fell into another silence, his brow thunderous. 'Lies and more lies, Mrs Rodd. I've never seen anything like it. But I'll admit to you that I brought you along because I'm not satisfied, and I know my superiors won't listen to me. Not unless she changes her story.'

'I am very relieved to hear it,' I said. 'I have been tormented by doubts, and by something else, a feeling I cannot shake off that the truth is before my eyes, if only I could see it!'

Twenty-two

THE DOOR TO MRS Sarah's cell stood open, and we heard the steady murmur of Mr Mallard's deep voice intoning the 91st Psalm.

'"He that dwelleth in the secret places of the most high shall abide under the shadow of the Almighty. I will say of the Lord, He is my refuge and my fortress: my God; in him will I trust. Surely He shall deliver thee from the snare of the fowler ... "'

I hung back in the corridor, but Mr Blackbeard had no such delicacy and stepped inside without knocking.

'Mrs Mallard – a word, if you please.'

I see them now, printed on my memory; those two thin, black-clad figures, sitting close together upon two hard chairs with their faces turned towards us.

'Can you not hear that I am reading the Bible?' Mr Mallard was indignant. 'Are we to have no privacy?'

'We've just heard a story that contradicts your confession, ma'am,' said Blackbeard, ignoring him and fixing his stern gaze upon Mrs Sarah. 'I have a couple of points I'd like to go over.'

'I was not told of this; on what authority do you burst into my wife's room without any warning?'

'You must forgive us, Mr Mallard,' I said. 'But if the matter is as important as we think, there is no time to waste.'

'Tell me what you've found,' said Mrs Sarah, looking at me intently.

'In two words,' I said, 'Cremorne Gardens.'

'Ah.' Pain flashed across her face, and then she raised her eyebrows at me, almost with humour. 'I should have known it would come out eventually.'

'My dear?' Mr Mallard was alarmed; he seized her hand as if to stop her flying away. 'What is this? You told me everything!'

'No, I'm afraid I didn't,' said Mrs Sarah tenderly. 'I'm so sorry, Titus. You married a very wicked woman. I told you a swarm of lies, because the whole truth was too shameful. You may leave if you like, but if you choose to stay, I should warn you that I will tell the whole truth now.'

'I don't understand,' said Mr Mallard. 'The crimes you confessed to me were unspeakable – what could possibly be worse?'

'You won't like to hear about my old life.'

'I am afraid of nothing; I have promised to walk with you through the valley of death itself.'

'Very well,' said Mrs Sarah. 'Perhaps you would care to expand upon "Cremorne Gardens", Mrs Rodd.'

'You went there after the performance, and apparently stayed all night,' I said.

'You was seen, ma'am,' said Blackbeard.

'Oh – by whom?'

'By the pair of turtle-doves next door.'

'Really? Dear me! Yes, I was at Cremorne Gardens, and I do recall that there was a couple in the next booth along; some city grocer and his fly-by-night.'

'The "fly-by-night" was Miss Paulina LaFaye,' I said. 'You did not know her, but she knew you.'

'LaFaye – that pert little wax doll! I daresay this is my punishment for trying to be discreet.' A smile twitched at

179

her mouth. 'The name of the man she was with is "Parkinson", by the way; I remember because she kept shrieking, "Oh, Mr Parkinson, do leave off!" And he spoke of a shop in Cheapside.'

I nearly laughed at this, and was ashamed of myself, for poor Mr Mallard was white with horror; I guessed that he had never heard his wife speaking in this way before.

'You were not alone,' I said.

'No,' said Mrs Sarah, 'I was not. I had arranged to meet a gentleman. His name is Jonathan Parrish; he had no involvement whatsoever in the death of my husband. He is a writer of plays by profession, and he is married; his wife is given to jealousy, which was the reason for our secrecy. I have known him for many years and we were once very close friends.'

'Miss LaFaye claims that you gave him a package of some kind.'

'If you think I gave him money, Mrs Rodd, I must remind you of my financial position, which you know better than anyone. The truth is that we met to return each other's letters.' She glanced at her husband's stricken face and her tone softened. 'I wouldn't describe them as compromising, exactly; they are, however, letters between lovers.'

'When?' asked Mr Mallard wretchedly. 'Why did you never mention him to me?'

'It was so many years ago, my dear. He was our business manager when we toured America.'

'Never mind that for the minute,' said Blackbeard. 'Was you and this Mr Parrish in that booth for the whole night, ma'am?'

'Yes,' said Mrs Sarah. (Her manner was steady, her speech was clear, yet I could almost hear the cogs turning busily inside her head; she was planning what to tell us.) 'We had a good deal to talk about.'

'And at what time did the pair of you leave Cremorne Gardens?'

'I don't know, whenever LaFaye said we did.'

'I'd like to hear it from you, ma'am, if you please.'

'I don't remember the exact time. It was very early in the morning.'

'And where did you go next?'

'Mr Parrish went back to his wife,' said Mrs Sarah, studying our faces with the utmost coolness. 'I took a cab home; I daresay the driver will remember me, since Mr Parrish paid him handsomely.'

'When did you kill your husband, then?' asked Blackbeard.

'Before I went to Cremorne Gardens.'

'But that's not possible!' I put in quickly. 'You cannot expect us to believe you killed your husband and then went out to supper! You wouldn't have had enough time.'

'And what about the blood, ma'am?' demanded Blackbeard.

I now had the strongest sense that Mrs Sarah was thinking on her feet; she took a hair's-breadth pause before she replied.

'There wasn't much blood. I washed my hands in the horse trough outside. Perhaps someone saw me. As for that little goose LaFaye, I wouldn't set much store by anything she says; she was too busy getting tipsy and fending off Mr Parkinson.'

'You went to a place of pleasure, knowing that your husband was dead!' Mr Mallard stared at his wife, as if seeing her for the first time. 'Are you truly capable of such hardness, such cruelty?'

'I'm capable of keeping my head,' said Mrs Sarah. 'I might have muddled up one or two of the details – what does that matter? I will plead guilty at my trial. The case is solved, unless you are going to accuse me of being innocent.'

'Mrs Rodd – Inspector—' Mr Mallard had now collected himself. 'I would be very much obliged if you could leave us alone. I would take it as a great kindness.'

'Ask me no more questions,' said Mrs Sarah. 'I have nothing more to tell you.' She took his hand and folded it in both her own, with a loving look that irradiated her with a kind of beauty.

I understood, as plainly as if she had said it, that she wanted to tell her husband certain things she had withheld from him, and I had the strange sense that Titus Mallard was more horrified by the existence of Jonathan Parrish than he had been by the murders.

'He's a queer customer,' said Blackbeard, once we were outside the prison. 'You'd think he'd jump at any hint that his wife was innocent. Instead of which, he acts like it's bad news!'

'Mr Blackbeard,' I said, 'she didn't do it.'

'That's your instinct, is it, ma'am?'

'I cannot imagine what she's up to – why she would willingly go to her death – but I know she is lying.'

The pavement was crowded; Blackbeard pulled us into the shadow of the prison wall. 'It's not enough, ma'am. Miss LaFaye's story don't count for much, seeing as she was asleep most of the night. Mrs Mallard and her man friend could have gone out and come back. You'll have to do better.'

'The trial is in two weeks,' I said, as forcefully as I could. 'If Mrs Sarah pleads guilty, she will be hanged and the true murderer will still be at large.'

'I'll tell you what, Mrs Rodd,' said Blackbeard. 'My personal opinion is neither here nor there. I'll be speaking to the two gentlemen, Parrish and Parkinson – and if it's all the same to you, I'll do Parkinson on my own. He might not like to discuss his little adventure in front of a lady.'

Twenty-three

THE INSPECTOR GAVE ME a brief account of the interview the following day. 'It was like pulling a tooth, ma'am. Parkinson was all in a flurry. First he denied he'd ever met Miss LaFaye, or ever been near Cremorne Gardens. He then begged me not to tell his wife, and he just about fainted when I spoke of giving evidence in court. But I had him cornered, and out it all came, pretty much as she said.'

'Was there any difference in his version of the story?'

'Just the one point,' said Blackbeard, 'though I don't know how much it counts, seeing as they were both drunk at the time. LaFaye said Mrs Sarah and her man friend was still in their booth when they woke up at six in the morning. Parkinson said they'd gone by then, and the voices belonged to another couple.'

'Did he know at what time Mrs Sarah left?' I asked.

'No, he did not. All he knew was that he had a thumping headache and a suspicious wife at home in Cheapside. It's not much, but enough to cast doubt on Mrs Sarah's tale – and Mrs Noonan's timekeeping.'

Mrs Noonan was still living in the rather dreary little square in Pentonville, and she was not pleased to see us on her doorstep.

'What do you want with me? I've told you everything, and now I wish you'd leave me be.'

'You told us a story, ma'am,' said Mr Blackbeard. 'And a very good story it was, saving the fact that it wasn't all true.'

'I don't know what you mean.'

'Come now, Mrs Noonan,' said Blackbeard. 'You can't go telling lies to the police.'

'I – I – haven't!' She was afraid, and made as if to shut the door in our faces, but Blackbeard had planted his foot on the threshold, and she had not the strength to prevent him pushing past her into the house.

'Please don't be alarmed,' I said, as kindly as I could. 'We have not come here to accuse you of perjury. It is simply that a new witness has come forward, and if she is telling the truth, you could not have seen Mrs Sarah at the theatre when you said you did.'

'Oh – but—' Her face crumpled and she burst into tears. 'I didn't mean any harm!'

The poor creature wept as people do when a weight has been lifted from their shoulders. Her meagre frame shook with sobs; she put her hands over her face and I was sorry for her.

'Are you alone, Mrs Noonan? Is there someone who could make you a cup of tea?'

'No, there's nobody here. I'm quite alone.'

She led us along the passage and down a flight of stairs to the kitchen, where she had evidently been sitting; the house and rented furniture were perfectly clean, but with few signs of human habitation, as if she had been a servant keeping the place on board wages. I had a sense of her immense loneliness, and wondered why she was not living with her daughter.

I set about the making of a pot of tea, and this was enough to stop her flood of tears; she almost wrenched the kettle from my hands in her eagerness to reclaim her

185

territory, and by the time she sat down with us at the table, she had fallen back into her usual state of listless calm.

Mr Blackbeard kept stony silence (apart from the slurping sound he habitually made when sipping his tea) for which I was grateful; she needed the gentlest encouragement to trust us with the truth.

'You must have been happy, Mrs Noonan, to see your daughter married,' I said.

'Oh, yes!'

'I have met Mr Betterton, and I liked him very much.'

'He's a good man, and he near enough worships Constance.'

'I find it surprising,' I said, 'that you do not live with her.'

'She's a great lady nowadays.' Mrs Noonan said this without rancour. 'And she sees to it that I want for nothing.'

'You spoke of your suspicion that the young lady was seeing a man; I take it that was Mr Betterton?'

'Oh – yes, yes, yes!' She had no more resistance. 'Constance and Tom were fighting, worse and worse, and she was cutting up rough about money; Miss Olivia told her a few things about Tom's financial circumstances and that's when Constance started making noises about taking herself off to another company. She didn't say anything to me; I heard it through the wall when Tom visited. I didn't know she was meeting Mr Betterton – or that he'd fallen in love with her. As I told you, ma'am, the time I visited you, I was sick with worry that he would throw her over and complete our ruination. I was telling the truth about going to the theatre that night, to have it out with her. I waited for her outside – just as I told you – and we did have a row before she went off in her carriage.'

She halted and her hands went up to cover her mouth.

'Did you see Sarah Transome, like you said?' asked Blackbeard.

'No.' Her hands fell back into her lap. 'No, I did not. I made that up.'

'But why?' I asked.

'I knew it was wrong,' said Mrs Noonan. 'And when Constance came out of the theatre, it was later than I said.' The tears welled up again. 'She was so very angry with Tom – God forgive me – I thought—'

'You thought she had committed the murder,' I finished for her.

'No – never!' She pulled a handkerchief from her sleeve and mopped her face. 'I was only trying to find out why she was so angry, and if she meant to ruin us!'

'Did you intend to tell the truth at any point, ma'am?' asked Blackbeard. 'Did you intend to lie in court? Did you intend to stand by when a woman was hanged on your say-so?'

He uttered the questions quietly, yet with a menacing undertone that made the poor woman cry out, 'Oh, I don't know what I intended, I was in such a fright! She's everything I've got!'

'Did you know the reason for her argument with Mr Transome?' I asked. 'Had he found out about her dealings with Mr Betterton?'

'I don't know – but she was so angry with Tom!'

This was the second time she had spoken of her daughter's 'anger'; I recalled Mr Transome's exhibition of fury, and wondered if actors were more given to the emotion than the rest of the population.

'She didn't confide in me,' said Mrs Noonan. 'That all stopped when we came to London. It was something about the theatre, and Miss Olivia, and the house in Herne Hill. I knew nothing, and that's why I lost my head. I wouldn't

187

have lied about Mrs Sarah if my girl hadn't kept me in the dark.' She clasped her trembling hands together. 'She won't get into trouble, will she? I don't care what you do to me.'

I was not entirely satisfied, but had a sense that Mrs Noonan would tell us no more for the moment, at least. I was glad that Blackbeard appeared to be of the same opinion. He gave her a terse lecture about the inadvisability of lying to the police and we took our leave.

Once outside on the pavement he became very still and fell into one of his longer silences. And then he gave his verdict:

'Hiding something!'

The day was wearing on; I had eaten nothing since breakfast and realized that I was giddy with hunger. Before I could think what to do about it, Mr Blackbeard had one of his flashes of thoughtfulness, and asked if I would care for 'a pie off the street'. I accepted most gratefully and he stopped the carriage to purchase hot mutton pies from a stall near the Angel.

Heaven only knew what was inside my pie, but it tasted delicious, and the act of eating made Blackbeard more talkative.

'It looks like a bit of a sideshow to me, Mrs Rodd.'

'How do you mean?'

'When push comes to shove, Mrs Sarah had time enough to kill a dozen people.'

'Don't you wonder what she was doing, all the time that Miss LaFaye was asleep?'

'No,' said Blackbeard. 'What does it matter? She confessed, and the Crown don't make a habit of arguing with people who've confessed. I will admit, however, that I'm curious about the new Mrs Betterton, and what she has to say for herself.'

'Indeed,' I said (busily brushing all traces of 'street pie' from my person). 'Quite apart from the murder, it's not every day that someone manages to overturn a bad reputation so thoroughly.'

'That'll be on account of the wedding ring, I daresay.'

'I'm sure you are right, Inspector; a marriage is a concrete and substantial fact that can often make people forget any unpleasant gossip.'

The Bettertons lived in Bedford Square in Bloomsbury, in one of those prosperous and solid houses that looked out over the pretty communal garden. It was an address of high respectability rather than fashion; as we waited upon the spotless front steps, I watched a nursemaid in the garden with her little charges, and thought it rather an unlikely setting for the former Miss Constance Noonan.

A young parlourmaid admitted us, and I gave her my card. We waited in the hall while she took it upstairs; she returned a few minutes later to show us into the drawing room on the first floor.

'Mrs Rodd – Inspector Blackbeard.' Mr James Betterton stood in front of a fine marble fireplace, in which a coal fire burned merrily. 'You know my wife, of course.'

'Mrs Betterton.' I bowed to her and she nodded back at me, throwing an anxious glance at her husband. 'I hope you will pardon us for our intrusion.'

Mrs Constance reclined in an armchair beside the tea-table in a robe of pale green silk, with her glorious hair loose and streaming down her back. She was splendidly beautiful, yet it was her husband who held my attention. Mr Betterton was quite transformed since our last meeting; happiness glowed from his every feature and had burned away at least twenty years, until he bore a startling resemblance to his son, the amiable Mr Edgar.

'Do please join us; you have found us in the middle of a hearty tea, for we have a performance tonight and this is how we prepare ourselves.' He told the servant to bring us cups and plates and would not hear of a refusal (I was struck by the contrast between this substantial meal and the rows of bottles I had seen in the dressing room of Mr Transome).

'You were surprised to hear of our marriage, I'm sure.' Mr Betterton smiled proudly at his new wife. 'You were not alone; everyone was surprised, including myself. I had long resigned myself to widowhood, and was a thorough-going old crock until Constance gave me back my youth.'

'You gave me back a great deal more, my dear.' She smiled at him, and I could tell that she loved Mr Betterton; it shone out of her like a stained-glass window with the sun behind it (naturally I recalled the manner in which she had gazed at Transome, and wondered how to bring his name into the conversation).

'We've just spoke to your mother, ma'am,' said Blackbeard.

'Oh?'

'She's changed her story, you see. Now she says she never saw Mrs Transome on the night of the murder. She says she lied to protect you.'

'My mother lied because she was afraid,' said Mrs Constance. 'She happened to overhear a serious disagreement I had with Tom.' She uttered his name quite easily, without changing colour or faltering. 'As you know, as you had seen yourself, we had a great many disagreements, mostly caused by Olivia and her jealousy.'

She stopped abruptly as the parlourmaid returned with a tray of extra crockery for myself and Blackbeard, and kept silence while Mr Betterton busied himself with the pouring of the tea (I wondered why Mrs Constance did not make the tea herself, but permitted her husband to wait on her).

Blackbeard took a loud gulp of his tea. 'Was this row about Miss Olivia?'

'No.' Mrs Constance eyed us steadily. 'It was a private matter, entirely between ourselves. I also exchanged angry words with my mother, when she waylaid me in the street after the performance.'

'And then you went off in a cab,' said Blackbeard.

'Let me tell you the rest, since it concerns me,' said Mr Betterton. 'A few weeks before Transome died, Constance approached me to ask if she might join my company. We met several times afterwards, but the final decision was not made until that night. Mrs Noonan has doubtless told you how our encounters became more frequent and longer. I must say most emphatically that there was nothing improper in the hours Constance and I spent together. We simply walked, or drove, through the empty streets, until it occurred to us that we loved one another, and would be more comfortable indoors.'

'He knew my history,' said Mrs Constance, with a celestial smile. 'I told him everything, and he forgave me.'

'There was nothing to forgive, my dear; although I don't wish to speak ill of the dead, Transome took advantage of you when you were very young.' The clock on the mantelpiece chimed the hour. 'I did not think it was so late; you had better go and dress.'

'Of course.' She jumped from her chair, no longer languid. 'I beg your pardon, Mrs Rodd; there is so much preparation before a performance!'

'I would not dream of delaying you, Mrs Betterton,' I said. 'Thank you for receiving us.'

Her husband's eyes rested upon her fondly as she left the room. 'See how she springs to life when she is about to go onstage! Her artistry is a miracle; I'm amazed every time.'

I was on the point of saying a polite farewell when Blackbeard said:

'Now you may speak ill of the dead, sir, if you please.'

Mr Betterton was startled. 'I beg your pardon?'

'You didn't like Transome, did you?'

'To put it bluntly,' said Mr Betterton, stiffening all over, 'no, I did not. It was mainly a professional thing. He was a very fine actor, but with too much of the traditional "barnstormer", and too little respect for the text – *Julius Caesar* with frightful songs and rows of ballet-dancers!'

'You didn't like his morals,' said Blackbeard.

'His immorality disgusted me. It was exactly the kind of shameless behaviour that gives my profession such a bad name. My parents were actors and they were also Christians; they did not believe the two were incompatible.'

'I observed the way you run your own theatre,' I said. 'I could not help contrasting it with Mr Transome's.'

'I believe I must put it as simply as this, Mrs Rodd,' said Mr Betterton. 'Thomas Transome was not a good man. His treatment of Constance was utterly reprehensible. He stands now before the ultimate judge and I will say no more.'

'Thank you, Mr Betterton,' I said. 'We will take up no more of your time, but I have one more question – what was the cause of the so-called feud between your two families?'

'Ah, the Montagues and the Capulets!' He was grimly amused. 'It happened thirty years ago, and does not reflect well upon either family. My father managed a theatre in Exeter; Tom Transome worked at the time for a competing establishment. Both theatres put on the same play and my father's had the greater success until Transome set fire

192

to the scenery, and came close to burning the whole place to the ground.'

'Are you certain it was him?'

'Oh, yes! Everyone knew it, though nothing could be proved.'

'That fits his wife's confession,' said Blackbeard. 'She reckons he set the fire at the King's.'

'I'm not sure I would go as far as accusing him of that,' said Mr Betterton. 'Actors don't make a habit of burning down their own theatres. When he set the fire at my father's, Transome was young and heedless and probably thought of it as a kind of game that got out of hand. Looking back, I now think my father's retaliation was too severe. I am sorry to say that he broke Transome's arm.'

'Good heavens!' I was intrigued to hear of such violence attached to the Betterton name.

'He was a hot-headed Irishman,' Mr Betterton said, with a rueful smile. 'He started out as a prize-fighter, and that part of his nature sometimes got the better of him. He soon repented, but there you have the cause of our famous feud.'

'I am surprised that Mr Transome kept it up for such a long time,' I said, 'even after his daughter married your son.'

'Ah, but it was Maria,' said Mr Betterton. 'And that he could not forgive – anyone but Maria!'

Twenty-four

'MRS RODD – I say, Mrs Rodd!'

It was the following morning, and the voice hailed me as I was walking down Wimpole Street. I had just emerged from a meeting with a certain wealthy lady who had dropped a few vague hints of a donation to the fund for Seven Dials; after an hour of hard work, I had managed to extract a written pledge for fifty guineas and was feeling tired but triumphant (I wished I could tell Matt, who delighted in my talent for 'screwing' money out of tight-fisted people). The weather was beautiful; warm and windless, with not a wisp of cloud in the pure blue sky. I had decided to award myself the treat of a walk in Regent's Park, and was on the point of hurrying off when I heard my name.

'Good morning, ma'am.'

'Mr Betterton!'

The sight of Edgar Betterton brought back my great anxiety about Mrs Sarah, which gnawed at me incessantly and had robbed me of my sleep the previous night.

He was on the pavement, beside an open carriage. I crossed the street to speak to him and saw that there was someone in the carriage; a young lady in a light-blue gown, whom I did not recognize until I saw her pale face and dark hair under the brim of her bonnet.

'Good morning, Miss Cordelia,' I said, 'I am glad to see you looking so much better! But I'm afraid you won't remember me.'

'You are Mrs Rodd, I think.' Her voice was soft, yet she met my gaze with those troubling eyes of hers, so like her father's that they looked strange in her little white face. 'I am a great deal better, thank you.'

'She has come on in leaps and bounds,' said Mr Edgar, smiling, as if he had not a care in the world and his mother-in-law was not about to be tried for murder. 'She will soon be up to going back onstage; my wife has set her heart on reviving her Rosalind, with Cordelia as Celia.'

'A charming idea,' I said. 'I hope your wife is well, Mr Betterton.'

'Thank you, she's very well.' Now he looked uneasy. 'Considering, you know—'

'Naturally I understand; this is a dreadful time for your family.'

'Maria distracts herself with professional matters,' said Mr Edgar. 'As far as she can. Look here, we're waiting for her now, and I'd rather you didn't mention anything about the trial if you happen to see her. She is meeting her doctor.'

'Is she unwell?'

'No – that is – she's consulting Sir Geoffrey Crabbe.'

'She wants a baby,' said Miss Cordelia.

'Sir Geoffrey has a great reputation for helping the childless,' I said (a little taken aback by her frankness). 'I'm sure she could not be in better hands.'

'He is very hopeful,' said Mr Edgar. 'He thinks her health will improve when the present sorrow is behind us. It depresses her spirits, you see.'

'That is only to be expected.' The subject was a painful one, for which I had nothing but sympathy; my own

195

childless state had made me very sad, and Maria had the additional pain of her mother's impending trial. 'I saw your father yesterday, Mr Betterton, and his new wife.'

'That's another thing you mustn't mention,' said Mr Edgar, his face reddening. 'Maria is still rather sensitive regarding the other Mrs Betterton. It's all the more awkward because my father simply doesn't understand; he says there can be no rivalry between members of the same family.'

How was I to reply to this? Had the man never heard of Cain and Abel? While I was casting about for a more suitable subject, Miss Cordelia asked:

'Will you be seeing my mother, Mrs Rodd?'

'Yes—' I began.

'Watch it!' Mr Edgar stood up straighter as the street door of the doctor's house opened, and his wife emerged on to the front steps.

Maria Betterton was soberly attired in a dress and bonnet of pale dove-grey, and these Quakerish clothes only emphasized her beauty. She shook my hand with distant, queenly politeness.

'Good morning, Mrs Rodd; may we take you anywhere?'

'No, thank you, Mrs Betterton. I ran across your husband and your sister quite by chance, and could not resist stopping; it is a pleasure to see Miss Cordelia looking so well.'

Her disdainful manner softened as she turned her gaze to her sister. 'Her recovery has been quite a miracle, just over the past few weeks, and a comfort to us, when everything else is dreadful.'

'Tell you what, my dear,' said Mr Edgar, 'you should ask Mrs Rodd to do something about Cooper.'

'Your father's old dresser?' I asked. 'What is the matter with him?'

'We've lost him.'

'I beg your pardon?'

'Cooper was chucked out of his lodgings, no one knows where to find him, and my poor wife is worrying herself into knots about him.'

'He could be on the streets, or ill, or in danger,' Mrs Maria cut in. 'Of course I'm worried! He loved my father, Mrs Rodd, and has been a part of my family since I can remember. I cannot bear to think of him dying in a gutter.'

'I would be happy to make enquiries on your behalf,' I said. 'The street is not the place to discuss the matter, however; I had better call on you at home tomorrow.'

'Thank you. Any time after two.'

'Usual rates,' said Mr Edgar.

'There will be no charge, Mr Betterton; it would not be appropriate in the present circumstances.'

'Oh, I beg your pardon. Money was the other thing I wasn't supposed to mention.'

Mrs Maria gave him a reluctant smile. 'Stop teasing and help me into the carriage.'

While Mr Edgar assisted his wife, my hand happened to be resting on the top of the carriage door next to Miss Cordelia.

She grabbed it, kissed it fervently and whispered, 'For Mamma!'

The house in Holloway had a pretty garden, and it was here that Mrs Maria received me, in the shade of a large apple tree (in the early years of the century, this part of London had contained many orchards). It was another sunny day, unseasonably warm and close; more like the end of the summer than the beginning. Mrs Maria was alone, sitting in a wicker chair with a book. She placed this on a little table at her elbow and gestured to me to take the other chair.

'We won't be interrupted; Edgar is in town somewhere and Murphy has taken my sister to the park.'

'I was very glad to see the improvement in Miss Cordelia's health.'

'It is my only source of comfort at this time, Mrs Rodd.'

She was dressed in the same plain gown I had seen yesterday, her hair was pinned back as simply as possible, and yet her splendid beauty gave everything she did an air of theatricality, whether she liked it or not.

'I don't know if you have heard,' I said, 'but your mother has changed some parts of her confession, and now admits that when she said she was at the theatre on the night of the murder, she was actually elsewhere. She speaks of meeting a man, by the name of Jonathan Parrish.'

'Parrish?'

'I wondered if you would remember him; he worked for your parents during their American tour. Perhaps you were too young?'

'I did not ask you here to talk about my mother. I cannot bear to hear anything about her. I have no desire to meet her new husband. As far as I am concerned, my mother is dead.'

'I quite understand, Mrs Betterton; you spoke yesterday of Mr Cooper.'

'I am nearly frantic with worry about him. We heard that Cooper was near to destitution and drinking himself to death, and I sent Edgar to his lodgings with some money only to find that he had been turned out into the street, and had apparently disappeared.'

'People do not often disappear,' I said. 'They often try to, but someone will always know where they are hiding. I don't think Cooper will be hard to find.'

'I hope to heaven you are right! In my worst moments, I fear that he has thrown himself into the river; he spoke of ending it all when my father died. If any harm has come to him, I think the remorse will kill me!'

'When I find him, what do you wish me to do with him?'

'He must come here,' said Mrs Maria. 'There is no room for him in this house but Edgar will find him a decent lodging in the neighbourhood.'

'Your concern for the man is admirable,' I said. 'I didn't know you were so fond of him.'

'It's not a question of being "fond" of him; I am trying to rebuild my ruined family, and Cooper is a part of that family. When my sisters and I were little children, he was our nursemaid. He washed our faces, bound up our grazed knees and mended our torn frocks. My very earliest memory is of Cooper putting me to bed in a basket underneath Papa's dressing table.' Her voice was softer now, and the hint of a smile played at her lips. 'The theatre was my true home, for as long as I can remember; it was quite natural to us to run around backstage, even when we were not performing.'

'What was Cooper's opinion of your marriage?'

'He took my father's side; we have not spoken since.' Mrs Maria's voice turned chilly and sour, and I was strongly reminded of her mother. 'Papa would have considered it a betrayal.'

'I heard something of your father's reaction to the news.'

'I wasn't there,' said Mrs Maria. 'Olivia was, however, and she told me all about the dreadful fuss he made.' She studied me in silence, and a look of indescribable pain flashed across her face. 'He loved me, of course; I should not have hurt him.'

'Mrs Betterton, are you able to tell me anything more of Cooper's whereabouts?'

'I can give you the address of his previous lodgings, and of certain taverns where he has been known to drink, and—' (A pause, more calculating than theatrical.) 'You should speak to Olivia.'

'Oh?'

'She saw to it that Cooper was given a job in her frightful theatre. He lost the job due to his drinking. Olivia may very well know where he is.'

'I beg your pardon, but would it not be simpler for you to approach her yourself?'

'She refuses to speak to me. I have no quarrel with my sister, Mrs Rodd. We offered to take her into our new company, but the roles were not good enough for her; she has elected herself as keeper of our father's flame, and now nothing less than Cleopatra will satisfy her. She is presently appearing at the Britannia Theatre in Charing Cross; it is a low sort of establishment, and I would not advise you to go there.'

'I know very little about the theatre, but is her acting really so bad?'

'You are sorry for her,' said Mrs Maria, with a sigh. 'You think we are unkind to her, perhaps deliberately holding her back.'

'No—'

'That is what Olivia believes; she has decided we are all against her. The truth is less dramatic; she looks well enough, she speaks well enough, but she lacks the spark that makes a great actor.'

'Spark?'

'I mean, the indefinable quality that demands the attention of an audience. Papa always maintained that it was something you were born with or not. He was sorry for her too.'

'It must be a hard thing for her to accept,' I said, 'as a member of such a celebrated family.'

'She does not accept it,' said Mrs Maria. 'She could live here, in a respectable house, playing perfectly decent roles in a successful theatre; instead of which she chooses to flaunt herself in various pieces of rubbish at the Britannia. I wish she would forgive us all, for we were close companions when we were little. And my poor Cordelia was once her darling."

'I shall drop a few hints on your behalf, Mrs Betterton; it is a shame when sisters are parted. Do you have an address for her, apart from the Britannia Theatre?'

'I do not,' said Mrs Maria. 'You had better leave a message for her at the stage door.'

'Very well,' I said. 'I hope I can soon bring you good news.'

'Thank you,' she said, very quiet and earnest. 'After everything that's happened, I need to keep those I love close by me.'

Twenty-five

THE NEXT DAY, EARLY in the evening, I was sitting in my brother's study in Highgate. I had my knitting, Fred had sherry and a cigar, and we were not thinking about murder. My sister-in-law was unwell (for the usual reason; the poor creature was expecting her twelfth baby) and lying down in her room. I had come to assist the governess and nursemaid in putting the little ones to bed, so that Tishy was able to devote herself to her mother. All was now quiet, inside the house at least; the close weather had broken into steady rain with rumbles of thunder.

'Thank you, my dear,' said Fred. 'You are our rock and our refuge; I told Gibson you were staying for dinner. I can't let you trudge back to Hampstead in this dismal weather.'

'I shall see to it that Fanny has her dinner upstairs. Really, Fred, you must not let her get so tired! She expects too much of herself, and it cannot be good for her, or the baby.'

'You'd better give her one of your stiff lectures. She never listens to me.'

'She must rest every afternoon,' I went on (choosing to ignore the jibe about my 'stiff lectures'). 'And I wish she would give her social ambitions a rest too; all those teas and dances and concerts are wearing her out.'

'Oh, you know Fanny,' said Fred airily, blowing out a smoke-ring. 'She always calms down about halfway through, and then she's an utter lamb.'

'You take her health too much for granted; you mustn't assume another safe delivery simply because she has gone through it so many times.'

The rain was heavier now, and my lecture was cut short by a crash of thunder loud enough to split the sky. As the noise died away, we could hear someone knocking urgently at the front door.

Mrs Gibson tapped on the door of the study a few minutes later and came into the room with a card.

'Mr Mallard to see you, sir; are you in?'

'Mallard? Yes, indeed.' In an instant my brother's manner hardened and sharpened. He took his feet off the desk, disposed of the cigar and stood up. 'I had an odd feeling we would be hearing more from him.'

Mr Mallard almost pushed Mrs Gibson aside in his eagerness to get into the room. He was soaking wet; his hat dripped in his hand.

'Mr Tyson, Mrs Rodd – I must speak with you at once. I cannot wait.'

'My dear fellow, come and sit down.' My brother removed Mr Mallard's sodden coat. 'Let me give you a glass of sherry.'

'No, thank you.' He was burning with purpose, and seemed not to be aware of his surroundings; he bumped into the furniture and had to be led to the armchair. I asked Mrs Gibson to bring us tea and gently wrestled Mr Mallard's hat from his clenched fingers.

'How may we help you, Mr Mallard?'

'Mr Tyson, you must defend my wife.'

'Must I? I thought that was all settled,' said Fred. 'George Pilton is to lead for the defence.'

'Pilton is the wrong man.'

'Why – what on earth is the matter with him?'

'He thinks she's guilty.'

'Oho!' Fred cried out, with an unsuitable rumble of laughter. 'Do you mean she's changed her story?'

'No,' said Mr Mallard. 'It is my own attitude to the story that has changed. I have admitted to myself that I don't believe her.' His lined face creased with pain. 'I said as much to Pilton this morning, and the man all but laughed in my face. He said his hands were tied unless Sarah pleaded "Not Guilty", and he left me in no doubt of his own opinion in the matter.'

'I can't say I blame him,' said Fred. 'That confession of hers is starting to look a little threadbare, but there's no point in tearing it to shreds; she insists that she committed two murders, and that's all the jury will care about.'

'They ought to care about the truth.'

'Mr Mallard,' I said, 'does your wife know that you are here?'

'She – she lied to me!' He turned to me with a look of amazement. 'She – she continues to lie – with a coolness that I now think absolutely brazen! But why is she so set on being hanged? That is the greatest lie of all – the one I cannot forgive!'

'Bless my soul, this is a new one!' said Fred. 'Let's get it straight – your wife says she's guilty, but you suspect her of being innocent?'

'Yes.'

'Have you confronted her with your suspicion?'

'I have not; I'm afraid she'll lie again and I cannot bear it.'

'Most men would be happy to discover their wives are not murderers.'

'You probably think I am ridiculous,' Mallard said, with a flash of anger. 'I can see how it looks – she has made a fool of me, and I don't care. I told her she should feel free to confess anything. It was a grand promise and God took me at my word; now he is testing me.'

The poor man was shivering, his few remaining strands of hair were plastered in stripes across his bald head, yet he clung to his dignity amidst the ruins of his broken heart.

Fred saw this and kindly dropped his 'courtroom' tone to insist that Mr Mallard drank a glass of brandy. He built and lit a fire in the empty grate, and Mrs Gibson brought in the tea tray. The fire took hold, I made the tea and drew the heavy plush curtains across the rain-splattered windows.

Mr Mallard had regained his composure by now, and he meekly accepted the plate of bread-and-butter that I put into his trembling hands. 'Thank you; I don't always remember to eat.'

'Where are you staying, Mr Mallard?' I asked. (I was a little ashamed that I did not know this.)

'I have a lodging in Highbury. I wanted to be as close to her as possible.'

'Naturally.'

'It's bare and somewhat spartan, but ideally suited to my purpose. I only go there to sleep. Though mostly I lie awake, staring at the ceiling like the lovelorn old fool that I am.'

This last twist of bitterness was not like him, and made me think about the enormity of the upheaval in his life since he met Sarah Transome.

'You are being too hard on yourself—' I began.

He cut me short. 'I know what people are saying, Mrs Rodd. I have tried to ignore the newspapers, the ballad-sheets and cartoons, but it is quite impossible. I have become a national joke.'

'I've been a national joke for years, my boy!' Fred said breezily. 'You'll soon get used to it.' He saw Mr Mallard's pained expression, remembered that the man had no sense of humour and added, 'This sort of thing goes away as suddenly as it blows up; try not to let it worry you.'

'Whatever the outcome,' said Mr Mallard, 'there will come a time when I must return to my duties as a clergyman, and I don't know how I am to do this. I don't even know how I can remain in holy orders. I have served my parish faithfully for many, many years, and now my curate writes that the people have turned against me and wish me to leave – and I fail to see how any of this mess can be God's will. I truly believed He had sent Sarah to me as a blessing. I believed He wished me to be happy, and then I came to believe he meant me to serve the harder purpose of helping a murderess to repent.'

'It is not like you to doubt the purposes of Heaven, Mr Mallard,' I said. 'Your faith has helped you through worse than this.'

'You remember my wife, of course – my first wife, I should say.'

'I do.' (I had a dim memory of a sweet, small, plain-featured young woman.)

'When Harriet died – and our poor little girl – I thought the grief would kill me. And yet I accepted God's will; the foundations of my faith were not shaken. Now I am tormented by doubts.'

My brother asked, 'What was it that made you suspect Sarah was throwing you a line?'

'I asked her, begged her, to tell me the whole truth about the night of Transome's murder. The new version of events came as a profound shock to me. It was the first I'd heard of this man, Jonathan Parrish. She admitted to me that she had loved him – she didn't even appear to be ashamed of the fact! I knew that she had committed the sin of adultery with Francis Fitzwarren. That was bad enough. To hear that she had done it again, and had not told me, was agony. What was worse, however, was her refusal to give me any satisfactory account of that night.' His eyes filled with tears. 'I am her husband; I thought we were one in spirit, and yet she will not trust me. Though I have no new evidence, I am now sure she did not kill Transome. My wife is innocent, Mr Tyson. She must be saved.'

'Someone killed him, and your wife had both the motive and the means,' said Fred. 'If she didn't do it, who did?'

'It can only be someone she would die to protect,' said Mr Mallard.

'Her children!' I said this almost without thinking.

'The daughters, eh?' Fred was very interested now. 'I understood that they were out of the picture. They all provided decent alibis for the night their father was murdered. As for Fitzwarren's murder, they were little girls at the time.'

'Maria was not a little girl.' My heart was beating hard, yet I strove to keep my manner calm. 'It is clear, however, that she was nowhere near the scene of the crime; either crime, I should say.'

'And I wonder about motive,' said Fred. 'As far as Transome is concerned, anyway. They were all in the habit of falling out with their father, and then making up – just look at Miss Olivia. She clearly adored the man, and she also depended on him for employment.'

I said, 'And Miss Cordelia was nine years old at the time of the first murder, and gravely ill at the time of the second.'

'The morning you came to Newley, Mrs Rodd,' said Mallard, 'that was the first time Sarah told me she had three children – and all professional actresses! I was deeply shocked and found her detachment very difficult to understand. I was a father once. My child lies in the churchyard, and I cannot even bear to leave her grave!'

The sorrow in his voice cut me to the heart and Fred whisked out his white silk handkerchief to blow his nose.

'I understood everything,' said Mr Mallard, 'the moment I saw my wife's determination to protect her daughters. The truth is that she loves them more than her life, but you must not let her do it!'

My brother, gazing intently at Mr Mallard, asked, 'Well, Letty, what do you think?'

At last – at long last – my famous instincts were awake again and sharp as knives. 'I have never been entirely satisfied with Mrs Sarah's impersonation of a violent murderess. Her manner has puzzled me since the day we met. She affected not to care overmuch for her children, yet I have observed her tenderness towards them, even when they were cold to her in return. If she has been protecting one of them from the gallows, it all makes far more sense.'

'I'm inclined to agree,' said Fred. 'I'll tell you what, Mallard – I'd be happy to defend your wife, whether or not she changes her story. I have no objection to confronting her with her innocence; I would positively enjoy persuading a jury to see her as a mother who is willing to die in order to protect her child. But I can't make bricks without straw, and I'll only do it if my sister can find some solid evidence of the true murderer.'

Twenty-six

'THE MORE I THINK about it, the more likely it looks,' said Mrs Bentley. 'Most mothers would happily get themselves hanged to save one of their children; I know I would. But which daughter? Cordelia was too young to commit the first murder, and too poorly to commit the second. That leaves Maria and Olivia.'

'Only if we are assuming there is one murderer,' I said. 'Cordelia could not have killed Fitzwarren, but we don't know enough about her movements on the night her father died to rule her out completely. I don't think anyone has bothered to question those who were supposedly in the house with her.'

It was after midnight and the two of us were sitting over the kitchen fire with our accustomed brandy-and-hot water; though I had told Mrs B not to wait up for me, I could not help being glad to find her wide awake when Fred's carriage dropped me back in Well Walk. I knew I would not be able to sleep until I had calmed the roar of confusion in my mind (it was at times like this that I missed my beloved Matt most cruelly; he was so clever at ironing out my tangled ideas).

'I reckon there's only one murderer, ma'am.' Mrs B refilled our glasses from the copper pan that was keeping warm on the hob. 'As the inspector always says, it ain't a common crime. What does Mr Mallard think?'

'He has never met his wife's children; he doesn't have a high opinion of any of them, because they are actresses. Poor man, he fell upon his dinner as if he hadn't seen a decent meal for months! I hate to think of him in his lonely room, brooding over the collapse of his blameless life.'

'He ain't the first man to make a fool of himself over a woman,' said Mrs Bentley. 'And he won't be the last.'

'No one who loves as sincerely as he does can be called a "fool". I will admit that he seems rather to have lost his head over Sarah Transome. The people of his parish have turned against him, and are unlikely to welcome him back, with or without his wife.'

'That's not how true Christians ought to carry on,' said Mrs B, shaking her head solemnly. 'Who do you speak to next, then?'

'To Miss Olivia; her sister thinks she knows the where-abouts of Cooper. You may help me here, my dear Mary; I suspect that Mr Tully knows more than he's letting on, but he is too wary of me after his experience at Newley Castle. I know he is in the habit of visiting you, however, and it would be useful if you could ask him a few of your artful questions.'

'Artful – I like that!' Mrs Bentley let out a rusty chuckle. 'I'm just a poor little old woman and nobody minds what they say in front of me. You can leave me to put the screws on him, ma'am, next time he drops in with one of his cakes.'

In those days before the building of the Thames embankment, the area of Charing Cross was a collection of crooked, dirty streets that ran from the main road down into the river. At low tide, the tainted mud gave off a most disgusting smell – thoroughly appropriate in a district notorious for immorality.

Great Scotland Yard was situated nearby ('They ain't your clever type of scoundrel here,' Blackbeard had once told me, 'or they wouldn't set up shop on the doorstep of the Metropolitan Police!'), and I stopped there to leave a note for the inspector, in which I asked for the address of Mr Jonathan Parrish.

I then went in search of the Britannia Theatre, at the end of one of those ramshackle streets, and when I found it, I saw for myself how far Miss Olivia had fallen; this lopsided wooden structure, half-sinking into the muddy riverbank, was many miles from her father's magnificent establishment in the Haymarket. It was flanked by two public houses of the worst kind, and covered with layer upon layer of tattered playbills that fluttered sadly in the breeze. The topmost layer – already faded – bore a crude picture of a woman wearing a crown and not much else, and the words: MISS TRANSOME PLAYS QUEEN CLEOPATRA.

In daylight the place was deserted and the doors chained shut. I looked around for a few minutes, fully aware of how incongruous I must appear in my sober black dress and bonnet. There was the narrowest possible gap between the theatre and the neighbouring public house. I squeezed myself through it and came to a battered door, propped open with a chair.

The interior was also deserted and as dirty as possible. I followed the sound of a solitary flute, tuneless and forlorn, to a tiny and windowless room. There I came upon an ancient man with white hair, who stopped playing when he saw me.

'I am looking for Miss Transome,' I said.

'She ain't here.' His voice was a toothless mumble.

'Could you tell me where I might find her?'

'Crown and Sceptre.'

'I beg your pardon?'

'Top of Venn Street.'

'Thank you.'

I left the theatre and hurried back to the relative civilization of the main street. The Crown and Sceptre was a large establishment, perfectly clean and respectable, but not the sort of place I would ever have associated with the queenly Olivia.

I asked the woman behind the bar, 'Is Miss Transome at home?'

'I'm not sure, ma'am.' She eyed me doubtfully. 'What name shall I tell her?'

'Mrs Rodd.' I gave her one of my cards.

She stared at this little piece of pasteboard, and turned it over in her hands. 'Beg pardon, ma'am, but are you after money?'

'Certainly not; this is purely a social call.'

'Just a minute.' She hurried away through a door that opened on to a steep staircase, returned a few minutes later and led me up to Miss Olivia's room.

'Mrs Rodd, you do have a way of turning up unexpectedly!' The young woman stood proudly in the middle of the floor, holding my card between two fingers. 'I warn you now that if you're here on behalf of my mother, you're wasting your breath.'

Her hair, a shade lighter than the raven tresses of her sisters, hung loose down her back, and she wore a dressing gown that was elaborately frilled but none too clean.

'My purpose is quite different,' I assured her. 'I'm here on an errand of mercy.'

'Oh?'

'Your sisters are very anxious to find Cooper, your father's old dresser. They have heard of his poverty and wish to assist him.'

'Oh, I see. Please sit down.'

The only chair in the room was hidden beneath a gaudy heap of clothes, which Miss Olivia threw on the floor. She sat down upon a couch that had not yet assumed its day-time character and was still mostly a bed.

'You see how I live these days.' She made another stab at hauteur, and only succeeded in looking sad. 'I'm sure you'll take a full account back to Maria.'

'Do you not wish her to know your address?'

'You may tell her if you like,' said Miss Olivia. 'Her opinion of me is her own affair.'

'Mrs Betterton told me you found employment for Mr Cooper,' I said, 'at the Britannia Theatre.'

'Yes, I did. Nobody else would have him on account of his drinking, but I could not bear to see him destitute when Papa loved him so.' Her voice broke a little over the word 'Papa'. 'He only lasted a week.'

'I understand he was turned out of his lodgings.'

'He was.'

'Do you know where he went after that?'

'He came to me, Mrs Rodd, and I found him a room here, above the stable. It's clean and decent, which is all that can be said for it, but the best I could afford.'

'You have been a good friend to him.' I found myself softening towards this prickly young woman more than I had expected. 'Your father would be happy to see it.'

'I hope so,' said Miss Olivia. 'Poor old Cooper took his death very hard; he kept saying he couldn't live without him. They met when they were both very young, and Papa was not the least bit famous. He told me once that Cooper had taken the place in his affections of his sister, my Aunt Eliza, who had lately died.'

'The last time I spoke to your father, he said that I reminded him of his sister.'

'He was paying you a great compliment.' She smiled a little and instantly looked younger and prettier, and less like an angry waxwork. 'He regarded her almost as a mother, and when she died, he missed being fussed over – you saw for yourself how Cooper fussed over Papa.'

'Your sister described him as your "nursemaid".'

'A typical piece of exaggeration but it's true that Cooper minded us when we were little, and we were all fond of him.'

'Is he here now, Miss Transome? Do you think he would see me?'

'I'm sure he would, though you shouldn't expect to get much sense out of him,' said Miss Olivia. 'At this time of day, you'll find him in one of a number of low taverns, telling tall stories about my family in exchange for gin. He's becoming quite a local character.'

'Mrs Betterton is anxious to take Cooper into her care,' I said. 'Would you have any objection to that?'

'Not in the least! To be truthful, I'd be happy to turn the responsibility over to someone else. I simply don't have the money to support another human creature. As it is, I struggle to pay the rent for my own room and board.'

'Did you receive nothing from your father?'

She sighed. 'His will is still being proved – or probed, or something of the kind – but there's not much point to it. He left nothing but debts. I saw the chaos for myself when I tried to make sense of his finances. Never mind robbing Peter to pay Paul, he simply robbed Peter.'

'Dear me,' I said. 'I take it that the Britannia Theatre is paying you a salary?'

'Ha!' said Miss Olivia bitterly. '"Salary" is too grand a word for it; what I get is a share of the takings.'

'Oh—'

'Do you know what that means? Your husband was a clergyman – imagine if you'd had to live on what you got in the collection plate! Sometimes it's just a heap of coppers with a bit of silver here and there, like raisins in a pudding. I can barely keep body and soul together.'

'My dear Miss Transome, there is no need for you to live like this! Your sister would be delighted to give you a home.'

'Yes, yes – and employment in Edgar's new theatre.' Miss Olivia held up her head proudly as her eyes filled with tears. 'Maria has never given me a single chance, Mrs Rodd. She wanted me to waste my time – and Papa's training – doing nothing but the most trifling little roles.'

'I know he devoted a lot of time to training your sister; did he teach you at the same time?'

'No, all I got were the crumbs under the table. Maria took up all his attention, and I believe she poisoned our father's love for me with her jealousy. It was a little better after she ran off with Edgar – better for me, I mean. Papa was quite broken by her betrayal. It was months before he could hear her name without weeping like a deserted lover.'

'Your sister's concern for you now is entirely genuine,' I said gently. 'May I take her your goodwill, at least?'

'I suppose.' Miss Olivia mopped her eyes with a grubby lace handkerchief. 'There's no real reason for us to quarrel. In the end Papa hurt me far more than she did. I offered myself to him, body and soul – and he turned me down flat.'

'That must have distressed you,' I said. 'Perhaps you were taking professional criticism too personally.'

'As far as my father was concerned, there was no difference between the professional and the personal. He was very kind to me afterwards, until Constance Noonan made her appearance.'

'Ah, yes; her marriage must have surprised you.'.

'Not really. She has her eye firmly fixed upon the main chance; I don't believe she loved Papa one bit.' Miss Olivia pursed up her lips and seemed to harden all over.

I allowed the silence to stretch out between us, wondering what could be done to save this young woman from the consequences of her own pride. How far did she have to fall before she returned to her family?

'Miss Transome,' I began, 'I know you don't wish to speak about your mother – but I don't see how we can avoid it. Have you nothing to say to her?'

'She killed my father. I have nothing whatsoever to say to her. She might as well have killed me while she was about it. My own life ended when he died. Perhaps my sisters feel differently, but it was so much worse for me! And it is so unjust, for I was the only one who didn't betray him. Maria and Cordelia both had their little intrigues; I thought only of him.'

'You implied to me that Miss Cordelia's "intrigue" with the musician – I forget his name – was not serious.'

'You mean Joseph Barber.' Miss Olivia shrugged miserably. 'It wasn't really serious, just a few rather overheated letters. Papa intercepted one of them and I daresay you can imagine his reaction.'

'The dance of rage,' I suggested.

'He was like a dervish. I had never seen him in such a passion. He berated Barber and warned him off in front of the entire company. Cordelia was very angry and that was the cause of their great falling-out.'

'Perhaps she loved Barber more than you thought?'

'It's possible that he is the man responsible,' said Miss Olivia. 'Though when it comes to the point, I simply cannot imagine she would make such a sacrifice for such a man – a common fiddler! I can barely recall what he looked like, except that he had black hair and a swarthy complexion, like an Italian organ-grinder. His real name is Giuseppe Barbarino.'

'Do you know if your sister and Joseph Barber kept in contact, after she left the theatre?'

'Since her illness, she hasn't been in a state to contact anyone.'

'Could there have been any other man?'

'Knowing both my sisters as I do, I'd say there could easily have been; we are all adept at deception. Look at Maria, and how she courted Edgar right under Papa's nose!' She was quiet for a moment. 'But Cordelia is the best of us and I find it very hard to believe she could commit such a dreadful sin. And I cannot bear to think how close we came to losing her.'

'She is making wonderful progress.'

'I'm glad to hear it.' Her face softened once more. 'Did you speak with her?'

'I wouldn't describe it as a conversation, but last time we met I saw at once that she had recovered her senses.'

'Does she know about Mamma? Does she ask about her?' Miss Olivia blurted this out as if she could not help herself.

'I'm afraid I don't know.' She was talking to me because she was lonely, and glad to talk to anyone, and I pitied her from my heart. 'Miss Transome, I wish you would at least communicate with your sisters – this is no place for you!'

'It's a hateful place. Everything in my life is hateful. You see how I am sinking into squalor. I have debts and no money to pay them and I daresay you know the common fate of solitary women with no money. I've managed to avoid that so far, but how long before I'm forced to seek a "protector"?'

'Get dressed and come with me now,' I said impulsively. 'Never mind your baggage; I'm sure Mr Edgar will come to collect it for you, and settle any outstanding bills. You can tell him where to find Cooper.'

'What about the Britannia? I'm doing two performances tonight.'

'I have seen the establishment, Miss Transome; it is no place for your father's daughter, and most decidedly no place for a young lady.'

She tried to protest, but so feebly that I saw she actually wished to be chivvied, and nagged at her until she had pinned up her hair and extracted a dress and bonnet from the tumbled heaps of clothes. I would not allow her to take more than one small bag containing her few coins and trinkets.

Once I had bundled her into a cab, Miss Olivia stopped holding up her head and her pride crumbled; she buried her face in her handkerchief and wept a few hot tears.

'I don't know how I shall face them. I have failed so badly!'

'This is no failure, Miss Transome,' I assured her. 'Your family will rejoice to have you back.' (I hoped this was true.) 'You tried to do too much by yourself; now you will have all the help and protection you need.'

'I suppose so.'

'And at this time, your place is with your sisters.'

'My mother's trial, you mean.' Miss Olivia dabbed at her eyes and the handkerchief disappeared into her bag. 'I think of it – and her – constantly. I am not heartless.'

'Of course not!'

'But I don't know her any more. First she disappeared, and everybody said she was dead, and then she suddenly came back to life, with a dreadful new husband in my father's place!'

'I am acquainted with Mr Mallard, and he is not "dreadful" in the least,' I said gently. 'He loves your mother, and believes she is innocent.'

'Because she told him so!'

'Not at all! She refuses to change her version of events. It's simply that some details of her confession turn out not to hold water.' As briefly as possible, I told her of Cremorne Gardens and the mysterious Mr Jonathan Parrish.

'Mr Parrish? Yes, I know him – he's a friend of Mamma's, though it's years since I saw the man. He used to meet us sometimes when we were out walking, and when I was a very little girl, Mamma took me to visit an old lady in Kensington who gave me cakes and candied fruits, and I think she must have been his mother.' Miss Olivia was interested. 'How funny – I'd quite forgotten until now. But he had no reason to murder my father.'

'At this stage, no one thinks he did.'

'I am confused, Mrs Rodd; why would my mother tell lies to condemn herself?'

'To protect someone else, perhaps.'

'Her children? Ha! She doesn't love any of us enough to make such a sacrifice.'

'You read her confession, I'm sure.'

'I did,' said Miss Olivia, with a shudder. 'A piece of self-serving hypocrisy – ornamented with untruths – except for the fire.'

'Oh?'

'I didn't want to believe Papa set that fire. When I was trying to make sense of his papers, however, I found a correspondence between him and a company called Imperial Assurance. He purchased a policy about six months before the fire, and they paid him a large sum of money afterwards.'

'I understood that he was not adequately insured,' I said (keeping my tone soft and sympathetic, and watching her closely).

'Oh, it wasn't "adequate", Mrs Rodd; the money was swallowed up in the ravening maw of his debts. But all he wanted was sufficient funding for his new venture at the Duke of Cumberland's – the theatre in which he would reign supreme, with Maria at his side.' For once, she was able to mention Maria without her usual bitterness. 'I'm afraid he did some very wicked things.'

'I'm afraid he did; James Betterton told me the story behind the so-called feud.'

'Papa never thought beyond the gratification of the moment,' said Miss Olivia. 'If he wanted a thing, he had to have it at once.'

'You were only a child at the time of the fire,' I said. 'I don't suppose you remember much about it.'

'I was fourteen. I remember how awful it was when they brought Papa home.'

'Were you aware of Maria's love affair with Frank Fitzwarren?'

'Well, of course!' Miss Olivia rolled her eyes with a satirical look that reminded me strongly of her mother. 'She's incapable of doing anything quietly. I had to hear all about it and occasionally act as a go-between. Frank was a good-natured sort, rather like Edgar Betterton – tall and fair – her "type" according to Papa.'

'Yellow-haired imbeciles,' I suggested.

'Yes! Oh, dear, you make me remember him vividly. I don't know whether to laugh or cry!'

'Were you surprised when Fitzwarren disappeared so suddenly after the fire?'

'I don't know. Maria made a dreadful fuss and I mostly recall her shrieks and swoons. Mamma said he ran away because she nagged him too much – though I never saw her nagging him. He only had to look at Maria and she melted like wax. It made Papa absolutely furious.'

'Were you surprised to learn of your mother's entanglement with Fitzwarren?'

'Not when I thought about it,' said Miss Olivia shortly. 'Both my parents were good at keeping things from their children. The theatre was our first home and we ran about backstage like three little mice but nobody told us anything, for fear of losing their employment.'

She looked so sad that I decided to change direction. 'By the by, Miss Transome, do you happen to know anything about the man who accompanied Miss LaFaye to the Cremorne Gardens: Mr Parkinson?'

'Polly has a number of admirers,' said Miss Olivia. 'All old and hideous, all with money and none of them bachelors. I could never tell them apart.'

We had left the crowded streets by now, and she became quieter and quieter as our cab approached Holloway. When we stopped outside Maria's house, she froze.

'Come along, Miss Transome!' I almost had to pull her hand off the window-strap. 'It is too late to be nervous!'

I rang the bell; the door was opened by one of the maids. Before I could say anything, a door inside burst open and a voice cried out, 'Livvy!'

'Cordelia, my darling!' Miss Olivia burst into tears and the sisters ran into each other's arms.

As the cab carried me back to Hampstead, I thought about the fiddle-playing Mr Barber (or Barbarino), wondered if he could be the true murderer of Thomas Transome and resolved to speak to him as soon as possible.

Twenty-seven

'**B**ARBER? JOSEPH BARBER?' Mrs Sarah turned the name over and allowed it to hang in the air. 'No, I have never heard of him – in either English or Italian. It's perfectly possible he had some sort of entanglement with Cordelia, but your guess is as good as mine. A musician, you say?'

'He plays the violin,' I said. 'According to Olivia, they had reached the stage of exchanging letters, one of which was discovered by Mr Transome.'

'Oh, dear; Tom must've hit the ceiling!' She paced to and fro in the tiny cell like a caged lioness. 'He was ridiculously jealous of any man who paid too much attention to the girls; he was absolutely out of his mind when Maria ran off with Edgar. After that, the mere prospect of losing Cordelia made him hysterical.'

'I have not spoken to Miss Cordelia,' I said. 'She is still fragile and I don't want to risk making her ill again. Do you know where I can find Joseph Barber?'

Mrs Sarah put a hand to her brow and I saw how thin she had become. 'The musicians are hired on a daily basis, from a public house near Soho Square called the Pillars of Hercules. And they are mostly Italians; that whole neighbourhood is swarming with them.'

'Thank you.'

'If he is the man responsible, I suppose we must assume that Cordelia is in love with him, and also that he deserted her most cruelly if she told him of her condition. I can quite understand why she couldn't tell her father, but I still don't see why she kept it from me; she must have known I would never condemn her! You saw her yesterday – how did she seem to you?'

'Very well, and very happy to see her sister.'

'I am glad to hear it,' said Mrs Sarah. 'I thank God for it. She has been so dreadfully miserable, ever since she left her father and ran home to me.'

'Where is Mr Mallard this morning?' I asked. 'I didn't expect to find you alone.'

She sighed, rather impatiently. 'He wouldn't tell me where he was going. He has some great mysterious plan, which seems to involve writing long missives to various important characters – quite useless, but I don't discourage him. Titus is one of those men who must be doing something. And I admit that I'm rather glad he's not here now. It makes him uneasy when I talk about my daughters – especially poor Cordelia. He cannot hide his horror that she was with child; he would love to hear that she was in that condition because someone forced himself upon her.'

'Do you think that's likely?'

'No, I do not. She kept quiet about it because she was protecting someone.'

'She is much better,' I assured her. 'She speaks, she walks, there is colour in her face. I wish you had seen her joy when she embraced Miss Olivia.'

'I'm grateful to you, Mrs Rodd, for rescuing Olivia from that frightful theatre – and from her own obstinacy! I hated to think of her in such a place. I hated to think of leaving her there after I'm hanged.' (She spoke of being hanged in an offhand way that made my flesh creep.) 'Her sisters are all she has in the world. Tom was sentimental about his girls, always telling anyone who would listen how he worshipped them but he was the cause of all their fallings-out. I don't care whether or not they forgive me. I pray that they can forgive each other.'

'Miss Olivia torments herself – and everyone else – with her jealousy. I was moved, however, by her kindness to the unfortunate Cooper.'

'They are all fond of the poor soul,' said Mrs Sarah. 'Do you know what will happen to him now?'

'Mr Edgar has promised to bring him back to Holloway.'

'Edgar's a good creature; I quite understand why Maria fell in love with him. That was my true reason for helping the two of them to elope. My motives were not entirely pure, but I didn't do it just to annoy Tom.'

The wardress, who stood guard out in the passage, rapped upon the open door of Mrs Sarah's cell. 'Visitor!'

And there was Mr Blackbeard, fresh from the outside world with raindrops glinting on his shoulders. 'Well now, if it ain't Mrs Rodd! I won't ask what you're doing, ma'am, but you've spared me the trouble of writing a letter. It's about your husband, Mrs Mallard.'

'My husband?' She sprang to her feet. 'What has happened to him – is he ill?'

'No, no, ma'am,' said Blackbeard. 'The reverend gentleman is as fit as a fiddle. You might not be seeing him quite as soon as you'd like, that's all.'

'Where is he?'

'He spent last night in a police cell, ma'am, which is in the neighbourhood of Hammersmith.'

'What?' gasped Mrs Sarah.

'My dear Inspector,' I asked, 'what on earth has he done?'

'He attacked a gentleman,' said Blackbeard. 'By the name of Jonathan Parrish.'

'No!' Mrs Sarah sat down heavily on the hard bed. She buried her face in her hands and groaned. 'Oh, the silly old – oh, my dear – if only he had listened to me! He thinks Jonathan is the true murderer, no matter how many times I tell him it's nonsense!'

'According to the report,' said Blackbeard, 'Mr Mallard waylaid Mr Parrish in the street outside his house. He shouted accusations of murder, and when Mr Parrish tried to get away, Mr Mallard struck him in the face, causing his nose to bleed.'

'This must be a mistake, Inspector,' I said, quite unable to believe the mild-mannered clergyman was capable of such behaviour. 'I have known Titus Mallard for years –' (I was about to add, 'and he couldn't say boo to a goose') '– and there's not a violent bone in his body!'

'My husband thinks I'm lying in order to protect Jonathan,' said Mrs Sarah. 'I beg you to believe that I'm doing nothing of the kind. He cannot understand why I kept up a connection with my old lover – why we continued to see one another, and write letters, when any decent woman would have cast him off.'

'I don't understand it myself, ma'am,' said Blackbeard.

'I didn't tell him the whole truth.' She was weary, as if she had suddenly let go of something. 'Which is that Jonathan is Olivia's father.'

'Oh—' I experienced one of those moments when light pours in, when many things fall into place. 'Of course!'

'You see why I kept it secret. I couldn't bear to break her heart. She loved Tom with such a passion.'

I recovered my voice. 'Did he know?'

'He could hardly have missed it,' said Mrs Sarah. 'Without being indelicate, it would have been obvious to him that Livvy was not his own child. He was happy to acknowledge her – he had one eye on business, of course, and his reputation as a paterfamilias – but he really did love her.'

'She told me she remembered meeting Mr Parrish when she was a child.'

'Jonathan has no other children, and begged to see her; how could I deny him?' She reached out to grasp my hand. 'For God's sake, Mrs Rodd, you know Titus; you know he doesn't belong in a police cell! You must help him, before I ruin yet another life!'

The sight was heart-rending. He shuffled into the outer office of the police station, blinking in the light, like an animal emerging from its burrow; an elderly clergyman in gaiters and shovel hat, and with a most unclerical black eye.

'You can take him away, sir,' the sergeant at the desk told Blackbeard. 'The other gentleman won't be pressing charges.'

'There's a piece of luck for you, Mr Mallard,' said Blackbeard, eyeing him sternly. 'Which I hope you appreciate! Personally, I'd be inclined to come down hard on a vicar who goes about attacking strangers in the street.'

'I – I – lost my head,' whispered Mr Mallard. 'He would not stop—'

All I could think was how amazed my dear husband would have been, to see his old colleague turned out of a cell like a common vagabond. I took Mr Mallard firmly by the arm and led him outside to the waiting cab.

He gathered his senses a little once we began to move. 'Mrs Rodd, I am thoroughly mortified. Sarah will be so angry with me!'

'The inspector and I have just seen her and she is not angry; she will only be glad to know that you are free.'

'You whacked the wrong man,' said Blackbeard. 'According to your wife.'

'I allowed myself to be carried away. I persuaded myself that he was a villain. A night in a police cell has made me see my wrong-headedness.'

'Yes, sir, it often has that effect.'

'Perhaps the moral aspect clouded my judgement. The very fact of his existence shocked me to the core. I could not bear to believe that the woman I loved had a habit of committing adultery.'

'You didn't mind her habit of committing murder,' said Blackbeard.

'She is innocent,' said Mr Mallard fiercely, clenching his fists. 'I know she is protecting someone. I thought it was Parrish. I thought she still loved the man, and I was jealous.'

'She is a mother,' I said. 'If she is protecting someone, isn't it most likely to be one of her children?'

'I don't know.' He was confused. 'They came as a shock, you see – three grown women – actresses! She doesn't like to talk about them. And I'm afraid I don't like to ask.'

'Well, you'd better brace up for another shock,' said Blackbeard.

'I beg your pardon?'

I gave him an account of our meeting with Mrs Sarah, doing my best to soften the revelation of Olivia's true parentage.

The colour drained from the poor man's face, and he looked so ill that I urged the inspector to stop at the next available stall for a cup of tea (these stalls were notoriously slipshod regarding the washing of cups, but I decided to take the risk). Mr Blackbeard halted the cab near Paddington Green, and the tea he gave to Mr Mallard was hot and sweet enough to revive him a little.

'My dear Mr Mallard, you are fainting away,' I said. 'When did you last have a proper meal? You had better come home with me.' (There wasn't much in the house, but Hannah could be sent out for fresh eggs and a quarter-pound of bacon; very fortunately, my last case had provided me with money enough to cover an occasional domestic emergency.) 'You need to rest before you return to the prison.' I could not allow him to face his wife in such a state. 'I can put a little witch hazel on your eye.'

'I see Parrish gave as good as he got, sir,' said Black-beard.

Mr Mallard did his best to gather the shreds of his dignity. 'I now regret that I resorted to violence. I am horrified to think that I drew blood. But you must interview Jonathan Parrish, Inspector. Sarah says he spent the whole night with her and I don't believe it.'

'I'll be having a word with him, sir, don't you worry.'

'I have accepted that I might not care for the truth when I hear it. My feelings are of no consequence, however, when weighed against the execution of an innocent woman. This is why Providence brought us together. What does it matter if one man suffers, as long as justice is done?'

I thought this was rather a harsh view of Providence, but did not have the heart to argue with him. He was half-crazed with exhaustion; his papery eyelids closed and he lay back in his seat like a crushed beetle.

'I don't know what my superiors are going to make of this, Mrs Rodd,' said Blackbeard. 'I've never seen a vicar with a shiner!'

'Is there nothing you can do, Inspector?' I lowered my voice, though Mr Mallard had fallen into a deep sleep. 'I am surer than ever that Mrs Sarah's so-called confession is nonsense.'

'She's a terrible sinner, that's clear enough,' said Black-beard (not lowering his voice in the slightest). 'She's told a heap of lies and had love affairs when she was married. But these ain't what I'd call hanging sins, or I'd have to string up half of London!'

'This man, Joseph Barber, had a motive for murdering Mr Transome – though it does sound rather like the plot of a light opera. I should very much like to speak to him.'

'No, Mrs Rodd; I can't have that.'

'I beg your pardon?'

'That neighbourhood ain't suitable for ladies.'

'We've had this argument before, Mr Blackbeard; you know I'm perfectly able to take care of myself, in any neighbourhood.'

'Hmm,' said Blackbeard. 'If you're dead set on it, do me one favour – don't go there without me.'

Twenty-eight

WE WENT TOGETHER, DIRECTLY after we had installed the unfortunate Mr Mallard in my house under the care of Mrs Bentley and Hannah (Mrs B rose to the occasion magnificently; he was sitting over the kitchen fire with a cup of tea before he was properly awake).

I admit that I was glad to have Mr Blackbeard's company, for the streets of Soho and St Giles were in those days notorious for desperate poverty, and all the crimes that commonly go with it.

'Dirt and devilry, ma'am,' said Blackbeard, with a certain satisfaction. 'Everywhere you look.'

He might have added 'everywhere you tread'; the roads and pavements were thick with filth and litter, and when I alighted from the cab in Soho Square, I resigned myself to the ruination of my second-best shoes.

'I ain't a-waiting here!' growled the cabby.

'You'll do as you're told,' said Blackbeard. 'Or I'll have that licence off you. If anyone bothers you, just tell 'em you're with me. I'm well known round here.'

I looked around at the decaying houses, the broken windows stopped up with old newspapers, the hollow-cheeked women and fierce, unshaven men. 'Where is this public house, Inspector?'

'It's down an alley off Greek Street, ma'am. Take a hold of my arm.'

I took his arm and we went down one of the wretched streets that led off the square. There were plenty of people about, yet they melted away in front of us, leaving our way miraculously clear; Blackbeard was indeed clearly 'well known' around here, and well feared.

'I was last here six months ago,' he told me cheerfully, as if we were strolling in the park. 'I had the pleasure of nabbing one of the biggest fences in London; nabbed him red-handed, ma'am, with a nice collection of red-hot stolen jewellery!'

'I remember the case; my brother defended him.'

'That's right, and it was on account of Mr Tyson he was transported and not hanged.'

He led me down a short, dark alley and we emerged into the court that contained the Pillars of Hercules. It was a small pothouse of the lowest kind, its walls covered with a black slime of chronic damp. The yard in front was crowded with listless, shabby men, all smoking furiously.

'These are the leftovers, the men who ain't been hired today,' said Mr Blackbeard. 'They all turn up every day at noon, and the people from the theatres come to pick out the fellows they want.'

'What a precarious way to make a living!' (My conscience smote me a little, for I had never troubled to look at the musicians in the orchestra pit, let alone wonder about their individual lives.)

Blackbeard glared through the smoke at a man nearby with a broken hat. 'Get me Mrs Bodge.'

'Not here,' said Broken Hat sulkily.

'Don't give me that,' said Blackbeard. 'She's always here for me.'

The man eyed him resentfully, then shuffled away into the crowd; a few minutes later the crowd shifted to make space for a meagre, sharp-eyed woman in a threadbare black gown, who was hastily wiping her hands on her apron.

'What do you want? I keep a respectable house these days and you've no call to pester me.'

'Nobody wishes to do that, Mrs Bodge,' I assured her. 'We merely wish to ask you a few questions, if you would be so kind.'

'My name's not "Bodge", it's "Boggi". My husband was an Italian.'

'I beg your pardon, Mrs Boggi. Do you know a young man named Joseph Barber, or Giuseppe Barbarino?'

'Yes, but you won't find him here.'

'We mean him no harm, I can assure you; it's simply that he may be able to help with an important case.'

She considered us for a moment, and then she shouted a stream of Italian (I am able to read the language, but could not make out a word of this). One of the men shouted something back.

'He was picked up this morning and he's at the Italian opera.' Her watchful face softened a little. 'He's one of the best players and usually the first to be picked – and he's no more a criminal than you are, Mr Blackbeard.'

'Who said anything about criminals? I'm obliged to you, Mrs Bodge; for once you're on the right side of the law.'

The afternoon was waning when Blackbeard and I arrived at the Royal Italian Opera House in Covent Garden. The fruit and vegetable market had packed up, leaving heroic amounts of litter behind it, and the great theatre had begun to assume its evening character. The street-sellers and hawkers were gathering outside, and in a few hours, wealthy music-lovers from the highest levels of society would be rubbing shoulders with the lowest.

'I daresay you're familiar with this place, Mrs Rodd.' Blackbeard peered at a framed notice for the night's performance. 'You'll have seen plenty of these Italian pieces; what might this be, when it's at home?'

'It's by Rossini,' I said. 'It means "The Thieving Magpie".' I was assailed by a memory, both sweet and bitter, of attending the same composer's *Barber of Seville* with my beloved husband, not three months before he died; we were guests of the Bishop of London, and we were nearly late because Matt lingered in the street to watch a Punch and Judy man. The music was sublime.

The stage door, at one side of the mighty building, was crowded with all kinds of people, from a celebrated lady singer attended by two servants to some decidedly down-at-heel musicians. Blackbeard asked for Joseph Barber; the door-keeper at first denied all knowledge of the man, but then found his name scrawled on a piece of paper and sent a 'call-boy' to fetch him.

After what seemed like a long time, he appeared, and we were face to face with the man who had (apparently) seduced Cordelia Transome. He was a young man, emaciated and sallow-faced, hugging his violin-case protectively. He would have been handsome if he had not looked so ill.

'I am Joseph Barber; what do you want from me?' His English was clear and fluent, with a faint accent. 'Have I done something wrong?'

The moment I uttered Miss Cordelia's name, his sallow cheeks reddened painfully. 'You have come to tell me she is dead.'

'Nothing of the kind,' I quickly assured him. 'She is very well.'

'I thank God for it.' He was pale again, and his eyes glazed over with tears. 'I heard that she was dying and I tried to find her. The letters I wrote to her were sent back to me, without a word of explanation. I was afraid she would think I had forsaken her but I have been sick, and could do nothing.'

'Let us talk outside,' I said, 'in the fresh air.'

The air outside was not particularly fresh; it was one of those close, still days when there is not enough wind to blow away all the unsavoury smells of the crowded city. Mr Barber looked a little less ghastly, however, once we had left the theatre.

'It was the cholera,' he said. 'It came to my street and many died of it. My brother died.'

'I am sorry to hear it,' I said. (That dreadful illness was imperfectly understood in those days and people believed it was spread by breathing tainted air; nowadays it is known to be caused by infected water, which makes it especially destructive in poorer districts where many share one tap.) 'Are you sure you have recovered fully, Mr Barber? You do not look well.'

'I am still a little weak but I must work.'

'Come and sit in our cab for a moment; you will be more comfortable.'

Mr Barber climbed into our cab with the air of one who has lost the strength to protest. I longed to give the poor thing a good cup of beef broth with a dash of brandy in it, as I would have done at home; I made do with a glass of wine and a mutton pie, brought by Blackbeard from the chop-house nearby.

'Thank you, ma'am. You are very kind.'

'Please try to eat a little, Mr Barber! You have had a fever, and should be building up your strength even if you don't feel hungry.' (I remembered that there was still one

jar of the beef tea I had made for Mrs Bentley in my
larder, and resolved to find a way of getting it to him; his
frayed clothes and transparent linen were evidence enough
of his poverty.) 'How long have you been ill?'

'My brother died six weeks ago and I became sick after
that.' He drank down the wine in a single gulp. 'I wanted
to die myself – we were three brothers, and now I must
make my way alone.'

'Dear me, life has been very hard for you,' I said. 'Did
you all come to London together?'

He nodded. 'We were born in Rome, where our father
played violin at the opera. He died seven years ago and we
came to London because we heard there was plenty of
work for musicians. My oldest brother died two years
later.'

The young man related this sad story in a quiet, matter-
of-fact way that made me very sorry for him. 'You were
afraid we had come to tell you Miss Cordelia was dead,' I
said very gently (the door of the cab stood open and
Blackbeard waited on the pavement, apparently not listening; this was a sign that he wished me to ask the questions).
'You had heard that she was ill?'

'I heard gossip and rumours; nobody could tell me the
truth.' Mr Barber took a cautious bite of the hot pie. 'She
cast me off and I did not know the reason; I thought she
loved me.'

He spoke as if he did not know that Miss Cordelia had
been with child, and my instinct told me that he was not
the man responsible; I would need to proceed with the
utmost tact. 'Could you tell me how you met her?'

'I worked at her father's theatre,' said Mr Barber. 'When
it is not the season for opera, I find work wherever I can
get it. Cordelia had to sing a song in Italian – she has a
very sweet voice, but her accent was not good, and Mr

Transome asked me to teach her. This is how we fell in love.'

'The two of you exchanged letters, I understand.'

'We did nothing wrong!'

'I'm sure you did not.'

'We wanted to be married.' Anger flared in his black eyes. 'But Mr Transome discovered one of my letters·and flew into a fury. Cordelia was his principal actress, and he would not let her throw herself away upon a poor "fiddle-player" – this was what he called me, though I have played my fiddle for some of the finest musicians in the world!'

'I know that Miss Cordelia quarrelled with her father,' I said. 'She left his theatre and returned to her mother. Did she contact you after that?'

'I wrote letters, I went to her mother's house, she refused to see me. The next thing I hear is that she is dying.' He grew thoughtful, and finished the pie as if unaware of what he was doing. 'I'm glad she is well. She would hardly know me now; they shaved my hair and my whiskers during my illness.'

'Did you try to contact her again after her father was murdered?'

'She was sick.'

Blackbeard coughed; a sign of impatience which I ignored.

'What were your feelings, when you heard of the crime?'

'I did not hear of it until some time later,' said Mr Barber. 'I was not in London.'

'Oh?'

'I was in Bad Gastein, a spa town in Austria.' He looked stronger now that he had eaten something. 'My poor brother was with me; we played in the orchestra at the casino.'

'That sounds rather elegant,' I said.

'The music was bad, but the money was good.'

'I'm surprised you came back.'

'The work ends when the season ends. Mr Transome was in his grave by the time we were home.'

'Tell him,' grunted Blackbeard.

I knew what he meant; it was time to tell Mr Barber the true cause of Cordelia's illness. I set about the delicate task with every ounce of tact I could summon, watching his reaction.

His eyes burned with pain, with anger and sorrow.

Not, however, with guilt.

'I did not do this – I am not the man!'

'Do you know who it might be, sir?' Blackbeard asked.

'No!' snapped Mr Barber.

A clock nearby struck the hour and he climbed out of the cab and hurried back to his work at the opera house.

'He is not our murderer,' I said. 'He was out of the country at the time.'

'Hmm,' said Blackbeard. 'If he didn't get the girl into trouble, who did? It stands to reason she was carrying on with somebody and that gives somebody a motive for bumping off her father. See if you can find out who it is, Mrs Rodd.'

Twenty-nine

IN THESE DAYS LEADING up to the trial, Mr James Betterton turned fifty and decided to celebrate his half-century by giving a grand evening reception. There was a great deal of talk about it beforehand, due to the fact that he had made a point of inviting all three of Thomas Transome's daughters. He wished the public to see that the old feud between the two families was at an end.

'Fifty, pish!' was my brother's comment. 'The man is fifty-five if he's a day, though his lovely young wife has taken years off him. And I can't help knowing that the reconciliation will do wonders for his takings at the various family box offices. It was a long fight, but the Bettertons won it hands down.'

'Still, it's kind of him to include the Transomes,' I said, 'and to make a show of it. They will need all the friends they can get if their mother is hanged.'

'My dear old boot, do try to forget about that woman, at least for one evening – a glorious evening, filled with ices and champagne and pretty young actresses!'

'I have no intention of forgetting Mrs Sarah. She is the reason I am here. There is every possibility that she is protecting one of her girls and I wish to observe them at close quarters.'

Fred had been invited to the reception, and I was attending in place of Fanny, who had gone to stay with her mother at Box Hill. The grandeur of the occasion had put me in rather a flutter; Mrs Bentley and I had spent the best part of the afternoon preparing my clothes, and I was now in an agony of elegance. My newest black silk gown was beautifully pressed, with my mother's diamond brooch twinkling at the neck. I wore my smartest (and least comfortable) shoes. Mrs B had scolded me into taking more than usual trouble with my heavy, straight, grey-streaked hair, which was now bundled smooth and tight under my very best lace cap.

The line of carriages took up all four sides of the square. Outside Mr Betterton's house, two policemen stood guard over the usual crowd of people who come to gawp at things. I must admit that my pulse fluttered with excitement as we took our places in the receiving-line that moved slowly up the staircase. There was a hum of conversation, there was music; everywhere I looked, I saw dazzle and glitter and fashion.

'Fanny will be furious about missing this,' Fred muttered beside me.

At the top of the stairs stood James and Constance Betterton. Mr Betterton looked handsome and youthful, but I had eyes only for his young wife. She wore a silk gown of palest sea-green that set off her vivid golden hair most strikingly, and a magnificent necklace of pearls and emeralds.

'What a stunner!' whispered Fred.

Constance shook the hands of her guests with the ease and grace of a duchess (I could not help recalling the house in Pentonville and her scandalous entanglement with Transome; she had discarded her old self like a snake shedding its skin).

Mr Betterton – all ablaze with happiness and pride – greeted Fred and myself, and rattled out introductions to the crowd of Bettertons alongside him. 'My oldest son, Marcus; his wife, Catherine; Edgar and his wife you know; my sons Philip and Charles.'

I moved swiftly along the line, shaking gloved hands.

If Constance had a rival, it was her stepdaughter-in-law; Maria wore diamonds in her lustrous dark hair, and the fashionable cut of her blue gown displayed the perfection of her white shoulders.

All the doors on the first floor had been thrown open, to make one large room. A small group of musicians played in one corner, while a regiment of hired waiters threaded their way through the crowd with trays of champagne.

'This must've set him back a few bob!' said Fred, gulping down one glass and immediately reaching for another. 'It's all part of his campaign to be accepted in society; he is determined to make actors respectable.'

It was certainly an interesting mixture of people. I had not expected to see anyone I knew, but found myself exchanging bows with several acquaintances, including a marchioness and a well-known liberal bishop, while Fred bowed to various members of the legal profession.

Olivia and Cordelia stood beside one of the windows. Despite the crush, there was a space around them; the same people who had shaken the hand of Maria could not quite bring themselves to acknowledge her sisters. I was sorry for them, and when my brother left my side to revel in champagne and pretty actresses, I hastened over to speak to them.

Cordelia was radiant in white; though she bore a strong resemblance to Maria, her beauty was of a different kind – more delicate, less fiery. Olivia wore rich dark red and was handsomer than I had ever seen her. Now that I knew her true parentage, however, I could not help noticing how different she looked, this cuckoo in the Transome nest.

'Isn't it frightful?' she murmured. 'I didn't in the least want to come.'

'Nor did I,' said Miss Cordelia. 'But Edgar is so kind, it would have been mean to refuse.' She had all the poise of an actress who is accustomed to the public gaze; she appeared to be fully recovered, yet she was trembling and fearful.

'You see, Mrs Rodd,' said Miss Olivia, 'to be a Transome is to be nobody. We are all Bettertons now. Maria said we mustn't wear mourning clothes, or we would spoil the party.'

'This must be an ordeal for you,' I said. 'I do think, however, that Mr Betterton is to be applauded for such a public act of generosity.'

'He has given us countenance, to be sure,' said Miss Olivia. 'He has shown the world that we are under the protection of his respectable family, and naturally we are grateful, though we've had to swallow a lot of humble pie, and it's not a taste I care for.'

'You are looking very well, Miss Transome; I hope you have forgiven me for kidnapping you.'

'Thank you, Mrs Rodd.' She coloured a little. 'You rescued me from the dreadful hole I had dug myself into, and my sister's house feels positively luxurious after that beastly tavern.'

The crowd shifted and eddied around us, and I saw that Mr Betterton was making a circuit of the room, with his wife on one arm and his daughter-in-law on the other.

'My dear young ladies!' He came up to our little group, wreathed in smiles. 'And Mrs Rodd – I trust that you are enjoying yourself, ma'am!'

'This is a splendid occasion, Mr Betterton.'

'I wanted to mark the start of a new era; my oldest son, Marcus, has just taken on Transome's old place, the Duke

241

of Cumberland's, and that brings my family up to three theatres – just look at my grey hairs!'

'Don't be nonsensical!' His wife gave him a radiant smile. 'I could swear that you look younger every day.'

'If that is true, you must take all the credit; you have granted me a new lease of life.'

This display of affection left all three Transome daughters looking pained, and I decided to change the subject. 'Has Cooper been found yet?'

'Cooper?' Mr Betterton looked blank.

'He was Tom's dresser,' said Mrs Constance, her interest quickening. 'Oh, poor man, what has happened to him?'

'He fell into drink and destitution,' said Mrs Maria. 'Olivia provided him with a decent lodging, but when we tried to claim him and bring him home, there was no sign of him.'

'It's good of you to concern yourselves,' Mr Betterton said, with suitable gravity. 'Too many faithful servants are forgotten.'

'Edgar has been searching for him in various drinking houses near to the Britannia,' said Mrs Maria. 'Without result as yet, but it won't be long; Cooper is only too well known in that neighbourhood.'

'As soon as he runs out of money,' said Miss Olivia, 'he'll be up to his old tricks again, telling tall stories for the price of a half-quartern of gin – who was where on the night of what.'

'Livvy.' Mrs Constance touched her arm briefly. 'Do please tell us when he is found; I should like to take a share of helping him.'

'Ah, my love!' Mr Betterton smiled down at his wife. 'Your heart is as golden as your hair!'

He bowed to us, then they moved away through the throng, smiling right and left.

'The man is quite besotted,' said Miss Olivia. 'That creature and her golden hair have turned his head as soft as butter, and now I must make a show of liking her.'

'Don't!' murmured Miss Cordelia.

'It's only too plain that she never truly loved Papa; she was always out for what she could get.'

'She seems to be very happy with Mr Betterton,' I said.

'As well she might, Mrs Rodd; she cares for nothing besides fame, and her doting old husband lets her have any role she wants.'

'I was impressed by her concern for Mr Cooper.'

'Let's wait and see how concerned she is when nobody's looking at her.'

The crowd around us shifted again and Mr Edgar appeared. 'Excuse me, Mrs Rodd – come along, girls – Maria wants you to have first crack at the refreshments, before the locusts descend.'

I had caught a glimpse of the lavish supper-table laid out downstairs; though it was still early, the drift towards it had already begun and would soon turn into a well-mannered stampede.

'A good idea,' I said. 'You look fatigued, Miss Cordelia, and should be sitting down.'

'I shall find you a chair,' Mr Edgar declared, laughing, 'by force, if necessary!'

Once again, I found myself thinking what a good-natured man he was; he attended to his wife's sisters with an instinctive gallantry, and his fondness for them seemed entirely genuine. If they did have to face the horror of Sarah being hanged, I would not need to worry that they would not be treated kindly (I tried to avoid thinking of how Mr Edgar would feel if the true murderer turned out to be his adored wife).

'Ah, Letty, here you are!' My brother fought his way over to where I stood. 'You must get yourself down to the supper-table before all the lobster patties have gone – but before you do, here is someone I know you are anxious to meet.'

The man he presented to me was tall and very elegantly dressed, with dark hair and fashionable side-whiskers. 'How do you do, Mrs Rodd; I am Jonathan Parrish.'

'Mr Parrish!' I saw his likeness to Olivia immediately; it seemed so glaringly obvious that I wondered if I would have noticed it without being told. 'Yes, indeed, I have been anxious to speak to you for all sorts of reasons, though perhaps this is not the place to do it.'

'An Inspector Blackbeard from Scotland Yard has been trying to contact me,' said Mr Parrish. 'I am not avoiding him; it is simply that my wife knows nothing about my encounter with that crazed clergyman.'

'It was kind of you not to press charges,' I said. 'It would only have made Mr Mallard's situation more pitiable. I hope you are quite recovered.'

'Quite recovered, thank you. My nose was not broken, only slightly bent. I told my wife a story about falling over in the street. She is frail, you see, and any sort of upset makes her ill. A policeman at the door would worry her dreadfully.'

'Naturally, I understand,' I said. 'Mr Blackbeard would be happy to meet you in any other place.'

'I shall be at the Princess Theatre on Monday morning, for a first reading of my new play. If he catches me there, I can speak with perfect freedom.'

'Thank you, Mr Parrish.'

My senses tingled with anticipation; I was intensely curious to know the truth about his night with Mrs Sarah. We exchanged bows and he left us; I watched his elegant figure as he made his way across the room. He sat down beside an old woman in a gown of glossy black silk sewn with jet beads.

'His wife,' Fred muttered in my ear.

'Surely not!'

'Looks more like his mother, don't you think? She's rolling in money, apparently, and keeps him on a pretty short string.'

He pounced upon a passing waiter to snatch two more glasses of champagne, and then hurried me downstairs for another go at the lobster patties (there was a dense crowd around the table, but Fred allowed no one to stand between him and his food, and he pushed his way through with cheerful determination). The supper was extravagant and delicious; I tried to remember as many of the dishes as I could, knowing Mrs Bentley would want every detail.

I was well satisfied with the evening's work and it was not yet done. When the food had been reduced to crumbs, the rooms upstairs were hot and noisy. My brother went off to flirt with actresses and I had a brief conversation with the liberal bishop.

It took me a few seconds to notice that something was wrong. The music stopped, a hush fell, and a space opened up in the middle of the floor. Miss Cordelia had fainted.

Maria – her face almost as white as her sister's – knelt down beside her, rubbing her hands.

I am never without my silver-topped bottle of smelling-salts, and I hastened to give it to Mrs Maria.

'Thank you; it is too hot and she was overcome.'

She waved the bottle under Miss Cordelia's nose so ineffectually that I took it back and set about restoring the young lady to her senses. In a very short time her eyelids fluttered and opened.

She whispered, in a child's voice, 'Mamma!'

Something made me look across the room, to the small group of musicians. One of them – a violinist – was staring at me, and I recognized the wasted face and black eyes of Mr Joseph Barber.

'It was certainly the heat,' I said quickly. 'She must have fresh air.'

Mr Edgar stepped forward to take the girl into his arms and bear her out of the room. Maria and I followed them up a flight of stairs to a bedchamber on the floor above, and while Cordelia lay down on top of the counterpane, I took it upon myself to open the window as wide as it would go. A breeze blew in, blissfully cooling.

'Oh, how dreadful of me!' Cordelia sat up, a little more colour in her face. 'I must apologize to Mr Betterton!'

'Nothing of the sort!' said Mr Edgar cheerily. 'He'll only want to hear that you're recovered.'

I wanted to talk about Mr Barber, and decided we would get on better without Maria's husband. 'Mr Edgar, would you be very kind and fetch a glass of wine? My dear, you really ought to rest.'

He left the room and I arranged the pillows so that Cordelia could sit up.

'You saw someone.' Maria took her sister's hand. 'Was it him?'

'Yes,' said Cordelia.

'I'm sorry. I wish I could have spared you.'

'I almost didn't know him; his hair has all gone and he is so thin!'

I did not think I had any right to break into this hurried exchange by mentioning my encounter with Joseph Barber, but watched the sisters as closely as I dared.

'I hope and pray he did not see me,' said Cordelia. 'The shame is too much to bear!'

'I know,' murmured Maria.

A look passed between them – an extraordinary look of mingled sorrow and complicity that I did not understand until much later.

Thirty

'**Y**ou had a busy evening, ma'am,' said Mr Black-beard. 'I'm obliged to you for snaffling this Parrish fellow.'

'He explained to me that he was only avoiding you to spare his wife's feelings.'

'Hmm, we'll see about that.'

It was eleven o'clock in the morning on the Monday after the Bettertons' reception, and Blackbeard and I had met at the Princess Theatre, in which I had seen James Betterton's *Hamlet*. The foyer was deserted; I peeped through a glass pane in the door to the stalls, where a circle of actors sat upon the bare stage like a constellation around Mr Betterton.

'Mrs Rodd – and I take it this is Inspector Blackbeard?' Jonathan Parrish was with us, very much as if he had been lying in wait. 'Thank you for meeting me here; shall we step outside?'

I had last seen him in evening dress, and he was every bit as elegant by day, though there were threads of grey now visible in his dark side-whiskers. He wore a green coat, beautifully cut to set off his fine figure, and a waistcoat of flowered silk that set off his very fine gold watch-chain.

'I hope we are not interrupting your work,' I said.

'They can do without me,' said Mr Parrish, with a smile. 'I am merely the man who wrote the play and my opinion counts for very little. If you don't object to it, Mrs Rodd, I keep a room nearby where we can talk comfortably.'

He led us down one of the side streets off St Martin's Lane, to a room above a shop that sold old books and maps. Though the staircase was dark and grubby, the room itself was surprisingly light and comfortable. There was a desk and chair, a well-ordered bookcase, a long sofa covered with gaily striped chintz and a small fireplace. Mr Parrish invited Blackbeard and myself to sit upon the sofa, while he sat down at his desk, flanked by the two windows.

'I like to write here,' he said. 'It is convenient for all the theatres, and I must admit that I sometimes use it as a refuge from domesticity; my wife objects to the amount of smoking I do when I'm working. She is a little older than I am and not in the best of health.'

'You know why we're here, sir,' said Blackbeard.

'You wish to know about the night of Tom Transome's murder,' said Mr Parrish. 'I assume you already know that Sarah Transome's so-called confession contains a number of untruths. I did not come forward sooner because my wife and I left for the Continent the very next day, and spent the winter in Nice. We have only lately returned.'

'When did you hear about it, then?' asked Blackbeard. 'I dunno how you managed to miss it, sir. That murder was everywhere – I daresay they heard of it on the moon!'

Mr Parrish reddened angrily. 'You think I stayed away like a damned coward, knowing I could help her? I only heard the fine details of the business when we got home.'

'I find that hard to believe, sir.'

'Nevertheless, it's the truth. There are plenty of newspapers available in the south of France, but our villa was miles away from Nice and horribly isolated; my wife wanted total seclusion. We had no visitors, no newspapers, not a whiff of the world beyond our walls. My wife wanted all my attention, every moment of my time. She is exceedingly jealous of Sarah. For all I know, she found out about the murder and deliberately kept it from me. I dread to think what she'll do when she finds out about my assignation in Cremorne Gardens – well, that can't be helped now. What do you want to know? Everything, I suppose.'

'You can trust the inspector to be discreet,' I said (a little shocked by the dismal picture he painted of his marriage). 'In your opinion, Mr Parrish, did Sarah Transome kill her husband?'

'She could have done it after we parted. I mean, it's possible. I know her well, however, and I've never seen any sign of such savagery in her nature.'

'At what time did you part company with Mrs Sarah?'

'I'd say five in the morning, or thereabouts.'

'Hmm,' said Blackbeard, 'that's not what we were told, sir. We'd better go back to the beginning.'

He rattled out a brief and rather crudely worded precis of everything we knew (or thought we knew) up to the moment of their parting.

Mr Parrish listened intently, and was startled to hear the identity of our witness. 'What, that little tart who was canoodling with Mr Parkinson of Cheapside? I beg your pardon for my language, Mrs Rodd. Sarah and I were amused and I wanted to put the pair of them into a play. The girl was as tipsy as a washerwoman! They were both sound asleep and snoring when we left.'

'You left?' I was dismayed; so much of our case depended upon Mrs Sarah being there for the entire night. 'At what time was this?'

He eyed us thoughtfully for a moment. 'Very well, you may have the facts, though they are not edifying. It was about two in the morning and we came – here.'

'Ah,' said Blackbeard.

'Our witness claims you stayed in Cremorne Gardens for the whole night,' I said, 'and were still present the following morning.'

'We were not. I certainly wasn't,' Mr Parrish said firmly. 'Your tipsy little witness saw someone else entirely.'

'Where did Mrs Sarah go after leaving here at five?'

'I have no idea. She didn't look as if she were planning to commit a murder.'

'Did you like Mr Transome, sir?' Blackbeard asked.

'Did I like him? I don't see what that has to do with anything but, of course, you have to look into the possibility that I am the guilty party. I can only assure you that I'm not. Transome and I were close associates at one time; he employed me as manager of his American tour and I liked him enormously. It was only later that we fell out.'

'You had a love affair with his wife,' said Blackbeard.

Mr Parrish winced at his bluntness. 'Yes, that was the beginning of my association with Sarah. A child was born – Olivia – and Transome was happy to acknowledge her as his own. It was probably the most decent thing he ever did. Unfortunately, Olivia was the reason for our eventual falling-out. A year or so after she was born, my wife found out about her. We had no children, she longed for a child, and so I tried to claim her back. Transome refused – again, to his credit, for my wife offered him a handsome sum of money.'

I was shocked that he could speak of this heartless transaction so casually.

'You continued to take an interest in her,' I said. 'Miss Olivia recalls meeting you when she was a child; she says you took her to have tea with a lady.' (I managed not to say that the lady was 'old' and that Olivia had assumed she was his mother.)

251

'My wife wished to see her,' said Mr Parrish. 'I didn't think Olivia would remember it, for she was a tiny thing – not more than two or three years old, a bright-eyed little pixie – we were both quite enchanted.'

His voice softened when he spoke of his daughter and I pitied his wife; I know too well the sorrow of being denied children, and I have the consolation of my dear nephews and nieces; Mrs Parrish had no such consolation, and Olivia was the one thing she could not buy.

'I think you are still interested in your daughter,' I said impulsively. 'And I'm glad of it; she is so dreadfully unhappy! She is also headstrong, however; did you hear of her adventure at the Britannia Theatre?'

He was surprised by this, and discomfited. 'That is something else I missed while I was abroad; I knew nothing about it until after Olivia had left the frightful place, but believe me, Mrs Rodd, if I had known … '

'Mrs Transome was seen to give you something,' said Blackbeard, 'while you was in the gardens.'

'Sarah was returning my letters,' said Mr Parrish. 'And I returned hers at the same time; she was afraid they could be used against her. That Noonan girl had started making noises about Transome getting himself a divorce, and she was looking for proof of Sarah's adultery. If she'd had her way, Sarah's name and reputation would have been ruined. I was once a student of the law, however, and I was aware – as Noonan was not – that Transome would never be granted a divorce because he had acknowledged another man's child as his own.'

I remembered that Miss Noonan quarrelled with Mr Transome on the day he was murdered, and wondered if this had been the cause. 'Is there anything more you can tell us, Mr Parrish?'

'Not at present. In case you are puzzling over whether to believe me or the tipsy Miss LaFaye, you really ought to talk to Mr Parkinson, the well-known grocer of Cheapside.'

'Thank you, sir,' said Blackbeard. 'I have already done so.'

Mr Parrish looked at him for a moment, and then said, with an effort, 'She didn't do it, and if you are working to establish her innocence, I want to help you.'

'Would you be willing to testify at the trial?' I asked.

'I wouldn't say I was "willing", Mrs Rodd; my wife will be beside herself. She knows nothing about my assignation that night with Sarah, she will hate hearing of it in public – all the same, if it's the right thing to do, I will do it.' He was quiet again for a long moment. 'Sarah is obviously protecting someone; I assume you have spoken to her daughters.'

'I cannot imagine her going to her death for the sake of anyone else,' I said. 'And two of her daughters had very public disagreements with Mr Transome before he died.'

'You'll have to go further back,' said Mr Parrish. 'Something happened at the time of the fire, or shortly after. God knows what it was, but Sarah and Maria have been at odds ever since.'

'Mr Transome forced Sarah into retirement, and made Maria his leading lady.'

'Yes, but there was something more. During our notorious night at the pleasure gardens, Sarah said she'd had a monstrous row with Maria on the night of the fire.'

I was confused. 'At the theatre? But Maria wasn't there—'

'Oh, she was there, all right,' said Mr Parrish. 'She was very young at the time, but not too young to be infatuated with Frank Fitzwarren.'

'You think she shot him?'

'Sarah might think so. She mentioned Transome's dresser – Cooper – and reckoned he knew more than he was letting on. You should talk to him.'

'Mr Cooper's gone a-wandering,' said Blackbeard. 'I'll be very happy to talk to him when he turns up. In the meantime, sir, I'm obliged to you for your help.'

Thirty-one

'COULD THIS NOT HAVE waited, Inspector? It is so vexatious to be interrupted in the middle of a scene.'

'Can't be helped, ma'am,' said Blackbeard.

'I can give you a quarter of an hour and no more.'

Maria Betterton received us in her dressing room like a god plucked out of the air in mid-flight; she wore a simple, everyday gown of sober green, made dramatic by her flowing masses of black hair. She sat down at one end of the long couch and gestured to me to sit at the other. Blackbeard stood at attention in front of the fireplace.

'I am most impressed by your new theatre, Mrs Betterton,' I said. 'The last time I saw the King's, it was in a very sorry state.'

'We spent a great deal of money, more than we intended. My husband insisted there could be no cutting of corners. He said it must be done properly or not at all.'

'It is magnificent.'

'Thank you. Does this visitation concern my mother?'

'No, ma'am,' said Blackbeard. 'It's about the night of the fire.'

'The fire? I thought that was all settled. It is just as my mother told you – I was at home in Ham Common with my sisters.'

'No, ma'am, you wasn't.'

'I – I beg your pardon?' She was rattled, and could not hide it. 'Mrs Rodd, what is this? You have heard my account of that night. I was under the impression that you believed me.'

'I've since heard other accounts, Mrs Betterton.' I spoke softly, yet wished her to know that I meant to have the truth. 'You were seen at the theatre after the performance, and heard to have an argument with your mother, concerning Frank Fitzwarren.'

She was silent for several minutes. When she spoke, she was quiet and matter-of-fact, 'Cooper told you.'

'Cooper has not yet been found. You must forgive me for saying this, but I now see why you have been so anxious to find him.'

'I hate to think of him spreading more scandal about my family,' said Maria. 'He is given to drinking, and it makes him indiscreet. My father-in-law doesn't care for scandal; I live by his standards these days. If it's at all possible, could you keep this from him, and from Edgar?'

She looked at me, but before I could reply, Blackbeard said, 'It's too late for that, ma'am. Let's have the truth now, if you please.'

There was a short silence, while Maria Betterton considered her reply.

'Very well; I did not tell you the truth.' Her manner was calm, but her breath quickened. 'I was attempting to save my reputation. The events of that night were shameful to me, and I did not think the whole truth would make much difference to your investigation. I am still convinced that my father murdered Frank Fitzwarren.'

'That's by the by,' said Blackbeard. 'We'll start again. You were at your father's theatre on the night it burned down and Fitzwarren was murdered.'

'Yes,' said Maria. 'We had planned to run away together – Frank and I, that very night – but everything went wrong. I had lately heard of my mother's disgraceful association with the man I loved. I was wounded, I was angry.'

'You were very young,' I said, 'to experience such volcanic emotions.'

'I grew up with volcanic emotions, Mrs Rodd; I don't know any other kind.'

'Do you remember how you heard of the affair?'

'It was more that I overheard it. Some of my fellow-actresses were gossiping too loudly. At first, I refused to believe it. I had made an idol of Frank, as girls do with their first loves. He couldn't bear to lie to me, however, and when I confronted him, told me it was all true. I was broken-hearted, and ended our engagement.'

'When was this, then?' asked Blackbeard.

'A week or so before the fire,' said Maria. 'Frank truly loved me and persuaded me to forgive him; to start afresh, and to end everything with my mother. I was to wait for him in the room of a friend who lived nearby, where we had a carriage waiting. He did not come and that was why I went to the theatre.'

'You could not have known,' I said, 'that Fitzwarren would be going on as an understudy that night.'

'No. I was most upset to find him still there, and thoroughly intoxicated.'

'Was your mother at the theatre when you arrived there?' I asked.

'I don't think so; my mother appeared while I was upbraiding poor Frank.' Maria was aiming for queenly dignity, yet I sensed the sorrowful ghost of that broken-hearted girl. 'She turned her anger upon me. My mother was jealous of me; my own mother, who ought to have been concerned that her young daughter was planning to run away to Gretna Green! She told me that my feelings for Frank were childish and worthless, and that she was the one he truly loved.'

'Did Fitzwarren defend you, or did he take your mother's side?'

'I don't think he was capable of taking anyone's side. My mother and I exchanged bitter words that could never be forgotten, never mind forgiven. Afterwards – after Frank vanished and everyone assumed he had deserted both of us – she did attempt to make amends.'

'Do you mean when she helped you to elope with Mr Edgar?'

'I – yes.' Her beautiful eyes moved between Blackbeard and myself, impossible to read. 'But we were never truly reconciled. As far as I was concerned, I had no mother. It is a mother's duty to protect her child. My mother could have saved me, and she did nothing until it was too late.'

'Your mother thinks you shot the man,' said Blackbeard.

'Me?' A wintry smile twitched at her lips. 'I suppose because she left the theatre before I did. I left very soon after.'

'Where did you go, ma'am?'

'The carriage was still waiting. Instead of running away to get married, I used it to take me home to Pericles Cottage.'

'You reckon it was your father who done the murder,' said Blackbeard. 'Did you see him do it?'

'No, as I told you, I did not know Frank was dead until you discovered his body. I blame my father because I've had all too much experience of his violent rages. His jealousy turned him into a madman.'

'And you're sure, are you, that it wasn't your mother that done it?'

'Quite sure,' said Maria. 'He was still alive when she left.'

'And what of the fire?' I asked.

'Papa set it himself, obviously.'

'I'd like to know why he made such a mess of it,' said Blackbeard. 'According to Miss Olivia, he did it to get his hands on the insurance money – but he nearly killed himself doing it.'

'Something went wrong, I suppose,' said Maria. 'I have wondered if Frank knew of the plan, or if he tried to stop it. This is mere speculation, however, since I was not present.'

'Were you aware that your father was entertaining one of the dancers on that night?'

'How elegantly you put it,' said Maria drily. 'No, I was not. When you find Cooper, he'll tell you that I tried to see Papa, and he stopped me; he stood before the door like the angel with the flaming sword. That's when I left the theatre.'

'Were you aware that Fitzwarren had asked Mr Betterton for employment?'

'Not at the time. I only heard years later. I think Frank might have told my father that he planned to leave, after I had gone. If he did, my father would have been beside himself with rage – but that is another question you should ask Cooper. It's my belief that Cooper knows my father was guilty, and that's why he is hiding now.'

'Stick to the facts, ma'am,' said Blackbeard. 'Did you see your father start the fire?'

'I did not.'

'Could Fitzwarren have done it?'

'It's perfectly possible,' said Maria. 'I can't give any facts, Mr Blackbeard. You will have to take my word that Frank would never have set the fire. It was not in his character; my mother will say exactly the same, if she really has started to tell the truth for a change.'

I was struck, once again, by her anger with her mother; eleven years and a happy marriage had not softened her. 'Do you recall the last time you saw Fitzwarren?'

She softened now. 'He was slumped upon a stool in the prompt corner. Ben Tully was feeding him a half-pint of coffee.'

'Mr Tully?' I was confused. 'Are you sure? He claims not to have gone into the theatre until after the fire started, when he went to rescue your father.'

'Do you think I could forget such a spectacle?' Maria asked sharply. 'You may not approve of the fact that I was planning to elope with Frank but I was very much in love with him, and my whole world lay in ruins. That final picture of him is burned into my memory for all eternity.'

There was a rap on the door; Mr Edgar put his head round it. 'You're needed onstage, my dear – beg your pardon, Mrs Rodd, Inspector.'

'Well now, ma'am,' said Blackbeard, once we had left the theatre. 'If Maria Betterton is to be believed, Sarah didn't kill Fitzwarren, and nor did she.'

'I'm prepared to believe Transome committed that first murder,' I said. 'The great puzzle is – who killed Transome?'

'We're left with the daughters; I'd better have another go at busting their alibis.'

'And you must leave me to speak with Mr Tully,' I said. 'He's had a long time to work on his story. Getting at the truth is going to be a delicate operation.'

Thirty-two

THE POLICEMAN KNOCKED ON my door shortly after four o'clock the following afternoon.

'Mr Blackbeard sends his compliments, ma'am, and he'd like the pleasure of your company, if convenient to you.'

'Yes, of course. Where is he?'

'Limehouse, ma'am.'

The plain police carriage waited at the kerb and I climbed into it with my heart beating high, for I knew that this hasty (and typically mysterious) summons meant the inspector had made a discovery. It was a long drive, which carried me through the city streets, down to the river and then several miles to the east of St Paul's Cathedral. Limehouse was known as a 'rough' neighbourhood, teeming with foreign sailors, rope-makers, sailmakers, ship's chandlers and coal barges; a mixture of commerce and crime. In Limehouse you could board one of the great steamers heading out to the Continent – and you could also get your head bashed in a dark alley.

From the safety of the carriage, I looked out at the forest of masts on the river, glimpsed in the gaps between the soot-encrusted buildings. We stopped, finally, outside a public house, built so close to the bank that the water lapped and swirled behind it. The establishment, though not the kind usually frequented by the widows of arch-deacons, appeared respectable enough.

Blackbeard was waiting.

'I'm obliged to you for coming, Mrs Rodd.'

'Don't mention it, Inspector – what have you got for me?'

'A dead body,' said Blackbeard. 'It was found in the mud at low tide, and I must warn you, it ain't a pretty sight.'

Without another word, he led me through the bar and into a kind of wooden lean-to at the very back of the house. The scant furnishings had been pushed against the walls to accommodate a large table, upon which lay the dead body.

There is a terrible stillness to a corpse that seems to make it the centre of all the stillness in the world. This poor creature was bloated and battered, and covered with a thick layer of mud.

'You know him,' said Blackbeard.

'It's Cooper.'

'Yes.'

Mr Transome's faithful dresser had gone to his long home. I said a silent prayer for his soul, and then moved closer to examine his corpse in more detail.

'How long would you say he was in the river, Inspector?'

'Two days, maybe three,' said Blackbeard. 'Not longer.'

'The body is swollen and discoloured; is that simply the effect of the water, or did you find any signs of injury?'

'I didn't see any, but it's hard to tell through the mud; I'll wait for the doctor's opinion.'

'What is your opinion, Mr Blackbeard?'

'Cooper was a drinking man,' he said, 'and I've pulled a few of those out of the river in my time. He could easily have fallen in by accident. He could have thrown himself into it deliberately. Or someone could have pushed him.'

'Murder. Is that likely?'

'You see how it looks, ma'am: it's another death we can't blame on Mrs Sarah.'

Night had fallen by the time we reached the prison. It was closed to all visitors, but this did not trouble Mr Blackbeard. He growled out a few orders, and Mrs Sarah appeared shortly afterwards, flanked by her husband and a wardress.

'Well, well, Mr Mallard,' said Blackbeard. 'Don't you ever go home?'

'I have a perfect right to hear what you have to say to my wife, Inspector.'

'All right, but we'll get on quicker if you don't interrupt.'

We were in a small room close to the main gate, minimally furnished with a few chairs and a table, and lit by a single oil lamp on a high shelf. Mrs Sarah, in her accustomed black dress, was a very picture of self-possession, but she was also watchful and cagey.

Her expression did not change when Mr Blackbeard told her about Cooper.

'I'm very sorry to hear it; he was a good man.'

'He was known to be a talker,' said Blackbeard. 'In particular, about your family, ma'am.'

'Oh?'

'It's my belief that someone drowned the man to stop him talking.'

'I suppose it's possible,' said Mrs Sarah. 'Anyway, you know it can't have been me.'

'What do you reckon he was talking about, ma'am?'

'I haven't the least idea; is this another attempt to accuse me of being innocent?'

'Don't!' Mr Mallard said, with more vigour and firmness in his bearing than I had ever seen in him. 'This hard, bitter character is not your true self, and I beg you to drop it – for the love of God, if not for me!'

'As I've told you a hundred times, what you call my true self *is* hard and bitter.'

'I can take a guess at what Cooper was saying when in his cups,' Blackbeard went on, as if he had not heard. 'I reckon it was the same thing Mr Jonathan Parrish let slip to me, ma'am.'

'Oh?'

'Which is that your daughter Maria was present on the night of the fire, and the two of you was heard to have an argument.'

'Maria?' She was defensive, she was prickly, and (I thought) cornered. 'Have you spoken to her? What did she say?'

'Never mind,' said Blackbeard. 'I want to hear what you say, ma'am. The truth, if you please. I've had enough of being lied to.'

'Heaven knows, so have I,' said Mr Mallard.

She gave him a look of affectionate exasperation. 'My dear, you go on about the truth as if you liked it, but when you actually hear it, you don't like it at all!'

'Mrs Mallard,' I said, 'would it help you to speak freely if your husband left the room?'

'No – I'm so dreadfully tired of all the covering up! Yes, Maria was at the theatre on the night of the fire. I found her there when I returned from Manchester Square in search of Frank.'

There was a silence as we all took this in.

'I lied to you, Mrs Rodd; my daughter had learnt of my entanglement with Frank. She was passionately angry and dreadfully wounded, and to my eternal shame I shrieked at her that Frank did not love her.' Her gaze dropped down to her lap. 'She shrieked back that he loved her more than he loved me – and so on, and so on. You have seen how Maria turns every situation into a drama.'

'She says she was all set to elope with Fitzwarren,' said Blackbeard. 'Did you know about that?'

Mrs Sarah glanced at her husband. 'I knew absolutely nothing about it, until that night. And before you ask, yes, I was very angry with both of them. Frank tried to stop us quarrelling, but – oh, poor man, he cut such a ludicrous figure! He was still in his costume and ridiculously drunk. Maria berated him like a fishwife, and she was still screaming when I left the theatre.'

'What time was this?' asked Blackbeard.

'I couldn't say precisely. I was too overwrought to take notice of the time.'

'Well, that's awkward, ma'am. If this ain't another falsehood, you confessed to at least one murder that you didn't commit.'

Once more, she flicked a glance at Mr Mallard. 'I did not kill Frank Fitzwarren.'

'You were afraid it was Maria,' I said.

'I was convinced of it. I simply could not believe Tom was capable of murder. I ought to have listened to my daughter – my poor daughter!' She was shaken; I had never seen her so upset. 'I hardly know how to tell you the next part of this story, for you will see what a bad mother I have been. Some weeks after Frank made off – or so we thought – Tom complained to me that his Rosalind was "getting fat". It was like a mist clearing from my eyes. I took a proper look at Maria and saw the reason for myself.'

'She was in the family way, was she?' asked Blackbeard.

Mrs Sarah nodded and her eyes glazed over with tears. 'Frank always swore to me that he never did more than kiss Maria's hand. God forgive me, I cursed him for being a liar and a libertine. Murphy and I took her to a cottage in the countryside. The poor baby – a boy – was born early, and died.' She was quiet for a long stretch. 'I'm not trying to make excuses for myself; I simply want to explain the reasons why I behaved as I did. Firstly, I burned with shame that I had ever loved the man who ruined my child. And my heart broke for Maria, in all her pain and sorrow. It was my opinion that she would recover quickest if she returned to her work at the theatre; she is so like Tom!'

'Was her father very angry with her?' I asked.

'Oh, yes. Without Maria, he couldn't open the new theatre. In the event, the loss of the poor baby worked out rather well for him, and he had the grace to be aware of this. He forgave her wrongdoing with Frank and showed her nothing but kindness, and the play was a vast success. The great rift between Tom and his golden girl didn't happen until she married Edgar.'

'You helped them, I believe?'

'I liked Edgar and I saw that Maria was in love with him, but holding back because she was ashamed of her past history. I took the risk of telling him, having a sense of his basic decency, and was most touched by his reaction; he said what was past was past and his feelings were unchanged.'

'Let us be clear,' Mr Mallard cut in eagerly. 'You claim you did not murder Fitzwarren, but took the blame because you believed your daughter had done it?'

'Yes, my dear,' said Mrs Sarah. 'That's about the size of it.'

'I knew it! I knew in my bones that Heaven could not have allowed me to love a woman who had slain her adulterous lover!'

'What about Transome?' demanded Blackbeard. 'Did you think that was Maria too?'

Mrs Sarah sighed, looking now very weary and a great deal older. 'No, of course not; I killed my husband. And he killed Frank – you can't accuse my daughter of a single thing!'

She would tell us no more and the interview was at an end.

Blackbeard and I left the prison in silence; he was wrapped in contemplation, and I was waiting impatiently for his verdict.

He said nothing until he had assisted me into the police carriage, in which he was sending me home.

And then he finally said, 'Lies, Mrs Rodd! Lies upon lies! And that woman is the worst of the lot. I daresay you're more convinced than ever that she's innocent.'

'Yes, aren't you?'

'I don't know what I think. Next time you're saying your prayers, ma'am, you might ask for one more clue to point us in the right direction.'

'I'll be happy to do so, Mr Blackbeard,' I said. 'But there's nothing to stop you making the request yourself – your prayers are just as good as mine!'

Thirty-three

'**Y**OU LOOK FAIRLY WORN out, ma'am,' Mrs Bentley told me next morning. 'I'll bet you didn't get a wink of sleep. This case has given you nothing but worry!'

'I'm afraid you're right; try as I will, I cannot make the pieces fit together.'

We were sitting at the kitchen table, in the process of making soup from a ham bone (my dear mother used to call it 'thrifty' soup; you can throw in any odds and ends without spoiling the taste, because everything comes out tasting of ham). The bone, along with two rather disreputable-looking onions, was simmering merrily on the range, while Mrs B and I cut out all the usable parts from a sorry collection of leftover potatoes and cabbages.

'You reckon Mrs Sarah is innocent of murdering her husband, and covering up for one of her daughters,' said Mrs Bentley. 'The question is – which daughter?'

'I have my doubts about all three of them.'

'You like 'em, that's the trouble.'

'It's more that I pity them; there is a sadness in that family that I sensed before Mr Transome was murdered. I wish I could put my finger on it. Maria is my most likely suspect at the moment; I have seen the violence of her emotions and her anger with her father.'

Mrs Bentley chopped busily; she thought best when her hands were occupied. 'Poor girl, I don't blame her in the least; whatever sins she committed, she paid for them many times over. It's no wonder she was so upset when the same thing happened to her sister.'

'The same thing?'

'Out of them three girls, two got themselves into trouble. It just goes to show that the theatre's a wicked place.'

This was a striking observation, but before I had time to think about it, we were interrupted by a loud knocking on the door. It was a policeman, bearing a note from Blackbeard; my heart rose up as if I had been a girl waiting for a love-letter.

Dear Mrs Rodd

Yr help wd be appreciated.

Yrs respectfully
T. Blackbeard

'He's been at it again,' said Blackbeard. 'He started a punch-up in a public house called the Duke of Buckingham by Villiers Wharf.'

'I did not do anything of the kind; this is persecution and slander!'

The inspector turned his sorrowful gaze upon the thin, trembling, dishevelled figure of Titus Mallard. 'You'll oblige me by keeping your mouth shut, Mr Mallard. I thought one night in a cell would be enough for you!'

We were in a police station in the old Hungerford Market (since obliterated by Charing Cross railway station) and Mr Mallard looked almost demented; his scanty hair hung in grey strings and one of his sleeves was torn at the shoulder.

'I will not be silenced! I went to that place in pursuit of justice, which you don't seem to care for in the slightest! I begged the officer to search for Mrs Quackington and the man arrested me!'

'Mrs who?' I tried not to show my dismay; had the poor man finally lost his reason?

'No, no, that's his professional name, as I was trying to explain—'

'You can go back in that cell, sir, if you won't keep quiet!' Blackbeard turned his back on the stricken clergyman to face me. 'I hope you can get some sense out of his ramblings, Mrs Rodd; the desk sergeant says he spent half the night shouting.'

'That's because I was drunk,' said Mr Mallard.

'*Drunk?*' I was horrified.

'I think I also sang some hymns.'

'Mr Mallard, what on earth has got into you?'

'I'll give you the full story, from the beginning,' said Mr Mallard, 'and then I would like to see my wife.'

Blackbeard took us into a small office, its walls lined with books and ledgers, where there was just space enough for the three of us to cram around the table.

'It was Cooper, you see,' said Mr Mallard. 'I wanted to know what he had been saying, and to whom he had been saying it. I believe he was murdered by the same person who murdered Transome, and this person must be found as a matter of urgency, to prove Sarah's innocence.'

'I wish you had not acted alone,' I said. 'Did you go anywhere else, apart from the Duke of Buckingham?'

'I visited several public houses in the district, and solicited information in exchange for gin; with hindsight I realize that I shouldn't have tried to match them drink for drink. I am not accustomed to it and was thoroughly intoxicated.'

'Did you hear anything useful?'

'Indeed I did,' said Mr Mallard. 'Several men told me I should look for a man named Samuel Watkins, who was known to be Cooper's closest friend and companion. He is a comical actor and goes by the professional name of "Mrs Quackington"; I understand that he once played old women in the pantomime. Before I got into the upset at the Duke of Buckingham, I had learnt that Watkins could be found in the King George, next door to the Britannia Theatre. You must search for him, Inspector.'

'Let's hear about the upset,' said Blackbeard. 'You punched one fellow and threatened another with a wine bottle. You attempted to attack a police officer with a chair. What was that all about?'

'Something quite different, I assure you. A personal matter.' Mr Mallard stiffened proudly. 'They were singing a certain popular song about my wife.'

Not for the first time I marvelled that one man could change so much. 'My dear Mr Mallard, this is no way to help your wife! Please promise that you'll try to stay out of trouble.'

'You must speak to this Watkins – discover who murdered Cooper—'

'Yes, yes, sir,' said Blackbeard. 'You leave it to me. Chasing after murderers is my business, not yours.'

Mr Mallard was unshaven and agitated, and in no fit state to see his wife. I put him in a cab to take him back to his lodging in Highbury, hoping he would get some rest and collect his scattered wits.

'Well?' I was impatient and excited, and pounced on Blackbeard the moment we were alone. 'What do you think?'

'He's definitely got a sniff of something,' said Black-beard. 'If you'd care for a stroll, Mrs Rodd, I'd like a word with this Watkins fellow.'

The King George, one of the public houses that flanked the Britannia Theatre, was deserted. I looked up and down the ramshackle street and saw not a sign of life; the only movement came from the heaps of litter – playbills, oyster-shells, scraps of broken glass – that stirred in the breeze from the river.

Blackbeard hammered on the door and shouted, 'Police!'

'There is no one here,' I said.

'Oh, they're here, all right,' said Blackbeard.

Sure enough, after a few more minutes of silence, we heard scrabblings and footsteps within, and the door opened a couple of inches to reveal a head of frowsty grey hair and a grizzled, unshaven chin.

'Mr Blackbeard!'

He made as if to shut the door, but Blackbeard planted his boot across the threshold.

'Don't fret, Harry, it's not you I'm after today. Me and this lady want to talk to a fellow by the name of Samuel Watkins.'

'Who?'

'We were told we'd find him here.'

'Never heard of him!'

'Harry's a fence in a small way, Mrs Rodd; that's why he's nervous,' said Blackbeard (managing to sound both conversational and menacing). 'He thinks I'll find stolen property – which I might, if I get riled enough to start looking for it.'

The heavy, scarred wooden door swung wide open at once.

'Just like *The Arabian Nights*!' There was a very faint glint of jocularity in Blackbeard's pebble-coloured eyes. 'What does that Ali Baba fellow say?'

'Do you mean, "Open Sesame"?'

'That's it, ma'am – the magic words!'

I stepped through the door and into the public bar. The air in here had an unpleasant reek of stale tobacco and the dregs of beer. Though the windows were shuttered and the room was in shadow, I saw that every surface was crowded with pint pots of common earthenware and bleared, misshapen glasses.

The grizzled Harry hurriedly smoothed his hair, pulled on a black jacket and took down one of the shutters; a dusty shaft of sunlight slanted across the room and lit up the remains of the night before.

'Sam's still asleep. He sleeps under the bar, and does certain little jobs for me in return.'

'Wake him up,' said Blackbeard.

My heart sank a little when our potential witness shuffled out from under the mahogany bar; he was rumpled and stained, dazed from sleep, and his hands shook.

'Give him a drink,' said Harry. 'It stops the shaking.'

It was painful to see the eagerness with which Mr Watkins grabbed his first glass of gin. He gulped down several more glasses in rapid succession, until he had taken the edge from his craving and had attention to spare for us. He was painfully thin, with plentiful dark hair and the ruins of good looks.

'We are making enquiries into the death of Mr Cooper,' I said. 'And you were a good friend of his, I understand.'

'I knew Charlie Cooper for the best part of twenty years,' said Mr Watkins. 'We met during my time in the theatrical profession. I'm retired now on account of the shakes, but I was once well known for my Mrs Quackington act. You might have seen me.'

'Did you see Cooper on the night he died?' asked Blackbeard.

'Yes – he had a bit of cash, and stood me a couple of drinks.'

'How did he seem to you?' I asked. 'Was anything troubling him?'

'Just the usual,' said Mr Watkins. 'There always came a point when he started weeping over Tom Transome and saying he had no more reason to live.'

'Do you think he committed suicide?' Blackbeard asked.

'That's what I assumed.'

'Can you remember the very last time you saw him?'

'It was a Sunday, two days before he was pulled out of the river,' said Mr Watkins. 'We didn't spend the whole night in each other's company. I had to collect the pots.'

'Was he alone?' I asked. 'Or did he have company at any point?'

'He was with a woman,' said Mr Watkins. 'She got him well and truly drunk, and they left together.'

'A woman?' I dared not look at the inspector, for fear of betraying my excitement. 'Can you describe her?'

'I didn't get much of a sight of her,' said Mr Watkins. 'She was all wrapped up in a cloak, and a veil over her face.'

'I remember her,' Harry cut in. 'She looked young, with a fine figure.'

I felt a little sick; this could only have been one of the Transome sisters. 'Did you see her face?'

'No, no, she kept that covered,' said Mr Watkins. 'But I heard her voice. The way she spoke, and the way she bore herself, left me in no doubt that she was on the stage.'

Thirty-four

'WE'RE GETTING ON, Mrs Rodd!' Blackbeard was brisk, if not cheerful. 'I'm of the opinion that one murder will lead us to the others.'

'I believe Mrs Sarah was telling the truth about the night of the fire,' I said. 'She didn't know that Fitzwarren had wronged Maria so dreadfully, not at that stage.'

'Hmm,' said Blackbeard. 'Might have been someone else.'

'I beg your pardon?'

'The father of that baby.'

'No! I refuse to believe Maria would behave so shamefully.'

'She was very young, ma'am.'

'She was a sinner, Inspector, but she was never depraved. I'd be prepared to swear there was no man but Frank Fitzwarren – and I'm very much afraid that she killed him.'

'And then she bumped off Cooper, to keep him quiet?'

'You know it's perfectly possible.'

Blackbeard stiffened, put his hands behind his back and sank into deep thought. I knew better than to interrupt him. We had left the public house and were stood beside a cab-rank on the Strand, and the inspector was as still as the stillness at the centre of a wheel.

Eventually, he said, 'I'd like to hear the truth about that fire, before we lose any more witnesses. Mrs Maria said

Tully was present before the fire took hold, and Tully says he wasn't."

'I will speak to him.'

'Thank you, ma'am,' said Blackbeard. 'Make sure you put the screws on.'

'You did not leave the theatre immediately after the performance, Mr Tully; you did not return only after the fire had started.'

Actor that he was, he could not hide his dismay. 'As I told you, I can't be entirely sure – my memory of the night is very imperfect—'

'I beg your pardon, but that simply will not do.'

'N-no?'

'No, Mr Tully. You may let me in or tell me on the doorstep, but I will have the truth.'

The afternoon was warm and I saw that he had been working in his little patch of garden; he had hastily put his coat on over a coarse apron with the handle of a trowel sticking out of the pocket.

He bit his lip nervously and stood aside to let me into his house. I marched into the drawing room – a mirror of my own, a few houses along – and sat myself down on the faded brocade sofa. Mr Tully gently pushed one of the cats out of the way to sit in the easy chair.

'I am not here to accuse you of any crime,' I said, softening my manner. 'I'm sure you would like to help Mrs Sarah.'

'Oh – yes.'

'I am now in a position to refresh your memory of that night, Mr Tully.' Briefly, never taking my eyes from his face, I related what I had heard from Sarah and Maria.

He was silent for several minutes afterwards.

'I do remember more than I admitted,' he said softly. 'I heard Sarah and her daughter having an impassioned argument about young Fitzwarren. They both appealed to him to stand up for them. He was so drunk that he could barely speak. It was the custom when an understudy went on – to stand him drinks and pour them into him, almost by force.'

'The more I think of him,' I said, 'the sorrier I feel for that young man! If he had not gone onstage that night, he would have been halfway to Gretna Green with Maria, long before Sarah came back to the theatre.'

'He was a decent young fellow,' said Mr Tully. 'I wish with all my heart that the other actors had left him alone. I ran out to get him a cup of hot coffee from the stall nearby. It helped bring him around a little.'

'Did you know of his plan to elope with Maria?' I asked.

'I had no idea, though he said Maria's name as soon as he could say anything. As far as I knew, he was expected in Manchester Square. I offered to help him out of his costume. He refused.'

'Was Fitzwarren alive when you went to the Fox and Grapes?'

'Yes.'

'And when you came back to the theatre?'

Mr Tully opened his mouth, but could not speak. His face, so expressive, was stricken and imploring.

'Who was present, Mr Tully? What did you see?'

'I – I—'

'It is too late to protect yourself,' I said gently, 'or anyone else.'

'I told the police that I went back after the fire had taken hold,' said Mr Tully. 'That wasn't true. Cooper came to fetch me, in a terrible state of agitation. He said, "Ben – thank God – I knew I'd find you here – you must come at once." I followed him back to the theatre. It was well after midnight by this time. Sarah and Maria had gone, and so had the little dancer, Miss Fenton. I found only Tom Transome and – and the dead body of Frank Fitzwarren.'

'You are certain he was dead?'

'Oh, dear me, yes, there was no doubt whatsoever. He lay face-down on the stage. The back of his head was bloody – oh, God, there was so much blood!' Mr Tully's lips quivered. 'Cooper was all a-tremble, but Tom was as cool as you like. He said, "She has done this. Sarah did this."'

'And did you believe him?'

'No,' said Mr Tully. 'I cried out something like, "This was Maria" – for I had seen the argument and knew her passionate nature. I knew Tom would do anything to protect her, but all he said was, "Never mind that now. Help me, or we are all ruined."'

'And what did he mean by that?'

'He wanted me to help him cover up the crime. Cooper was in on it too. The three of us, under Tom's direction, dragged Fitzwarren down the stairs to the old cistern under the stage. It was no easy task; the trapdoor was heavy and had not been lifted for years. Cooper was weeping and babbling about the blood; the pool of blood on the stage, the trail of blood down the stairs. Tom said something like, "I'll see to it," and then he sent us both out of the building and I went back to the Fox and Grapes. And the rest is more or less what I told you. Someone said the King's was burning; I knew Tom was still inside. And so on.'

Mr Tully sighed and was silent.

Once more, I marvelled at the devotion Tom Transome had inspired in his actors. 'You saved his life, and nearly lost your own in the process.'

'I'm not a brave man by nature,' said Mr Tully. 'To this day, I couldn't tell you what got into me.'

'Where was Cooper during all this?'

'He told me, much later, that he had gone down to the river to get rid of Tom's pistol.'

'Did Transome start the fire?'

'I didn't see him do it,' said Mr Tully, very quiet. 'But he more or less admitted it to me afterwards – rather pluming himself on his presence of mind.'

'He assumed, I suppose, that the money he gave you from the benefit performance had bought your silence?'

'I'm ashamed to say that it did buy my silence, Mrs Rodd – what other choice did I have? If I'd been a better citizen and told the police, how on earth would I have lived? I was a penniless cripple.'

I ran this new version of events through my mind for a moment, never taking my eyes from Mr Tully; he was afraid and unhappy, I decided, but with a kind of relief in his manner that suggested he was telling the truth at last.

'I find it quite extraordinary,' I said, 'that Mr Transome was not more fearful the body would be discovered when the King's Theatre was renovated; was he never tempted to go back and remove it once all the fuss had died down?'

'We never spoke of it,' said Mr Tully. 'Tom behaved as if it had never happened. He had a talent for rearranging events in his mind. His reality was the stage, and he never could pay attention to anything else for very long.'

I remembered Mrs Noonan saying something similar. 'He was a reckless man; he nearly killed himself when he set that fire.'

'Impulsive,' said Mr Tully. 'He never considered the consequences of what he did.'

'Do you truly believe he was shielding Maria by accusing her mother?'

'You know Sarah,' said Mr Tully. 'She is no murderess. Whereas Maria is the image of her father; she is what Tom would be, had he been born female. And I myself saw her screaming at young Fitzwarren.'

'Did you see her threaten him, or attack him?'

'Well, no; not exactly – please, Mrs Rodd, please don't have anyone arrested on my say-so!'

'I don't think you have given me enough to have anyone arrested, Mr Tully.'

'I know that I am a criminal,' he said. 'I assisted in the covering-up of a murder. I took money for keeping my mouth shut. Will I be charged?'

He was indeed a criminal, yet I did not like the idea of such a fragile little man being arrested and locked up, and assured him that I would do my best to prevent it.

That evening, I spent a long time in my own drawing room, gazing at the painting of Matt and turning things over in my mind.

Three people could have murdered poor Frank Fitzwarren. It was more than possible that Maria was guilty. My beloved husband, however, would have warned me not to overlook the obvious.

And the 'obvious' candidate was Tom Transome.

But if he killed Fitzwarren – who then killed him?

Thirty-five

A NOTE CAME FOR ME, in a shaky, uphill hand.

Dear Mrs Rodd

Please help me to see my mother. She will not allow me to visit her in prison. Maria says I must not, but if she is to be hanged, I cannot bear to think that I will never see her again.

Yours respectfully
Cordelia Transome

I duly wrote to Mrs Sarah, and was surprised to receive the following reply:

Dear Mrs Rodd

My wife is now refusing to see her daughters. I do not believe, however, that this means she does not wish to see them. If Miss Cordelia comes, I will make sure that she is admitted.

Titus Mallard

———

'Quite right,' said Fred. 'Let's hope the poor little thing isn't scared into fits by her new stepfather.'

My brother was friendly with the governor of Holloway Prison, and used his influence to arrange a meeting between Sarah and Miss Cordelia the next afternoon. We travelled to Maria's house in the large and somewhat cumbersome carriage he used to transport his regiment of children. The cushions were frayed and strewn with crumbs, and I sat down upon something hard and painful that turned out to be a wooden elephant on wheels.

'Mallard is hoping for something that will finally break Sarah's confession,' said Fred. 'I hope, for both their sakes, that he is able to relax his moral outrage when he comes face to face with that poor little girl.'

'He was a father once himself.'

'Perhaps Miss Cordelia wants to talk about the rascal who got her into the family way. Are we absolutely certain it wasn't the Italian fiddler?'

'I am certain,' I returned. 'I know you like to laugh at my "instincts" but, if you had spoken to that young man, you would see how unlikely it is. He loves her deeply and sincerely, and would never hurt her in such a way.'

'In which case, my dear, you will have to admit that the girl is no better than a streetwalker.'

'Fred!'

'Don't get on your high horse. The fact remains that somebody did it, and it probably wasn't the Holy Spirit.'

'Really, Fred, how could you? Think what Papa would say if he could hear you!'

'He might use different wording, but he'd be of the same opinion.' My brother (puffing one of his nasty little black cigars, despite my objections) blew a plume of smoke out of the window. 'Maria got herself into exactly the same scrape eleven years ago, with Frank Fitzwarren. One can only conclude that Transome's daughters have the morals of alley-cats. I might persuade a jury to believe that one of them was a wronged innocent, but not both.'

I wanted to argue, but something tugged unpleasantly at my memory; hadn't Mrs Bentley said the same thing? 'Their morals – or lack of them – have nothing to do with committing murder.'

'I must say, I'm a little surprised to find you so advanced in your thinking,' said Fred, grinning at me through a veil of smoke. 'What would Papa say to that?'

This was a low blow, I thought; our beloved father, kind as he was, would not have wavered in his condemnation. As a country clergyman, he often had to marry couples who already had babies well under way by the time they reached the altar, and such casual immorality always grieved him. 'He would have reminded us to treat sinners with compassion, remembering that the merciful shall obtain mercy.'

We had arrived at Maria Betterton's house in Vale Crescent. Cordelia waited at the front gate; the sight of her slender, black-clad figure, so delicate and so mournful, sobered my sentimental brother in a moment, and he threw away the cigar to assist the girl into the carriage.

Her hand, when I took it, trembled. 'Maria is angry with me, and won't come outside; that hasn't changed my mind. I want to see my mother.'

'Of course you do,' I said. 'It is only natural.'

'You mustn't think too badly of Maria. She and Edgar have been so good to me, so forgiving of my disgrace, but she is quite obdurate.'

I wondered if she knew of Maria's own 'disgrace'. 'Your mother will be very happy to see you.'

'She told me not to come and I don't care. I can't let her go without one last kiss.'

'Keep your spirits up, my dear,' Fred said, as kindly as if he had been speaking to Tishy. 'Never say die; we are not beaten yet.'

'She didn't kill Papa. She loved him.' Cordelia wore a thick black veil upon her bonnet, which she now pulled down over her face; she kept silent behind it for the rest of the short journey.

A dozen or so seedy individuals – the usual loafers, gawpers and penny-a-liners – ran up to Fred's carriage, rudely shouting questions ('Who is she?') and trying to look inside. Fred drew the blinds and then they pounded the carriage doors with their fists.

'Ignore them, Miss Cordelia,' said Fred. 'They are hungry for a story, but we have nothing for them today.'

She was utterly composed, yet I sensed her fear and was very glad to be safely through the gatehouse. Inside the prison, we were met by a wardress and led to a bleak visitors' room, furnished with a table and chairs and a large Bible.

Mr Mallard was there, quite alone; I was glad to see a great improvement in his appearance since our last encounter. His hair was neatly trimmed, his linen was crisp and clean, and he was altogether restored to the man I had known in Herefordshire – the somewhat stern and uncompromising man, as I now remembered.

'My wife does not know you are here,' he said. 'I have gone against her wishes. I don't believe it is healthy for her to hold her children at arm's length.'

'This is Miss Cordelia,' I said. 'Shall I assist you with your veil, my dear?'

I did not like the expression on Mallard's face, as if he had a bad smell under his nose. Gently, and with a great desire to defend the girl, I helped her to put back her veil.

She curtseyed to her mother's new husband. He took a step back and I thought he was moved, against his will, by her youth and her beauty.

'Cordelia,' he said gravely, and they shook hands. 'You have been ill; I am glad to see that you are recovered.'

'I … thank you, sir.' Cordelia was uneasy, only too well aware of the shameful nature of her illness.

'I very much hope,' said Mr Mallard, 'that you and I may be friends.' He did not sound very friendly. 'I hope that we may pray together.'

The door opened and Mrs Sarah came into the room. One look of dismay crossed her face, and then she melted into tears and mother and daughter were in each other's arms. I was greatly moved to see Sarah's haggard looks so irradiated with the joy of holding her child that she was positively beautiful.

'My darling – you shouldn't have come – oh, my darling – my baby!'

'Mamma – I wanted you so—'

Cordelia would not be separated from her mother; Sarah sat down and Cordelia knelt at her feet with her head buried in her lap.

Sarah murmured, 'Forgive me, little puss. I should never have left you!'

'Why did you?'

'I had to make things right.' Overcome with feeling as she was, Sarah was still aware of her audience; her husband, for one, was watching her with hungry intensity. 'One day, you will understand that I did this for the best.'

Cordelia raised her head. 'You didn't kill Papa, I know you did not!'

'If you believe your mother is innocent, you must help her,' said Mr Mallard. 'Let us pray that the truth will reveal itself.' He knelt down upon the flagstone floor and folded his hands.

'Pish!' said Fred.

'Mr Tyson!' Mallard gaped at my brother with absolute outrage.

'Praying won't get us anywhere. Stand up, man!'

Mr Mallard stood.

'Miss Cordelia.' Fred pulled up a chair and sat himself down beside the mother and daughter. 'You are very sure that your mother did not kill your father.'

'She did not,' said Cordelia from where she knelt. 'I don't say it because she is my mother.'

'Did you read her confession?'

'I did, and found it a great lie. My father murdered Francis Fitzwarren.'

'It does begin to look that way,' said Fred, in the silken tones he used to coax something from a witness.

'You cannot possibly know anything about that!' Sarah said sharply.

Cordelia looked steadily at my brother. 'Papa told me.'

'*What?*'

'He was in one of his tempers and it came out. He had just discovered Giuseppe's letters.'

'My dear,' murmured Sarah, 'this can do no good.'

'Giuseppe told Papa that he loved me and wished to marry me,' said Cordelia determinedly. 'I never saw him so angry; it was worse than when he lost Maria. He struck my face. Giuseppe struck him back and, while they fought, Papa shouted about how he had killed that idiotic Frankie Fitzwarren. "I shot him when he turned his back on me and so I'll shoot you if you lay one finger on her."'

'Oh, God,' said Sarah.

'Mr Tully has adjusted his story,' I said, 'and admitted his part in the events of that night. There is little point in continuing to defend your husband. That part of your confession, relating to the first murder, is fiction, which casts doubt upon other parts relating to the second.'

'Poor Ben.' Sarah stroked her daughter's hair.

'Let it go, ma'am,' said Fred. 'Change your plea to "Not Guilty". We will discover the true murderer of Tom Transome and have these charges dropped.'

'The Italian,' Mr Mallard blurted out suddenly. 'He is your murderer! Go and take him up – and God have mercy on him if he does not confess!'

'How dare you!' cried Cordelia.

'Mr Barber was out of the country at the time,' I put in quickly.

'The man is a scoundrel,' said Mr Mallard. 'He is the villain who shamed this young woman!'

'He did not!' Cordelia rapped this out with surprising force. 'He'd rather die!'

'This is depravity beyond belief,' said Mr Mallard. 'Do I understand you correctly? You are either defending one villain, or admitting that there is another!'

Cordelia scrambled to her feet. 'Mamma, I love you very much, but I don't want to see this hateful man again.'

She ran out of the room and the interview was over.

Thirty-six

I MUST NOW PAUSE, TO warn the reader that my account of these murders is about to descend into yet greater darkness. In relating the facts, I must touch on subjects most emphatically not suitable for young, impressionable people, nor for those who have led sheltered lives. I do not write for publication; my family and friends are my public, and my beloved niece, Tishy, is usually the first to read of my experiences. This manuscript, however, will be put straight into the hands of her husband, Sir Patrick Flint. I trust him to know what to do with it – if I do not decide to burn it first.

The puzzle of Cordelia, and the angry words she had flung at her stepfather, gnawed at me all through my journey back to Hampstead. Fred, unwontedly meditative and grave, for once left me to my thoughts. I had no idea where to look next amidst such a forest of motives, but Providence works in all sorts of unexpected ways.

When I got home, I found a note from Inspector Blackbeard.

Dear Mrs Rodd

The man Samuel Watkins is dying and wishes to see us. The carriage will call for you at nine tomorrow, if agreeable to you.

Respectfully
T. Blackbeard

Watkins had been taken to the Grimaldi Hospital and Almshouses in Edmonton, in those days still a small town on the outskirts of the city. The hospital, named after the celebrated clown who died in poverty, was a collection of low buildings behind Church Street, built a few years before in the Gothic style.

Blackbeard awaited me at the main gate, beside a row of clean and attractive almshouses, each with its own door and one little window (thinking of my committee for Seven Dials, I couldn't help wondering how much they had cost to build, and whether they were expensive to maintain).

'It's a charity for actors and suchlike,' said Blackbeard. 'When they need a place to live – or to die. I beg your pardon for the hurry, ma'am, but he ain't got long.'

The red-brick hospital building at the quietest end of the grounds was larger and more imposing than the houses, yet still had an air of homeliness and tranquillity. Over the fireplace in the entrance hall, I was interested to see a portrait of James Betterton; while I was gazing up at that handsome face, a clergyman came to meet us. He introduced himself as William Forbes, and eagerly explained that Mr Betterton had contributed a great deal of money to the Grimaldi Trust for destitute actors.

'Betterton has been extremely generous,' said Mr Forbes. 'More to the point, he has been energetic and active; the fact that the funds were raised and put to use so quickly is due to him.'

'I know Mr Betterton,' I said, 'and he strikes me as a man of great sense and decency. Can you tell me how Samuel Watkins came here?'

'He was admitted the day before yesterday, and came from the infirmary of a workhouse; the chaplain sent him here knowing his theatrical background.'

Mr Forbes led us along a tiled corridor that ran down one side of the building. It was very quiet and orderly; through open doors I caught glimpses of hushed wards and soft-footed nurses.

'Poor fellows, they come here for a good death, which is all we can do for them,' said Mr Forbes. 'Watkins is pretty much wide awake – as drinkers are sometimes, in their last hours – and he's worried about the state of his soul. He claims he has something to tell you, Inspector.'

'Might you know what it is, sir?'

'I don't, and I warn you not to take anything he says too seriously.' Mr Forbes halted outside a door. 'His wits are wandering and he comes out with all sorts of nonsense.'

There were four beds in the square white room, each with a still figure upon it; all were wasted and meagre, and struggling with their last breaths.

Samuel Watkins was in the bed closest to the door. I sat down in the chair beside it, and was startled when he grabbed my hand with his shaking claw. His eyes snapped open and disconcerted me with their feverish brightness.

'Well, Sam,' said Blackbeard, standing over him, 'do you know who I am?'

'Policeman,' rasped Watkins.

'And I am Mrs Rodd,' I said. 'We spoke to you about the night you saw Mr Cooper.'

'Yes, yes.' His eyes moved between our faces. 'All green outside the window here.'

'Very nice too,' said Blackbeard. 'Now, what've you got for me?'

'They won't give me a drink – I don't care that it hurts like swallowing hot coals – just a little glass of something.'

'You saw Cooper on the night he died,' said Blackbeard. 'You saw him with a young woman.'

I had no great hope of getting any sense from this pitiful creature, but the inspector's bracing tone seemed to bring him back to himself. His watery eyes turned to me as if drawing me into focus.

'Poor Charlie! He was never right after Transome was gone.'

'You told us that the woman was an actress,' I prompted gently. 'You heard her voice.'

'More than that,' said Watkins. 'My memory is all at sea these days, and sometimes I can't tell if I truly saw a thing, or the thing was just a phantom; when the shakes are upon me, I see demons and goblins, as real as you are. But there was a picture that stayed with me and wouldn't be banished.'

'A picture?'

'She walked outside with Charlie Cooper and I saw her face; the wind lifted up her veil.'

Though I kept my composure, my heart leapt. 'Did you know her, Mr Watkins?'

'She was young, and what a beauty! A voice like an angel, she had, and the figure of a queen.'

'That don't get us very far,' murmured Blackbeard. 'Come now, Sam, was it one of the Transome gels?'

'Charlie kissed her hand – the rings on her fingers—'

'Did you see the colour of her hair?' I asked more urgently.

'Golden,' said Watkins. 'Bright as the sun!'

'Golden?' I gasped this out, for the light poured into my mind so suddenly that I was winded.

'Hmm.' Blackbeard folded his hands behind his back. 'Bingo!'

'Constance Noonan.' I uttered the name as soon as Blackbeard and I were out of the hospital and the tumult in my brain had begun to settle. 'Constance did away with Cooper.'

'Steady, ma'am,' said Blackbeard. 'Let's take this nice and slow. What's her motive?'

'Number Three on your list – fear of discovery. Cooper knew something, and this is why Constance asked after him at that party. It was when Olivia said he was telling tall stories.'

'What did he know?'

'Something that would place her near to the scene of Transome's murder,' I said. 'She did it, Inspector. The more I think of it, the more the pieces fit together! Constance Noonan killed him, and Sarah confessed to it because she believed she was protecting one of her daughters.'

'Hmm,' said Blackbeard. 'Not a lot to go on, Mrs Rodd; poor old Sam won't be in any state to give his evidence in court, and no jury would believe him if he did.'

'We know that Constance argued with Transome on the day he was murdered.'

'He argued with just about everybody, ma'am; I need more than that. I can't arrest the woman on the word of a poor old drunk.'

'You must talk to her mother again,' I said. 'And do it quickly, before Constance can get at her – if she has not already done so.'

Thirty-seven

THE JOURNEY FROM EDMONTON was a long one, and seemed even longer to me; the city traffic was heavy, and it was well into the afternoon when the police carriage drew up in Pentonville.

Margaret Noonan was at home, and she opened the front door to us with her accustomed meekness, though her fear was now quite plain to see.

'What do you want now?'

'Inspector Blackbeard has a few more questions to ask you, Mrs Noonan.'

'I've told you everything I could.'

'May we come in?'

'I – I don't know – it's not convenient.'

'Don't give me that,' said Blackbeard. 'You've been telling lies again, Maggie.'

'No!'

'I can ask my questions at the police station, if you'd like that better.'

Mrs Noonan, rigid and trembling, wrapped her arms around her body. She looked into our faces, and stood aside with a kind of despairing resignation for us to enter the house. Blackbeard led the way down to the kitchen and planted himself in front of the range.

'Sit down.'

She dropped into a chair at the table and I took the chair opposite. 'We're concerned with the death of Mr Cooper,' I said. 'Can you tell us where you were on the night of Sunday the fourteenth?'

'I was here,' said Mrs Noonan. 'With Constance.'

'Not with Constance,' said Blackbeard. 'She was seen somewhere else, buying gin for the murdered man – careful what you say!'

Her hands flew to her mouth; she made a strange, choking noise and tears spilled from her eyes. 'She was here with me, just me and her, I swear it on the Bible!'

'I'd keep the Bible out of it, if I was you,' said Blackbeard. 'Constance ordered you to cover for her, didn't she?'

'No!'

'And properly put the frights on you, by the looks of it.'

The poor, faded creature saw that she was cornered, and broke down into a passion of crying. Blackbeard simply watched her as she put her head upon the table. After a few minutes had passed, he cocked one eyebrow at me.

'Mrs Noonan,' I said gently, 'you will be in very great trouble unless you tell us the truth. It is too late; you cannot shield her now.'

She sat up, and said, through her wrenching sobs, 'She told me we'd be ruined if I didn't lie for her. I don't know where she went or what she did; only that I was to say she was here the whole evening.'

'It looks like she assisted Cooper into the river,' said Blackbeard. 'I could take you up as an accessory to murder; do you know what that means?'

'I didn't dare say no to her,' wept Mrs Noonan. 'I've never dared, since she was a little girl. She's so set on getting on, nothing's allowed to stand in her way, and the business with Tom Transome only made her worse! I tried to talk her out of it, but there was never any use telling Constance what she didn't want to hear!'

'What was her quarrel with Transome?' I asked. 'You admitted that she was angry with him; was that simply because he couldn't marry her?'

'That didn't bother her, not to begin with.' Mrs Noonan pulled a handkerchief from her sleeve to mop her streaming eyes. 'He came to see her at the theatre, and dazzled her with promises; she was to be rich and celebrated, and he told me that if I said *one thing* to spoil it, we would all be ruined, and was that what I wanted? He spoke so soft and sweet, he swore nothing would ever come out. And I couldn't stand against both of them.'

'She threatened to leave him,' said Blackbeard. 'Was that why they fell out?'

'He wouldn't let me tell her,' said Mrs Noonan.

'Tell her what?' I asked.

'I'm a terrible sinner, Mrs Rodd. I lived in dread of it coming out – oh, I was in such a fright when I heard them fighting!'

I saw Constance in my mind's eye, in all the splendour of her beauty. 'Did she believe he could divorce his wife, because of Sarah's adultery?'

'I don't know what she believed, but Tom must've let out the truth,' said Mrs Noonan, with another rush of tears. 'He knew it almost at once, after he saw her on the stage and found out that I was her mother.'

'Knew what?'

'He – he was her father.'

'You're very quiet, Mrs Rodd,' Blackbeard told me, once we were back in the carriage. 'I've never known you so quiet, or so short of opinions. You're shocked, that's what.'

'I am shocked, naturally,' I said, 'but not surprised. The moment Mrs Noonan let it out, the likeness between the two of them was so plain to me that I wondered how we could have missed it. Her eyes are blue, yet they are shaped just like Transome's. She has the same bearing, the same presence and the same temperament.'

'Along with the same habit of doing away with people she don't care for.' Blackbeard had the serenity that settled around him when he was on the point of closing a case. 'That's what caused my confusion, ma'am; I set out looking for one murderer instead of two. Transome shot Fitzwarren, and when he was bumped off himself, we looked at his daughters – the wrong daughters, as it turned out. It's queer that the one from the wrong side of the blanket should be the one most like him.'

'Do we have enough to set Mrs Sarah free?'

'Not my department, ma'am.'

'Do we at least have enough to take up Constance?'

'I reckon so,' said Blackbeard. 'My superiors like things neat and tidy.'

'Poor Mrs Noonan! I hope she won't suffer any more than she has to; must you charge her with anything?'

'I'm inclined to leave her alone, seeing how helpful she's being now.'

'She has had to live with the disgraceful knowledge that Transome made advances to his own child! How am I to pray for the soul of such a man?'

'Hmm,' said Blackbeard. 'Disgrace of that sort is more common than you might think, ma'am.'

The depravity, the immorality of the man had shaken me to the core, and made me recall certain incidents from my past life as the wife of a country clergyman that I had done my best to forget; I wished with all my heart that I could talk to Matt now.

The afternoon was advancing. Blackbeard took out his large pocket-watch of dented silver. We were headed for the Princess Theatre, at which James Betterton and his wife were to give a performance of *Much Ado About Nothing*.

'You are tired, Mrs Rodd,' he pronounced. 'And I have one or two things to see to before I pounce on her. If you have no objection, I'll park you at a respectable chop-house for half an hour.'

I was bone-weary by this time, and giddy with hunger, and I had no objection whatsoever to being 'parked'. The carriage dropped me in a street close to the theatre, at a chop-house that had a coffee room for the accommodation of ladies. I was very glad to refresh myself with a cup of tea and a shilling plate of roast beef with bread-and-butter.

Blackbeard came to collect me a short time later, and offered me his arm through the crowded street; darkness was falling, and the stage door of the Princess Theatre was like the opening of a beehive, busy with workers coming and going. No one took much notice of the two policemen the inspector had placed outside.

'The play's due to start in an hour,' said Blackbeard. 'Here's why I need you, ma'am – I can't be doing with anybody getting on their high horses and obstructing police business.'

'You mean Mr Betterton,' I said. 'I can't help pitying him for what he is about to hear.'

'He'll get over it,' Blackbeard said briskly. 'He ain't the first old man to get took for a ride.'

We entered the theatre; the man who guarded the stage door attempted to stand in our way, but Blackbeard barked out the single word 'Police!' and marched straight past him.

The area behind the scenes hummed with industry; there were sounds of hammering and a trumpet playing, and actors swarmed up and down the stone staircase. Blackbeard thumped twice upon the door of Mr Betterton's dressing room, and barged in before anyone gave him permission.

The tableau that greeted us there was very striking. Mr Betterton stood over a young woman in a gaudy bonnet, who was sobbing loudly into a handkerchief. Constance lay upon a couch in a dark blue dressing gown, her blessedly noticeable golden hair in cascades around her.

'Mrs Rodd, Inspector Blackbeard,' said Mr Betterton. 'This is unexpected, and somewhat inconvenient; could you wait until after the performance?'

'No,' said Blackbeard.

If Mr Betterton was startled by his abrupt manner, he did not show it. 'Very well; you must excuse me for one minute.' He turned his attention back to the sobbing girl. 'You do understand me, I hope? I cannot allow you to bring your baby to the theatre. It's against every regulation and could lose me my licence.'

'Oh, sir – I'm sorry, sir!'

'Well, see that you don't do it again. I'll pay the laundress's mother a few pennies to sit with the child.'

'Thank you, sir!' She ran from the room.

'I beg your pardon,' said Mr Betterton. 'Some matters can't wait. That poor creature nearly suffocated her child by trying to hide it in a drawer. Won't you sit down?'

The room had changed since my last visit; the walls were papered, the furnishings were of finer quality. I sat down in a new armchair covered with flowered chintz, thinking that the new Mrs Betterton had made herself very comfortable.

'It's a shame she's not married to the father of her child,' Mr Betterton went on, perching at the end of the couch beside his wife's feet. 'But I saw no point in condemning her after the damage was done. Now, how may I help you?'

'It is Mrs Betterton who may be able to help us,' I said, as lightly as possible.

'Me?' Constance sat up properly. 'What do you mean?'

'We have been making enquiries about the death of Mr Cooper.'

'He fell into the river,' said Mr Betterton, 'possibly by accident.'

I kept my eyes pinned to Constance. 'Two people have told us that they saw you with him on what was very likely the night he died.'

'This is absurd!' said Mr Betterton quickly. 'We are actors, and all our nights are spent at the theatre. My wife is never out of my sight.'

'It was a Sunday, sir,' said Mr Blackbeard. 'The four-teenth, two days before they found Cooper's body.'

Mr Betterton was startled, and shot one uneasy glance at Constance. 'Sunday was the day I drove out to Nor-wood to visit my father. I slept there and returned the next morning.'

'I was at my mother's house in Pentonville,' said Constance. 'You can ask her, if you don't believe it. We spent the whole evening together.'

'These two witnesses reckon they saw you at the King George in Tide Street,' said Blackbeard, 'buying drinks for Mr Cooper.'

'Who are these witnesses, Inspector?' Mr Betterton demanded. 'Are they respectable?'

'No, sir, not in the least,' said Blackbeard. 'But they've got eyes and ears, and if they say they saw your wife, I have to take notice.'

'My dear?' He looked at Constance, his eyes begging for reassurance.

She was sulky for a moment, and then sighed irritably. 'Oh, this is all so tiresome! I didn't say anything because it was a private matter. I wanted to help the wretched man. I went to that public house because I'd heard that he drank there.'

'You – you went there?'

'I'm sorry, James; I know I should've told you, but you don't like me to speak about my old life, or anybody connected to it.'

'I understood that Transome's daughters were more than willing to take care of Cooper,' I said. 'Why did you not take him to Mrs Maria's house?'

'He refused to go,' said Constance. 'Naturally, I did my utmost to persuade him, and he would have none of it. He kept up his disapproval of Maria for Tom's sake. I couldn't think what to do except give him money.'

'How much?' asked Blackbeard.

'Ten shillings.'

'Most generous,' I said.

'It was the least I could do for him,' said Constance. 'You have seen, Mrs Rodd, how well my husband treats his underlings; I was ashamed that I had neglected a good and faithful servant.'

'My dear girl!' Mr Betterton breathed a little easier. 'There was no need to put yourself in such danger!'

'You was seen buying him drinks,' said Blackbeard.

'Yes, I did buy him a few drinks,' said Constance. 'To stop him breaking into the ten shillings.'

'You was seen to leave with him, ma'am.'

'He was heavily intoxicated; I didn't like to leave him in that horrid place, so I coaxed him outside for a breath of air. We parted soon afterwards. Since you like to know every little detail, I'll add that I had kept a cab waiting nearby, and I went home. That was the last I saw of Cooper, and I don't believe he meant to throw himself in the river. I think he must have fallen in by accident.'

'I wish you had confided in me,' said Mr Betterton, smiling at her. 'I trust that you're satisfied, Inspector.'

Blackbeard ignored him and kept his grim gaze fixed upon Constance. 'I've just had a talk with your mother, and very interesting I found it.'

'Oh? I shouldn't believe everything she says.'

'The only lies she's told me are the lies you made her tell – such as you spending the evening of the fourteenth in Pentonville. And I'm glad to say she's seen sense and changed her story.'

'I don't have to listen to this,' Constance snapped. 'I have a performance to prepare for.'

'No, you don't.'

'James – make him go away!'

Mr Betterton's handsome face was looking uneasy, with the first stirrings of deep disquiet. 'I have no power to get rid of the inspector, and I don't wish to; let us by all means hear what he has to say – although I must know if our performance can commence as usual.'

'Yours can,' said Blackbeard.

'I beg your pardon?'

'Hmm, what's the word?' Blackbeard's manner was polite to the point of geniality, while his face was as icy as the North Pole. 'What do you call the person that has to go on when someone is indisposed – like Fitzwarren did?'

'An understudy,' I said softly.

'Thank you, Mrs Rodd. The play can carry on, but you'd better call Mrs Betterton's understudy.'

'No!' cried Constance, with a passionate stamp of the foot that eerily recalled her true father. 'That part is mine; tell them, James!'

Betterton asked, not looking as if he wanted to hear the answer, 'Why can't my wife perform tonight?'

'Because I'm going to arrest her for murder.'

'NO!' Constance grabbed a glass ornament from the mantelpiece and hurled it violently into the fireplace. While the rest of us gaped, she blindly seized anything she could break, with a torrent of bad language; I was reminded, more forcibly than ever, of Transome and his 'dance' of rage, and the unfortunate Cooper saying he was too late to save the mirrors.

Mr Betterton caught and held his wife's arms, until she was a little calmer, though still furious.

'James, what's the matter with you? He can't arrest me! Why is everybody so bothered about that stupid Cooper? You're glad enough he can't spread any more gossip about Maria! I only met him to discover what he knew. Anyone who says they saw me push him into that river is a liar!'

'What did Cooper know?' I asked. 'I wonder if it was connected to what your mother told us, regarding your parentage?'

'That's my business!'

'She gave us the true reason you were so angry with Tom Transome,' I went on, 'which I believe is the reason you killed him.'

'I did not kill him!'

'This is nonsense – slander!' Mr Betterton suddenly looked years older. 'Why would Constance kill him?'

'I didn't need him,' said Constance. 'I could succeed without him.' She shook off her husband's hands impatiently. 'I told Tom I was not his property. He was very angry, and told me that I was indeed his property – that I belonged to him because he was my father.'

Mr Betterton was thunderstruck, and could only stare at his wife.

'Say something!' Constance snapped at him. 'Am I to be blamed for this? Am I to be blamed because my mother was stupid and my true father was a damned villain? Tom didn't see how he had spoiled everything – the life we were to have together, the parts I was to play – he wasn't the least bit ashamed of himself! He said he had taught me everything – given me everything – as if I couldn't even exist without him!'

'At the time of his murder,' I said, 'you had already made plans to leave his company.'

'So what if I had? I'd met James by then. He promised me the roles that I deserved, he was free to marry me, and he didn't have a pack of jealous daughters obstructing him at every turn! He could give me exactly what I wanted, and anyone else would have done the same!'

'You could have told me, my dear,' Mr Betterton said, very quiet. 'You are not to be blamed for Transome's villainy.'

'He said I couldn't go, that he wouldn't allow me to go – not to a new theatre, not to another man!' Constance took her husband's hand. 'Why must people spoil things?'

There was a brisk knock at the door, and a voice called out, 'Half an hour, sir!'

Constance released Betterton's hand and took several deep breaths. 'I must get dressed – I must ring for Higgins to bring me my gown. My headpiece takes fifteen minutes to put on, and my paint, I have not done my eyes. We must hurry, James, or we won't be ready.'

I watched, in absolute fascination, as the beautiful young woman stood before the glass, smoothing her hair, studying her reflection, as if the upset had finished and Blackbeard and I had simply evaporated.

Mr Betterton was also watching her, with an expression of dawning horror that I will never forget. His voice, though perfectly modulated and controlled, was a shadow of itself. 'Did you not hear the inspector? There can be no performance tonight.'

'Don't be silly!'

'Inspector, Mrs Rodd, excuse me for one minute. I must speak to my theatre manager.'

Pale and stern as the most tragic of heroes, Mr Betterton left the room. All three of us – myself, Blackbeard, Constance – listened in silence as he gave his order that the performance was to be stopped. Around us erupted a wave of cries, a bell ringing far off, a tumult of running feet.

He returned and fixed his eyes upon his wife.

Constance stared back at him, astonished. 'What is this? What on earth are you doing? You cannot turn my audience away now!'

'You lied to me,' said Mr Betterton. 'You ordered your mother to lie on your behalf.'

'I told you why!'

'Did you kill the man Cooper?'

'Can I help it if a drunken man falls into the river? Oh, this is all nonsense.'

'I am afraid,' said Betterton. 'I am very much afraid that you did kill him – and Transome.'

'Maria killed Tom,' said Constance, impatient and scornful. 'Your son's wife is a jealous whore.'

The word made him wince. 'Don't speak of Maria.'

'You believe her word against mine?'

'You have lied to me,' said Betterton. 'I chose to believe you because I loved you, I trusted you. And the worst of it is that you have involved me in your lying. You did not leave Transome's theatre when you claimed to have left it on the night of his death. You persuaded me to back up your version of events. It is all the more bitter to me because my love for you made me ignore my own doubts.'

'You're talking like a fool!' cried Constance, in a passion once more. 'Like the soft-headed old fool they all call you behind your back! Well, I won't let you. I'm going to find Higgins this moment – stand aside!'

This last was to Blackbeard, who stood before the door.

'James, this is your theatre; tell this man to get out of my way! You're as bad as Tom; he tried to stop me and laid violent hands upon me! You saw the bruise on my arm! He said that if I ran away, he would tell everything – every-thing! – and my career would be finished in the blink of an eye! Oh, he tried to talk sweetly and kiss me – I only picked up the dagger to defend myself!'

'Dear God.' Mr Betterton began to weep; not in any stagey way, but like a woman or a child.

'Didn't you hear me, James? Oh, stop your snivelling! I was defending my honour, which is more than you ever did!'

'You were not defending yourself with Cooper,' I said. 'He did not threaten your honour.'

Constance turned to me, her eyes hot and blazing. 'How do you know, you old witch?' (I am paraphrasing; her actual words were too obscene to print.)

'Now then,' said Blackbeard. 'Constance Betterton, I'm arresting you for the murders of Thomas Transome and Charles Cooper.'

Thirty-eight

'WILLIAM GREAVES HAS TAKEN her on,' my brother told me. 'He will try to persuade the jury that she killed Transome in self-defence, but it won't wash; good old Flinty is over the way, and he won't let them forget the other murder.' ('Flinty' was Patrick Flint, then a rising barrister in Fred's chambers.) 'You know his style, my dear; all hellfire and damnation. If you're planning to pray for her, you'd better start now.'

'I'm too hot to mind your irreverence,' I returned. 'In any case, I'm already praying for her. She will certainly be hanged.'

It was a warm evening, the tail end of a sunny day, and we were in Fred's large back garden, sat on the low wall of the vegetable patch, recovering from a ferocious game of 'tag' with most of his children (the two oldest boys were travelling on the Continent with an uncle on Fanny's side).

'I'm sorry for old Betterton,' said Fred. 'Anyone could see he was wildly in love with that young harpy.'

'He's a thoroughly decent man too. I've seen for myself his generosity; Sam Watkins died in an excellent hospital that was funded mainly by Mr Betterton.'

'A broken heart's a dreadful thing for a man of his age. I did it the sensible way and, by the time I met Fanny, I'd broken mine at least twice. Oh, you women – the trouble you cause!'

'Don't provoke me until I get my breath back.'

The game had broken up and the boys shouted and wrestled on the grass, while Fred's daughters did ring-around-the-rosy at a safe distance.

'Sarah will be here soon,' I said. 'She is very grateful to you, for managing the business of her release so quickly.'

'That's because I let the Home Secretary beat me at billiards. Seriously, the charges didn't stand up. All eyes are now turned towards the fair Constance, who seems to be rather enjoying the attention than otherwise.' Fred mopped his brow with his handkerchief. 'Did you have any success with Maria Betterton?'

'She sent me one of her firecracker notes, to the effect that she did not wish to see her mother.' I was unhappy about this, for I had come to like Sarah, and to honour her determination to protect her children. 'I confess that I hoped for a full reconciliation.'

'She doesn't want to meet her stepfather,' said Fred. 'And I can't say I blame her; Mallard quite clearly thinks his new-minted daughters are harlots.'

'Fred, really!'

'He has a point, my dear; most people would look askance at those girls, with their decidedly shady histories.'

'Titus Mallard is a clergyman,' I said. 'It is his duty, as a Christian, to forgive sinners – why are you smiling?'

'It's just that I'm constantly surprised to see you so easy-going about sin, as if one brush with the world of the theatre has loosened your morals.'

I told him firmly that I was not in the least 'easy-going' about sin, and marched indoors to set my cap to rights before Sarah's arrival. My brother, with his genius for teasing me, had touched a nerve. Before my acquaintance with the Transomes, I would have been the first to condemn them, yet all I could see was their dreadful sadness.

This was not due to any loosening of my morals, however; I preferred to believe that the case had broadened my mind and increased my compassion. We are all sinners, and we will all come to judgement in the end.

The arrest and approaching trial of Constance had distracted the gossips and scandal-mongers; she was the new sensation and Sarah was able to leave prison without too much public attention. Fred banished his wife and children to the upper regions of his capacious old house; Mr and Mrs Mallard were to be received in his pleasant drawing room.

They arrived without fanfare in a cab, and I was struck by how much they had changed. Sarah, elegantly dressed in black silk, looked decidedly older; her face was lined, her dark hair threaded with grey. Mr Mallard, by contrast, was a man reborn. He was calm, and a kind of sober happiness had ironed away his anguished creases.

'Heaven has shown us great mercy, Mrs Rodd. We must thank you for your kindness throughout this grievous business.'

Sarah startled me by greeting me with a kiss. 'I shall always be grateful – we neither of us expected this outcome when we first met.'

'No, indeed,' I said. 'Do you know where you will go now?'

'I shall take up my duties as the wife of a clergyman,' said Sarah (with a droll twitch of her eyebrows that gave me an unholy desire to laugh, though her husband noticed nothing). 'Never a role that suited me; you must be my model now.'

'We are returning to Newley,' said Mr Mallard. 'The recent circumstances have softened the prejudices of my parishioners. We are setting off tomorrow, after my wife has taken leave of her daughters today.'

'Will they come, Mrs Rodd? Will any of them come?' Sarah asked.

'Miss Cordelia promised to come, and Miss Olivia,' I said.

'But not Maria?'

'I'm very sorry.'

'I can't say I blame her,' said Sarah, sad but resigned. 'She has known too much suffering.'

'My dear, you must be strong,' Mr Mallard put in firmly. 'Remember, there can be no forgiveness without true repentance.'

'Titus, I've told you a hundred times,' said Sarah, 'my daughters don't need my forgiveness.'

He stiffened crossly. 'Your youngest child, for one, has offered no apology for her rudeness, and does not even seem to see that an apology is called for.'

The subject was clearly a bone of contention between them; it was a relief to be interrupted by the sounds of a carriage drawing up in the street outside, and a loud knock at the front door.

Mrs Gibson, Fred's housekeeper, came into the room to make the surprising announcement:

'Mr Parrish and Miss Parrish.'

A moment later, they made their entrance – Jonathan Parrish, dressed in the deepest mourning, and Miss Olivia.

Olivia was very smart, and the knot of chronic dissatisfaction had melted from her brow. I was glad to see how freely she ran to embrace her mother.

Sarah held her child in her arms, weeping with joy. 'My darling girl!'

'I was beastly to you, Mamma, but I've missed you so dreadfully!' With a new self-possession that made her very handsome, and very like her true father, she curtseyed to

Mr Mallard and held out her hand. 'I am Olivia, Mr Mallard.'

He shook her hand briefly, and without a word.

'My wife has lately died,' said Mr Parrish. 'It was a sudden death, as peaceful as anyone could wish for, and I have claimed my daughter. She is now under my protection.'

'I have cast off my old life,' said Miss Olivia. 'I've had enough of the stage, and trying to be an actress.'

Mr Mallard found his voice at last. 'Mr Parrish, I owe you thanks for your forbearance. I should not have attacked you as I did.'

'Please don't think about it,' said Mr Parrish.

The two men exchanged bows; the urbane Mr Parrish with a glint of humour when he caught Fred's eye. Mr Mallard turned to ice.

There was another knock at the door. Miss Cordelia had arrived, escorted by the faithful Murphy. Mrs Sarah kissed them both, wreathed in smiles and utterly oblivious to her husband's disapproval.

'I never was so glad to see anybody in my life!' declared Murphy. 'Oh, you've led us all a merry dance!'

'Please forgive me, my dear,' said Sarah.

'There's nothing to forgive; I'm just too filled with thankfulness to bear any grudges.'

Fred said, 'Thank you for coming, Mrs Murphy, and my housekeeper will be happy to entertain you downstairs.'

'Oh, no, sir,' Murphy said decidedly, still smiling. 'I'm staying right here, if you please.'

The faithful dresser planted herself beside Mrs Sarah.

'But of course you must stay,' Fred said quickly. 'You know this family better than anyone.'

'Better than they know themselves, sir.' Murphy was excited and impatient, as if the words were ready to jump off her tongue, and a memory stirred in me; something about Transome treating his daughters as 'playthings'.

'This is like waking up after a nightmare,' said Cordelia. She turned to Mallard, her cheeks flushing red. 'I must beg your pardon for my behaviour the last time we met.'

'You displayed a certain self-will.' He would not take the hand she offered. 'And a disregard for your wrongdoing.'

'Don't be hard on her,' said Sarah, with a flash of her old spirit. 'I begged you not to be hard!'

'And I begged you not to expect me to condone flagrant immorality.'

They were both angry now, and I was worried that they would break into an argument, when they were stopped short by yet another knock at the front door.

'Hullo,' said Fred. 'Are we expecting anyone else?'

Sarah was very still. She put a hand over her mouth, and stared at the door of the drawing room with a mixture of apprehension and yearning. There were voices out in the hall, and then the door burst open.

'Maria!' whispered Sarah.

It was (as Fred said later) quite a tableau. Maria held fast to the arm of her husband, and I found myself distractedly thinking I had never seen her look so beautiful. Mother and daughter did not move towards each other, but stood on opposite sides of the room, frozen like a pair of statues.

The silence deepened, and I felt I had to say something to break it. 'Mr Betterton, I hope your father is well.'

'Oh – er – thank you, Mrs Rodd.' Mr Edgar was very red about the face, and striving to be as determined as possible, but he was flustered and nervous. 'He's horribly cut up. I've never seen him in such a ghastly state, not even when my mother died. He's doing everything he can for Constance and his health's holding up pretty well.'

'I am glad to hear it; please give him my respects.'

After a spell of breathless quiet, Maria released Mr Edgar's arm.

'Edgar made me come. I was afraid to see you.'

'Afraid?' echoed Sarah.

'I was afraid of what I would say to you. I can't bear the silence any more. Edgar says I should speak.'

'She told me,' said Mr Edgar, looking steadily at Sarah and turning a deeper shade of red. 'She thought I would turn away from her if I ever found out.'

'I don't understand.'

'Thank God – now at last it comes out!' cried Murphy. 'Tell the truth, Miss Maria darling, for I never dared!'

Again, Sarah said, 'I don't understand.'

'It was only a glimpse I caught,' said Murphy, breathing hard. 'But it was enough. I saw him in the glass on the landing, before he shut the door. I saw how he laid his hands upon you.'

'I – I don't—' Sarah was pale to her lips.

'I tried to forget it, Mamma,' said Maria. 'I tried with all my might and nearly succeeded.'

'The baby,' said Sarah. 'But Edgar knew about that.'

'Mamma, did you truly, honestly believe Frank was responsible?'

'Naturally, of course. What else was I to believe?'

'I guessed that Cordelia was in the same condition – though she denied it – and that was my reason for removing her to my house. I knew perfectly well that the Italian had nothing to do with it.'

Cordelia burst into tears.

Maria cried out, 'See what he has done to her!'

Once more, that tombstone-slab of silence fell across the room. A realization began to dawn upon me –

something I had pushed away to the very back of my mind, that sickened me to the marrow.

I murmured, 'Perhaps my brother and I should leave, so that you may speak freely.'

'I want you to hear this, Mrs Rodd,' said Maria. 'I want you to know that we are not the great sinners you believe us to be. You think we are shameless, when it was our shame that kept us quiet.'

'You have done nothing wrong,' said Miss Olivia. 'I am at fault, for refusing to see what was under my nose all those years – when I might have seen it, if I hadn't made him into an idol.'

'He said I had to do something nice for him,' sobbed Cordelia. 'I didn't think it was nice – I thought it was disgusting – but he said he had a right, and that me and Maria were his perfect beings, and he loved us more than anyone.'

Olivia moved across the room to put her arms about her sister. 'I didn't count as a "perfect being"; now I know why. I was not his daughter.'

Cordelia fell into a storm of weeping, as if she had not been able to weep thoroughly until now. I gave Olivia my smelling-bottle. For what seemed to be a long time, we listened to her wrenching sobs in silence.

'Damn the man to hell,' said Mr Parrish.

'Amen to that,' said Fred.

Maria, though tears streamed down her face, was composed. 'Did you really not know what he was doing, Mamma?'

'No!' Sarah cried out. 'I swear it – but I might have, I should have saved you – if I ever suspected, I pushed it away – my darling, I should have known!'

After everything that had happened to her, after weeks languishing in the shade of the gallows, Sarah was finally broken. She held Maria to her as if she would never let her go. The rest of us tried to understand what we had heard – that Transome had violated his own, beloved girls.

The tragedy at the heart of this family of tragedians was laid bare at last.

The Holy Spirit moved amongst us, however, in the somewhat surprising shape of Titus Mallard; that sacred tongue of flame awoke in his nature a tenderness it had not known since he laid his own little child to rest.

He went to Cordelia, picked up her hand and gently said, 'I see it now; forgive me for condemning you.'

The workings of Providence only amaze me more as I grow older.

Mr Mallard turned out to be a good, kind husband to Sarah and a decent, if distant, stepfather to her daughters. Greatly to the fascination of his parishioners, this rigid man came to consort with actresses and even ventured into theatres. He had the blessing of little faces about him, and little voices waking the echoes in his dull home, when Sarah's daughters became mothers themselves.

Maria Betterton's first son was born six months after the scene described above, and this is how I came to number a celebrated actor amongst my godchildren, much to the amusement of my family. Miss Cordelia married Joseph Barber, Miss Olivia (now a wealthy woman, due to her father's late wife) married a baronet.

Maria and Cordelia – Transome's 'perfect beings' – continued to perform on the stage, with great success, as did the unfortunate Mr James Betterton.

'Naturally, I considered retiring,' he told me, 'but acting is meat and drink to me, Mrs Rodd, and I am only fully myself when I am on a stage; this much I have in common with Tom Transome. I shall never stop praying for him. I pray for her too.'

By 'her', he meant Constance, whose hanging was the sensation of that year. Good man that he was, Mr Betterton took care of Mrs Noonan for the rest of her days, and he even paid for a new tombstone when Tom Transome's grave fell into disrepair.

Sarah Mallard still maintains, all these years later, that her performance as a clergyman's wife is one of her finest. We are two old women now, and probably look exactly the same to those who do not know our histories, but she has never lost her air of youthfulness – nor her ability to make me laugh at unsuitable moments.

I have not made up my mind what to do about this story – whether or not to burn it.

Patrick was startled the other day, when I told him what I had been writing so busily.

'It was a dreadful business; I hated seeing that young woman sent to her death, richly as she deserved it. I'll warn Tishy that she may not care to read about this particular case of yours, but you mustn't put it on the fire. The truth is the truth, and burning your story won't make it vanish.'

His two daughters, my beloved great-nieces, ran into the room at this moment, and drove away all that was sordid and sad, like a sweet breeze blown from Heaven.

Afterword

IN THE MIDDLE OF the nineteenth century, when this novel is set, the British theatre was beginning a long process of gentrification. Thomas Transome belongs to the Georgian tradition, which Charles Dickens sent up so hilariously in *Nicholas Nickleby* and *Great Expectations*; a tradition that survives to this day in the form of the Christmas pantomime. Audiences booed and hissed, and the style of acting was coarse with a large helping of ham.

James Betterton is an early example of a new style of performer, far more intelligent and naturalistic, as exemplified by the likes of William Macready, Fanny Kemble and (a generation later) the Terry family. Educated people were rediscovering the plays of Shakespeare, and demanding truer interpretations of the great roles, without additional songs and dances or tacked-on happy endings.

It was a long time, however, before professional actors were accepted as respectable members of society; even now it is possible to find people who think the words 'actress' and 'prostitute' are interchangeable. This basic indignity is one reason (along with a chronic lack of fame and fortune) why I gave up my own brief career on the stage. I was increasingly uncomfortable with the fact that I was being paid to do things with my body, when there were always those who thought this should include more than simply moving and speaking. Mrs Rodd, who clearly has a soft spot for actors, would have given the Me Too movement her wholehearted support.

Kate Saunders

Acknowledgements

It only takes one person to do the actual writing of a book, but quite a crowd of people to make it fit for publication. I owe thanks to Alexandra Pringle, Alison Hennessey, Caradoc King, Millie Hoskins, Amanda Craig and Marcus Berkmann. Also to my beloved family, Bill, Louisa, Etta, Ewan, Ed, Charlotte, Tom, George, Elsa, Claudia and Max.

A Note on the Type

The text of this book is set in Baskerville, a typeface named after John Baskerville of Birmingham (1706–1775). The original punches cut by him still survive. His widow sold them to Beaumarchais, from where they passed through several French foundries to Deberney & Peignot in Paris, before finding their way to Cambridge University Press.

Baskerville was the first of the 'transitional romans' between the softer and rounder calligraphic Old Face and the 'Modern' sharp-tooled Bodoni. It does not look very different to the Old Faces, but the thick and thin strokes are more crisply defined and the serifs on lower-case letters are closer to the horizontal with the stress nearer the vertical. The R in some sizes has the eighteenth-century curled tail, the lower-case w has no middle serif, and the lower-case g has an open tail and a curled ear.